To my family, for reading to me.

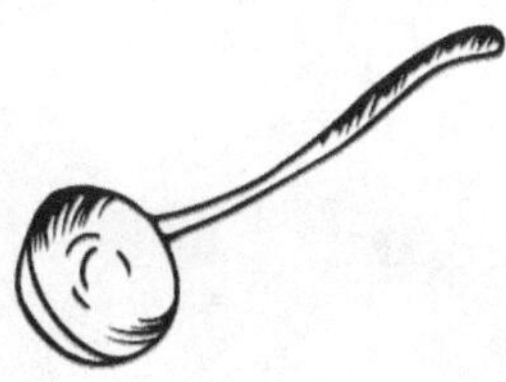

And, to my husband, for feeding me.

Borosia
Silk
Isles
Glas
RUGGED M
SEA
OF DEATH
Silver Narrows

THE EVERY STONE

BOOK ONE OF THE GEMPENDIUM

E.A. SANDROSE

This is a work of fiction. Names, characters, business, events and incidents are the products of the author's imagination. Any resemblance to actual persons, living or dead, or actual events is purely coincidental.

Map artist: Renflower Grapx

ISBN-13: 978-1-7331709-1-8

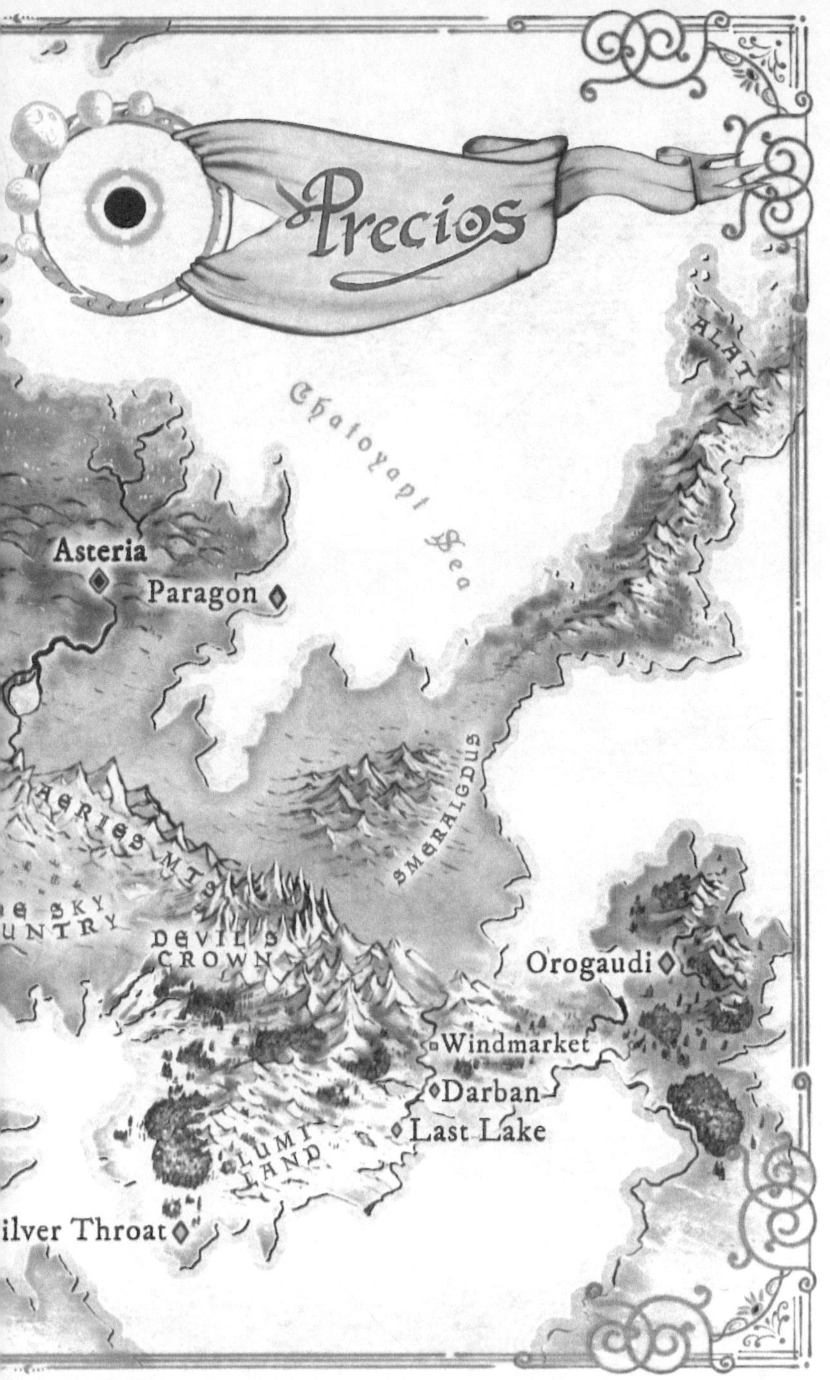

Precios
Chatoyant Sea
ALAT
Asteria
Paragon
SMARAGDUS
Aeries Mts.
Sky Country
Devil's Crown
Orogaudi
Windmarket
Darban
Last Lake
Lumi Land
Silver Throat

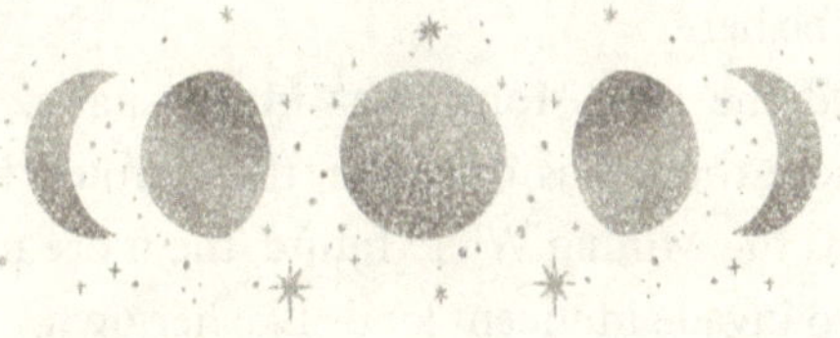

Yrund hated gems more than she had ever hated anything. No—that wasn't true. She hated the mine boss more than she hated gems. And she hated the memluk guards. And the Mining Wield who had sent her to die in this death hole they called Devil's Crown.

Her lantern flickered, momentarily turning the pocket of cave black.

Bogging hell. She was almost out of firemoss.

Another day returning empty-handed. Another day being beaten or dangled over the cliff while the mine boss screamed for the guards to drop her. Only now, they finally would.

Yrund swung her pick one last time, saying a prayer to the Great Sky, an utterly pointless act so far underground.

The shock of metal against stone reverberated through her as her pick cleaved into the wall, shattering the rock. And there, as if she had willed it, was the vein—a jagged line of white stone like fat cutting through mutton. She held her breath and swung again, sending a shower of rocks to the floor. As they fell a blue flash caught in the light.

Yrund's hands were so cramped she had to pry them off the

pick's handle to pluck the rough gem from the rubble. The crystal was hardly bigger than the tip of her pinky finger, its planes the soft blue of a summer evening. Yrund let out the breath she'd been holding. Maybe her prayer had been heard after all. As fast as the hope filled her, it drained back out like a bucket with a hole—if the Sky cared about the prayers of a goat herder, she wouldn't still be here.

She turned the blue stone over in her palm, relieved and annoyed. Where there was one gem, there would be more, and the more gems the Mining Wield found, the more memluks they could afford to invade innocent lands like her own.

Yrund tucked the blue crystal under her tongue before she could lose it. Some sort of seefire, maybe, though whether it was a valuable vagary or just a forget-me-not, she couldn't say. Her family were gem shy. They didn't believe in using rocks to solve their problems, not unless it involved a sling and a yote. The people of the Sky Country still followed the Way. Not like the lazy, spoiled, bug-eating Asterians—using gems to ease and cheat their way through life. It made her blood seethe to know she was risking her life just because some vain northerner wanted violet eyes instead of blue or couldn't remember their grocery list without a gem aid. But as quickly as her rage came, it fell away again, too heavy for her tired body to hold.

Yrund rocked her head from one shoulder to the other. After the long, cold hours crawling through the damp labyrinth of caves that cut through the mine, her muscles had forgotten whether they were stone or flesh. In the lantern's low light, she looked more like an old woman than a girl, her dark eyes sunken, her back stooped, her skin as light as butter tea after so many months in the dark.

Still stiff, she collected her pack and tools, then followed the chalk marks that would lead her back out, the second lesson the other ratters had taught her when she had first arrived—mark your escape. The light flickered again. Crap on crap! The first lesson was not to run out of firemoss. After filling her lantern with nearly the last of the fuel, she squeezed herself out the hole she'd come in, spidering her way between long spikes of rock that met between floor and ceiling like a giant's bite. The scent of wet rock guided her toward a gaping chasm, two towers twisting upward from the center like frozen lovers, cursed mid-embrace. Yrund didn't believe in eye-eyes and peskies, but if there were any place in the mine that spirits might dwell, it would be here in this bottomless darkness.

She circled the chasm's edge, toes gripping like fingers, until she reached a fan of ham-colored crystal marked with chalk. She swung herself over it and into a vertical chute, startling a bat from sleep, its soft wing brushing against her cheek as it flapped off. Yrund wished she too had wings to fly away. Lantern clamped between her teeth, she felt her way down the rock chimney, wedging elbows and knees out as anchors as she stretched to find her next toehold.

At the bottom, she landed in a tunnel so full of rubble she could touch the ceiling. From there it was a matter of crossing the loose boulders without one turning and crushing her. The trick was to move either very fast or very slow. At the end of the tunnel was a wooden barricade, an X of rotting wood marked with skulls, warning other miners away from the closed floor. Ratters were not so lucky. Not even the last ratter.

She was still rabu. Still one of the damned. If she died, it would be a mere inconvenience to the men that ran the mine, just as it was when the other ratters died. The faces of her dead friends came back to Yrund as if they stood before her. Pit, Ang, Lora. All gone. Yrund shook her head as if it might clear the ghosts away. Grief was a distraction the mountain would not forgive.

Her lantern hissed, almost out of fuel. Yrund cursed, slipping beneath the blockade and into the main tunnel. Stinn, the Asterian in charge of ratters, was nowhere to be seen. It wasn't the first time he had left her; perhaps the man thought she wasn't coming back, fallen down a crevasse or stuck in a hole. Or suffocated by cave gas. There were countless ways to die underground, and the bones of dead ratters to prove it. More likely, though, he had snuck off for a game of keeps with one of the memluks. The ex-pirates nearly always preferred gambling to working, unless working meant violence—that they enjoyed. Had it been earlier, Yrund would have taken a nap, but her shift would be ending soon, and she had to hurry if she wanted dinner.

Then a new thought occurred to her—without Stinn, there was no one to watch her on the walk back to camp. Without Stinn there was no one to watch she didn't slip away. She and Pit had talked many times about escaping. It was too late for her friend now.

But not for her.

Yrund began to run, following the tunnel's convoluted path upward, skidding around corners. She pulled herself up the rusty spikes that served as a ladder, ignoring her usual curiosity about how the Mining Wield had ever gotten so much heavy equipment here with their light airships. One tunnel gave way to another as she raced up the mine's floors. She could just smell the first drafts of fresh air when her lantern blew out. Bogging firemoss. Yrund reached for the walls, just as Pit had taught her, counting the turns back. Left, left, right, duck, left, left, right, left… Her pack bounced against her spine as she ran through the mountain. Right, left, right again. She knew the way out as if it were painted in her mind.

A gong sounded in the distance, starting off a cascade of bells. Right, left, left—a torch sputtered in the tunnel ahead. She would miss dinner, such as it was, but that didn't matter now. If she really ran away, she would probably miss many meals in the days ahead. The light increased and other workers appeared, dark silhouettes in the shadowy tunnel.

Yrund squeezed past the trudging prisoners, only slowing

when she passed a guard. In the entrance chamber, she unpacked her sack of tools, then pushed her way through the stinking bodies to the large map drawn across a flat wall. With a nub of chalk, she added a mark where she'd found the vein, then erased it. Then put it back. It pained her to help the Mining Wield find a single gem, but she couldn't risk a beating now.

As one line of prisoners stumbled out of the mountain into the night, heads hanging, another shift of men and women shuffled in, past Brandul, the mine boss. The slope-shouldered Asterian perched on a rock outside the entrance, too absorbed with a mottled green crystal he wore around his neck to even look up. The amulet hung from a long silver chain, bright against the mine boss's coat, a garment so stained, the golden eagle of the Mining Wield was barely visible. Without his gems, he might have been mistaken for one of the rabu. He was as dirty as his prisoners, the nails at the ends of his ringed fingers black with dirt, his posture bent from hours of looking at small jewels. Yrund despised him—the only man in camp with a bath barrel, and he never used it. His hair was dark with grease, his skin a sour yellow. Pit had said it was a side effect of the short-handled strikers at his belt—ornately engraved gem-powered weapons that could spit lightning like venom. In front of the mine boss was a dented metal bowl, worn smooth with handling.

"Well?" Brandul asked, letting the amulet drop back against his chest.

Prisoners who had not yet turned in any gems they had found during their shift had one last chance. Yrund pulled the small blue stone from under her tongue and dropped it with a clatter on top of a half dozen others. Brandul snatched the gem back out before it had even settled, tilting it one way then the other in the light of the lantern, his mouth open slightly.

"You found the vein? In the caves?" His bloodshot eyes, already large, grew wider as they shifted from the stone to Yrund. "Did you put it on the map?"

Yrund motioned toward the entrance chamber. Of course she had.

"So, I was right." With a flick, Brandul tossed the blue gem back. Not a precious vagary, then. He would have set that aside. "You should have listened to me before."

That was a lie. Yrund hated liars. It had been Stinn's idea for Yrund to search the caves. The mine boss had been against it.

"Where's Stinn?"

Yrund shrugged. She wasn't the memluk's keeper.

"Useless mute," said the mine boss, scratching at his pants.

Useless bugnuts, Yrund thought right back. She wasn't mute. She just didn't have anything to say. What was the point? Talking and crying were the two things that annoyed her captors the most. So she did neither. Pit was the last person Yrund had spoken with. He'd taught her everything when she'd first arrived —the correct way to swing a pick and how to use the color of the bedrock to find the gem-bearing vein. He had reminded her of her cousins, full of jokes at the guards' expense. Now, he was gone. Swallowed up by the mountain along with all the other ratters. All except her.

"Then tomorrow you'll blast." Brandul picked up the mottled green stone that lay in front of him, rubbing it with his thumb.

Blast? Bile splashed up behind Yrund's ribs.

"What's that? Do you wish to say something, rabu?"

Yrund's teeth cut into her lips as she forced her mouth shut.

"It's too bad there's no one to help you. Perhaps if you had done your job last time, your friends might still be alive."

Yrund's fists squeezed tight. It was the mine boss that had given the orders to blast beneath an unstable floor.

"Well, such was their Way. Don't cry. I thought you sheep-eaters liked blowing things up."

Yrund wasn't crying. She was imagining plunging her thumbs through the Asterian's eyeballs.

Brandul waved the next prisoner forward.

Yrund was dismissed.

Fists still balled, she got back in line. Her family had never touched the bridge over the Jaggedy River, whatever the wields said. But they had paid anyway. For the thousandth time her mind wandered over the night of her capture, trying to find the chink where it had all gone wrong, the moment that, if she had just seen it, the horror could be undone. The day had been warm and the grazing good, so she and her cousins had taken their time returning from the upper pasture while the suns lingered on the dusty pink horizon. It was after twilight by the time she had herded her sheep into their pens, the stars pricking through the sky one by one. Inside, her little sisters were already getting into their beds. As always, her grandmother sat by the stove in the center of the room, telling them a story. Yrund greeted her with a kiss, her cheek like soft leather beneath her lips. The scent of dinner still lingered in the round house.

"Oooh! You made dumplings." Her mother's curd dumplings were famous, their edges fried to a crisp in mutton fat then sprinkled with browned onion.

"Watch your boots," warned her mother in her quiet voice. "You're getting mud on the rugs. And take off your father's hat before you lose it. It's as big as a bucket on you," she said, filling Yrund a bowl of butter tea.

Yrund pulled off her felt boots but stubbornly left the wide-brimmed hat on as she knelt at the low table in front of the stove. Her father was away trading, and she missed him.

"You're very late tonight," observed her mother. "Are they running out of forage so soon? Maybe you should try going east tomorrow."

"There's plenty of grass still." Yrund inhaled as her mother filled a plate with warm dumplings and fried onions and set it in front of her.

"That means you were racing your cousins. You cannot watch the herd if you are running to Tala and back again, Yrund."

"The dogs were still watching, and, Momma, Otur's new horse is so fast. You should see how he flies…" She picked up a dumpling.

Her mother was not listening but had held up a finger. "I think I heard the gate. Go check, Yrund, and make sure it hasn't come open. I put a batch of cheese out to dry this afternoon, and I don't want those dogs in it."

Yrund groaned. She hadn't even had a bite yet. "I shut the gate tight! And put the wire over."

Her mother's head tipped ever so slightly back as her arms crossed.

"But it won't hurt to go and look," said Yrund hastily, setting the warm dumpling back down.

Outside, she shut the thick blue door behind her and waited for her eyes to adjust to the moonless night. Without a sound, a gloved hand closed around her mouth.

Yrund tried to scream, but the grip was too tight. Something soft was crammed between her teeth and a musty bag dropped over her head. Rough ropes wound around her ankles and arms. And then, chaos—dogs barking and yelping, her sisters scream-ing…her cousins and uncle shouting from next door to run, run!

But it was too late.

Yrund forced herself to breathe as she came back to the present. She wished they *had* blown up the Mining Wield's bogging bridge. Yet, now was not the time for revenge. Let the mine boss say what he wanted. She was leaving, and soon— before they realized the missing Stinn meant no one was watching her.

Up ahead, a loud whoof of air escaped a prisoner as he collapsed to the ground, the fist of a giant memluk guard suspended over him. Another memluk hauled him back up, and they continued the nightly search within the circle of torches outside the mine's entrance. First, they parted the man's hair, then peered into his ears, looked up his dust-inflamed nostrils, under his tongue, and on down the length of his entire body. The prisoners wore little except a threadbare sarong and menacing silver snake bracelets around each wrist. There were few things as hotly traded in camp as an article of clothing. They'd been provisioned, if it could be called that, for the sweltering heat of the mezmerald mines of Smeralgdus. Then, with no explanation, the wield's airships had veered south instead of north—to the snow-covered peaks of the High Aeries where a sarong was no match for the towering mountains' ill-tempered weather.

Soon, it was Yrund's turn to be searched. She stood in the circle of light, amusing the memluks when they lifted her skinny arms to see underneath, and she came right off the ground. One of the memluks made a joke in Douarr, the gargling, bone-crunching tongue of the guards from across the Long Sea. The men were captives themselves, prizes of the ongoing Spice Wars, and much valued by the wields for their size and fierceness.

The large memluk thumped Yrund's head playfully, making her ears ring. His grin was interrupted by a pink scar that jagged from temple to mouth, just missing a thick red beard woven with jewels the colors of a storm-cast sea. She'd heard the other memluks call him Melmeth, but Yrund thought of him as Gem Beard. Trails of tattoo sailboats looped around his suns-darkened wrists and neck, merging seamlessly with the embroidered islands and coastlines on his leather vest. His chest was a tangle of stone amulets, and more talismans hung from his broad belt, which was overloaded with clanking weapons and tools, including a broad and deadly-looking hammer as long as Yrund's arm. On his feet were the largest boots she'd ever seen, made of fur and hide and hammered disks of metal, dagger hilts glinting from their tops.

Seeing Yrund didn't understand his joke, Gem Beard flapped his arms, cocking his head in and out like a chicken. Yrund could tell she was being insulted, whatever the language. "You could feed us more!" she wanted to scream, but the guards didn't speak the language of her people. They didn't even speak Trade Tongue. Too stupid to learn, no doubt. Not that the memluks seemed to have any desire to converse with the rabu they were in charge of, not when a shove would do. Pit had tried to explain the hierarchy of Asteria's prisoners, mercenaries, and servants to Yrund once. It was nearly as confounding as their system of wields, which controlled everything from mining to sewers. Ratters weren't supposed to talk, but with most of their shifts spent deep in the crevices of the mine where no adults fit, there had been no one to stop them.

Gem Beard clucked some more, braids waggling, then went on with his job, prying apart Yrund's fingers to see if a small rubily or moonsstone had been secreted between them. An involuntary complaint escaped her when the rough hands moved on to her feet. She sucked the sound back.

"You won't laugh when we cut off your toes and make you eat them because you tried to steal one of the wield's gems," threatened Brandul as he stopped to watch on his way back to camp. The gems in his bowl had been emptied into a worn leather pouch that hung from his neck beside his other talismans.

"Don't forget the ears," he reminded the guards. When the memluks ignored him, he said it again in Douarr.

The men turned to stare him down, each twice his size. The mine boss had the slack muscles of one who had others do his bidding. His jeweled hand moved to one of the strikers on his belt, but the guards did not break eye contact. They knew he wouldn't shoot them. They were too valuable. The scarred memluk feinted forward. Brandul retreated.

"Carry on, then," he commanded from the safer distance.

With a smirk, the men returned to their task.

The mine boss slapped a man that made the mistake of being within reach and stomped down the valley toward his tent, where he would spend the rest of the night counting and recounting piles of raw gems.

The memluks continued their search, not forgetting to check Yrund's short hair or under her snake-shaped anklets. She'd been too small for her captors to fit the scaled manacles around her wrists. The first day they'd been put on at the rabu market in Wyn, she'd tried to pull them off, but the resulting jolt had been so strong, it had knocked her over. Now, she touched the anklets with their unblinking jeweled eyes as rarely as possible, though the cold metal made her legs ache. The other prisoners watched from under their bowed heads while the memluks pulled on Yrund's ears to peer inside. They all knew the penalty for stealing a gem from Devil's Crown. The skulls of previous thieves had been turned into lanterns to remind them.

Satisfied, Gem Beard pushed Yrund out of the circle of light.

YRUND BLINKED at the sudden dark. Two faintly glowing ribbons lined the trail down the mountain's side, switching back and forth toward the camp of tents pitched between piles of tailings and trash in the valley below. Yrund stopped along the darkest part of the trail, where the echo of the river beneath the cliffs blotted out the sounds of men, and she was alone with the stars. She had spent many nights back home gazing up at the constellations while out with her goats. The Sky Country was aptly named with its high plains and long views, while at Devil's Crown the heavens were reduced to a meager bowl between snowy peaks. Bracing against the wind, Yrund searched the eastern horizon for her favorite constellation, the Kite, barely visible in the east, its starry string hidden by the mass of mountains. To the west, wisps of cloud furled like sails around the Great Ship before they blew on. Once again, Yrund willed the tiny specks of light to reverse time and return her to where she belonged. But the stars ignored her, blind to anything but their own light.

Tomorrow you'll blast—the words repeated in Yrund's head as she dropped her gaze to the glowing ropes beside the trail. The one bordering the cliff was as thin as her pinky finger, its greenish light wan. Deadlines, the rabu called them, though they didn't look deadly to Yrund. Clever, perhaps, with their mysterious luminous fibers—the Asterians were nothing if not clever—but deadly? No, that was just what the wield wanted them to believe. The real reason nobody ever crossed the ropes was because of what lay on the other side.

For beyond the deadlines, beyond the ragged cliffs and the rushing river, still loomed the peaks of Devil's Crown, sharp as blades, their dizzying crests disappearing into the clouds. Impassable without an airship like the ones that had brought them.

Impassable for most maybe, but Yrund had spent her life scaling rocky crags with her goats.

She took a small step toward the edge, checking the sky once more for her bearings. The Sky Country couldn't be more than a thousand miles from here. She could be there by summer. After all, her family were nomads—travel was her birthright.

Even uncaring, the stars would still guide her.

Though the journey would not be entirely straight. To the east, the direction of her home, lay the Saltlands, a flat expanse with neither water nor trees. To the north stretched the Gem Road, with its regular patrols of wield men and bandits. And to the south was a land of storms, full of wolves and woodwilds. At least, that was what the other ratters had said. Yrund was afraid of wolves, but not woodwilds. They were no more real than eyeeyes and peskies.

She took another step, the wind whistling through her sarong pushing her onward. No one would even notice she was gone, not until her next shift.

Tomorrow you'll blast.

Yrund made up her mind. She was going home, deadlines be

damned. With a thrill of exhilaration, she lifted her foot for the last step to freedom—

"Nope, you don't." An enormous hand yanked her back by the neck. "Stop your kicking, or I'll throw you over, see if I don't."

Yrund dangled in midair for a long moment before being tossed onto the trail.

"Son of the Sea Mother, you really are an idjit." The moonslight outlined the pinkish-white scar running down Gem Beard's face. "Thought for sure it was gonna be one of those Lumi that went first." His accent was so thick, the memluk sounded more like he was growling than speaking Trade Tongue.

"You could've cost me a nice little moonystone," Gem Beard went on, wagging a big finger at her. "I didn't bet on no scrawny chickens."

So, the memluks had a wager going over which prisoner would escape first. She should've known. Those idiots would bet on anything and everything, from how far they could spit to who had the biggest knife. Yrund glared up at the guard, the disappointment so bitter she could taste it in her mouth. All she wanted was to go home. Back to her goats and her pony and the scrub-covered hills. Back to being a child. Back to the arms of her family. Yrund lifted her face up to the Sky, wondering why it had abandoned her. As if to taunt her, the clouds parted to reveal the Wild Mare bucking and sparkling against the night.

"What the sea snakes are you looking at? The Bringers back?"

The Bringers—those mythical beings whose boats could fly between the stars. Superstitious memluks. Yrund looked for the Horsefly constellation behind the mare's tail.

"What are you always looking at the blooding sky for? Is it the stars?" Gem Beard pushed Yrund down the hill toward camp. "Can't eat stars, you know."

Yrund's stomach grumbled its agreement. But her eyes lingered on the twinkling bits of light the wields of Asteria had yet to claim.

The gong rang across the predawn valley, waking Yrund from one nightmare into another.

Tomorrow you'll blast.

Tomorrow was today. She cursed Gem Beard as she sat up in the near dark, listening to someone piss on the side of the tent's wall. Whoever it was laughed, making a joke in Douarr. Yrund's head hurt. Her eyes hurt. The metal snakes around her ankles hurt, but still she forced herself up, rolled her pelt, and hid it in the shadows. Pit had stolen it for her. Pit who was gone. Perhaps she would join him.

Yrund slipped out into the cold, ahead of the other prisoners, who grumbled and groaned as they woke. Someone had already broken the ice on the barrel outside. Teeth chattering, she washed herself.

Wake now, wake.
Get out of bed.
Shake the sleep and dreams
From your head.

Light the fire
Fill the kettle—

The gong sounded again, interrupting the song in Yrund's head, the song her mother had sung every morning of her life.

She wondered what her mother was singing now. And where? Her cousins, her mother, her sisters, her aunt—they had all been captured. The last Yrund had seen them was at the rabu market in Wyn, where prisoners were sold like a yak or a camel.

Yrund wound back through the camp, hurrying toward the already long line outside the cook's tent. There were rarely enough rations for those who were late. She sniffed. The air was full of the acrid scent of rancid oil and baked grain. Bug biscuits. Again. The cook spent more time playing keeps than cooking. Even the guards were losing weight. The prisoner waiting in front of Yrund caught her eye as she too sniffed the air. Yrund hadn't seen the woman before. Her light skin was deeply freckled, her lips blistered. Part of the river crew, Yrund thought with a rush of jealousy. Yrund had barely seen the suns since they had arrived. She glanced at the woman again, taking in the gray-green eyes and long braid tied carefully with a bit of rag. It was a small act of defiance to stay neat in the mine, and Yrund admired her for it, swiping her fingers through her own hair a few times before she gave up.

When Yrund finally got her two rancid biscuits, she ate them quickly before another prisoner could take them from her, holding her breath as she chewed and swallowed. Except for a mug of worm-colored tea, they were all she would get until dinner. Yrund disliked the red tea, how it jumbled her mind so her thoughts would not stay still, how it made her muscles twitch. But the drink was warm, and it staved off hunger, at least for a few hours.

When the memluk foreman bellowed, they fell into ranks, a

whip flicking above their heads as they filed by the mine's second-in-command, a razor-mustached Asterian named Veng who was best avoided. Unlike the mine boss, Veng was all muscle with taut, shimmery skin the color of brass, the result of who knew what gem. He was much smaller than the memluks, but Yrund had seen him sparring with them for fun, using his feet against their fists. Footfighting, Pit had called it, and Veng was as fast as a spit snake.

Brandul stood beside Veng, counting and scratching—his only two talents as far as Yrund could tell. Every day there were prisoners that did not have the strength to walk up the mountain. If they were lucky, they would spend the day by the river sorting and smashing rubble carried out from the mine. If they were too weak for even that, they would be thrown off the cliff, sometimes still screaming.

Yrund stopped to drink from the tank by the trail. The water barrels in the mine were not filled as often, and though this one tasted of metal and dirt, it was fed by the nearby stream and was the freshest in camp. She did not see the eight feet of rough leather slicing toward her as she lifted the dipper to her mouth, but she felt it as it burned through her flesh. Veng laughed as Yrund flinched, water splashing down her front.

Without thinking, she flung the heavy dipper at the man. The dipper hit him in the face, splitting the skin below his eye. The other prisoners gasped. Veng reached up in disbelief, blood darkening his fingers.

"Corpse!"

He raised the whip a second time, but Brandul jerked it away from him. "I need the rat today."

Yrund watched herself as if from a distance. What had she done? A freckled hand pulled her back into line, and they started up the mountain, the hint of first dawn just beginning to light the sky. Yrund's feet moved all on their own, step after step, switching over and back, up and up, the faint green deadlines leading the way.

As they ascended, someone began to sing. Another voice joined in, and then another. Soon an invisible choir echoed through the valley, untethered in the twilight.

> *Oa-a-a, oa-a-a,*
> *Are you coming?*
> *Through the stars*
> *We will fly*
> *On our Way*
> *In ships of moonlight*
> *With diamond rudders*
> *Back to our home*
> *Back to our home*
> *Leave those bones*
> *No grave can hold us*
> *We're going home*
> *In ships of light.*
> *Oa-a-a, oa-a-a...*

A weak tenor rose apart from the other voices as if the man's soul was already lifting away from his body. Yrund put her fingers in her ears.

INSIDE THE MINE, the prisoners peeled off into work crews, picking up tools and supplies stored within the domed entrance. Jostling with the others to get equipped, Yrund filled a rough pack with a canteen, several chunks of white chalk, and as much firemoss as she could cram inside. It took a small fight to get hold of a lantern and a starter. When she'd tested to make sure they both worked, she checked all her equipment again. Miles underground was not the place to find you had forgotten something important. Like her pick. Yrund wrestled her way through to extract one from the dwindling stack, then flung her heavy pack over her shoulder, looking around for Stinn. He was late again, probably hungover, which was fine with Yrund. She was in no hurry to begin blasting. The walk up the mountain had given her time to think. Maybe there wasn't anyone waiting for her back in the Sky Country. Maybe she would never get home. But damn the Way, she was getting out of this mine. If she made it through her shift, that was…

After filling her canteen, she waited near the survey wall, where hand-drawn charts and maps of the mine spread a little farther each day. As she feared, Brandul had already marked today's blast site. She cursed him, then herself for not escaping when she'd had the chance, though that was as much Gem Beard's fault as her own.

The big memluk towered nearby, cracking seeds between his teeth as he slowly copied something from the wall onto an oilcloth. Yrund kept her distance from him as the other prisoners dispersed like ants into the mountain, the sound of their hammers echoing up from the hive of tunnels below. Still no Stinn. He must have forgotten her again. Yrund paced, wondering what to do. It was just her and the big man now. Gem Beard cleared his throat, and a wad of seed shells landed inches from Yrund's toes. Bogging ugly memluk.

She tried to ignore him, washing the raw burns Veng's whip had left across her legs. At least she had the water tank inside the entrance to herself. She drank as much as she could hold. That had been stupid of her, throwing the dipper at Veng. He would not forget the insult.

One more reason to leave—or it would be her own skull smoldering with firemoss in the alcoves. The skulls had a morbidly cheery look, flames dancing out of the eye sockets in the drafts. Yrund snorted and hawked the mucus in her throat into the back of her mouth. Using her tongue as a funnel, she launched the spit out. It sizzled as it hit one of the skull lanterns.

One of Gem Beard's eyebrows lifted as he calculated the distance out of the corner of his eye.

"You're with me today," he growled, finishing up his map. "I didn't ask for this job, and sure as thunder didn't ask to do it with the likes of you, you got that?"

Yrund did not ask what had happened to Stinn. Drunk, no doubt.

"Can you hear me?" Gem Beard thumped her up the side of the head.

Yrund jerked back, nodding.

"Just mute, huh? Good. Less backtalk than that other little twerp, what was his name—Tip?"

Pit, thought Yrund. His name had been Pit.

"Here's where you're going to blast first." Gem Beard used a gnarled thumb to indicate a chamber Yrund had explored weeks before. He looked at her to see if she understood.

She didn't. His accent sounded like he had a mouthful of nails. Or snails. Or both. In fact, between all the extra consonants, it sounded like he wanted to blast the chamber below the one where she'd found the vein. She corrected him, pointing at the X where Brandul had put the mark to blast.

Gem Beard, in turn, pointed to the hollow chasm with the cursed lovers. "This here's near the vein?"

Yrund nodded.

"Then forget what the *fynrryg* mine boss said—unless you want the mountain down on your head. That's how level two got blooding shut down in the first place. Only safe way in is to make a shaft up to the vein from below."

He erased the mine boss's mark, drawing a new blast line between the two chambers. "Get it now, dumb donkey? Then we'll tunnel through to the shaft you've made from the back side of level three. Avoid that holey nonsense in the middle completely."

Yrund looked at the big memluk as if he had a brain worm. Brandul would serve them both for dinner when he found out.

"What? You want to die today?"

Yrund shook her head.

"Me either, so don't listen to that crazy bugpot. For a man born to the Mining Wield, he doesn't know twiddles about mining. Thinks there's a blinking allystone hidden behind every rock. Allystones of all things! Crazy as a moon nut. Why do you think they sent Veng along to watch him?"

Yrund didn't know what an ollystone was. Some kind of tyrmaline? Those were for sleeping. Or was it eating? She could not believe how many varieties of gemstones there were or that anyone could keep track of them all. You would need a guidebook just to get dressed. Not to mention, she'd yet to hear of any gem that was truly useful. "There's no stone that will do the laundry or gather the firedung," as her mother had always said. Though sometimes Yrund secretly wished there had been. Just as she wished now for a stone that would make all the wields disappear.

"If you ask me, he shouldn't have spent his savings on any gemcrack finder agyt that couldn't point the way to more wellos," said Gem Beard. "That's where the money is, what with this new shortage—if it is even a shortage. Could just be another trick, like they tried with the alat out in Orogaudi." His beard shook. "Never know what those bugeaters will try next. Asterians are cheats and don't ever forget it."

Yrund nodded. She didn't need anyone else to tell her that.

"Still, they wouldn't be poking around in these old cloud mines if their own weren't running dry…" Gem Beard topped off his canteen and attached it to his belt, checking all his knives and hammers were in place. "Well, are we going to stand here all day yawping or are you ready?"

Yrund drew her own map on a scrap of cloth, marking the new blast sites in the order the memluk had said. Gem Beard checked her drawing before unlocking the explosives, wrapping the small sticks carefully in empty sacks, and padding them with firemoss. Then he gathered a fuse wheel and hand drill, and the rest of the gear they would need. He was more thorough than even Yrund had been, and as cautious, holding his lantern on the opposite side from the bag of explosives, which, unlike Stinn, he had chosen to carry himself. At this rate, she just might survive.

The scent of the mine engulfed them as they stepped through the dark entrance, faintly metallic with traces of decay and a whiff of far-off water. The farther they went, the narrower the tunnels, with Gem Beard's shoulders soon scraping the sides.

"Give me a mast-snapper any day compared to these blooding walls everywhere you look. Rock, rock, and more rock. And not a cup of alat anywhere. It's worse than being locked in the bilge. If it wasn't for all the jewlies…" He didn't finish the thought, distracted by a large pair of eyes so cleanly cut into the wall, it was impossible to make out the tool marks. The memluk touched one of the amulets hanging around his neck. There were similar eyes carved throughout the mine, and as with the others, the floor below had been turned into a makeshift altar by the equally superstitious memluks and rabu.

"Weird-looking little buggers, aren't they? Always watching. They give me the jeeblies." He poured a small offering of seeds onto the floor, mumbling something in Douarr. As he stood up, he knocked his head on the low ceiling. "For pissake! It's like the place was built for a two-year-old."

The mine's tunnels were small, many no more than five feet high, but that was still well over the height of any two-year-old from the Sky Country, thought Yrund. Just how big did memluks get?

"Allyright, then, hurry up! There's jewlies to find."

Yrund waited until the big man disappeared around the

tunnel's curve. Then, without the slightest hesitation, she scooped up the seeds from the altar and crammed them in her mouth.

✳ ★ ✳ ✦ ✳

"A HUNDRED AND eight days on that alat-forsaken island. Just me and their captain, sworn enemies, fighting over a rotten seal carcass. If it hadn't been for the hurricane bringing all those birds, we'd have eaten each other next. As it was, we..." Gem Beard's voice disappeared into the shaft as he tipped his head down to see where he was going.

Yrund climbed down after him, testing each spike before she let go of the one before.

"Hoy, hoy!" shouted Gem Beard. "Did your mother drop you on your head?"

Yrund peered stupidly over her shoulder at him.

"Wait till I'm down! If you blooding slip, we'll both be scraps."

Yrund scurried back up the spikes, annoyed with herself and the memluk, who, of course, was right. The day had barely begun, and she was already off her game.

"Outlanders!" he said, as if he wasn't one himself.

As the mine's ceilings grew lower, Gem Beard's swearing grew louder. Occasionally, a faraway rumble or banging would signal another crew at work.

"That spit-for-brains Stinn," Gem Beard complained as he picked his way down the fourth shaft, bottom unseen, carrying the pack of padded explosives. Sweat matted the hair around his face. "Should be him down here, not me. Just had to try and cheat an Astrini..." He cursed again in Douarr. "And don't tell me Veng isn't one of those sneaking spies for hire. With all that fancy foot-fighting and those cobaline knives. Sick blasturd put a star right between Stinn's teeth before he cut out his..." The memluk's voice drifted away in the depths.

So—that was what had happened to Stinn, thought Yrund. And she'd thrown a bogging water dipper at Veng. An Astrini. Who killed memluks.

Gem Beard was making up a rhyme when the tunnel opened up again.

There once was a man from Douarr
Who had a fearsome long scar
A good-looking feller
With boots of fine leather
But of ladies he loved only his Mar.

"That's pretty good, huh, chicken?" he called out.

The sea's finest captain...

He paused, searching for a rhyme.

Yrund had never known anyone who could talk so much. She wished he'd shut up. Her armpits were cold with sweat. She'd never blasted by herself before. What if she made a mistake? What if she dropped the bag?

Yrund followed the memluk's light around a bend, almost running into him. The big man had gotten himself stuck in the narrow tunnel. He took a deep breath and popped himself through.

"Fartfogger! I hope I can get back—Sea Hammers weren't built for this." He went back to his verses. *"The sea's finest captain?* No, no. Nothing rhymes with that. Let's see—*the sea's finest sailor*...nope." He switched to Douarr to finish his composition. Or maybe he had something stuck in this throat. It was hard to tell the difference.

They reached a fork that led to two diverging holes, and the big guard could go no further. He took out his map, checking their location against the markings chalked onto the rock around them. Satisfied of where they were at, he slowly lowered the bag of explosives to the ground, waiting until it had fully settled before letting go. The blast sticks smelled of sulfur and body odor. Or maybe that was her. Yrund ran through the blasting protocol in her head.

"Know what to do, little stink? Don't go drilling too deep, but none too shallow either, and make sure every hole is done before you put in the charges. Tie on your fuses last. Then get your butt out. Don't get the sticks wet, don't bump them, and for Mother's sake, don't drop any."

Yrund wiped her damp palms across her sarong. She'd forgotten the sticks couldn't get wet. Her lips felt numb.

Gem Beard handed her a drill and a reed straw.

"Might take you five lanterns. Or ten." He pinched her thin bicep, his scar puckering in a frown. "Maybe twenty if the rock is hard." Yrund hoped not. She didn't have that much firemoss in her pack.

"Stupid job for a kid. Going to take all day." The memluk made himself comfortable, pulling a book and the rest of the bag of piney seeds from his pockets. Yrund watched him split a seed between his teeth. The sharp, buttery scent of the kernels made her stomach howl.

"What are you staring at now?"

Yrund tried to take her eyes off the food, but it was impossible.

"You want some seeds, is that it?" He poured a trickle into his palm, as she stood there salivating. "Allyright. I'll give you some—as soon as you bring me back a gem." He shoved the seeds into his mouth, shells and all, then laughed, shells spraying.

"Now be off or the jellies can have you!"

Bogging memluk, cursed Yrund. She lifted the explosives gently to her front, heart thumping. As she entered the right-hand tunnel, she prayed to the Sky he would choke. Behind her, already muffled by the surrounding rock, she could hear the memluk singing.

Jellyfish scrambled
Jellyfish baked
Jellyfish jellied
In a nice cake.

CHAPTER THREE

At first, the tunnel's ceiling was just high enough for Yrund's head to clear, but soon the path twisted into cave, an unpredictable labyrinth of rock dangling with mineral spires. With every step, her stomach clenched harder, scenes of the last time they had blasted burning in her mind. An entire floor collapsed. Three ratters gone. Because of the mine boss's impatience. Yet his words haunted her. She had been the eldest. She should have protected them. Her mind turned the memory of her friends over like a tangled knot as if thinking about it hard enough would undo what had happened. But as the passage shrank, she had to bring herself back to the present. Or she would be next.

Her lantern gave off a boggy scent as it slowly burned, illuminating only a few feet in any direction. Hemmed in on all sides, Yrund dropped to all fours, scooting along on her hands and knees. She'd seen other rabu lose their nerve in the mountain's claustrophobic spaces, and most of them had never even been to the caves, a maze of hollows within the mountain far more dangerous than the mine with its torches and solid floors. Here nothing was constant except darkness.

In the low light of her lantern, every shadow looked like a crevasse. Yrund advanced an inch at a time, cursing as the way grew slippery. The bag couldn't get wet. But as she hitched it awkwardly up behind her, her knee lost its grip and the bag bounced across the rock overhead. Yrund cursed, but Gem Beard must have wrapped the sticks well, for there was no fiery explosion.

She rested her head back on the limestone, heart thumping. This was no place for a girl of the Sky Country to die. Yet again, she wondered how her Way had brought her to Devil's Crown. Or perhaps there was no Way. Maybe life was all chance. For she knew with certainty she had never done anything to deserve this. It was the wields who had come to her land, building their useless road, taking her family. The Sky People hadn't asked to be invaded by a bunch of gem-grubbing northerners. They were herders—they didn't even use roads. And despite what Brandul said, they hadn't blown up the Jaggedy Bridge, though she was beginning to wish otherwise.

But this was not the time for thoughts of home or revenge. There was work to do. Whatever she thought of Gem Beard, his plan was better than Brandul's.

Yrund pushed on, talking to herself as she climbed past the chasm with the towering stone lovers, their frozen rock faces hidden in the darkness. *Don't bump the bag. Don't drop the bag. Don't get the bag wet*, she repeated.

Finally, she reached the chamber Gem Beard had marked on the map, the bag of explosives still intact. She set the blast sticks down as if they were made of glass, drying her hands on her sweat-soaked sarong. Then she refilled her lantern. Four loads of firemoss down.

She surveyed the pocket-sized cavern, too low to stand, even for her. There was no sign of the vein here. It was the only reason she'd put it on the map. Misleading the mine boss was one of her few pleasures—only now Brandul was growing impatient. Yrund took a sip from her canteen and hoped Gem Beard knew what he was doing.

Yrund got out her pick and the hand drill and tucked the straw from the memluk behind her ear.

Don't bump the bag...

It was a slow job drilling even one hole deep enough for a charge. Each of the holes had to be angled slightly so the sticks wouldn't fall immediately back out. Yrund alternated arms to ease the strain, first tapping the drill with the hammer end of her pick head, then turning it a quarter way. Tap, turn, tap, turn.

Jellyfish scrambled.
Jellyfish baked.
Jellyfish...

What was it that came next? The memluk's song was just the right rhythm for drilling, though Yrund had no idea what a jellyfish was. She tried to imagine the small trout in the rivers near her home made of jelly instead of scales. Did they have bones, these jellyfish, or teeth? She'd never seen the ocean, but if she could trust the tattoos of sea monsters on Gem Beard's arms, it was a dangerous place. She stretched her arms, imagining for a moment what it would be like to travel the world—not as a prisoner but as a free person, seeking adventure and riches. It made the time pass, daydreaming of other lands, far away from the wields' reach.

Periodically, she used the straw to blow dust away from the hole she was digging. *Don't bump the bag. Don't bump the bag.* The memluk's words circled in her head like anxious birds. She burned through four lantern loads, then five, the pile of firemoss in her sack fast diminishing. Once, she prodded a hole with the straw to test its depth and dislodged a small pink gem. Rubily? Korundum? Nothing that would make her job easier. She set the gem aside and returned to drilling, only stopping to massage the cramps from her hands.

Tap, turn, tap, turn.

Her eyes burned from the dust.

When she finished with the holes in the walls, she started on the floor below. She was on lantern load eight, or maybe it was nine, before she was finally done. Yrund wiped her brow, smearing mud across her forehead, where the sweat and dust mingled.

It was time. She might have said a prayer to the Sky if she had believed it could hear her. Or cared.

Her fingers felt thick and clumsy as she opened the pack with the explosives and unwrapped a charge, releasing the scent of eggs and clay. *Don't drop it. Don't bump it. Don't drop it.* She bit off a piece of fuse line long enough to reach the exit, tied it to the blast stick and slid it slowly into its hole, stopping it up with a wad of firemoss. Only twenty more to go. When the last charge was securely in its hole, she tied the web of lines and the end of the spool together, trying to keep her hands steady. Just one tug and the sticks would fall from their holes, detonating on impact with the hard rock below.

She drank the last of her canteen and packed her gear, picking up the pink gem she'd found. Maybe Gem Beard would stay good to his word and trade it for some seeds. She tucked the stone beneath her tongue and wiggled back out the way she had come, spooling the roll of fuse line out behind her. Even without the bag of explosives to carry, there was no relaxing. She planned every motion before she made it, keeping as much slack in the blast line as possible.

Gem Beard was fast asleep when Yrund finally reached him, snoring like a bear in his winter den, his lantern burnt out. She set down her gear, dizzy. She should have been relieved she'd gotten all the way back without blowing herself up, but as she waited for the memluk to wake, one worry was soon replaced with another.

Veng was not done with her. Veng, the Astrini, who had killed Stinn over a game of keeps. The thought of Stinn prodded something in Yrund's mind. She looked over at the sleeping memluk. With Stinn gone, he was the only thing between her and escape.

Gem Beard's large mass stretched from wall to wall, blocking the way back. Bogging memluk. There was no way past him.

Yrund lifted her pick. One good blow through his eyeball should do it.

She crept closer, the pick tight in her hands. It was not the first time she had imagined killing one of the wields' men, though usually it had been Veng or Brandul.

Yrund stood over the sleeping guard, gathering her courage. It had been memluks just like this one that had ripped her from her home. With a steadying breath, she raised the pick up.

Gem Beard's eyes opened, and Yrund was on the floor, her foot in the big man's fist. She rolled her whole body away from him, breaking his grip, but now the pick was under her. The memluk seized her wrist. Yrund rolled again, trying to keep her hold.

Gem Beard giggled. "I've never wrestled with a chicken before," he said, twisting the other direction.

Yrund cursed him as she strained to get the pick back. Wrestling was a passion in the Sky Country, but months of starvation and a day drilling had made her arms weak.

The memluk propped his head up with his free hand. "You done yet?" he asked, his grip threatening to break her arm.

Yrund let go before her wrist could snap.

With a chuckle, the memluk rolled over and went back to sleep, Yrund's pick tucked inside his armpit.

Yrund slumped to the floor, cradling her sprained arm, wondering if it was broken. Would she never win? The wields had a thousand eyes, a thousand arms. They could afford the loyalties of men like Gem Beard and Veng while rabu like her had nothing.

She picked at the scabs on her knees, then examined the raw whip welts on the backs of her legs. When she had tired of that, she picked the dusty strips of boogers from inside her nose and wiped them on the sole of Gem Beard's mammoth boot. Then, eyes drooping, she leaned her head against the wall.

KABOOOOOOOMM!!! BOOOOOM! A blast of hot air exploded past Yrund, loosening rock, which fell about them like rain. She jumped up, ears ringing. Gem Beard had his palms over his own ears, roaring with delight. Obviously, he'd lit the fuse.

Yrund shook her canteen, mouth dry with dust, but it was still empty.

"You sang my song in your sleep," Gem Beard told her. "Got the words all wrong." Nevertheless, he seemed pleased. "Guess you're not mute after all."

Yrund glowered at him, her arm still sore.

"Don't be mad at me, now—you're the one that botched the job. Next time, don't make a shadow on the feller you've a mind to end. And don't stand there thinking about it for so long. If you need to kill someone, just kill them and be over with it." He made a hammering motion. "Course a little squirt like you might be better with a blade. Just like a Yavani—cut yer fella's throat before he ever wakes up. Or, if you really want to be like the high wielder's lady assassins—you'd slip a gembane under his pillow. Not my pillow, understand." He squinted at her. "Unless you want to go to whatever outlander heaven you pray to in a thousand pieces."

Yrund nodded her head, then shook it.

"Good," said the memluk.

Yrund didn't bother to tell the memluk that all bodies were

cut into pieces back home. How else were the birds supposed to deliver your soul to the Sky? But she would never use a gem to kill her enemies. She wanted to feel their warm blood on her hands.

Gem Beard handed her his waterskin.

Yrund was so thirsty she forgot she still had the pink gem hidden under her tongue. It went down with the stale water. She choked as she tried to unswallow it, but the stone had gone down too far.

"Uh-ho, now." Gem Beard reached for the evil dagger on his belt and squinted at her. "You find a jewlie somewhere?"

Yrund coughed, pointing under her tongue, where it used to be.

"Must've been a big one," the memluk observed, the blue stones in his beard glimmering in the lantern's light. "Stealing or keeping safe to give to Melmeth?"

Yrund tried to explain but couldn't speak. Some of the water had gone down her windpipe. She pointed down her throat, where the gem scratched as it descended, then at his waterskin.

"Maybe you were going to give me the jewlie? Maybe not." Gem Beard scraped the edge of his knife against a callous on his thumb, making the metal zing.

Yrund wondered if he was going to cut it out right there.

"When that jewlie comes out"—he made a face—"you give it to me, not to any other blasturd. Not Brandul, not anyone. To me, got it? If not…" He gestured with the blade across his stomach. "Not planning on spending the rest of my life in these blooding mines."

By the time they got back to the mine's entrance, the second shift had already started. A half dozen memluks loitered by a fire outside, playing gembles and insulting one another. Gem Beard tossed a few of his own round gemstones into the game, collecting two and losing one, before he steered Yrund down the mountain, keeping her firmly to the middle of the trail.

"No stars tonight, my chicken," he said as he rattled his new gembles in his fist. "No stars tonight."

He was right, thought Yrund. She should have killed him when she'd had the chance.

THE EVENING GONG was ringing its last brassy note as Gem Beard dropped Yrund off at the cook tent. "Better you than me," he said, wrinkling his nose at the combination of body odor and scorched grease wafting out the door.

"Don't forget—I'll expect that jewlie in the morning." He poked her in the stomach, where the gem Yrund had swallowed sat churning. "Hope you're regular."

Yrund cursed the memluk's entire lineage. For once, she wasn't hungry, but if she didn't eat, she would never make it through the next day. She fished a dented cup from a barrel of dirty water, dunking it a few times to dislodge the bits of food that still clung to it.

Inside, smoke obscured the firelit prisoners, who ate with their heads down, trying not to draw the attention of the guards, some of whom were already drunk. Yrund stood in line to have her cup filled with the same thin soup the rabu got every night. Bean, maybe? The camp cook had boiled it so long it was hard to tell. There was no salt and no spice, save the flavor of any vermin that had fallen into the pot, a lucky bonus. Yrund had not been so appreciative the first time she'd found a pile of bones and fur in her soup. Disgusted, she had set the cup back down on the table, only to have it snatched up by another prisoner who'd crunched the bones with feral relish. Now, she was not so stupid.

She scanned the tent for Veng, but the Asterian had either already eaten or skipped dinner to join the crowd of gamblers swearing and hooting in their quarters. Even so, she picked the two tallest prisoners she could find to sit between. The rabu silently made way for her on the bench, both giving her a small nod. No one had ever done that before.

As Yrund sat down, her whip wounds raw against the rough wood, she felt the eyes at the table shift toward her, a few with awe but most with pity. One skinny prisoner elbowed his neighbor, touching a finger to the cheek below his eye. They had heard about the morning's incident with Veng. Yrund's stomach did a flip. Sooner or later Veng would find her, and when he did… She had seen the man nearly drown Pit in the dishwater barrel once after the boy had talked back to him. And he'd killed Stinn over a mere game. Yrund forced the grainy soup down, each swallow harder than the last.

Dinner was no longer the pleasure she had grown up with— there was no meat, no herbs, no cheese. No butter tea to wash it all down. No loom by the stove. No grandmother with a pipe. No sisters in their beds. No father. No mother. No laughing.

No singing.

Yrund closed her eyes tight, trying not to remember and…not to forget.

Something dropped into her lap, and she returned to the present, feeling to see what it was. To her astonishment, it was an apple—small and bruised—with a single bite taken out of the side. She clutched it as if it were a gem. There was only one man in camp that would throw away an apple, the only man with an entire crate of fresh fruit in his tent. She knew how hard it must have been for one of the rabu to give up such a precious find and what it meant that they had. They thought Veng was going to kill her. Yrund took a defiant bite from the apple.

"No!"

Yrund froze. She hadn't seen the mine boss come in.

"No, no, no!" said Brandul, looking around accusingly. The prisoners cowered at their tables, shoulders hunched.

Hurriedly, Yrund hid the apple beneath the table, swallowing the rest of the bite whole.

The mine boss stalked through the tent. "The airships will return in less than two weeks, and we are not even close to the wielder's quota! We are short on seefires, topaz, pomegarnets, moonsstones, rubilies..." He pinched a prisoner's exposed ear. "Are you even listening?" Yrund leaned deeper back into the shadow. "I have never seen such a feeble lot of workers. Or memluks—you're as pathetic as the rabu," he addressed the single guard left in the cook's tent, apparently too inebriated to join his comrades in the noisy game of keeps outside, though Yrund noticed Brandul did not translate his lecture into Douarr. Even drunk, the memluk could still rip off the mine boss's head.

"Wielder Damantine did not send me here for potch and paffle," Brandul went on. "This mountain is holding the most precious stones on Precios, yet you haven't dug out enough to even pay for your keep. Perhaps I should take away your meals until you do." He rubbed his thumb against the long green crystal hanging from his neck, calming himself. "Do not think the wield has been unfair. It is only because of the mercy of the Mining Wield that you still live to atone for your crimes against the commonwield. Your Way is not to shirk the path of justice but to accept it with..."

Yrund rolled the apple over in her hand as the mine boss droned on, stuck on one of his usual tirades about Asterian superiority. She lifted the apple to her mouth, aware the other prisoners were watching, and tore into the sweet flesh. The apple was mealy and overripe, but Yrund ate it all, down to the seeds and core.

"And in case you don't remember me telling you yesterday, let me say it again"—Brandul unwrapped a speckled white stone and held it up—"the river crew is not to save any more mouse agyt!" The last few words came out in a squeak. A muffled snort escaped from the table behind them. Brandul snarled, throwing the agyt out the door, then unwrapped another stone that looked identical to Yrund's eyes. He lifted it for everyone to see. "*This* is what you are to keep—milk agyt and milk agyt only."

Based on the twitching lips around her, Yrund guessed the river crew knew exactly which stone they had been collecting.

"As you no doubt heard, we blasted today, so that means all of the day shift will be clearing rubble on level two tomorrow."

Yrund sat up. What? Level two? That wasn't where they had blasted. Had Gem Beard not told the mine boss yet? All the defiance drained out of her. There was no rubble to cart out, and it would be at least another day of blasting before there was.

"So, enough wasting time. We've found the vein. Go get me the gems."

When the mine boss finally dismissed them, Yrund stopped at the tank outside her tent to wash her face and tend to the blisters the day's drilling had left across her palms. Normally she had to fight her way for a place at the water, but tonight the other prisoners let her through. Having everyone think you were about to die had its privileges, but if Veng had meant to get his revenge tonight, he was late. If he didn't hurry, Brandul would beat him to it. Or Gem Beard—there was still the matter of the pink gem. Yrund had almost forgotten about it, but now she imagined she could feel the stone inside her, bobbing among the fermented apple and watery soup. Her head spun. She searched in her dark corner of the tent for the pelt Pit had given her. Another rabu must have taken it. As she rolled herself against the moldy side of the tent for warmth, she caught a whisper of voices outside, too faint to understand.

YRUND WOKE IN THE DARKNESS, clammy and shivering, the damp seeping into her bones from the ground beneath the moldy tent. Yak balls. Her stomach felt like it was being stirred with a dirty spoon—probably Brandul's revenge for eating his garbage. The woman next to her was talking in her sleep, begging for more soup. Yrund burped, the remnants of dinner lapping at the back of her tongue.

She rolled over again, trying to return to sleep, but the churning was growing stronger. A flush of nausea ran up her throat and jaw. She lay as still as possible, hoping it would pass. She couldn't get sick. She wasn't even allowed out of the tent at this hour. But her stomach was not going to stay down. Whatever bit of poison it had ingested was climbing back out, and rapidly.

DOUBLED OVER, Yrund stumbled out of her tent, cursing the camp's cook to a long and soup-induced death. It was not the first time she had been sick since her capture, what with the Mining Wield's poor care of them, but this was more than her stomach. Her head was spinning so badly she could hardly see, missing the path to the latrine trenches in the dark. She turned back, confused.

A man stepped out of the shadows, blocking her way.

"Look what I've found, out scurrying in the night," said Veng. "It's the little rat."

Bogging hell.

Yrund clutched at her abdomen, pointing toward the latrines. Or were they the other direction? A fresh wave of sweat broke across her forehead.

"You know, you're—not—supposed—to—leave—your—tent." He stressed each word like a teacher admonishing a student, a very drunk teacher that was.

Yrund pointed a finger at her throat. Couldn't the blasturd see she was going to be sick?

"Now why are you making faces at me? Is it the black eye? Don't you like it?" he purred. "You gave it to me." Boozy fumes of something sharp and fermented wafted downwind.

Yrund tried to duck past him, stomach contracting, but the ground was tilting away. Instead of going around the man, she lurched into him.

Veng staggered, then caught her, grinning like a wolf that had found his prey. "Oh, you want to dance, do you?"

Was he swaying, or was it her? He licked her cheek, and she gagged, trying to twist free, but up and down had ceased to have any meaning at all. Her eyes were dice in a cup.

"This is even more fun than I thought it would be," sang Veng, accompanied by the metallic zing of a knife slipping from its scabbard.

Yrund stepped back, tripping over her own feet and into the rough canvas of a tent. She bounced and fell. Blindly, she searched for something to defend herself with. Anything—a chunk of rock or a tent peg. As if the Sky had finally heard her, her fingers closed around the wood of a handle. A shovel from the weight of it.

As she heaved the heavy tool up, Gem Beard's words came back to her: *If you need to kill someone, just do it.*

She was trying, but the world was a spinning whirl. She held the shovel in front of her, jabbing at the two Vengs, unable to tell which was real. He laughed, and she spun toward the sound, the jagged edge of a blade raking across her ribs.

She jabbed again, making contact with something soft.

Veng cursed, swinging his leg to kick her so hard the wind was knocked from her lungs. Yrund dropped to her knees, the shovel falling from her grasp. He kicked her again. And again.

"Are you ready?" A boot jammed against Yrund's shoulder, crushing her into the dirt.

She could feel a hand closing over her mouth.

"An eye for an eye?" Veng cooed as his knife pierced Yrund's skin.

Yrund bit down. Blood and bone filled her mouth.

Then she vomited.

Veng reared back, screaming as he clutched his hand. "My fing—"

He was cut off by the sound of a shovel bouncing off something hard.

Yrund vomited again, her stomach turning itself inside out until nothing was left.

"Come now," someone whispered. "You can't stay here." Cool hands helped Yrund sit up, wiping her mouth with her sarong.

Yrund turned dizzily to see the freckled face of the woman from the breakfast line that morning. The woman with the braid. "Can you walk?" she asked, her strong arms lifting Yrund up to stand.

Yrund's eyes were settling now, the scene before her coming into focus. Veng lay slumped where he had fallen, a crystal flask gaping out from his coat pocket and his dagger in the dirt. Against the tent behind him leaned a shovel.

"I would cut his throat if I thought you wouldn't take the blame," said the woman as she pulled Yrund away from the scene. "Pray to Irsil he falls down a shaft." She led Yrund back down the dark path to the water barrel outside her tent, hastily washing the blood from Yrund's face and sarong. The woman looked back frequently over her shoulder as if someone were waiting.

Yrund shivered in her wet sarong, too weak to help, barely able to stand.

"I'm sorry," Yrund thought she heard the woman say as she finished her rough scrubbing and pushed Yrund into her tent.

Yrund collapsed in her corner, dreaming the memluks were laughing while her mother screamed.

CHAPTER FOUR

Yrund felt almost warm, light shining through her eyelids with a red glow. One eye opened to take in the bright, empty tent. The other was swollen shut. *Bog it!* She had missed the morning gong! Must have missed all the gongs. How had the guards not found her yet?

She sat up, wincing. There was a shallow gash across her side, the blood a strange blue in the tent's light, and boot-shaped black bruises across her ribs. The night came back in a dizzying flash. Veng. Yrund touched her puffy eye, fingertips tracing the edge of the knife wound below. If it hadn't been for the woman with the braid…

Yrund crawled to the tent flap, almost blinding herself when she lifted it.

Suns and blue sky!

And a very big memluk.

"Tried to wake you earlier, but you were out like a possum," said Gem Beard. The memluk was sitting bare-chested in the sunslight, embroidering his vest with a needle and thread. His red hair was wet and his shirt was drying on the rock beside him.

"Boss said cut off your stinking feet so we could reuse those anklets, then throw you off the cliff." He looked closely at his work, rubbing his thumb across the knots. "Wasn't too happy we changed his plan."

The hair on Yrund's arms lifted like prairie squirrels on alert.

"However, he's a perfect idjit. We need a ratter, and you're the only one left. I convinced him we gotta see how much good yesterday's blast did before we start tunneling through all holey-poley." He pointed his needle at her. "So, you're going to go back in and have a look-see. Maybe set some more charges. Find something blooding good before this hellhole freezes over. Winter won't be long now." He lifted his beard at the clouds accumulating to the south. A trace of rain was in the air. Yrund could smell it, too, along with the nearly forgotten scent of suns-warmed dirt and grass and soap. Gem Beard had had a bath.

One of the beads woven into his beard caught in the sunslight, shimmering blue and green like waves over deep water. Yrund examined the maps of islands and shores tattooed across his war-scarred body. Had he really been all those places? she wondered. She'd never seen the memluk in full light before. He was younger than she'd thought, thirty at most, his eyes crinkled prematurely by a life at sea and shifting between green and blue with little sparks of gold.

"What are you staring at? You're not so pretty yourself this morning, you know."

Yrund touched her swollen eye, then shifted her gaze away from the memluk to take in the snow-capped peaks around them. They were arranged like a crown seen from the inside. A deep green lake lay in the center of the high aerie, its shores lit with firemoss and ice plant. Into the lake poured a river, along which prisoners were crushing and sorting ore. Above it all was the searing blue sky.

"Enough sitting around staring at the clouds," said Gem Beard, biting off his thread. He put the needle in a small case, then retrieved his shirt. Last he put the vest back on, admiring the new ring of peaks across the shoulder. "We've got jewlies waiting for us."

Yrund's heart sank. Her first look at the suns in months, and it would soon be over.

"Speaking of which"—Gem Beard groaned a little as he heaved himself up, rubbing at his back—"where's *my* jewlie?"

The jewlie! Yrund had forgotten all about it. Where was the jewlie? She touched her abdomen, scenes of the night coming back to her—Veng and his knife, the blood, and the vomiting. Bogging hell! Could the stone still be there? What if someone else had already found it?

Gem Beard held out his hand as big as a pan, waiting.

Yrund gathered her torn sarong, then used the tent pole to pull herself up.

"Well?" said the memluk. "Where is it?"

Yrund motioned for Gem Beard to follow her, retracing the route to the latrine she had taken the night before. There was no missing the place she had been attacked. Veng was still there, passed out in the shadows of the tent, the flask at his side.

Yrund dug through the stinking puddle of blood and vomit curdling beside the man, searching for Gem Beard's jewlie, and then she saw it—a hint of pink beneath the muck. She wiped the lumpy gem on her sarong and held it out to Gem Beard, but when she tried to stand, she fell right back over, eyes spinning.

✦ ✦ ✦ ✦

GEM BEARD GUFFAWED as he held the gem up to the suns. "This is what you swallowed? A spinyl? What the sea snakes did you do that for? This will make you sicker than bat curry in a hurricane. You're not supposed to swallow a spinyl unless you've been poisoned. Don't you know anything?"

Yrund started to shake her head, then stopped, the motion too much to bear. She watched Gem Beard wrap the pink gem in a wad of tree gum he pulled off his boot. Then he flipped open the pommel of one of his hammers and stuck the gum-covered gem up inside.

Veng moaned from the shadows.

With a practiced motion, Gem Beard smacked the hammer against his fist, sealing the pommel's secret hollow back up.

"Bad night with the bug juice?" he asked Veng, knocking the man's outstretched boot with his own. "You missed all the fun."

Veng woke, cursing as he tried to raise a hand to the back of his head, where dried blood had formed a cap.

"You tangle with a cliff leopard or something?"

"Not a leopard—a rat. Help me up!"

Gem Beard waited a moment before giving the man his wrist.

"Must have been a big rat," said the memluk, shaking the Asterian off as soon as he was standing.

Veng examined his mangled hand with a hiss of real pain. Deep tooth marks went clear through two swollen fingers, one of which drooped at an odd angle. "Not a real rat. The girl, you fool —that mangy little outlander."

"This one?" Gem Beard asked with a guffaw, tipping his beard at Yrund, who was doing her best to hide behind him. Veng swung around to glare at Yrund, his eyes shot with red. His knife still lay in the dirt. He kicked the blue blade up with his toe, catching the hilt in his good hand.

"Corpse! I'll kill you!"

Yrund leapt back, keeping the memluk between her and the circling Veng.

"Are you joking me?" Gem Beard hooted. "This morning just keeps getting better. You're telling me this little chicken got the best of you?"

This caught Veng off guard. His glare darted to the big memluk now.

"The best of me? She didn't get the best of me..." He wobbled his head, his unshaven face muddled by hangover and pain.

"Uh-huh, moons weren't up until late last night. Would've been pretty dark out here. You sure it wasn't those two southern fellers you caught trying to escape?"

"Escape? You mean the Lumi?" Veng said, absorbing this news.

So someone else had finally done it, thought Yrund despondently. That would make her own plans all the harder. The guards would be watching now.

"The men or the woman?" asked Veng.

"Just the fellers. Guess she was late."

Veng didn't like that. "I bet on all three!" He winced as he tried to move his hand.

"That's how it goes. Though, I wouldn't have guessed them for biters…"

Sweat shone across Veng's face as he braced his wounded hand against his chest. "I'm telling you—it was the rat that bit me! Look at her. Only a cobaline blade could leave that stain." He pointed at Yrund's swollen eye with his dagger, the sunslight catching its blue sheen.

Face now serious, Gem Beard took Yrund's chin in his big fingers, tipping it up to the suns. Then he examined the boot marks across her shoulders. "Let me see what's under that," he said, pointing to the torn sarong, which Yrund was clutching between her fingers.

Bog them all, thought Yrund, letting the fabric fall open to reveal the long dagger mark across her ribs. The raw wound was edged with blue as deep as ink.

Gem Beard made a small sucking sound with his teeth. "*Mzryllyck* blasturd," he said under his breath.

"See?" Veng was on one foot now, his other ready to strike.

Yrund ducked behind Gem Beard, wondering if she could get one of the hammers off his belt.

"Hold up—you can't kill her yet." The memluk stood his ground between the two of them. "Not until the blasting's done.

Unless you want to send the wielder a pigeon before we get back that says we don't have his stones?"

With a sound of disgust, Veng flipped his dagger back into its scabbard.

"Leolin Damantine can put a pigeon up his..." Veng made a rude gesture, starting his hand bleeding again. "Kicking little mute!" he said, advancing towards Yrund. "Don't think I'll forget this."

"You want to stand around blooding and whining or you gonna let me sew up those fingers?" asked Gem Beard.

INSIDE THE MEAL TENT, two memluks and the cigar-smoking cook were playing jump-jewel on a board carved straight into a table's plank. The game pieces glinted in the sunslight that cut under the tent's rolled-up sides. Melmeth guided Yrund in toward them, his hand around her neck like a noose. The cook hacked when she stood up, the table shaking under her weight as she leaned to spit on the floor of her own kitchen.

"Melmeth," she said in Trade Tongue. "I don't see you here often." Her grimy apron had stains on its stains, but in her ears were shiny gems the size of buttons and as bright as grass, and around her wide waist was a purse made of scraps. She might have been a prisoner, but she was an Asterian prisoner and that came with privileges.

"Morning, Tmina. You still have that mallowkite? We've got a little sewing to do."

Veng sagged down on a bench. "And something to drink."

"What happened to him?" asked the cook, her piggy eyes wide.

"Run-in with those Lumi," said Gem Beard, as if that explained it all. Yrund noticed he didn't mention her own part, though she couldn't say whether that was for her sake or Veng's.

Tmina wobbled her head, a custom Yrund had observed

among the few Asterians at the mine. "Gone now." The cook opened the purse at her waist, picking through its contents with dirty fingers until she found what she wanted—a smooth green stone the size of a thumbnail. "One mallowkite." She placed the marbled green cabochon on the rough table.

"Think you owe me a moonystone, too," said Gem Beard before Tmina could close her purse.

The cook took a puff on her cigar, then slid over a shimmery blue stone from her keeps pile.

Clucking with satisfaction, Gem Beard slipped the moonsstone into a drawstring sack he wore around his neck with all his other amulets, then tossed the mallowkite to Veng, who placed it under his tongue. The Asterian's hand looked even worse up close, half of his right ring finger barely attached by white tendon.

Yrund's stomach churned. Had she really done that?

Yes—and she would do it again. Veng had been about to carve her eye out. She shivered to think what might have happened if the brave woman with the braid hadn't shown up. Brave Braid had saved her. Had she also escaped? Yrund hoped so.

Gem Beard said something in Douarr to the other two memluks in the tent. After a quick round of rock, rabbit, lichen, one of the pair let out a groan. He was the youngest of the guards, and though the second in height after Gem Beard, his reddish beard was still short. Inexplicably, Pit had liked him, no doubt because he let the ratter gamble with them at night. The young giant fished a flask from his vest and brought it over. Gem Beard said a few more words in Douarr that seemed to provide consolation. Lips twitching, Short Beard sidled back to the other memluk and whispered in his ear.

"What did you tell them?" demanded Veng.

"You know. About those southern dolts."

"What about them?"

"Like Tmina said—gone now."

Veng did not look convinced. He took a long pull of the flask as he watched Gem Beard heat first an embroidery needle to red in the cookfire's coals, then the blade of his heaviest knife.

"What's that for?"

"See for yourself. Not even a bloodstone could save the end of that finger."

Yrund skittered back as Veng threw his empty flask at her head. "Count your fingers now, rat! When Brandul's done with you, I'm going to take them all."

WHILE GEM BEARD finished his gruesome work, Yrund pretended to watch the game of keeps that had restarted, trying to ignore Veng who was oddly oblivious to the pain now that he had the cook's green stone. His eyes traced her features like two arrows.

"Five!" Short Beard gathered up all the stones on the table while the cook wished him a short trip off the nearby cliff. Yrund noticed she didn't say so in Douarr, which the cook knew better than anyone in camp, having been in the Spice Wars herself, though in what capacity it was hard to imagine. The woman had a disdain for work.

To Yrund's gratitude, Veng had finally passed out, either from the drink or gem, or both. No longer being watched with those hateful, bleary eyes, she stretched to get a better view of the peaks, hoping she might spot the Lumi prisoners that had escaped, but the view from this side of camp was too limited to see more than a triangle of ridge. She wondered why the guards were so relaxed with rabu on the loose. Did they not expect the escapees to survive the high mountains? Or had they already caught them? No, that was unlikely. She knew memluks well enough to know they wouldn't have been able to resist parading their prize around in front of the camp like a cat with a lizard.

"Maybe you could get that ratter breakfast," Gem Beard called to the cook as he finished his work on the unconscious Asterian. Tmina reached for a burnt bug biscuit.

"Not that—give her some meat." Gem Beard unclipped the large brass meal cup from his belt and tossed it to Yrund.

"The captain know what you're up to?" the cook asked around the cigar in her mouth, one eye wrinkled against the smoke.

"Brandul wouldn't feed his own mother if she were starving, and I need a ratter that can stand up today."

The woman shrugged. "It's your head, not mine." She ladled Yrund a cup of cold meat soup, then tapped her cigar's burning end on top. Yrund blew the ash off. There were a few lumps of stringy marmot swimming in the greasy, unseasoned broth. The memluks added their own salt, from little pinch pots they carried in their vests and did not share with lowly rabu. Yrund missed her mother's cooking almost as much as she missed her mother— barbecued marmot stuffed with wild mint and spring onions with a side of curd dumplings.

She took her meal to the edge of the tent, drinking in the sunslight. It would have been a glorious day if she hadn't been a prisoner. Little snow drops and monkey paws and other wild- flowers decorated the mossy banks of the river below, and across the valley the willow leaves were already beginning to turn golden. She could hear the calls of a pair of eagles hunting over- head, high above the noise of the river and the clang of tools on rocks. Even the trash piles outside camp were dotted with violet bells and yellow bulbs. Back home she would have picked them, weaving a wreath for her favorite goat, who would blink sweetly with her golden-green eyes while eating any flowers that drooped low enough over her ears to reach.

"Don't lick my cup!" said Gem Beard, clipping Yrund on the head and taking the empty mug back. Veng was splayed out across the table behind them, his hand wrapped in cloth while the memluks tossed the severed half of his finger back and forth like a keeps stone. Seeing the cook was distracted with the fun, Gem Beard slipped a dusty jar of chili flakes from her stores into his pocket. Then he pushed Yrund back outside. One of the memluks saluted as they left, gnashing his teeth at her.

"Still can't understand how one little chicken could knock out an Astrini all on her own," said Gem Beard as they made their way out of camp. "Or why you didn't just cut the blasturd's throat. He'll be out for you now…"

All the more reason to leave. Yrund gazed up at the crown of mountains that rose around them. The peaks were even steeper than she remembered, cragged with snowy caps, but to the south, where the suns shone, little white dots were grazing on patches of brilliant green grass. Mountain goats! She craned her neck to pick out the path the sure-footed animals must have taken to reach the pasture above the cliffs. It would not be easy to find their slim footholds, but if there was one thing Yrund was born for—it was to follow goats.

"Faster, little fart, or we'll never get there," called Gem Beard, beginning the steep climb up the mountain.

Yrund dragged behind him, taking it all in. In her treks down from the mine every night, she had entirely missed the narrow ledge that cut across the cliffs above the river. It would not be hard to reach, just a short drop past the deadlines. A patch of lilies fluttered beside the trail like tethered stars glorious in the sunslight, a pair of blue-backed ravens pecking at strands of something red. Yrund stopped. Amid the delicate white flowers lay two charred skeletons, meaty flesh scorched down to the bone.

"Watch yourself!"

Yrund's head spun as if she'd swallowed a spinyl again.

The men's faces were melted black masks, mouths open mid-scream.

"Told you not to cross those lines, didn't I?"

Yrund did not move. "What h-happened?" she asked, voice croaking from disuse.

The memluk gaped at her, his scar shining white in the suns. "You got something to say?"

Yrund cleared her throat and tried again. "What happened to them?"

"What happened? The gem-sucking Mining Wield happened. There's no getting in their way or out of it. There's no escape for your lot—not with those snakes on," he said, pointing to Yrund's anklets.

Fury filled her. "You bet which of us would die first?"

"Nope—we bet which of you would try to *escape* first. Dying's easy."

Yrund stared into Gem Beard's blue eyes, willing him to burst into flames.

"Don't look at me like that." He stared right back at her. "I warned you about those deadlines not two nights ago."

"You did not!" Yrund was shaking she was so angry. "You only kept me from going over so you wouldn't lose your bet."

Gem Beard tried to remember, then shrugged. "Well, I still saved your scrawny tail, so shut your beak."

Yrund looked anew at the metal snakes that bound her ankles, the individual scales and cold blue eyes glinting in the light. Then she looked up at the mountain goats scampering along the peaks. She would never be free.

She would never go home.

"Now hurry it up. We've got jewlies to find."

Yrund moved to the center of the trail, following in the memluk's dusty boot prints. Though the sky blazed, the valley had turned ominous, the rocky cliffs casting shadows at every turn.

CHAPTER FIVE

At the mine's entrance, Yrund paused to stare up, burning the blue sky into her memory. Then she raised her arms in salute to the suns and began to sing.

Oh the suns,
Oh the light,
Oh the warmth,
Oh, Oh, Oh,
Oh the day!
The suns are here!

With a final look back, Yrund stepped from bright day into the perpetual night of the mine, green dots swimming in the black space of her pupils. Blast it! She couldn't see a thing. She bumped into one wall and then the other until the sound of Gem Beard's exasperated swearing told her which direction to turn.

"Nuts! You aren't supposed to look at the suns. Everyone knows that. You'll burn your eyes out."

Yrund squeezed her eyes open and closed, trying to adjust to the dim light. Gradually, spots still lingering, she made out the large memluk shaking his beard at her.

As they packed their gear, Gem Beard handed her a second canteen to fill for herself, something Stinn had never allowed. "Don't swallow any more jewlies. Next one could be a nepenthe."

He didn't have to worry. Swallowing a gemstone was already on Yrund's list of things never to do again.

When they reached the fork where Gem Beard had waited for her the day before, they found only one tunnel remained. The other had collapsed overnight, spewing crushed rock. The memluk carefully set down the explosives and dug through the rubble, picking out small bits of pink crystal. Spinyl. Yrund felt queasy just looking at them, but Gem Beard was nodding.

"Yup, yup. On the right track. One more round of blasts should do it." As he stood up, he grimaced. "Oww, my back can't take this for much longer. Stooping and bending all day—it's mole's work." He tried to reach around his girth to massage a spot near his spine just under his heavy leather vest, but his arm wouldn't bend that far. He searched for a rock jutting out from the wall at the right height, but couldn't find one. "Here, you, give me a hand."

Yrund felt as if she were moving through thick water. There was no escape—not for her, not for anyone. She set down her equipment with a clank.

"Wake up!" Gem Beard snapped his fingers in front of her face, but Yrund barely blinked. "What's wrong with you?"

Yrund turned away.

"You still upset about those men? Don't be—they were crimi-nals, or else they wouldn't have been here."

"I'm here, and I'm not a criminal." Yrund's voice was rusty, foreign to her ears.

"No? Your people didn't blow up that bridge over the Jaggedy? 'Cause someone did—it was all over the posts."

"It wasn't us!"

"Doesn't matter. You did something that pissed off the wields. Now you're here."

"No, I'm here because of all of you that can't pick your nose without a gem to help you!" she said angrily, the act of speaking releasing a rush of feelings she'd been trying to keep penned.

"You poor blooding fool," said Gem Beard, looking at her with pity. "You think the ladies are just gonna give up their rubilies and pearls 'cause it's little squirts digging them up? Or a Sea Hammer his guidestones? Not a chance. This planet runs on gems. And one little rabu isn't going to change that."

"But it's the rabu that dig up those gems."

"So?"

"So—there's more of us than them. We could do something!"

"What?"

"We could say no."

Gem Beard snorted, the small motion making him reach for his back again. "Not while the Sea Hammers work for the Mining Wield, you can't."

"The Mining Wield captured you, too, didn't they?"

"No, they blooding did not!" Gem Beard's nostrils flared, then retracted. "The Borosians did. The Mining Wield just bought us."

"What's the difference? You're still prisoners."

"Prisoners!" scoffed Gem Beard. "We can leave anytime we want."

"Then why don't you?"

"Because they pay us not to, is why not. A pirate's life isn't all gemshine and burning down towns, you know. We're at sea in suns and storms for months at a time, nothing but salt terns and ocean..." He went quiet, remembering.

"Sounds better than being down here," said Yrund, waving at the rock walls imprisoning them.

For a moment it looked like the memluk would agree, but only for a moment. "What are you—a freewielder? Mind your own Way," he snapped. "Now, are you going to help me out with this sore back of mine, or do I need to give you a thump?"

Yrund dug her knuckles into the memluk's spine, but it was like trying to massage a wall.

"I didn't say tickle me, did I? Use some strength."

Yrund switched to her fists, leaning in with all her weight.

Gem Beard tried to crane his neck around to see what she was doing. "That's all you got?" He sighed. "You'll have to use those stinky little feet."

Yrund lifted a foot up into the air, trying to keep her balance, but it wasn't even close to reaching the memluk's back. "Not like that, you idjit. I have to lie down first. You walk on it, get it? You try to kick me again, and I'll drop you down the next shaft." He winced as he lowered his bulk to the floor, only to find his belt of knives and tools in the way. He cursed in Douarr, shifting them and his heavy hammer to the side.

"I'll walk on your back if you give me some of your piney seeds to eat."

"What is this? A mutiny? You don't get to bargain. You're lower than chum slick. Think I liked you better as a mute."

Yrund crossed her arms and leaned back against the wall. Like he'd told Veng, they couldn't kill her yet. She was still the last ratter.

"Fine. You can have some seeds—when you're done."

It wasn't as easy as Yrund might have thought, walking on someone's back. "Oooh, hoo, hoo! No tickling!" Gem Beard yelled when her foot slipped and her toes dragged across his side.

She used the wall for balance until she got the hang of it, wedging her arch over the muscles along his spine. Hopping her way up his ribs, she finally felt something pop. Gem Beard exhaled with relief and rolled over. "That's better. Now help me up." She grabbed his calloused hand with both of hers and leaned back with all her weight. Slowly the memluk rose to sitting.

"Blast this mine," he said, wiping his face.

"I want my seeds," said Yrund.

He fished around in his vest and tossed a sack to her.

Yrund poured out a generous, but not too large, handful of seeds and gave the rest back.

"Allyright, don't get comfortable," Gem Beard said, leaning against the wall and getting out his book. "We still have another chamber to blast." By *we*, he meant *she* did.

Yrund repeated her journey of the day before, no easier than it had been the last time. But when she finally reached the chamber where she had planted the previous charges, it was not just unrecognizable—it was no longer there. Yrund lowered the sack of fresh blast sticks to the floor and inched forward to hang her lantern over the edge of the new crevasse their work had created. Gleaming blue and violet crystals ran like mold across the chasm's veined sides, spiraling down into the darkness. Yrund dropped a rock over, waiting for it to hit bottom, but not a sound came back.

With a sickening crack, she chipped off the bit of gem she could reach with her pick and sat back on her haunches to inspect it. The gem was bright on its broken edge, turning from violet to blue depending how she held it. A vagary, she guessed, and there were more—lots more. She hated to help the wield in their greedy hunt for more stones, but she had to bring something back. Yrund leaned back over the hole and chipped off one more crystal. One for the mine boss. One for Gem Beard. Not so much they could be done with her, but not so little they would whip her. Like Gem Beard had said—she had to think five moves ahead, though right now she could only think one. Once Brandul had recovered his quota, there was nothing to keep him from letting Veng have her.

Gem Beard was engrossed with his book when Yrund returned. Or maybe he was asleep. It was hard to tell with his head tipped down toward the page. Yrund set her pick down, keeping her distance. She cleared her throat.

"Hey." No response.

"Gem Beard?"

He held up a finger, continuing to read. Finally, he closed the book. "About time. Where's the fuse line?"

Yrund held out the sack with the gems. She had left the blast sticks that had been inside it under a dry rock.

"What's that you've got in there? A spider? Some nepenthe?"

She wished. Yrund opened the sack for him, offering one of the violet crystals out on her palm.

"If I'm not a squid's…would you look at that!" Gem Beard rubbed his thumb against the crystal's raw edges, holding it closer to the lantern light. "That's as big a vagary as I've seen. Shame there's just one."

Yrund shook the sack that held the other crystal. The memluk dumped the second vagary out. "There's two?"

"One for you. One for Brandul," explained Yrund.

Gem Beard whooped, dancing her around the tunnel, his back pain forgotten. "With a stone like this, I could spend the rest of my days eating crabs and drinking rumgem," he gloated. "What do you think about that?"

Yrund's shoulders fell. "That's good for you," she said wearily, blotting the blood running down her ribs with her sarong. The blue gash across her ribs had broken open again.

"But not for you, huh?" The memluk rolled the rough crystal between his fingers, feeling its weight. "You know, sometimes rabu have a way of finding new owners at the end of the season. If they pull their oar right…"

Yrund wondered what that meant—pulling her oar right.

Gem Beard slid the violet gem inside his hammer's handle. "And go back to keeping their mouths shut like good little mutes."

That she understood.

"Good. Now, what was it you called me—Gem Beard? I like that. Gem Beard. What's that rhyme with? Feared, steered, skeered…"

Weird, Yrund thought to herself, but didn't say so out loud. The memluk made up a new song on their long trek back up to the mine's entrance.

They call him Gem Beard!
A pirate most revered!
Born of fire and thunder,
Over the seas he wandered,
The wind his only home,
Oh! The wind his only home.
Helping lost ships
To lighten their loads,
Oh! Lost ships to lighten their loads,
Of wheels of ripe cheese,
And baskets of bees,
And stones of seefire and toad.

"You like it?"

Gems of toad? Yrund considered what he'd just said about some rabu getting second chances before she answered. "Mmm… not bad."

"But not good?" he grumbled.

"I didn't say that. The beginning was all right."

Gem Beard sang through the last part again.

Wheels of ripe cheese,
And baskets of bees…

"What comes next?" he asked as he disappeared up a shaft's ladder. "Did I get to the oranges yet?"

As Yrund followed him up, she wondered how much she could trust the memluk. She had seen memluks buying rabu at the market in Wyn after her capture, and though she wasn't keen on being anyone's property—surely it was easier to escape from one obnoxious pirate than the entire Mining Wield. Maybe her Way had finally changed.

. *. * ☆ ✳. ✹ *.

FOR THE FIRST time since her capture, Yrund woke with something akin to hope. Gem Beard was waiting outside the meal tent just as he'd said he would. He waved Yrund to the front of the line.

"Three biscuits today, Tmina," he told the cook, ignoring the mumblings of the rabu they'd cut in front of. "Got a big day ahead of us." He broke off a piece of Yrund's breakfast, sniffed it, then took a bite.

"Bleh!" He spat the rest out and wiped his mouth. "Tastes like slug shat."

Yrund didn't disagree, but she ate the biscuits anyway. With Gem Beard by her side, no one would dare steal them, but she could feel the eyes upon her. Brave Braid was not among them. On the night shift again, Yrund hoped. She shivered.

"You cold? Hoy, there, give the rat your shirt," he told a man waiting in line. The shocked prisoner took a moment to react. Gem Beard pulled it off him and threw it to Yrund. "There you go."

Yrund didn't want it. The other rabu would hate her enough for the extra biscuit.

Gem Beard slapped her ear. "You said you were cold."

Yrund avoided looking at the prisoner as she put the shirt on, still warm from his skin and stinking of his sweat.

"Don't think your new pet will last," said Veng, sidling out of the cook's tent. "She still owes me." He raised his bandaged hand, and Yrund saw he had one of Brandul's strikers on his belt.

"Tell you what," said Gem Beard. "When we're done, you can have her finger, and that taw of mine you been wanting—the azuline one."

Yrund went cold again despite the shirt, imagining the pain of losing a finger.

"You're just a memluk. It isn't for you to decide," Veng pointed out.

Gem Beard wobbled his head. "You saying she's not for sale? Guess I'll bargain with Brandul for her, then. My mistake."

"Why do you want her so bad?" asked Veng suspiciously, staring Yrund up and down. "She looks like a boy. Hasn't even grown her teats yet."

Yrund covered her chest with her arms, then let them down again. There was nothing wrong with her body.

"You're as sick as they're born, Veng," said Gem Beard with disgust. "And stupider than I would have thought. Every rabu you kill is one less worker. Less workers is less gems. Less gems is less pay."

"Less pay for you maybe, memluk. I'm wield by blood."

"Yeah? We'll see how far that gets you when the Mining Wield runs out of gems."

Veng laughed. "The Mining Wield will never run out of gems. But you can have her, Hammer Melmeth, in exchange for the taw, a finger—and an eye. *Her* finger and eye," he clarified. "Not someone else's. I know how clever you think you are."

"What would I want a one-eyed ratter for, huh?"

"That's my price," said Veng.

An eye? thought Yrund. She might have cost him a finger, but Veng's eye was fine. There was barely a hint of a bruise left from where she had thrown the cup at him.

"We'll talk later. There's mining to do," said Gem Beard, pulling Yrund away.

"Don't you worry," the memluk said when they were out of earshot. "Every Asterian has a price. Even a blasturd like Veng. You just find me another one of those vagaries, and you've got a new friend. An eyestone for an eye—how could he resist?"

The right stone had bought her Gem Beard. But Veng? The

only stone Veng deserved was a gembane. She wished she knew more about the poisonous stones. In the meantime, it would have to be a seefire. At least she knew what those looked like. And where to find one.

Gem Beard sang as they hiked up the mountain, swinging his hammer into his fist for percussion.

Jewlies, jewlies, jewlies!
Sunday is rubilies,
Moonsday azulies,
Tidesday a topaz,
Waysday a...

The memluk's good mood did not last long. Brandul was waiting for them inside the mine's entrance chamber. The mine boss jabbed the wall map with his striker. A yellow-green gem shone sickly from a crystal window in its side. "I told you to blast straight through. What's all this about tunneling through from level three?"

Gem Beard bushy eyebrows crossed. "You and I discussed it—we're risking collapse going straight in. 'Specially now. The crews already started blasting the new tunnel last night."

"And only cleared ten feet! At that rate, we'll never make it in time."

"But they found a whole bucket of pomegarnets and moonystones, not to mention those seefires."

"You think I'm here for a few seefires?" Brandul asked, turning to tap Gem Beard with the snout of the striker. "The airships will be back for us any day! We—are—going—straight—through!"

The memluk raised his hands. "You saw what happened last time. Lost three ratters—could've been a whole crew."

"Three ratters? Three ratters?! You think I care about losing rabu? That's what they're here for, you thickheaded pirate! To die! Leolin doesn't intend to waste his precious ships on a bunch of spent rabu."

Gem Beard rocked back on his big boots, eyes narrowing. "What about my men? I thought we were going to Smeralgdus next."

"Your men are. The rabu are not."

"Not if you blow them to pieces, you *rppty* idjit! I've got six Sea Hammers down there right now."

"Then go get them out!" Brandul screamed, the striker flailing.

Yrund turned on her heel to follow Gem Beard, her mind reeling at the mine boss's words. He was going to leave the prisoners behind.

"Not you, rat! You have work to do."

Yrund looked helplessly at Gem Beard. He shook his head, cursing in Douarr. "Sea Mother, forgive me…" Then he turned his back on them and left.

Yrund watched as the big memluk abandoned her. She should have known. He had never meant to help her. He had only wanted more gems for himself.

Brandul put away his striker and dragged a dazed Yrund to the map. "Now, listen to me. I'm the one in charge at this mine. You're going to blast here. Understand?"

Yrund shook her head no.

Brandul jabbed the wall again. "Here, you goat-eater! Here!"

Gem Beard was right. It was bad enough before, but now that the crews had already started blasting level three, going through would be suicide.

Brandul touched the green stone he wore around his neck. "They can go to hell, all of them, laughing behind my back. Let them stay with the rabu. They'll be so hungry by winter, they'll be eating each other alive—if they don't freeze first." He laughed, a short angry bark.

Yrund recoiled as the mine boss continued to rant, mumbling to himself, his lips wet with spit. "But I will have the stone. And

Leolin can go to hell... I will be the high wielder. I am the man Niloofar deserves, not that father-killing traitor..." Brandul unlocked the explosives trunk, filled two bags tight with charges, and shoved them into Yrund's arms.

Yrund barely caught the heavy load, fear moving like cold nettles through her limbs.

Brandul collected the rest of their gear, and Yrund watched him as if in a dream. He had only picked up one lantern and carried no map.

"Now, rat! Now!" he said, pulling out the striker again, urging her onward into the darkness of the mine. "The airships are coming!"

It was a struggle to keep up. Though not nearly the size of Gem Beard, the mine boss had long legs and was propelled by a fever-like fury. He yelled at every line of rabu carrying gem-laden rubble out the opposite direction. Yrund watched them pass her by, their faces glazed. It was as if they were already dead. Their eyes knew. Their bodies just hadn't yet fallen.

Yrund adjusted her precarious grip on the explosives, wondering why she bothered. If she dropped one, it would hardly matter—they were all going to die anyway. The only joy would be knowing she'd taken the mine boss down with her.

But she could not bring herself to do it. Not here, so close to the others.

With a new idea in her head, Yrund followed Brandul down the mine's tunnels, hardly noticing how far they had traveled until Brandul stopped in front of a shaft closed off with a large X. Yrund's heart jerked. At the bottom of the shaft lay the collapsed floor where the other ratters had been smothered.

Brandul pulled his finder's agyt over his neck, the silver chain sparkling in the flame of the lantern. Sweat had formed a greasy slick across his brow. He breathed heavily, tongue pressing against his lips as he watched the green-and-white amulet twitch, then slowly point down, its white tip aimed straight into the shaft.

"Yes…" Brandul's long nose followed. "I knew it. There's an allstone in this mountain, and the beautiful Niloofar shall have it."

As if any gem could make someone love Brandul. It was too much. How one man could be allowed to trade a hundred lives… Yrund stared hard at the mine boss's exposed back. All she had to do was drop the bag she was carrying, and just like that, it would all be over. Violence, then peace. But despite her trembling arms, she could not let the bag go.

Yrund set the load down, wondering what was wrong with her. Hadn't she wanted revenge? On Brandul yes, answered a voice in her head. But why should she have to die? Why not just get rid of the mine boss? He wasn't even paying attention to her, his attention all on his finder stone. She crept forward. Just one push…

Something sharp sank into Yrund's back. At her cry, Brandul whirled from the shaft's edge, flicking one of the spurs on the back of the striker over with his thumb. A spear of light projected from one of the holes in the end like a fang. Yrund ducked behind the bag of explosives, her only cover.

"Look at that, Bran. The rat was going to push you over." Veng emerged from the tunnel behind them, a gleaming throwing star between the thumb and pointer finger on his bandaged hand.

Bogging slinking Asterian, thought Yrund, reaching back to pull out the disk of metal wedged into the muscle by her spine and slicing open her finger. She was between the two men with only the bag of explosives to shield her, and poorly at that.

Veng threw the second disk, which spun into Yrund's shoulder hitting bone. She sucked back the pain, searching wildly for a way out. With a grunt, she picked up the bag with the blast sticks as Brandul advanced. Better Veng's stars than the striker, she decided, keeping the explosives pointed toward the mine boss.

"Crazy rat!" Brandul scrambled up the tunnel toward Veng, clearly assuming she meant to drop the bag. Once again, Yrund considered it, thinking of the ratters who had died just below them.

"You haven't got it in you," sneered Veng. "You still want to live too bad. I can see it in your eyes."

"He's Astrini!" Yrund said to Brandul in a desperate burst. "He's here to spy on you." As she talked, she inched backward toward the shaft.

Brandul's already bulging eyes grew even wider. "Do you hear that, Veng? The mute says you're Astrini."

Veng laughed merrily, another star out. "You think he doesn't know who I am? He arranged for Leolin to send me."

Of course. Had she really thought she could turn the men against each other?

Yrund's heart steeled over. She had nothing left but hate. "You can dig up as many jewels as you want, but you'll still have nothing! No one will ever love you, not the memluks, not Veng, not Niloofar Damantine—not a single woman on this planet. And no one and no stone will ever change that!" She threw the bag.

It clattered on the floor in front of the men, dumping picks and hand drills. Yrund stood stunned, blood dripping down her body. She had picked up the wrong bag. The sack with the explosives was still resting harmlessly by Brandul's feet.

Brandul raised the striker's beam level with her face. "Oh well. At least you'll still be dead."

Bile-colored lightning ripped over Yrund's head as she dove down the shaft.

✳ ✦ ✳ ✦ ✳

Yrund twisted as she fell, flinging her arms out to reach one of the protruding ladder spikes flashing past. With a shoulder-wrenching jerk and scrape of skin, she caught herself, swinging over the dark depths of the cold shaft. The rusty metal twanged as it began to pull loose.

Veng peered over the edge at her.

"Better run, little rat," he said, holding up what looked like a blast stick.

Bogging hell, what had she done? A scatter of dirt fell across her head.

"One…"

The spikes gouged Yrund's body as she half fell and half swung from spike to spike, bloody hands flailing for the next handhold.

"Two…"

Yrund let go.

The ground rose to hit her like a team of horses, taking her breath away.

Get up! She couldn't see anything in the black abandoned tunnel. She reached for a wall, stumbling over rocks.

Far above Veng's voice echoed down.

"Three!"

CHAPTER SIX

The explosion was deafening, the sound echoing off the walls like a giant's hammer. Yrund raised up her arms to shield herself from the spray of rock, ducking in the blackness. For a moment, the tunnel held. Then far away, there was a second explosion. Bogging hell! That must have been the pile of blast sticks she hadn't used the day before, the ones she had left piled by the vein. She just had time to think of her mother and her horse before the floor collapsed, swallowing her whole.

YRUND FELL between the mountain's gnashing rock teeth, tumbling head over tail and screaming curses until she somersaulted into what felt like a pile of sharp glass. Dazed, she lay moaning, ears buzzing like a basket of angry bees, eyes blinded by harsh sunslight. Her nose burned with the smell of blast sticks and blood. It was a long time before she could do more than whimper, but gradually the pain focused itself from every part of her to a distinct constellation of points, the one in her shoulder finally too much to bear. *Bogging Veng!* One of his metal stars was still stuck in her back. With great effort, she sat up, contorting herself to yank the sharp weapon loose. She hissed as it tore her flesh, then flung it away, wiping her tears with a sticky hand.

Blooding hell, it was bright. She shielded her eyes, understanding slow to break.

Sunslight!

There was sunslight! She was free! Yrund stumbled to her feet, forgetting all else. The mountainside must have split—there was a way out. She scrambled toward the suns, slipping on the sharp crystal beneath her, cutting herself anew.

No, not the suns.

Disappointment crushed Yrund as she peered through her fingers.

It was just a gem. A very bright, very large gem, lying between two halves of a cracked rock shell, as if it had just hatched.

Yrund took a step closer. She'd heard of sunsstones before but never actually seen one. She'd no idea they could illuminate so much. It was the first truly useful gem she'd yet run across. Curious, she reached out. The gem rang like a bell at her touch, startling her. Yrund stepped back, but the sound did not stop. On the contrary, the chiming grew louder, echoing through the enormous crystals growing up from the floor. Yrund spun, taking in the shining cavern that rose around her like something out of a moonstale. The gem's music surrounded her, filling her with delirious light, the notes building until the entire cave seemed to thrum. Yrund's mouth opened as if she were possessed.

The mountain was singing—and she knew the song. The mountain was dancing—and she knew the steps. She was the mountain. She was the stone. She was a sun spinning through the sky. She was a star shooting through the night. She was a sparrow, a tree, a drop of falling rain.

She was dust. She was nothing.

She was everything. She was alone.

She was one. She was alive.

She was dead.

Chaos, order, rhythm, misstep. Faster and faster, patterns upon patterns. The steps merging, the music tangling.

Her feet stumbled. Her voice cracked.

She couldn't keep up. The light flickered. Faded.

Then it was gone.

Yrund wept, just a leaf caught up by the wind, then dropped back to earth.

CHAPTER SEVEN

Yrund woke to the cry of an injured animal. Oh no, had she been sleeping during her watch? Had a wolf gotten one of her goats? She coughed, and the crying stopped, replaced by a buzzing ting like a bee stuck inside a bell. She could not tell if her eyes were open or closed, all around her was so black. The air smelled of burnt hair and something else she couldn't place for a moment.

Explosives.

She wasn't back home. She was still inside the mine. There were no scampering goats. No whinnying pony. No hills, no pasture, no suns, no sky.

She was trapped, alone and underground with no way out. She would never see her family again, never hear her mother singing at the loom. Never hear her father whistling as he strode up and down the hills observing their flocks and herds. Never see her grandmother leaning against the family's blue door frame, watching for her to come home with the herd.

Yrund sobbed, tears running down her face and tickling her ears. When she raised her hand to wipe them, something moved in her palm.

"Aaah!" she yelped, flinging her hand as she sat up.

"Aaah!" the thing yelped back, holding firm.

Were peskies real after all?

"Let go!"

"Leggooo. AAAAaaaa!" the thing repeated.

Yrund shook her hand lightly, tentatively.

Whatever it was, wasn't very big for a monster. Don't panic. It was probably just a bat that had fallen from its perch. Or a spider...

She closed her other hand gently around it, expecting teeth or claws, not a burst of light. In her hands glowed a stone as big as a walnut. Had she seen the gem before? A curl of memory rose as if from a dream, then vanished. No, that was impossible. Even a gem shy girl like herself would remember a stone such as this. It was like every beautiful thing she'd ever seen rolled into one—water and lightning, coals and sunslight—the colors shifting like a sky on fire. She ran one finger across the stone and the light went out. She stroked it again, and the light went on. On, off, on, off.

"What in the yak's wool are you?" Some sort of sunsstone obviously.

"Yaaa-aak?" said the stone, and Yrund nearly dropped it. The gem blinked at her, and she stared back in wonder. She didn't know gems could talk.

"Holy beetle. You must be worth a fortune," said Yrund, light-headed. The guards would chop each other to bits fighting over such a stone. She spent a while rolling it around in her hand. The rounded indentations fit her thumb just so, no matter which way she held it. Every time she turned the glittering gem, a new face appeared, the brilliant green of moss by a stream, the soft gold of dry grass. She turned the stone over and over, the sparks within lifting up into the darkness. Yrund had to tear herself away, remembering where she was.

This was the trouble with gems. All they did was distract

people from what really mattered—like the fact there had still been a cave-in. Yrund shone the gem's light around like a lantern, expecting a dark tunnel filled with rubble. Instead she sat at the bottom of a deep and shining cavern growing with blades of giant gold crystals. At their bases grew clusters of pomegarnets and spinyls. Or maybe they were rubilies.

She held the light up higher. There was a hole in the ceiling near one of the crystals. The tunnel's floor must have collapsed, though how she had survived impaling herself on one of the crystal spears… She must have slid down the one nearest to her. That had been lucky. More than lucky. She could have broken her neck. Her clothes were in tatters, stiff with dried blood, but she couldn't find any wounds, only the deep blue ink of Veng's blades like a ragged tattoo. She touched the places where his stars had struck her, confused. Just how long had she been asleep?

Beneath her was a bed of moonsstone. And the broken shell of a cracked egg. No, not an egg. The pieces were made of stone. She held the gem next to it. Was that where it had come from? She tried to fit it back in, but the stone squawked.

"Okay, okay," said Yrund. She didn't want to go back in the dark either. There was so much to see, so much to feel—a whole world to eat.

Wait a moment—what? Why had she thought that? Yrund had a sudden sense her mind had been interrupted with someone else's thoughts. She palpated her head, wondering if she had hit it, but it seemed fine. More than fine. She felt wonderful.

That didn't seem right either. How could she feel wonderful? She was trapped down here. Even a pretty cage was still a cage. She needed to get back to the mine. She had to find Gem Beard and warn him about Brandul's plan. Maybe he wouldn't care about her or the rabu, but he would care about his memluks.

She got up, swinging the stone like a torch. The light narrowed to a pinpoint, then widened until it burst into scatters like a cloud of fireflies. "Wows!" Yrund took a step back without thinking, and her foot dropped into nothing. She teetered backward, waving her arms to catch herself, barely regaining her balance. "Bogging hell!" A chasm stretched down behind her—dark and bottomless. "That was your fault!" she told the light.

The gem seemed chastened, focusing in a solid beam as Yrund picked her way across the sharp crystalline floor away from the chasm. "Ooh, ah!" she complained as spikes of gem stabbed into her bare soles.

"Oowah," said the stone in her hand.

Beyond the crystal forest, a small stream cut through the cavern, clear and green in the gem's light. Yrund set the gem down on the bank, then cupped her hands to drink. The water was cold and tasted of minerals, and she filled her hollow stomach as if she had never drunk before. When she was full, she let the water drip between her fingers, mesmerized at the way it flowed across her skin, catching the light like a liquid jewel. She splashed her face. What was wrong with her? She couldn't just sit here playing like a child. She had to get back. She cursed. There was no way she could reach the hole she had fallen through, and even if she could, the floor above could be entirely caved in.

The first wave of panic hit her. She was still going to die. Without thinking, she began to yell, "Help! Help!"

"Elp-elp!" cried the gem, and Yrund realized how silly it sounded.

Nobody cared about a buried ratter.

"Gems! Gems! Enormous gems! Rubilies! Vagaries! Wellos!" However slim the chance she would convince Gem Beard to rally his men against Brandul, it was still better than starving to death underground. "Allstones!" she yelled. "Allstones!" If that didn't bring them, nothing would.

"Allystones!" repeated the gem like a funny bird.

Yrund sat back on the bank as if someone had punched her. What if the gem really was an allstone, whatever that was? Surely, that was worth her life. Yrund tipped the gem gently with a finger, watching its inner lights twinkle. Just the thought of Brandul holding it filled her with revulsion. Gem Beard? No—not him either, the traitor. If they came for her, she would just have to put it back in its egg, hide it somewhere they would never find it. Poor thing. Back in the dark.

As if it had read her mind, the gem tipped away from her, rolling down the bank.

"Hoy," said Yrund. "Where are you going?"

The gem plunked into the stream with a splash. Yrund jumped in after it, but when she bent to retrieve the stone, a jet of water shot up and hit her in the face. Yrund wiped her eyes. It looked like there were jewels everywhere, the way the gem's light rippled and bounced exuberantly through the waves.

There it was. No, there.

She grabbed and missed again. A much larger plume of water came up in a geyser and doused her completely. Yrund sputtered as the gem spun around her, encircling her with bubbles.

"Hoy, hoy, hoy," it sang as it swam, and Yrund was filled with the giddy sensation of bubbles bursting over her.

What was going on?

The gem looped around her legs, examining her snake-shaped anklets. Then it prodded one, sending a shock of pain through Yrund's leg.

"Stop that!" she said, splashing the stone away and rubbing at her ankle.

The stone swam back, bumping her gently as if it were sorry.

"It's okay," said Yrund. This was getting strange. Too strange. She was talking to a gem. She understood talking to her pony or her goats or the Sky, or even the trees sometimes...but a gem? And yet, she felt as if she understood the stone, and the stone understood her. Perhaps that was the property of this particular gem. Pit had said there were gems that could change your eye color or your mood, though he'd never mentioned anything about talking or swimming.

The gem floated downstream, humming to itself.

"Hoy," said Yrund again, splashing after it. "That's the wrong way!"

But the gem was not listening.

"Hoy, hoy, hoy…hoy, hoy…hoy," sang the stone as it disappeared around the bend, taking its light with it.

* * * * *

YRUND PLUNGED through the stream after the stone.

"Wait! Please!"

The gem bobbled along ahead of her, its light playing against the cave's formations. Waves of delight washed through Yrund's mind as if she were seeing everything all for the first time—rocks, ripples, stalagmites. They looked just like mushrooms without their caps. Mmm, mushrooms.

No! Concentrate, she told herself. One wrong turn and they would be lost forever. They would starve. Or at least, she would starve.

The gem slowed but did not stop zigging and zagging through the water like a drunk fish. Was it laughing? Did gems laugh?

"Listen to me—we have to go back." There was still a chance one of the rubble crews might hear her yelling, still a chance she could convince Gem Beard to help her.

"Hoy, hoy!" The stone beckoned her on, and Yrund had a vision of little blue crabs skittering along the stream's bottom.

Her stomach twisted with hunger. There were crabs down here? She took an involuntary step forward. No. Focus. She needed that light.

She had tamed wild animals before. Why not a gem?

Yrund began to sing:

Find myself a licorice root
To chew all through the night.

The suns will come up rising
Over the hills at dawn.
Now I have the sky to chase
Across the grassy steppes where
You, my love, will be waiting
Just over the horizon.

It was a song her father had taught her to calm the herds.

The gem blinked rapidly on and off, humming the last note.

"You want to hear the song again? Then we have to turn around," said Yrund, backing up through the current. They had lost too much time already.

"Song?"

"I'll sing, but only if we go back."

The light dimmed, and Yrund had a flash of herself trying to put the stone back in its egg. Then giving Gem Beard the vagary.

No wonder the gem didn't trust her.

And should it?

Yrund stood in the middle of the stream as the water flowed around her.

Could she really promise she wouldn't trade the stone for her life? Or would she betray it—just like Gem Beard had betrayed her?

It's not the same thing, she argued with herself. It was just a rock. No harm would actually come to it. The wields loved gems. It would probably be treated better than she had ever been, taken to Asteria and set in some fancy necklace. They might cut and polish it, but that was…

The thought of being cut made Yrund's entire body tremble. It would destroy her.

Not her—the stone, she reminded herself, but the terror lingered as if it were her own.

"All right, I won't take you with me, but I have to go back." Back to the dark to wait for someone that might never come, for someone who would probably kill her anyway. Yrund could not force herself to turn around.

"Where are you going, anyway?"

A vision of searing blue sky and rolling hills flooded Yrund's mind.

"What? The Sky Country? That's where you want to go?" No, that was where Yrund wanted to go. The current pulled against her legs. She hadn't really thought about where the stream might lead. Not to the Sky Country obviously, but maybe there was another way out of the mountain. Water did flow downhill, didn't it?

"That's insane." Yrund shook her head.

"Innnsaane," repeated the gem happily.

"That's not a good thing," said Yrund, but the light just blinked and floated back downstream, the little line of crabs in its wake.

YRUND BURPED, stomach bulging. The crabs had been crunchy and sweet, and bits of shell still stuck between her teeth. Bog Brandul and Veng and Gem Beard. She would find her own way out. She had a light and water and food...

"Sing!" said the gem.

So they went—deeper into the mountain, following the flow of water, voices echoing. The stone was all excitement, curious at every new pool and cascade, swimming easily where Yrund had to pick her way carefully down the slippery rocks. The stream split once, then twice, Yrund trying to keep track of each fork.

Always the stone stayed just out of reach, demanding more songs. It had found the right person. Sky People loved to sing. They had herding songs and journey songs, weaving songs and cooking songs—songs for springtime when does were fat and greedy, and songs for their just-born kids with their nubby little heads. There were songs for birthing and shearing and remembering to close the gate—that was a special one of her mother's. The music came unbidden, painful and precious. It was easier to carry something in your head than on your back, her father had always said.

Singing was the backdrop of Yrund's childhood, that and the sound of weaving. Her mother would take the loom outside when the weather was fair, or inside when it was not, the rhythm of the shuttle as familiar as her own heartbeat. The women of the steppes knew hundreds of weaving chants between them, each one a pattern of their family's life, one for thunder and one for rain, one for the spring between two hills and one for the clouds in the deep endless sky, but Yrund rarely sang them herself. As the eldest child, her days were spent with the herds and flocks.

The gem bumped Yrund's leg. She had stopped singing, her thoughts turning to all she had lost.

"That's all I know," said Yrund. Which was not at all true, but she no longer wanted to remember what she could not have. Not yet. Not until they got out. "Nothing more about home." And none of those miserable songs from the mine, the ones the prisoners sang as they worked, full of despair and resignation. Even Gem Beard's stupid songs were better than that. The gem bumped her again, harder. It was as bad as a little goat.

She guessed she could sing one of the memluk's songs. She had not forgiven Gem Beard, but if it would make the gem shut up...

"All right, all right, but don't say I didn't warn you."

Oh, a bucket of sugarcane rum
Is good for the Sea Hammer's tum,
But unless you like sitting
And endlessly shitting,
Stay away from bat curry, ho-hum.
Bat curry will wear out your bum.

The stone bounced up and down for more.

"Really? That's what you want to hear? Fine," said Yrund. "There's plenty more of those if you can stand them. *There once was a feller with crabs...*" The gemstone hooted along. There was just no accounting for taste, thought Yrund.

✴ ✦ ✷ ✴

FOR WHAT SEEMED LIKE DAYS, they followed the water down and down and down into the mountain. Yrund was afraid they had passed all hope of exit and were traveling far beneath the earth, but the gem was always calm, always moving exactly as if it knew where they were going.

From one turn to the next, the landscape of the stream changed, the walls sometimes rough and scabbed with mineral protuberances and just around the following bend as smooth as marble. Sometimes the way was narrow and sometimes wide, winding its way over a silty floor that held the shape of Yrund's footprints in perfect suspension. As they went, the gem made up its own song:

> *Oh da bucket da da da da bum,*
> *Good for Sea Hummer's rum.*
> *You, you like the shitting*
> *And da da da sitting.*
> *Stay away from dat bat curry hum.*
> *Bat curry will wear out you bum.*

"How is it you can sing and talk?" asked Yrund. "I didn't know gems could do that."

"Talk?" repeated the stone.

"You know—use words."

The gem didn't answer, not that Yrund had expected it to. So far, the gem's side of their conversations had been mostly nonsensical, but it calmed Yrund to hear someone else's voice.

Yrund's nose wrinkled. The stream had emptied into a pool, which stank of rotten eggs, the ceiling low and dangling with strands of yellow mucus. They stung her skin as she tried to duck beneath them. The gem's light glowed eerily through the still water, illuminating small piles of bones.

"I don't think we should go this way," Yrund called, her eyes watering.

But the gem was far ahead, now curiously circling a bubbling vent crusted with orange minerals.

"Get away from that!" she tried to yell, her voice growing hoarse, her lungs burning with every inhale.

She tripped after the gem through the warm water, the strands of yellow slime blistering her shoulders and face where they touched her.

"Come back!" Yrund wheezed, unable to see where the light had gone.

Then the stone was back, bumping her leg. Yrund stumbled as she tried to scoop it up, her limbs clumsy. The light swam downstream toward the pool's edge, then back to her, flashing brightly. "Ho-hoy…ho-hoy!" Yrund struggled on, following the sound, her feet dragging through a dam of skeletons at the end of the pool. "Hoy! Hoy, ho-hoy!"

Yrund collapsed over the piles of tangled bones and back into the stream's flow. The water carried her forward, washing her eyes and skin and going up her nose. She sputtered, trying to get her breath as the air finally cleared.

The stream was moving faster now, whisking her along in flashes of light and dark as the gem bobbed through the waves.

Yrund tried to get her legs underneath her, but the current was dashing like a horse without his reins, other channels joining their own, some hot and some cold, brewing fog as they combined. It was all she could do just to keep her head above water, catching breaths between waves.

For a few moments, she swirled off to the side, caught up in an eddy. The gem passed her by, its light spinning through the clouds of steam.

"HOY HOY HOY!" it called, and then Yrund was pulled after it, bumping from wall to wall as the stream's tunnel narrowed, then turned black, a great sucking sound racing toward her.

Crap, crap, crap, crap... Unseen waves tossed her from side to side. Not good, not good at all—the air was wet with spray, the sucking growing louder. Yrund took in the biggest breath she could hold, and then the river swallowed her, too.

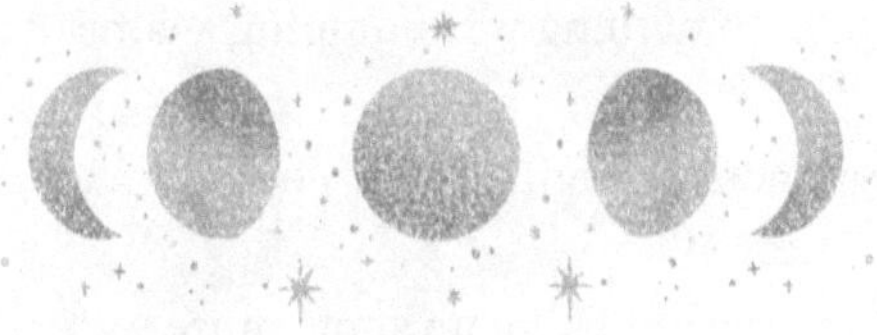

Yrund spun through the submerged tunnel at the current's mercy, her arms flailing away from her. Of all the ways she'd thought she might die at Devil's Crown, drowning had not been one of them. Had she really survived Brandul and Veng and the cave-in to die now? Like this? The sheer unfairness and absurdity filled Yrund with rage. This was not her Way! She fought the river as it ripped her from the tunnel in a deafening spray. For a moment, she was weightless, suspended over a waterfall lit by the falling gem. Then she too was sucked down in the plummeting foam, crushed and spun, so she could not tell which way was up or down. She struggled to swim free of the churning force. Red pain flashed behind her eyes as her lungs cried for air.

Don't try to wrestle the river, she heard her father say. *If you fight it, you will drown.* She was standing with him on the cliffs above the Jaggedy River, whirling and white-capped. His worn felt hat was tilted low over his face against the setting suns. *It will pop you out in the end if you just let go,* he said. He knew. The river had pulled him under once when he jumped in to save a ewe.

Yrund let go. The current shot her to the surface, carrying her away from the pounding fall and onto a rock beach. She collapsed in the shallow ripples, coughing up water. Bogging hell, this mountain hated her.

.✳.✦ ✷. ✸✳.

WHEN SHE WOKE, something was bumping against her side.

"Sing?"

Yrund had never imagined she could be so glad to see a gemstone.

"He…llo," she said, burping up some more water.

"El-lo," said the stone, its light beaming off the vaulted ceiling of an underground lake, so vast Yrund could not believe the mountain still stood. The white crash of the waterfall echoed in the distance, but her stomach echoed louder. Yrund and the stone explored their end of the lake, searching for breakfast.

She wondered how much time had passed since the cave-in. Had anyone even cared she was missing? Probably not. She was just another rabu. She waded around the lake again, her heavy snake anklets dragging against the current. Even if there was a way out of this mountain, which she was beginning to doubt, that would only make her a fugitive, something she had ignored in her earlier dreams of escape.

"Hoy," said the gem, shining its light behind Yrund.

Thousands upon thousands of tiny jewels were sliding across the walls. Not jewels. Snails! With luminous shells as clear as glass. Yrund pried one off the rock and touched the tip of her tongue to its slimy underside. It didn't taste like poison.

The shell was thin, the insides chewy.

Yrund had never eaten a snail—it tasted like the lake but with texture.

"What do you eat?" she asked the gem, which was spinning itself across the water.

"What you eat!" it sang. "What you eat! Ooodle ooh-du-doo-doo-doo."

"No, really—I was asking you a question," said Yrund, exasperated and inexplicably dizzy as if she too were spinning around like a crazed fish. "What do *you* eat?"

The stone stopped splashing and floated back to her. "Eat-eat-eat," the stone sang, enjoying the sound. It was learning words quickly, especially songs, though how much the gem actually understood was unclear.

"You know what eating is, right? You put something in your mouth, like this snail, and you chew it up and swallow it, and then your body...well, I'm not exactly sure what happens next, but you get strength from what you eat. Like dung for the fire."

"Dung...duh...dun...dung..."

"Never mind," said Yrund, rolling her eyes at herself. What had she expected? The gem didn't even have a mouth. Sound just emanated from it, like a bell that had been rung from the inside.

The stone blinked. "You," it said simply. "I eat you."

"Me?" said Yrund. She made a derisive sound with her tongue. That made no sense.

The gem floated closer, and Yrund's ears buzzed. The breakfast she had just eaten came back to her, the crunch of the snails' delicate shells and their chewy meat sticking between her teeth. And that wasn't all. She could feel the water of the lake soft and cool against her shins, the waterfall roaring as it pummeled her, and waves of other sensations—the burn of nearly drowning and the deep grief of missing home. A shiver ran up her wet arms.

"What? You can't eat those things. They're...they're..." What were they? Memories? Experiences? "They're not food, all right? You can't eat what I eat. Or what I feel. Or hear. I'm me. You're you." Whatever that was. "That's not how it works."

The gem made a movement akin to a shrug, then floated away to skip back and forth across the river.

Yrund returned to hunting for breakfast, perturbed. This was what came of talking to gems. And there it was, she realized, the thing that had been bothering her all along—she was talking to a gem. That couldn't be normal, and even if it was—what did she know about gems?—that didn't make it right.

Her place was in the Sky Country. She wouldn't even be here if it wasn't for gemstones like this one.

As they made their circuit around the lake, Yrund's mood worsened. As far as they went, there were only slime-covered walls and snails—no tunnels, no adjoining chambers, not even a little wormhole that might lead someplace new. The high walls curved back toward the crashing waterfall—the only way in.

Yrund returned to the rock beach and slumped down, letting the water loll around her as the truth set in. They were trapped. When the light bumped Yrund, she pushed it away. This was the stone's fault. It had led her down here. She should have never followed it. She was no better than an Asterian—enticed by the dazzle of a gem. If she had just put it back where it belonged, the rubble crew would have rescued her by now. Instead, she was going to spend the rest of her life in the dark, eating snails and talking nonsense with an addled rock until first her mind gave way then her body. Horror mixed with bitterness.

"Hoy?"

"Go away," said Yrund.

The gem bumped her again.

"I said go away! If it wasn't for you, we wouldn't be lost!" And not just lost inside a mountain with no way out. "If it wasn't for stupid, useless gems like you, I'd still be with my family!"

Without thinking, Yrund snatched the gem and threw it as far as she could across the lake.

For a moment, a few luminous circles rippled where the stone had fallen. Then the light snuffed out.

IMMEDIATELY, Yrund regretted what she had done. Her eyes sparkled with the memory of light as the darkness surrounding her like a living thing, its breath damp from the mist of the waterfall.

"Hello?" Her voice echoed weakly back to her. "Hello?" she called again louder. "Are you there? Can you hear me?" The lake's gentle current no longer seemed so gentle, the fall's crashing water echoing from every direction. "I'm sorry I threw you." Yrund began to shake as the cold ran up her legs. Did she really want to die alone and in the dark? Even the gem's company was better than that.

"I...I shouldn't have said those things. You didn't send the wields to the Sky Country to build their useless road." Though why the Asterians had come was still a mystery. The Sky Country didn't have any mines. "My people don't use gems," Yrund tried to explain, her words absorbed by the darkness. She doubted the stone could even hear her anymore. "We did once, a long time ago..." At least, that was what her grandmother had told her. "But the gems made us lazy and greedy, fighting and stealing from each other instead of tending to our herds. They made us lose our Way." Just as she had lost hers.

Yet what was the alternative? Was she supposed to have put the stone back in its shell and waited for Brandul and Veng to find her? Or wandered blindly until she died of thirst or fell down a crevasse?

"The truth is—I wouldn't have survived at all without your light." Yrund wrapped her arms around herself. "I'm sorry...it's not your fault we're trapped." It was the Mining Wield that had brought her to Devil's Crown, not this silly rock.

"You've actually been a pretty good friend." Even as Yrund said the words, she knew they were true. The gem was the only real friend she'd had since the other ratters had died. That Lumi woman, Brave Braid, had saved her life, but Yrund knew almost nothing about her except her kindness and her courage. And

Gem Beard… Gem Beard had never cared about anyone but himself.

Yrund's head hung in the darkness. Maybe the stone had gotten them lost, but at least it had stayed with her—right to the end.

Now she was alone, more alone than she had ever been. Possibly more alone than any human on Precios. She turned in the river's current unable to see her own hands, her mind detached from her body. If only she could see the sky one last time—that deep, sunslit blue infinity with its dog-shaped clouds and squawking crows. To lie against her pony's warm back in the blowing grass. She'd never even gotten a chance to say goodbye.

Yrund took a breath and began to sing.

Listen, the Sky is calling
All the heavenly horses home
Go, my friend, and join them
Ride the suns' wind
I'll catch up in a moment
That's all this life is
Just a moment
And then we ride the wind.

The light was so small Yrund thought it was a snail at first, just a glimmer beneath the water. Then it rose up like a star falling backwards.

"Ride the wind!" the stone sang.

"We will," said Yrund, immeasurably glad to have her friend back. "When we die…" That was if her soul could ever find its way free of the mountain. Morbidly, she wondered how long that might take. Or would her bones lie forever with those of lost bats? Would the snails eat her flesh?

"Die?" asked the gem, circling around her.

"Yeah, die. Death, dead, no longer alive."

"Alive? What, what?"

Yrund considered the question, without impatience or annoyance. They had all the time in the world now.

"Alive is…" What was alive? Breath? Blood? A heart? "I'm alive." Yrund wiggled her fingers to prove it. "So are snails and crabs and birds and trees. Even the Sky."

"Am I a-liiive?" asked the stone, savoring the word.

"Yes," said Yrund after a thoughtful pause. "You're alive, too." She couldn't say how she knew it, but she knew it just the same, just as surely as she knew her goats were alive or her sisters. "You should have a name. I have a name. I'm Yrund."

"Ah-rroond?"

"Y-rund."

"Eh-roond?"

"Yrund!"

"Uh-rhoond!"

"Close enough," sighed Yrund. "Now, what is your name?"

"Orrrrrund!" said the stone, playing with the sound.

"It's *Yrund*, and we can't have the same name. How would we know who was who? No, you have to have your own name."

"Alive," suggested the gem.

"That's not a name. Not a normal one anyway. Not like Yrund." She considered the options. "I don't know many gem names. There's spinyl—definitely not that," she said, remembering her night of vomiting. "And seefire." She wobbled her head. She hadn't thought about the names of gems before. "Rubily. Violette…"

"No."

"No?" That was a new word for the stone.

"All right, what else?" asked Yrund, wishing there was something besides snails to eat. "Thistle? Petal?"

The stone didn't like a single one of the names Yrund had been so proud to give her goats. Nor did she like any yak, horse, or dog names.

As they talked, Yrund waded around the lake's edge, looking at the walls one more time. "How about Oyyn? Or Lyrma?"

The stone dimmed.

"Really? Those are my aunts' names."

Yrund began another circuit of the lake. If there wasn't a way out why didn't the waterfall make the cavern fill up? And why was there a current if there was nowhere to go?

"How about Erdene?" asked Yrund between dives. "That's nice." Yrund blew some water out of her nose before she sank back down.

"No," said the stone, who, strangely, Yrund could hear underwater as if the voice was as much inside her as out. Small holes pocked the cave's walls beneath the waterline. Yrund examined them closely in the gem's light, reaching her arms inside the dark depths. She nearly choked when something reached back. But it was just a crab.

"Suvana's a good name," Yrund suggested next when she came up for a breath.

"Noooo."

"I liked that one. Huh. What about Aniliana?"

"Huhm."

"Getting closer," said Yrund. The farther around the lake they swam away from the waterfall, the bigger the holes below the water grew. "How about Lella? That's a good one. Or Elia. That's pretty, too."

The gem shot out a burst of light like a firework. "Orelia!"

"No, I meant, *or* Elia," she said, wiping water from her burning eyes.

The gem spun around in the water, zizzing sparks and beams. "Orelia! Orelia!"

"Not Orelia…" Yrund groaned. "What kind of name is that? It sounds like a medicine."

"Orelia!" declared the stone, but Yrund was no longer listening. The faintest light was shimmering through the water. Not from the gem or a snail or even a fish. It was something else, something she had only seen once since she'd arrived at Devil's Crown. She dove, hands churning to keep herself down as she stared at the sunslight breaking through the gloom.

"Orelia!" said Yrund, popping back up. "Orelia!"

"Yrrrrund! Yrund!"

"There's a passage under the water! I think it goes outside!"

The gem swirled around her. "Hoy, hoy!"

Clutching the gem tight in her fingers, Yrund dove back down again, paddling and kicking toward the light. When they rose, it was into a cold and narrow cavern, its far wall split by the dazzling rays of dawn.

CHAPTER NINE

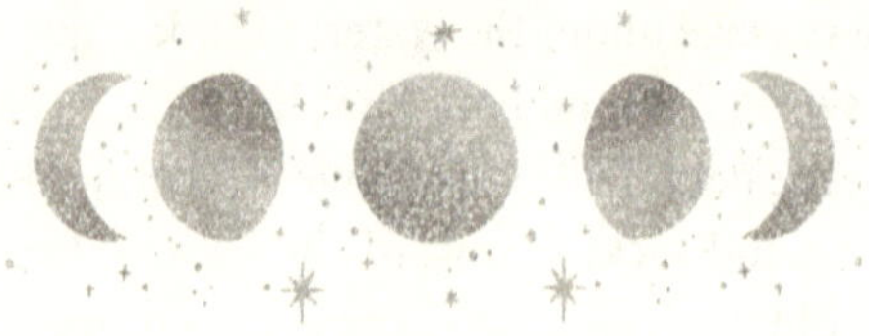

Yrund's bare toes sank into the cool earth as she braced against the autumn wind, her hair wild and eyes shining. Oh, beautiful Sky! It was an upside-down sea, bottomless and blue. One step off the mountain's steep side and she would float away. A pair of kestrels kited by on thermals like errant fish.

The gem crowed from her perch in the crook of Yrund's arm, her surface shimmering like yellow fire. "Orelias!"

"Where?"

"There!"

"Those are the suns." Yrund lifted her arms in greeting, the morning song of her people sweet in her mouth.

Oh the suns,
Oh the light,
Oh the warmth...

When she was done singing, she surveyed the rest of the world spreading below her. Small springs trickled out from the mountain and down moss-covered rocks toward a silvery creek lined with red and orange trees. Behind her was the ragged crack from which she'd escaped. There was no mining camp and no mine, no sign of any humans at all, only a staircase of crimson-foliaged mountains descending to the south. They had actually done it. They were free—no Brandul, no Veng, no memluks, no prisoners—Yrund's heart clenched recalling all the rabu the Mining Wield meant to abandon. Brave Braid would die as soon as winter came, and there was no way to get back to warn anyone, not without an airship. And Yrund didn't even have a coat or shoes. The cliffs of Devil's Crown rose impenetrably behind her until they were hidden in cloud.

"What suns eat?" asked Orelia, breaking through Yrund's thoughts.

"What *do the* suns eat?" Yrund corrected her. "I don't know. I never thought about it." It was like seeing the world for the first time. Did the suns eat, or were they themselves the food?

Her stomach twisted with hunger. She would need to find food and shelter before night fell.

"Are *the* suns alive?" asked the stone.

"I don't know that either. They give us light."

"I give light. I are alive," said Orelia with a superior tone.

Yrund swallowed. She had put this off as long as she could. "I appreciate everything you've done for me—I do, but it's a long way to the Sky Country, months at least, and anything could happen trying to get there—tigers, wolves, snow. Worse, the wields might catch me."

The stone made a sound like a fart.

"You don't understand. They would take you away from me if they found us together."

"Hoy hoy?"

"Why? Because gems are valuable to them, and that's what they do—they take." Yrund didn't know what kind of gem Orelia was—a sunsstone of some sort? Certainly not the allstone Brandul was looking for—even such a repulsive man as himself wouldn't give Niloofar Damantine a gem that liked to fart—but even a sunsstone that could fart must be worth quite a lot. In fact, someone like Gem Beard would probably consider it a bonus.

Yrund rubbed her watery eyes, unused to sunslight. "What I'm trying to say is that I can't take you with me. And you wouldn't want me to, not if you knew what they did to gems…" Yrund shuddered at the thought of Orelia being cut.

The stone turned from gold to angry red.

"It's not what I want," Yrund tried to explain. "But I cannot hide a gem that talks and sings. If you were plain like this"—Yrund picked up a flat gray stone at her feet—"I could carry you anywhere." Even home, where gems were forbidden, she thought wistfully. "I'm sorry…but you can't come. I won't put you back in the dark—I can leave you right here, where you can watch the sky and see the suns rise and set."

Yrund put the stone on the ground. She didn't want to say goodbye to her new friend, but when she let go, the gem stuck to her palm, not budging no matter how hard she tried to pry it off.

"Orelia," she pleaded. "You have to stay."

"No," said the stone again. "I am plain."

Yrund almost laughed. A stone of such fire and color could never be plain, and yet as she watched, the gem's contours roughened, its luster gone. In her hand was the homeliest rock she had ever seen, pitted and gray. She rubbed it with her thumb, and the stone sparkled for one forgetful moment before growing dull again.

"That's…" She didn't have the words. "I didn't know you could do that." But still—the gem was not hers. It belonged to the Mining Wield. It would be stealing to take it. Stealing from those that had taken everything from her. "You can really stay plain and hidden like this?"

"Plain," the stone said solemnly.

"You promise."

"Promise."

"Unless no one else is around," amended Yrund. It might not

hurt to have a little light sometimes. They did have a long journey ahead.

"Who else?"

"Other humans. I'm not the only one like me. There are more of us, but not all of us are good. Some people are dangerous. Understand?"

"Are there more of me?"

"I don't know." But she hoped not. One Orelia was enough to handle.

Gem in hand, Yrund slipped and slid down the mountainside, using clumps of moss and thin tree trunks as handholds. When she finally looked back, she couldn't see the cave's entrance at all —just a rocky slope rising into cliffs.

Down along the silver river, she searched hopefully for something to eat, poking into rotten logs and prying back brambles in search of late berries. But the few she found were seedy and dry. Nearby was a pile of dark bear scat, still fresh. Fox prints, too, skulked across the trail. Yrund picked herself up a solid stick. Foxes were not a problem. But where there were foxes, there were wolves and cliff leopards.

"We need to find someplace to camp before it gets dark," she told Orelia. Thick gray clouds were sliding over the mountains. "Then we can start a fire." A fire! That would cheer her. Based on the suns, they were south of Devil's Crown, land of wolves and woodwilds, according to Pit. "After we find a good place to camp, I'll make myself a sling," she decided. She could use her sarong. She didn't believe in woodwilds, but she knew firsthand what wolves could do.

"Hu, hu, hu," laughed the stone, who wasn't listening, distracted by the sight of a long-eared squirrel chasing a chipmunk.

Yrund eyed the animals with hunger. That sling would have more than one purpose.

As THEY HIKED, Yrund wondered how far it was to any villages or towns. Days? Weeks? She would have to stay wide of any she found. The snakes around her ankles would give her away as a rabu at a glance. She would need to fashion something to hide the anklets. But she could think about a disguise later. For now, she was determined to be grateful.

She had dreamt for so long of escaping from the mine, she could not believe she was out. Every sound was loud to her ears —the burble of the creek, the sparrows calling in the thickets— her nerves raw at the newness of it all.

"What what?" the stone asked again and again as they followed the stream down the valley.

"Leaves," answered Yrund, kicking through them in search of any mushrooms. She settled for a squirming pile of termites she found beneath an old log. The insects were carrot-like and sweet, intriguing the stone, who seemed to savor each bite far more than Yrund. How the stone could tell what she was sensing still baffled Yrund, as if she were a mother bird feeding her chick everything she swallowed. At least she didn't have to urp it up for the gem.

Yrund searched for fish along the cold stream's banks, but the darting prey were too fast to be caught by hand. And too small for a bow even if she'd had one. What she needed was a net. Perhaps later she would make one with grass, but the gathering clouds turned her attention from food to shelter. Mountain storms were no joke, something she knew well from her years spent herding. The riverside path took them through a grove of pale-trunked trees, their dry leaves scattering like paper moons as Yrund sped up her pace.

"What what?" asked Orelia.

"Trees."

"Treeeees!" called the stone, introducing herself. "I am Orelia."

"Most people don't talk to the trees," said Yrund.

"You talk to the suns."

"That's not the same."

"Why?"

Yrund sighed. It was like traveling with her little sisters.

"What is that one?" An image of one of the pale trees she had just walked past flashed through Yrund's mind.

"That's a tree too."

"You said we can't both be Yrund. How can they both be Tree?"

Yrund tried to explain how plants were different from people. That each type had a name but not each individual tree.

"What type of trees is them?"

"Are they," Yrund corrected.

Yrund didn't know. The Sky Country contained deserts and hills and waves of small mountains, but it was also a windy land, more welcome to grasses and shrubs and the occasional oaks or nut pines. "Moon leaf," she invented.

And so they continued on, Yrund making up names for everything she didn't know.

"Purple willows."

"Puuurple," enthused the stone, trying out the shade on itself.

"Purple is not plain," scolded Yrund as a scatter of raindrops landed across her shoulders. Bogging hell, it had gotten cold fast. The track beside the river turned muddy as she began to jog, searching for a weather break. It was not until the valley took a turn into a boulder-stacked canyon that she finally saw the perfect spot to make camp, sheltered from the wind and sideways rain. Only someone else had beaten them to it.

A plume of smoke curled tauntingly above the rocks.

"Blast," said Yrund, ducking back behind a tree. There hadn't been any smoke before.

"What what?" asked the stone.

"Someone's there."

"Blast!" said the stone, too.

Yrund wiped the rain from her eyes, considering what to do. She was a fugitive. A nearly naked fugitive. Until now, this aspect of her appearance had hardly registered with her. There had been no one to see or care that her sarong and the shirt Gem Beard had purloined were so destroyed they were hanging in ribbons. But modesty was the least of her concerns. What sort of person would be camped in these isolated mountains with winter looming? Maybe a trapper or hunter. The thought of meeting another human jarred her senses after so many days alone in the mountain.

She picked up a gnarled stick, heavy enough to hit someone with. Then, staying low, she climbed the wet rocks above the stranger's camp, sliding forward on her belly until her forehead and eyes hung over the granite outcrop. A puff of steam caught her right in the face.

There was no fire. And no camp—only a small hot spring, its warm, moist air funneling up through the rocks.

Yrund leaned over to see better and slipped off the rain-slick rock right into what felt like a pot of lumpy fur soup.

The pool went from perfect calm to instant chaos, flailing limbs tangling with her own. Then she was pushed under as something large and foot-like stepped across her head. What the—

Spluttering, Yrund rose and wiped her eyes, ready to fight, but there was nothing there but the stone, the waves in the pool already subsiding. She felt around underneath her, but there too was only rock and warm water.

"Orelia!" said Yrund, trying to draw the bobbing gem back to her.

"Hoy, hoy!" piped the gem, its light casting long shadows across the grotto's slick walls.

"Stop it!" hissed Yrund. "What if it's still out there?" Just because they'd scared whatever it was off didn't mean it wouldn't come back. A bear—or worse, a rock tiger—wouldn't let a bit of water get between himself and a nice dinner. Unfazed, Orelia continued to splash and play, making golden circles of bubbles.

Cursing the stone, Yrund pulled herself out of the warm water. It was sleeting now, and her numb hands fumbled as she gathered fist-sized stones, piling them up beside the pool. If the creature returned, she would be ready. If it didn't, she was halfway to breakfast. Not until the stack reached mid-shin did she allow her stiff and shivering body to ease back into the spring's sheltering warmth, the rain running in cool rivulets down her face.

At first her head jerked and heart leapt at every moon shadow or sound. But as the heat soaked deep into her bones, Yrund's eyes began to close. Soon her head slumped back against the pillow of moss, visions of hungry predators replaced by dreams of juicy grilled squirrel.

✴ ★ ✳ ✴

IT WAS STILL night when Yrund woke, a full moon shining down between the patches of cloud and steam into the mirror of the pool. The rain had finally stopped, though the wind was still whistling. Or was that the wind?

"Orelia?"

"Yrund," said the stone, light contentedly pulsing from the large hand in which she rested.

Yrund's heart jumped against her ribs as if it might break through. An enormous furry man sat across from her, holding Orelia and dangling his legs in the warm pool. He was bigger even than Gem Beard, with a blunt leathery nose and round dark eyes.

Woodwilds weren't real. Woodwilds were just stories. Like yowis. Or eye-eyes.

The creature cleared his throat and nodded politely at her.

Which was not at all what Yrund had expected. In her grand-mother's tales, woodwilds were howling demons that sucked the blood from goats. She was definitely dreaming. Or perhaps she'd knocked her head when she had fallen into the spring. Her cousin had once smelled marmot cooking for weeks after he had been thrown off his horse.

"You are from the Sky Country," the creature said, his voice smooth and melodic.

Yrund's head wavered back and forth in disbelief.

"You are not of the Sky People? Did your friend tell me wrong?"

Her friend wasn't supposed to be talking at all. Nor was this… this monster.

"I—I am," Yrund finally said, head still shaking. It was a dream —just a dream. Or was it a nightmare? Didn't woodwilds eat people?

"Then, may you find good pasture," the enormous man said in the ritual greeting of the Sky Country.

"And may your herds multiply," answered Yrund automati-cally, trying to wake herself up.

"And yours." Every time the woodwild's mouth opened, Yrund could see a full set of ivory teeth counterpointed by a pair of sharp fangs. The creature held Orelia up admiringly, whistling, and Yrund could feel the gem's pride cut through her own disap-proval. Yrund cursed. The goat was on the roof now. Though she didn't know if she was more annoyed the stone would let someone else hold her or that she had broken her promise to stay plain.

The woodwild set the stone lightly on the water, where Orelia floated.

"The Sky People are notable wrestlers," said the hairy man, surprising Yrund.

"We are," Yrund said, hoping she looked fierce, not wet and wrinkled. So he did know about her people.

"Yes, I saw Yrdin Tcheeletter compete at the Sky Games last summer. Her falcon dance was magnificent. Twenty opponents in one day." He sounded impressed. "Those she had defeated lined up and sang to her."

Fastest, strongest, most persevering.
Today, you won, you won, you won,
With courtesy, and dignity, and honor.
Now you are the lion, our lion.
You won, you won...

Yrund knew the song well. It was the finale of every wrestling match in the Sky Country.

With cour-te-sy, and dig-ni-ty, annnnd ho-nor!
You won, you won.
Li-on, liii-onnnnn, you won!

The woodwild extended his hairy arms wide for the close of the song, lifting his legs from the water. Bits of bark and leaves and other things Yrund couldn't identify hung from his fur. When the song was over, Orelia cheered, but Yrund did not. She was too busy staring at the woodwild's feet. Or the lack thereof.

"What happened to your feet?" Yrund asked in horror, taking inventory of her own limbs, which all still seemed to be present.

Chuffing, the woodwild lifted a dripping, nearly invisible foot out of the water to show her. "They're merely clean."

In a stomach-dropping instant, it all came together. There must have been a woodwild in the hot spring when she jumped in. "Woodwilds can't be seen?"

"Not when we're clean," said the woodwild. "And we prefer to be called woodwins—not *woodwilds*—if you don't mind." A small branch stuck out from behind his matted ear. He certainly looked wild. "I've just returned from a long trip," he explained defensively, removing a few leaves.

"What happens if you are seen? Wood*wins*, that is."

"That depends…we're not spotted often. In fact, we take great pains to avoid humans."

"Why?" asked Yrund.

"'Humanity is an abomination upon the planet,'" he said, as if quoting someone.

"Oh?" That didn't sound good. "Then how come you're here talking to me?"

The woodwin tilted his furry head at her. "I think the more pertinent question is how are *you* here talking to me?"

"Me? I…just wanted to get warm. I was going to build a fire—"

The woodwin made a choking sound. "You started a fire?"

"No. I was going to," Yrund repeated. "But since it was raining, I went looking for shelter first and found this hot spring."

"That is something, at least," said the woodwin, clucking his tongue. "But the mystery remains—how did you arrive?"

That was a question Yrund realized she wasn't at all prepared to answer. Was she really going to tell a total stranger she had run away from the Mining Wield? The wields paid bounties for escaped rabu. "I was out with my herds and got a little lost," she lied.

"The Sky Country is nearly a thousand miles from here." He looked at her strangely. "You, ah, didn't go to sleep in a tree, did you?"

"No," said Yrund, perplexed. Why would that matter?

"You do not have to tell me…" The woodwin coughed, the ruff under his chin rising up and down. "But I must warn you, the Thinkers will not find that a satisfying answer when they hear a human has been found in the Hidden Woods."

"The Hidden Woods?"

"Do you really have no idea where you are?"

"No, not exactly," Yrund admitted. "South is all I know."

"South, yes. But to be more precise, you are in the private sanctuary of the woodwins. No human has ever been here before." He let the significance of this revelation sink in.

"Why not?" asked Yrund, afraid of the answer.

"As I said, woodwins do not love humans, and our land is extremely remote—there are no roads to get here."

"If I'm not supposed to be here, what will you do to me?" asked Yrund, imagining a dozen gruesome fates in an instant.

"That is for the Thinkers to decide," the woodwin said. "I am only a Listener. Though at least you didn't start a fire."

"Why is that?"

"Trees are sacred to woodwins. You are lucky a Doer didn't find you before I did."

Thinkers? Doers? What an odd race the woodwins were. "Ah…there might have been one of your people here when I jumped in."

The woodwin's eyes grew bigger.

"More than one, maybe," she added, remembering how tangled it had all seemed.

Was he laughing? It sounded more like a sneeze.

"I look forward to hearing who such a small girl chased away. News of your arrival has already spread, then." He pressed his fingers together. "That means the Thinkers will be gathering. It is an unprecedented event for a human to enter one of our enclaves. I must admit I do not understand how it was you made it across the Double Deaths."

"What are the Double Deaths?" asked Yrund.

"The two rifts our wilderness lies between," he said, as though this was common knowledge.

"I didn't pass any rifts. I came from the mountains."

"But the High Aeries are not passable by any human."

Yrund had no doubt that was true. For anyone that went over them. Under them was another matter. "I didn't know this was your land, I promise. If you show me the way out, I won't come back." Her voice rose.

"I'm afraid that isn't up to me."

Sensing Yrund's emotion, Orelia began to blink.

"I could have sworn the Sky People were gem shy."

"They are," said Yrund, her guilt like a weight.

"But not you?"

"I am. It's just…this gem saved my life."

"Really? That must be very difficult for you."

"It is," said Yrund. "I was raised believing that gems would make you lose the Way."

The woodwin trailed his hand through the water, sending Orelia on a small wave toward Yrund. "I was raised believing humans would make us lose *our* Way."

Yrund looked up at his shiny, dark eyes. They had more in common than she had thought.

"Is it true? Has this gem made you lose your Way?"

"I'm not sure I believe in the Way anymore." Yrund rubbed the stone with one finger. "I only know that if it wasn't for Orelia I'd be more than lost. I'd be dead."

"Aurelia, did you say her name was?" asked the woodwin. "How appropriate—golden light."

The stone trilled.

Yrund stared at her. Orelia meant golden light? Maybe it wasn't as bad a name as she'd thought. "Will the Thinkers take her from me?"

"Gems do not have the same effect on us as they do on humans, but a stone such as yours would make an undeniably tempting offering for the Great Oak."

Well, there were probably worse things than the gem being given to a tree. Still, the thought of losing Orelia was unbearable to Yrund, like losing a limb. "What if I don't want to give her up?"

"What else do you have to barter?"

Barter? Yrund drooped. "I don't have anything else."

"Of course you do."

"I do?" she asked, trying to ignore the wash of strange sensations pouring through her—as if she was swimming through blades of soft grass. "Stop that," she told the stone, who was looping through the invisible fur on the woodwin's legs.

"Huh, huh, huh," chattered Orelia.

"As much as they might abhor humans, the Thinkers have one weakness when it comes to your species."

"Which is what?" asked Yrund, trying to refocus her mind.

"Your ability to tell stories, and I suspect that yours is a very good one. After all, how else would you be here?"

"The Thinkers would trade my freedom for my story?" Telling her story would mean admitting she was a fugitive. She felt a sudden chill despite the heat of the pool.

"Your freedom? That I don't know. But your life? It might be possible." The woodwin wobbled his head. "Particularly when the council hears what news I bring…" He lifted his blurry feet back out of the water, letting them drip for a moment, before getting up. Standing, he was taller and broader than any memluk, fully twice Yrund's height and twice her breadth, too, though he appeared less to be standing than floating, what with the bottom portion of each leg appearing to be entirely missing. "Tell me— what is your name, little human?"

Yrund sat up straighter, trying not to show her fear. "Yrund, Daughter of Wian of the First Moon and Gantul of the Badger."

"Yrund. Very good. I am—" He whistled a song that brought to her mind a picture of a magpie, blue-black feathers ruffling in the wind.

But when Yrund puckered her own lips to repeat the sound, the best she could conjure was a grackle. The woodwin winced. "Why don't you call me something a human can pronounce?"

"Like what?" asked Yrund.

"Humphrey, perhaps?"

CHAPTER TEN

The sky was a pearly gray with a hint of metal at its edges. Yrund got out of the hot spring with her back to the woodwin, wringing out her tattered shirt and sarong as best she could. Then she remembered her anklets, now in full view. Yrund turned like a deer, wondering what to do, but it was too late.

Humphrey was already staring at the snake-shaped bracelets around each of Yrund's ankles. Yrund shuffled one leg behind the other. How would she ever explain those to the Thinkers?

The woodwin whistled with reverence, turning his attention away from her to the suns as they broke over the mountains, lighting the steam rising off the spring like golden smoke.

Unexpectedly, Yrund's arms and voice lifted and her mouth opened to greet the morning sky. She hadn't meant to do that. Lack of sleep and food was having the strangest effect on her. A wood wren fluttered over to listen as Orelia joined in the ritual song.

The woodwin nodded when they were done. "Few humans remember the Way any longer," he said. "The Sky People are some of the last."

Yrund wrapped her arms, once again her own, around her

wet body, shaking with cold. "H-how d-do you know so much about the Sky Country?"

"I am a Listener. It is my job to keep tabs on humans," Humphrey said, grooming his fur with his fingers. He found the branch behind his ear and pulled it out. "It's easy to see and hear quite a lot when no one knows you're there. In fact, it can be extremely entertaining."

"*You* don't sound like you hate us," said Yrund.

The woodwin thought about this. "It's true. I'm not as convinced as my brethren that all humanity is lost."

Yrund considered Devil's Crown and all the horrors that just a year ago she would not have believed possible. "We can be very evil, too."

"Yes, humans have a lot to answer for. More than they know, but I cannot deny that humans are quite ingenious too. Flutes, for instance," he said. "And books." He glanced at something behind him—an old rucksack, patchworked sides bulging.

"I seem to have, ah, picked a few things up on my last trip," said Humphrey, retrieving the pack with a long arm. "Perhaps some of them would be useful to you."

The woodwin produced a red bundle that, when untied, revealed a hard piece of cheese, some dried sugar currants, and—wonder of wonders—a clay pot of pickled fish.

"What what?" asked Orelia from the edge of the pool where Yrund had left her. Yrund scooped her up and brought her over to join them.

"Please help yourself," said Humphrey. So Yrund did, politely at first, then ravenously.

"Hoy, hoy!" said Orelia at the new flavors. The fish was delicate but pungent, and the cheese—Yrund could not believe anything could taste so good—salty and buttery. It took all her willpower to leave some for the woodwin, who only ate a few currants, then licked the sugar off his fingers. Yrund distracted herself from staring at what was left by playing with the red fabric in which the picnic had been tied. It was as soft as wild rose petals and embroidered with bright flowers.

"Pretty, isn't it? Silk. From Borosia, if I'm not mistaken." Humphrey shook the crimson garment out to reveal a woman's night-robe. "Much too small for me." When he tried to reach a hairy arm through one of the sleeves, it only came up as far as his wrist. So he draped it around his neck like a scarf, admiring the sheen for a moment, before noticing Yrund's expression. "I don't suppose you could use it?" he said, unwinding it from his shoulders and holding it out to her.

The red robe was so long on Yrund it nearly dragged across the ground, but it was warm for the weight. And it had a pocket on each side. Yrund had a weakness for pockets. Orelia oohed and aahed, entranced with the fabric's rich tones, then turned herself crimson to match.

"I must say—she's more like a moodfish than a stone."

"She promised she would stay plain...," said Yrund with exasperation.

"Around humans," clarified Orelia. "Humphrey is a woodwin."

Yrund supposed she could not argue with that. But even so she dropped the gem into one of the robe's deep pockets. For a brief and disorienting moment it seemed to be Yrund herself who was sliding down into the soft silken depths.

"It must be difficult not having fur," the woodwin observed.

"I've never thought about it before. Why don't humans have more hair?"

"Defective," said Humphrey, as if this were obvious. "Like your tiny feet. You couldn't stomp anything with those..." Once again his gaze returned to her anklets. "Are you still hungry? Would you like more to eat?"

"Yes!" said Orelia. "More to eat!"

"Hush, it isn't polite to ask for more," Yrund said, though her stomach was still growling. If there was ever a time to practice her manners, it was with a race of beings that already believed humans were an abomination upon the planet.

"It's fine. I wouldn't have taken them if I'd known it was fish. I prefer neeps," Humphrey said, handing over the rest of the jar. At every bite Yrund took, Orelia chirped with pleasure.

Humphrey rummaged through the rest of the pack. "Perhaps I have something else you might like. I don't mean to pick things up, but…you humans are so careless with your belongings."

"But I can't," protested Yrund, nevertheless curious. "Those belong to you."

"Oh, pshaw, nothing belongs to anyone," said the woodwin. "Not truly. Besides, the Thinkers don't really approve of me collecting human artifacts. Though I find the study of such things essential to understanding your species." Were pickles and silk robes essential to understanding humanity? Yrund wondered as Humphrey pulled an etched brass telescope with filigreed casings out of the pack and held it out to her. "Perhaps you can explain this item to me. I'm at a loss for what it does."

Yrund examined the ridgeline across the valley. Her grandmother had a telescope for hunting with her falcon. It had been her most prized possession besides the bird, and occasionally, when they were being good, she had let Yrund and her sisters look through it. "The lens seems just fine—I can see a raven up on top of that scraggly tree."

Humphrey turned where she was looking. "That's not a raven. That's a sooty hawk," he said.

"You can see that far all on your own?" asked Yrund, lowering the scope in amazement.

"Of course," Humphrey said. "Can't you?"

"Not even close," said Yrund. Any thoughts she might have had of escape disappeared. There would be no eluding the keen eyes of the woodwins.

Humphrey dumped the remaining contents of the pack out onto a rock beside him. "There are a few things I admit are still mysteries," he said, poking at the pile. "Maybe you can enlighten me. Like this, for example." He picked up a carved piece of shell fringed with narrow teeth.

"That's a comb," said Yrund. "And this is a thimble. It's for sewing." She rolled the tiny silver cup between her fingers. The maker had engraved a small fox across the side. Her mother would have liked that.

Humphrey pushed the shell comb into the fur above his ear, where it stuck out at a rakish angle.

"How do I look?" he asked, teeth gleaming.

"Very unique," she said truthfully. "Ooh—a book!" And it was in Trade Tongue! *The Silver Thread* by Humphrey Deforest." She looked up at the woodwin.

"I liked the name," he said bashfully.

Yrund opened the book to its middle, burying her nose in the sweet grass scent before reading a few lines out loud:

Sail the silver thread
Through the space between the stars,
Between dawns and noon,
Time and night,
Where the scents of acorns and atoms
Mingle on the stellar wind.
Sail, sail between the stars.
Made or born, earthbound or risen,
All the same.

Yrund closed the book and looked at the cover again. There was a drawing of a sailboat floating through the stars embossed on the front.

"What do you think?" the woodwin asked her.

"Of the poem? I like it," said Yrund. "Though it does make you feel all loose inside, doesn't it?"

"You may keep it if you wish. The Thinkers do not approve of books."

"Why not? You said woodwins love stories."

"Because of the trees."

"So woodwins don't have any books at all?"

Humphrey's head wobbled. "Not as you know them, no. We have other methods of recording what we need to."

"What's acorns-and-atoms?" interrupted Orelia, quoting the poem back to them.

"She likes new words," said Yrund. "An acorn is a type of nut," she told the stone. "Maybe an atom is too…"

Hearing the word *nut*, Orelia began to sing one of Melmeth's obscene ditties.

Beware the pirates of Douarr,
Especially the one with the scar.
He'll cut out your guts,
While scratching his…

Yrund stopped her with a tap to her pocket. "That's enough."

"That would give the Thinkers something to think about," chuffed the woodwin.

"Humphrey, have you ever heard of a gemstone that could talk or sing?"

Humphrey's ears swiveled. "No. But then again, there are many things that sing when humans aren't around."

"So you don't know what kind of stone Orelia is?"

"My knowledge of gems is somewhat limited since we don't use them. She has aspects of both vagaries and sunsstones—something new, perhaps? However, if you want to keep her in your possession, you'll have to be more discreet. Shiny things have a way of disappearing on Precios."

Yrund suspected shiny things had a way of disappearing around

Humphrey, who had the silver thimble balanced on the tip of his carrot-sized pinkie. "Do you hear that, Orelia? No singing, no talking. From here on, you're going to have to be plain and quiet."

"Hmmph!" said the stone, disgruntled.

"All yours, then," said Humphrey repacking the rucksack and pushing it toward Yrund.

"You're really sure?"

"Quite," he said, setting off.

Yrund swung the lumpy sack up onto her back and followed the woodwin out of the grotto. Humphrey's feet might not have been visible, but his footprints were, as wide as shovel heads and twice the length. They passed through a crop of rustling trees and onto a well-trodden trail.

"Thank you for the food and the things," Yrund said to the woodwin's back, trying to keep up. She hadn't had anything that was all hers since she'd left home except her hated snake anklets.

"You're welcome," said Humphrey. "I only hope you are allowed to live long enough to enjoy them."

ALL MORNING and most of the afternoon, they wound over and across golden valleys, tacking always to the south, a far horizon of cloud-obscured earth. To the east and west, the mountains stretched into more mountains like soldiers on guard. Leaves blew past them in the wind. Winter was advancing, and the animals of the forest were getting ready, jays and chipmunks foraging for seeds, big-eared deer fattening themselves on grass.

Humphrey stopped several times throughout the day to scratch his back against a rough-barked tree. "Oh, that's nice. You should try it."

"Maybe later," Yrund said, sitting down, glad for the rest. The woodwin had set a furious pace with his great strides, and with the snacks from the rucksack long gone, she was famished—

again. She considered how quickly her fortune had changed. She hadn't even been free of the mountain for a day before being captured—by a creature right out of a moonstale, no less. And while Humphrey might not hate humans, she was about to be tried by a council that did.

"I've been thinking," said Humphrey, leaving off his scratching for a moment, scraps of bark still clinging to his coat. "You won't tell the Thinkers I gave you the rucksack, will you? Especially not the book?"

"I won't tell them if you promise you won't let them eat me," said Yrund, reaching out her hand to shake on it. Time with Gem Beard had taught her something.

"Eat a human? What a vile notion." The woodwin sounded thoroughly disgusted. "I've never understood how that rumor got started. Imagine how bad you taste." He stuck out his tongue. "We might knock your heads in, or stomp you, or give you to the Great Oak, but you can be certain you won't be dinner."

Yrund's hand wavered.

"But I'll try to make sure it's over quickly if they do," the woodwin promised, his enormous hand closing around hers. His fur was softer than she expected, the pads of his fingers dry and smooth.

"We probably shouldn't dawdle now they know we're on our way," he said, letting go and setting off again.

Yrund wondered how the other woodwins knew they were coming, but Humphrey had proved his species could see eagle-worthy distances, and what a view the woodwins had—an infinity of mountains lit with orange and red forests.

A herd of elk grazing in a meadow swung their black heads to watch them as they passed. The woodwins' haven was full of animals Yrund had not seen the day before—spotted skunks and striped foxes with bushy tails and countless birds, whistling back and forth with the woodwin as if they were having a real conversation. When they reached a small creek, Humphrey turned, following alongside it. The narrow trail looked like a dead end until the creek bent, joining a slow river meandering down from a hidden valley.

As they ascended, the river slowed into pools, dammed at both ends with woven branches and twigs. Yrund tried not to fall into one of the holes carved along the soft grassy banks, but it was hard to keep her eyes on the trail. Something brown and sleek was swimming toward them. Humphrey waved, and the animal brought down its broad leathery tail with a flat and echoing slap on the water.

"What was that?" asked Yrund.

"A rainkeeper, though you might call them dam builders."

"I've never heard of them."

"There are very few left anymore. Humans consider them pests—very foolish. Your kind couldn't have survived a day on Precios if the rainkeepers hadn't been here first."

"What do you mean? Haven't humans always been here?"

Humphrey shook his head. "Is that really what they teach you?"

"Yes?"

"Then it's even worse than we thought."

They balanced their way over an enormous dam, piled up with driftwood and chinked with mud, crossing to the other side of the river, which had been dammed into a long staircase of ponds. Yrund stared into one, mesmerized, the water so still she could see every cloud above, until a golden-green trout broke the surface sending perfect circles of ripples across the inverted sky. Beside the pools were long baskets like nets that looked as if they could be raised or lowered.

"Do woodwins eat fish, then?" she asked, remembering the jar the woodwin had shared, though in hindsight she hadn't actually seen him eat any.

"Not often," said the woodwin mysteriously.

Along the borders of the fish ponds sprouted lilies and cattails and bunches of wild mint that smelled of wet dog fur.

All plants that should be over by fall.

In fact, the farther they went, the warmer the valley grew.

"Why does it feel like it's still summer up here?" asked Yrund, climbing up a rock that blocked the trail and startling a marmot.

"The warm season is long in the Hidden Forest," said Humphrey. "But it will be over soon—even here." The woodwin whistled a greeting to the marmots, who whistled noisily back.

Looking at the fat golden creatures, Yrund wondered what the next meal would be. And when? One well-aimed rock, and they would have lunch, but then she remembered that the strange woodwins did not make fires. If they didn't eat humans or fish or marmots… "What do you eat?"

"We eat lots of things. It depends on the season. The berries are good now," said Humphrey, pointing ahead. Past the ponds, the river tumbled freely, its sides thick with dark, berry-strewn brambles. "Help yourself."

Yrund plucked the purpley-black fruit until her fingers were swollen with stickers and so stained it was as if she'd dipped them in a bucket of violet dye. The berries were tart and sweet and warm from the suns.

After the brambles, they passed a field of strange hoops woven with growing vines. Yrund could not see their purpose. One creation was so large it stretched between five tree trunks, a perfect hole in its center. Beneath it, from the forest floor, sprung hundreds of white mushrooms, fat caps radiant in the dappled light.

Then Humphrey split away from the river valley and up a steep side canyon, shaded with tall firs that loomed like angry guards. In a flat clearing halfway up they came upon a series of great stone arches leading nowhere.

"What are those?" asked Yrund, her lungs still burning from the climb.

"They are called..." The woodwin answered with a whistle that enlightened her not at all.

"What are they for?"

"No time for questions now," the woodwin said, stopping in front of a wall of pine so thick Yrund could not see what lay beyond. "We have arrived."

He looked down at her, face unreadable. "Whatever happens, I want you to know I enjoyed our conversation today. It turns out that talking with humans is even more interesting than listening to them."

CHAPTER ELEVEN

Humphrey whistled twice, and the branches in the green wall blew aside. "Ready?"

Yrund tiptoed into an oval glade, more indoors than out, enclosed by living trees and carpeted with fragrant needles. Pale light trickled through the high ceiling, illuminating drifting motes. She drew in her breath—at one end of the dim chamber was a stone altar, gleaming with something wet and dark red.

Humphrey motioned for her to sit down next to him. Yrund took off her pack and sat, unable to take her eyes from the altar. Had the woodwin lied? Were they going to eat her after all? She looked to him for reassurance, but the woodwin appeared equally unsettled, his short ears twitching.

Yrund bumped him with her elbow, raising her eyebrows at the shell comb still stuck in the fur behind his ear.

With a spasm, Humphrey flicked the comb out and into Yrund's lap.

Yrund dropped the trinket into her pocket on top of Orelia, who gave a small blink.

If you can hear me, Yrund silently prayed to the Sky, *please make Orelia be good.*

They waited for what seemed like an eternity, Yrund unsure what to do with herself. When Humphrey crossed his legs, she did the same, double-checking the snake anklets were covered by her new robe and trying not to look over at the red altar.

Finally, the branches at the entrance rustled and bent. The others had arrived. Yrund couldn't see the woodwins that entered, not clearly, but she could hear the soft huff of their breath as they took their places around her, and she could see the pine needles rearrange on the floor.

She made a swipe with her fingers at her tangled hair, wishing she had used the comb while she still had the chance. Pairs of eyes floated above her, sending a tingle down her back. She didn't know where to look or how to sit, the eyes following her every fidget.

A long whistle called the assembly to order. Yrund straightened her spine and locked her hands together in her lap as Humphrey exchanged greetings with the unseen Thinkers—a combination of whistles and squirrel-like chatters.

Someone close by made a loud yawning noise as if they were bored. Then they began to hum. It took a few bars before Yrund recognized the tune as one of Gem Beard's songs. *Orelia!* But the woodwins gave no sign that they'd heard, continuing with their whistling as if she and the stone weren't even there. *Shhh!* Yrund thought silently, begging the gem to behave.

From the shift in the woodwins' tone, it appeared the discussion of what to do with the human had begun. Humphrey started calmly, gesturing occasionally in Yrund's direction, his whistles sounding smooth and reasoned, but as the minutes passed, the other woodwins grew impatient. A volley of notes flew back and forth.

Yrund pressed her sweaty armpits to her sides, afraid the council could smell her fear. There was no mistaking the ill will toward her, but Humphrey kept calmly on.

"I have persuaded the Thinkers to let you speak for yourself. You may start with how you came to our forest."

He nodded for her to begin.

"I—" Yrund cleared her throat. "I was just passing through on my way home. I didn't know I was in your land. If you show me the way out, I promise I won't come back."

Humphrey translated her words. The flurry of whistles that came back nearly deafened Yrund. She covered her ears. The air was a blur of invisible arms waving their protest.

"I am having a hard time convincing the Thinkers you speak the truth. There are only two ways into the Hidden Woods—past the Quick Death Gorge or past the Slow Death Gorge, neither of which we thought was passable for a human."

Yrund let out a resigned breath. Humphrey had already seen her anklets, and unless she gave the woodwins an explanation soon, the wields would not be her first problem. "I didn't come over the gorges. I don't know anything about them. I came from the mountains above the hot spring."

Humphrey absorbed this for a startled moment before translating.

There was a palpable silence from the Thinkers too and then a long derisive whistle.

"Even we do not attempt to scale the cliffs of the Aeries."

"I didn't go over the mountain. I went under it—there are caves that connect Devil's Crown to your forest."

"Devil's Crown?" The woodwin rocked his body back and forth. "That mine has been closed for many hundreds of years," he said. "And there are no roads in or out."

"We were taken in airships."

There was a surprised rumble among the woodwins when Humphrey translated what she had said.

"So the Asterians are using airships to reach our mountains." He did not look pleased. "You say you were transported there? It was not your choice to go?"

"No. We were prisoners. I was captured when the Asterians sent memluks to raid my home. I would never have left the Sky Country. Not to go to a horrid dark mine to dig up gems we don't even use."

"And those bands around your feet—those are to do with the Asterians?"

"The Mining Wield has them on all the prisoners. If there's a way to take them off, I have not found it." In her mind, Yrund could still see the burnt bodies lying by the side of the trail back at Devil's Crown. "There's something in them that strikes you like lightning if you step over one of the deadlines they put around the camp. Some Lumi men died that way trying to escape."

"May we see them?"

Yrund stretched out her legs so the council could examine the metallic snake bindings with their blue gem eyes. The Thinkers flinched as one, releasing low sucking sounds of disapproval.

"Of all the human inventions, this is one of the most despicable."

After some conversation among themselves, one of the Thinkers at the back whistled out a new question.

"They are perplexed how you escaped if you could not get these chains off?"

Yrund explained about Brandul and the cave-in and her arduous journey through the mountain with no mention of Orelia, only a sunsstone, though she didn't doubt Humphrey could fill in the blanks. The Thinkers, however, were more concerned about the workings of the mine.

"There are humans still up there? Prisoners, like you?"

"There might be. The wield meant to leave us all, even the memluks. We were already low on food, and with winter coming..." Those that remained would die fighting over the meager supplies that were left.

The Thinkers did not seem as concerned about the death toll

as what route the airships took when they came and went. Yrund described what she could remember of the bleary journey in, then answered a dozen more questions about the numbers and habits of the memluk guards before the woodwins returned to whistling among themselves.

Yrrrund? said Orelia.

Yrund's mind rippled like wind on a stream. She clutched at her pocket, but the woodwins ignored the interruption, continuing to whistle back and forth over her head.

Yrund? said the stone again, even louder this time.

Yrund panicked, head swiveling to see how the Thinkers would react to the talking stone this human had brought into their council. But there was no pause in their high-pitched discussion. It was as if they hadn't heard the stone at all. Which was impossible.

Yrund! said Orelia for the third time, so loud Yrund's teeth quivered. Still, not even Humphrey sitting right beside her seemed to hear.

Shhh! Yrund thought back at the stone.

I am being shh, said Orelia, her voice tickling the deepest parts of Yrund's mind.

No, you're not! Yrund thought back silently. Could other gems communicate this way? she wondered, realizing once again how ignorant she was about the stones the rest of the planet took for granted.

Humphrey spoke again, jolting Yrund back to the matter at hand. "The Thinkers would like to know what crime it was that made the Asterians take you prisoner."

Yrund's nostrils flared. "There was no crime. They say we burned down the bridge over the Jaggedy River, but my family was at the Sky Games. Ask anyone. We got there early to trade and left late because of a cousin's wedding."

"Your family was captured because of the bridge over the Jaggedy?" Humphrey repeated, looking troubled. "Why would the wields blame the Sky People? That bridge is not in your people's land."

"Because that bridge is the beginning of the wield's new road through the Sky Country, a road they know we don't want. We don't even know why they're building it—it doesn't go anywhere."

"Why do the Asterians ever build roads?"

"But we don't have any mines in the Sky Country. Just clay."

"Perhaps it is not something in the Sky Country they want, but something farther south."

"What?" asked Yrund. "There's nothing down there but sheep herders and storms."

"The *what* of it remains a mystery to us, too." Humphrey translated everything Yrund had said back to the Thinkers, but they were not satisfied. "They do not understand why your family would oppose the road. Most countries have welcomed the Asterians, who bring gems and other goods that humans crave."

"We don't use gems, remember. And even if we did, we still wouldn't want to be taxed for a road we'll never need. We're herders, not carters—we go where the grazing is."

This seemed to hit a note with the Thinkers. "Tell us more about your home," said Humphrey.

So Yrund told them—about the Great Sky and the clouds like mountains, about the juniper hills and the sheltering desert springs, about her herds and flocks and her horse and her family.

"My mother is of the First Moon People. My father is of the Badger Clan. I have three sisters and a grandmother, plus an aunt, uncle, and cousins who we travel with."

For the first time, sounds of approval came from the council. Ancestry seemed to mean something to the woodwins.

"Before the wield men took them, my family had twenty-nine goats." Yrund counted on her fingers. "Twelve sheep, two yaks, five horses, and two dogs…"

She told the Thinkers about their little round house that could be rolled up onto a cart and moved from pasture to pasture. And she told them about her mother's loom. She told them how her father took her weavings to trade with neighbors to the east and to the west. How the Asterians came promising their road and wealth, and how the Sky People politely declined, and how the Asterians came back with memluks and forced the Sky People to dig. She told them about the night of her capture and how she'd been wearing her father's hat, how they had bound them and taken them.

Finally, she was back where she'd started.

Yrund stopped, her throat dry.

The light was growing dim within the vaulted, green room.

One of the Thinkers got up, the air blurring, and lifted a red-stained bag from behind the altar.

Yrund's blood slowed. "You said if I told them my story, they wouldn't kill me."

"I said they wouldn't *eat* you…"

The bag opened, spilling a pile of dry resin globules onto the stone table. Then the Thinker added a handful of golden dust, and the hardened sap began to smolder, casting the sanctuary in its red glow. The spice of pine filled the air like the richest of perfumes, heady and dense.

Humphrey unfolded himself to standing.

"I think we might go and find some dinner."

What? Yrund got up, utterly confused.

"They're going to let me go?"

"That I cannot say," said Humphrey. He whistled, and the branches closed behind them. "But the Thinkers need time to think. There are matters far beyond what to do with one little human that remain to be discussed tonight."

AS THEY EMERGED from the pine canyon, a growl tore through the twilight. Humphrey chuffed as Yrund jumped. "Past time for dinner."

"That was you?" said Yrund, whose own stomach was grumbling.

"The Thinkers sometimes forget such lowly things as eating."

They turned at the creek, the last light shining silver off its surface, traveling up the valley into a grove of the largest trees Yrund had ever seen. A whistle called out from the distance. Humphrey answered.

"They have made a place for you to stay tonight. Come," he said, leading her through the gloaming to a tree on the grove's edge. Hanging from one of the oak's enormous branches was an elongated basket shaped like a gourd with a hole in the side near the bottom. On the ground was an actual gourd full of water along with a tray made of twigs, heaped with bronze-colored apples and nuts and mysterious leaf-wrapped rolls—enough to feed three of her, at least.

Humphrey apologized for the small portions.

"Do you really have to go?" The thought of being left alone did not make her easy.

"The wields have been up to more than reopening old mines, I'm afraid. There is trouble in the west that still needs relaying—it's why I returned." He swiveled the mouth of the hanging basket toward her. Inside was a bed of lichen and moss. "You can sleep here, but do not wander off—a human will not be welcome in the village."

"I won't," promised Yrund, putting her rucksack in the swinging basket. "Humphrey," she called after him as he turned to leave.

"Yes?"

"I would never tell the wields about your land. I promise."

The woodwin nodded. "I'll return when the Thinkers have

made their decision. You told a good story—that is worth some-thing—and you were polite. For a human."

"So you couldn't hear Orelia, then?"

"The stone?" asked the woodwin, perplexed. "No, not once. Why?"

"No reason… Um, one last thing," said Yrund. "Where should I go to…uh, you know?"

Humphrey waved his arms. "Anywhere you like. It's good for the soil."

Yrund blushed. It was fine for invisible woodwins to pursue their business out in the open, but she was not invisible.

"Humans are shy about the most curious things."

"Easy for you to say—none of you can see each other."

"What? Woodwins can see each other just fine."

"You can?"

"Of course. In fact," he said, taking two long strides into the forest, "I see a little woodwin there behind that tree." He whistled sternly, and Yrund heard something scampering off in the dark-ness. Humphrey returned, head shaking. "Doubtless she's never seen a human before."

Any ideas Yrund had had about escaping in the night disap-peared. Even in the dark, the woodwins could find her.

After Humphrey departed, Yrund sampled her dinner. The leaf rolls were filled with a dry paste rolled in sweet flakes. The first bite was fine, and the second, but by the third her tongue had begun to prickle, so she put the roll down—whatever it was might be good for woodwins, but not for humans. The apples, however, were crisp and tart, nothing like Brandul's mealy speci-mens, though a few were so tart as to be inedible.

"Ichh!" Yrund flinched at an especially sour bite at the same time Orelia said, *Mmmmm.*

Yrund looked around—the gem was still in her pocket, yet she could feel Orelia yearning for another bite. And she could hear the stone talking in her head—just like she had done in the meeting with the Thinkers. It was a peculiar sensation having someone else there inside her, displacing the natural current of her thoughts.

Yrund didn't know much about gems, but even she knew that was strange. *How are you doing that?* she thought to the stone. *How are you in my head?*

How are you in me? retorted the stone as if the accusation could go both ways.

Shhhh!

Something was moving in the forest. The rising moons had turned the grove silver with deep wells of shadow behind every trunk. Yrund stared into the darkness, letting her eyes adjust. There, hiding between the trees, was a small woodwin covered in striped brown fur. Small being relative—the creature stood several inches taller than Yrund with muscular arms as long as her own legs. Another shadow wavered, and a second woodwin stepped out. Then a third and a fourth.

Moving slowly, Yrund held out a walnut from her dinner as a peace offering. The woodwins drew closer, and a hand darted out to touch her.

"Hey now," said Yrund, backing into something strong and furry that pushed her right back. They were all pushing and pinching her, prodding at her skin and tugging on her hair. "Stop that!" she cried, swatting the hands away.

"Oww!" said Yrund. A leathery hand had slapped her back. "That...is...enough!" She climbed up into the shelter of the basket, soon realizing her mistake as the little woodwins pushed it between them like a swing. Then, they began to wind the basket up, chattering and snuffing like behemoth squirrels. One turn, two...three...seven... The woodwins let go at eleven.

Bogging hell! The moons and trees whirled around Yrund, the basket spinning like a top. As soon as she slowed, the woodwins wound her up again. Orelia laughed, delighted with the new game, which didn't stop until a lampbeetle glowed on. The mob of woodwins abandoned Yrund to give chase, tumbling after the twirling insect. The basket, once released, unspun itself the other direction. Yrund clutched the sides until the swinging slowed, watching dizzily as another lampbeetle dipped in through the door and hovered above her. Her hands reached of their own accord to catch the insect between her fingers. What the hell? She was like a doll, her limbs moving against her will.

Aah, said the stone, admiring the lampbeetle's orange light.

Orelia! Let me go. What are you doing?

Thbbbt! said the stone, and Yrund's hands relaxed, releasing the insect, which looped up into the night.

I don't know how you are in my head, but you are absolutely not allowed to go messing with me like that because you haven't got your own hands, Yrund lectured the stone. *I don't make you do anything you don't want to do...* Well, she had asked the stone to look like a plain rock and stay hidden, but that was just it—she had asked. She hadn't forced the gem. *Are you listening to me?* Yrund demanded of the stone as another lampbeetle floated by.

I can do that, said Orelia, and in an instant, Yrund's robe began to glow.

"No, Orelia!" said Yrund out loud.

But it was too late. Strong hands tipped Yrund out of the basket, sending both her and the glimmering gem tumbling across the ground. One of the little woodwins scooped it up with a happy squeak before another woodwin stole it away. Orelia laughed and blinked as the woodwins tossed her back and forth, keeping the gem just out of Yrund's reach.

"Give it back!" Yrund shouted, but the merrymakers ignored her, including Orelia.

"Fine." She gave up. What did she care if they took the stone? She shouldn't have it anyway. Yrund bent to gather up the contents of Humphrey's rucksack, which had also spilled, but soon those items too were ripped from her hands. She was not big enough or fast enough to compete with woodwins, even juveniles, who were whooping and stomping in a wild circle, holding the shining stone high.

Yrund leapt up into the hanging basket to avoid being trampled as the little woodwins, whistling and chuffing, danced around the oak and then off into the woods with their prize.

Disgusted, Yrund settled back in the moss, watching the lampbeetles fly up toward the moons. Deep down she had known this would happen. She should have left the stone in the mountain. Yrund had thought they were friends, but she was wrong. Orelia was still a gem, and gems could not be trusted.

CHAPTER TWELVE

Yrund! Yrund!

Yrund's eyes snapped open at the gem's screams, terror flooding in.

"Orelia?" Yrund leapt out of her hanging bed only to find she was still alone beneath the creaking oak. It was late, with three moons risen, but far off she could hear wild whistles and chanting. "Orelia?"

Noooooo! cried the gem.

"I'm coming!" called Yrund, running through shadowed ferns and moonslit trees. The gem pulled her onward like a beacon towards the center of the oak grove, where a softly glowing village of vine walls rose from the forest floor. Yrund slowed as she entered, overcome at the sight. Fox moss strung the mammoth halls in living chandeliers, illuminating rooms full of blurry figures, who whistled in shock as Yrund dashed past. The village, like the Thinkers' enclave, was as much indoors as out, the dwellings opening into a mazelike garden dotted with small ponds turning with water wheels. Beside them, gray in the moonslight, were trellises of squash and long marrows.

Yrund!!

She splashed through the pools and tore through vines, careening around human-sized baskets and clay water urns, following the gem's call right into the heart of the village, where a great tree stretched nearly to the stars. Yrund skidded to a stop. The woodwins were chanting and tossing Orelia up and down in front of a shimmering black doorway, not in a house, but in the tree itself.

"Stop!" yelled Yrund, rushing in and twisting at the arm of the striped woodwin holding Orelia aloft. The little woodwin shoved her aside, dangling the gem toward the tree's opening, which Yrund could now see was not really a door at all but a hole, darker and deeper than any chasm in Devil's Crown. The cold and empty nothing within made Yrund shudder, as if she were about to fall out of herself, out of existence entirely. Horror and indignation combined within her like a cold flame. The wood-wins were no better than the Asterians, toying with her and the gem as if their deaths were just some amusement. Was her life worth so little to Precios? That she could survive all of Devil's Crown just to be extinguished now by this strange and evil door?

Yrund's fury ignited, bursting through her in a raging storm, and then, somehow, it was in the stone too, a blazing ball of blue light. The woodwin shrieked, dropping the gem and beating away the flames licking at his fur.

The woodwins turned as one, stampeding over Yrund to get away from the fire.

Yrund wrestled her way through the fleeing mob, throwing herself onto the burning woodwin. They rolled across the dirt in front of the tree, Yrund smothering the flames with her robe even as the woodwin fought her.

They rolled and struggled until Humphrey was pulling her off and other hands reached down to carry the howling woodwin away.

"Come now—you should not be here," said Humphrey.

"They...they took Orelia! They were going to throw her

into…into…" Yrund gestured wildly at the huge oak, but the shimmering doorway was no longer there, just a dead-end hollow in the trunk, a pile of acorns and flowers at its base like an altar. She reached her arm in. Nothing but cobwebs and leaves.

"Where's the gem now?" asked Humphrey.

Yrund turned around, disoriented.

Orelia lay in the dirt where she'd fallen, looking as innocent as a plain gray rock.

YRUND WOKE with a start at first dawn, cold and damp with dew, the basket swinging in the morning wind. She had been awake most of the short night, looking up at the stars through the oak forest and worrying. What had happened to the little woodwin? What would happen to Orelia? The gem was clutched so tightly in her hand Yrund could barely move her fingers.

Sitting up, she saw someone had made a ring of crossed twigs and leaves on the ground around the tree. A warning to keep her in or to keep others out?

Outside the circle stood a fence of blurry woodwins, their eyes watchful. Each one held a large gourd filled to the top with water. Humphrey, alone, stepped over the ring of leaves.

Yrund dropped down from the basket to meet him, heart thumping.

What what? asked Orelia, sending a tingle of sensation through Yrund's head.

They must think we're going to start another fire, Yrund thought back, hiding the stone in her pocket.

"Good morning," said Humphrey, which seemed an oddly normal thing to say under the circumstances.

"Good morning," said Yrund. "How…how is he? The one who got burnt?"

"*She* will be all right," said Humphrey. "A little singed, but no real damage luckily."

That was a miracle, thought Yrund, remembering the intensity of blue flames. Her scorched robe still smelled of charred hair, though she too had escaped any injury. "What will happen to me now?"

"That is for you to decide," said Humphrey, his deep eyes considering her.

"Me?" Yrund didn't understand. "Don't the Thinkers think I'm an ab…abom…?"

"Abomination. They do—you brought fire to our forest."

"I didn't mean for that to happen. I didn't know I—she could do that."

"So it seems, or you would not have tried to put the flames out, but the danger remains."

"I'm sorry," said Yrund, for she was. "But it looked like they were going to throw her into a terrible hole…" She recoiled at the memory of it. "It was there in the tree! I swear!"

Humphrey's fur ruffled uncomfortably. "I cannot explain what you saw. At night, in the forest especially, the eyes can play many tricks. You were not the only one, or ones should I say, at fault—the little ones had been forbidden from going near you, or the Great Oak, but they are not very good Listeners yet. Or Thinkers. I'm afraid we all start out as Doers. Nor did it help that they had stolen a pot of honey beer. It was only half-fermented, but it no doubt emboldened them. I had hoped," he went on, "that your coming here might have been a sign from Aya that there was a way forward—an opportunity to convince the Thinkers there are still humans that follow the Way, but…" His shoulders drooped slightly. Clearly, he took the failure upon himself. "At any rate, it's time for you to leave."

"For where?" asked Yrund.

"The council has instructed me to escort you to the nearest human settlement, under the condition—" He paused. "You take the binding eye oath never to speak of our woods or even our existence to another human. If you cannot swear to this, the Doers are prepared to take their chances…and exterminate you."

"You can't take me to a human settlement," said Yrund, panicking. "I'm still a fugitive. If the wields find me, I'll be sent back to the mines." If she wasn't *exterminated* by the Mining Wield first.

"The Lumi are no friends of the wields. They will give you shelter; I am certain of it."

The Lumi? Like Brave Braid and the men at Devil's Crown?

"How do I take this…binding eye oath?" asked Yrund nervously.

"First you must say the words." Humphrey led her through the oath to keep the Hidden Woods secret, which involved several gruesome types of death if she were to break it.

"And lastly," he finished, "do you agree to the debt owed by you to our good and tree-loving peoples? That in return for your life, you promise you will give aid to any woodwin, at any time, and in any way that is required of you, even when such aid does not serve human aim, as long as it serves the woodwin? On penalty of not just your death but also that of the First Moon People and the Badger People, including your mother and your father, Wian and Gantul?"

Yrund swallowed, cursing herself for giving the council her real name. "I…"

Humphrey waited.

"Yes. I accept the debt."

"Now, you will be bound by the eyes."

Yrund felt herself begin to sweat. "It will not hurt. I assure you. But it is necessary. Please, hold out your hands."

Trembling, Yrund held her hands out.

Humphrey turned them over, palms up, and whistled. A blurry figure broke from the circle and approached, carrying a tiny clay bottle with a stopper. Despite the cloaked fur, there was an air of age in the woodwin's movements that reminded her of her grand-mother. From nowhere the creature pulled out an instrument with a sharp point at the end. With a ritual-like whistle, she—for that was Yrund's guess—dipped the end into the clay bottle, then drew a wet mark on both of Yrund's palms. Two eyes stared up at her.

"These eyes are the sign of your debt to us. And a reminder you will be watched. You are bound by your oath today as witnessed by this tree and these—" He whistled the rest.

If the woodwins were satisfied, they gave no hint—the circle still stood silent with mistrust.

"When do we leave, then?" asked Yrund, sensing it was time.

"I think now," said Humphrey, brushing a fallen leaf from his fur. "Our valley does not reflect the weather that will soon be falling upon the south." He handed her back the rucksack the little woodwins had stolen the night before. She could see he had added packets of wrapped leaves to the contents.

The circle parted for them to pass. Yrund followed Humphrey out of the great grove and back up the valley. It wasn't until they reached the creek that she looked down at her hands again. The eyes were still there. She wiped at the design, but it did not come off. As if the snakes around her ankles weren't enough… And yet, unlike the heartless creations of the Asterians, there was no malevolence in these eyes.

Nor was there warmth.

There was only waiting, for a debt to be filled.

✳ ✳ ✦ ✳ ✳

THE SUNS HAD both risen when they reached the rainkeepers' vast dams, the light tinging the valley the ochre of late summer. Upstream, a line of blurry forms bent to gather reeds from the shallows.

"Hey—how come I could see the little woodwins but not the

big ones?" she asked, curiosity overcoming her worry for a moment.

"You can see the young because of the unfading. With each generation we are losing our protection. Our ancestors never had to bathe at all. In fact they abhorred washing, but by the time I was born we had no choice. Now, most of the little ones are born with no camouflage at all."

"No wonder you don't want humans in your forest," said Yrund as they walked across the interwoven bridge of driftwood and branches, which had been polished to a pleasing smoothness by the water.

Orelia whistled something in woodwin, a note of contriteness to the song.

"Fire, in the right season, is a gift. But not from men. Or gems," he added.

"Why did you stand up for us?" asked Yrund.

"Someday we may need humans more than we think. We were not brought to Precios to be executioners."

"What do you mean—you were brought here?"

"We were all brought here."

"By who? Surely you don't mean the Bringers. Those are just stories."

"Just like woodwilds? Moonstales and myths often contain more truth than you realize. Have your people really forgotten where they came from?"

"We came from the Sky," said Yrund.

"So you did," said the woodwin. "In great ships to start again. Do you know why?"

"No," Yrund echoed. Nobody asked *why* about myths, did they?

"Because," said the woodwin, hopping from the dam to the trail. "Humans burned down their last home."

"How do you know that?" asked Yrund, leaping after him.

"We know many things humans have chosen not to remember. Seven hundred years is not so long for us."

Seven hundred years! Yrund hurried after the woodwin, questions bubbling like boiling water.

The temperature dropped as they left the woodwins' protected valley, the leaves of the forest outside already turning from russet to burgundy, scattered by a brusque wind that crept through the blackened holes in Yrund's red robe.

"You said the woodwins weren't brought here to be executioners. Why were you brought here, then?" asked Yrund when they paused at the crest of a sharp ridge, the wind in their face.

"Our job was—is—to keep humans to the Way," answered Humphrey. "Among other things."

"Which Way?" asked Yrund. There were many Ways on Precios, including the Way of the wields—that the strong should rule the weak.

"The true Way."

"Which is what—not cutting down trees or starting any fires? How would we cook or stay warm? We're not built like woodwins." And too bad in this chill. She could use a fur coat.

"The Way is not about rules but balance. Humans were given a second chance here—to test whether they were bees or locusts."

"*Baskets of bees…*" Orelia began to sing before Yrund shushed her. Her family might not have been farmers themselves, but Yrund knew what locusts could do to crops.

"We've failed the test, haven't we?"

"Many of you. But not all. The Sky People are an exception. And the Lumi. There are others—the Outer Glasians, the Tolrukim…"

"But not the wields," said Yrund with a flush of vindication.

"Not all the wields are without merit. Even the Mining Wield once followed its own constraints, but the Age of Gems changed that—for Asteria and the rest of the planet."

"What do you mean the 'Age of Gems'? Weren't there always gems on Precios?"

"Oh yes, and they were mined far before humans arrived."

Yrund recalled Devil's Crown and all the heavy equipment in its hollows. And the eyes carved into the walls. Once again, she checked her hands. The woodwins' ink was indelible, impervious to spit or an inadvertent slip in the creek, a dark brown stain outlining the watching dark eyes. She wondered if there was a connection between the woodwins and the mine, but woodwins were taller even than memluks. They would never have fit in the short tunnels that Gem Beard had said were built for children.

"Are you saying we weren't the first ones to come to this planet?"

The woodwin walked on, his fur blowing around him in the wind. "Of course not. The signs are everywhere, or they were. Most have been destroyed or hidden, an unwelcome reminder that not all species last, especially those that lose the Way. The wields believe they are the exception, emboldened by their inventions and the powers gems have given them."

Yrund's head felt like it would split. "Why bring us to a place with gems, then?"

Humphrey blew through his lips, producing a horsey sound.

"The minerals of Precios did not affect humans in the beginning," he explained. "You were like us in that regard or doubtless you would not have been brought here. Over time, however, your receptivity to the planet's stones began to grow."

"While your invisibility began to lessen."

"You see the problem. Our ability to protect you from yourselves grows harder every year."

Yrund slumped down on a wind-smoothed rock, her mind an avalanche of questions.

"We probably shouldn't dawdle," said the woodwin, looking south at the clouds.

"Look," said Yrund, staying put. "I've never heard any of this before. I'm not saying I don't believe you, but how could humans have all just forgotten where we came from, who we used to be?"

"They have not all forgotten their history. Why else would your people be gem shy?"

"Why didn't the Bringers come back to check on us?"

"They did in the beginning." Humphrey watched as a V of winter geese flew over. "But then they disappeared."

"Leaving you here with us."

"That was partly humans' fault. We used to have a way back to our own planet. But humans destroyed it."

"Humans," tsked Orelia.

Even more reason to hate us, thought Yrund. "How long since the Bringers disappeared?"

"Almost four hundred years."

"So, what happened to them?"

"That, no one can say. Perhaps they abandoned us both. Perhaps they're just late."

Four centuries late? Yrund was growing fond of Humphrey, but he was as superstitious as Gem Beard. And yet, could she really say he was wrong? "And if the Bringers do come back and find out we're locusts, not bees? What then?"

"Precisely," said Humphrey, setting off once more. "What then?"

The more questions Yrund asked, the more she had. "Who are the Bringers? Where are they from?"

"I have answered all that I can for now," said the woodwin, waiting for Yrund to descend a chain of boulders in their path. "Now it is your turn."

"What can I possibly tell you?" asked Yrund, using a clump of bright moss for a handhold.

"You can start with everything you know about airships."

The morning took them south through forests of wind-stripped trees, losing leaves to the autumn gusts like books losing pages. The golden piles scattered as Yrund waded through them after the untiring woodwin. Yrund was sure she had disappointed him with just how little she understood of the wields' airborne contraptions. In the two unhappy trips she had taken, drugged and cramped between other prisoners, the first one with a bag over her head half the trip, she had not thought to pay attention to such things as turn-shafts and bellow foils. She couldn't even tell him what gems were used in the airship's wheeled engines.

"Do you really have to take me to the Lumi? Can't I just go home?" she asked, when they finally paused for a lunch of apples from the rucksack. "I know which way to go." She pointed east, where the mountains descended, little siblings looking up to the High Aeries.

"To the Sky Steppes?" said Humphrey, nearly choking on his apple. "A human cannot walk there from here. The Slow Death Gorge blocks your way. Beyond that are miles of bogs, and after that the cliffs of Skerry Strait. Unless you are a bird, that way is impassable. Your only course back home is over the Quick Death Gorge to Lumi Land, then the Gem Road round in the spring—through Asteria." He scratched a map on the ground with a twig.

The disappointment was like a weight. The airships that delivered the rabu to Devil's Crown had covered even more distance than Yrund had realized. Home was not only farther than she'd hoped, but only reachable through the land of the enemy.

"You said no human has ever crossed either of your gorges."

The woodwin's hairy face turned up into a smile. "They haven't."

EACH DAY THEY CONTINUED SOUTHWARD, hiking from sunrise to sunset and sleeping in tree hollows at night, first a mix of pine and oak and then only evergreen as the forest changed. Humphrey had an uncanny ability to find these living shelters just when they needed one. They provided shelter from the rain and wind, and only a few bark mites had crawled through Yrund's scalp as they slept. The woodwin also had good eyes for the dried mushrooms that squirrels had speared on branches for the coming winter.

Once, Humphrey made a detour into a side valley. "Wait here," he said at the edge of a meadow dotted with domed baskets. When he loped back, he held a dripping chunk of honeycomb still buzzing with bees. It was nearly the best thing Yrund had ever eaten—spicy and chewy and wriggling with sweet, nutty larvae—and far preferable to some of the provisions in the rucksack, which included more tongue-prickling balls of what Humphrey said was acorn paste and yellow strips of a jerky-like fungus that made her feel light in the head.

For her own part, Yrund contributed to their meals by pulling up late wild onions when she saw them, and the occasional handful of sweet gooseberries the bears had missed.

Every morning when Yrund woke, she marveled at the progress they were making and how different the forest looked from evening to first light. Occasionally they ran across more of the woodwins' strange arches or boulders arranged in eccentric circles, or Humphrey would whistle with a blur in the distance, but no one approached them, whether from council edict or general disdain of humans.

As the days passed, the mountains descended ahead of them, dropping into valleys, then hills, and then on the fourth day, they reached a wide plateau strewn with short, wind-twisted pines. Beyond that, Yrund could not see, for the horizon was concealed by long rolls of cloud that did not seem to move.

"Here we are," said Humphrey, stopping so suddenly Yrund nearly ran into him. She had been distracted by a black dot among the clouds.

Yrund stepped back with alarm. The ground had turned to sky.

"What is that?" she asked, though a sinking feeling in her stomach told her she already knew.

"The Quick Death Gorge." A large raven flapped down next to them, cawing at Humphrey as if they were old friends.

If Yrund had to choose between a slow death and a quick death, she supposed it would be the latter. She crept back to the edge. The sides of the gorge were only yelling distance apart but so vertical and with such a drop between them only a bird could have crossed it. The way really was impassable.

"Ready?"

"Ready for what? To fly?"

Whistling happily, Humphrey began to fish around for something in a hole beneath a nearby tree.

"Ah-ha," he said, getting back up, holding what looked like knotted loops of white gauze. Then he hung the makeshift harness over an almost invisible line of more gauze that stretched from around a giant boulder out into the empty space above the canyon. Yrund retreated. She didn't know what he was doing, but she didn't like it. The woodwin stepped into one of the hanging loops he had made and then the other, putting his arms through the opposite side of the flimsy-looking arrangement. "What are you waiting for?"

"That's how you're getting across?" Yrund's throat felt dry.

"That's how *we're* getting across," said Humphrey as though nothing was amiss.

Yrund's legs went wobbly.

Oooh! said the stone with excitement.

"You aren't afraid of heights, are you?" asked Humphrey, surprised.

"No, I'm not. But that isn't a height," said Yrund, pointing at the gorge. "That's a depth. There's a difference."

"Ah yes, I believe in Lumi Land they do call it the Bottomless Depth," he said. "Or is it the Bottomless Death? I can't remember. Anyway, here goes—hop on!" He finished his adjustments and stooped for her to get on his back. "No time to waste. Chop the onion as they say; there's weather coming in."

"Yes, chop chop," said Orelia, who it appeared had no qualms about heights or depths.

"As who say?" asked Yrund, stalling, though she too had noticed the advancing darkness. For a brief moment one cloud looked like it was moving opposite of the others. "Do you see that?"

"See what?" said Humphrey, shading his eyes.

"The clouds look weird."

"The Southern Glories, they're called. One of the only standing roll clouds on the planet. Hard to see now, but quite impressive."

Yrund looked over the edge of the gorge again, and the nothingness of it overcame her.

"You do not have to leave our land, but I can promise what will happen if you stay. The Doers are persistent and resourceful—even with your stone's fire, they will likely find a way to kill you in the end."

"Why did they let me go, then?"

"Because I convinced the Thinkers you were worth more to us alive. Who better to report on humans than another human?"

"You mean, I'm to be a Watcher like you."

"I can tell the Thinkers you've changed your mind. They may grant a merciful execution."

"No, I'm not breaking my oath."

"Then we really shouldn't dally," he said as lightning flashed in the distance.

"Dally," said Orelia, trying out the new word.

"Bogging hell," said Yrund under her breath as she transferred Orelia from her pocket to the rucksack, knotting the top twice. Then, ignoring every screaming instinct within her, she climbed onto Humphrey's back and wrapped her arms around him, twisting every finger and toe into his thick, soft fur.

"Not so tight." The woodwin coughed, and Yrund loosened her grip around his neck. "That's better. Off we go, then!" With that, Humphrey leapt right off the cliff.

For one heart-stopping moment, they fell free until the harness caught the line and they were flying across the gorge, the silvery gauze above them humming like a plucked harp string. Humphrey whooped, and Orelia joined him from the depths of Yrund's pack.

"Awwooooooo!" sang the gem.

The opposite cliff was rushing toward them so fast Yrund turned her head away, closing her eyes tight, but the line swung up again at the last, slowing their hurtle to a crawl. Her relief was short, for just a few yards from the edge they began to reverse direction, the woodwin's gauzy harness whizzing backward across the thin line until they hung bouncing above the middle of the gorge.

"Huh," said Humphrey when they finally came to a stop. Far below in the shadows, something was roaring.

"Huh? What do you mean—'huh'?" asked Yrund, her voice high. All around them was absolutely nothing.

"It must be the extra weight... No matter." The woodwin began to pull them back toward the south side, his enormous arms bulging with each swing.

"What's down there?" asked Yrund, taking a quick glance, then regretting it.

"The Skerry River. It flows that way to the sea." The woodwin let go with one hand and pointed to where the gray canyon curved away into a thick bank of clouds.

"Could you hold on with both hands, please?"

"Don't worry—this is spider thread. There's nothing stronger. The potato farmers in Finsalir use these to get across the West Jaggedies." Humphrey jounced up and down, testing their weight on the line as Orelia whistled with glee.

"Long way to the bottom, though," Humphrey said, spitting and watching the saliva fall. Yrund closed her eyes until they began to move again, the woodwin hauling them hand over hand the rest of the way. He heaved them both up onto the gorge's south ledge, and Yrund scrambled away from the chasm.

"I can't believe you have to cross that every time you want to come or go," she said, still shaking.

"Oh, this isn't how woodwins get across," said Humphrey.

"You said this was the only way out!" Yrund's voice rose another note higher.

"It is for humans."

"Then how do you usually go?" Did woodwins have their own airships?

"We have our ways."

"Do it again!" begged Orelia.

"No," said Yrund, having to sit down for a moment. They were all insane. "Wood*wild*," she muttered under her breath.

"I can hear you," said Humphrey as he untethered the harness and tucked it under a rock. Something white fell onto his leathery nose.

The storm had arrived.

"How much farther?" asked Yrund again, who had no sense of where they were going or how far they had come. The trees all looked alike, floating in the snowy fog like skeletons. They had been hiking through snow for hours now, and she could no longer feel her feet.

"That depends whether the Lumi are still rounding up their herds in the mountains or have left for the southern lowlands."

"Are you sure they'll take me in?" asked Yrund, breath turning to frozen crystal in the air. She pulled her robe tight, the scarlet color muted by frost.

"I think you'll find the Mining Wield is especially unpopular in Lumi Land. Besides, would your people turn away a child?"

"I'm not exactly a child. I'm thirteen." Fourteen soon.

"A lost soul, then?"

"No," she said. But this was not the Sky Country. "And what am I going to do with Orelia? What if she forgets to be plain?"

The gem whistled something in woodwin.

Humphrey chuffed, nearly invisible now as the snow sloughed his fur clean. "I'm sure she learned her lesson," he said with far more confidence than Yrund felt. It was annoying the gem and the woodwin could converse without her, whistling back and forth like gossipy birds.

The sunless gray sky grew darker as if a shadow were passing overhead.

Humphrey looked up. "Do you hear that?"

Yrund did. It was the sound of an airship.

The wooden prow of the ship cut through the ghostly low clouds like a hangman's lantern. A bulging-eyed man leaned over the side, holding something out in his hand.

The mine boss no longer wore the golden colors of the Mining Wield but the blues and browns of Roads and Ways. Even still, there was no mistaking him. Brandul had found her. And he still had his finder's agyt, which was tilting toward Yrund as the airship glided past.

Yrund willed her legs to run.

She should have known, she thought, cursing—she should have known the Mining Wield would never let her go.

"It's the rat!" Brandul cried, pointing down at her. Beside him stood Veng and two men, bows at the ready. "I told you she wasn't dead! The rat has the allstone! Shoot her! *Shoot her!*" As he screamed, he jabbed out his agyt toward her.

The allstone? What was he saying? She didn't have any gems but Orelia, and Orelia wasn't an allstone. Not that Yrund knew what an allstone was, but surely Brandul, of all people, wasn't looking for a mouthy gem with no sense.

"Run!" yelled Humphrey, and Yrund's limbs came back to life, propelling her into the cover of the trees.

"There, there!" yelled Brandul as the ship passed over her, the agyt rotating in his hand. "See? I told you she had it! Shoot her! Drop the stone, you rat! Drop it, I command you!"

Never. She would never give Orelia to a cruel and craven man like Brandul. She might have been a gem, but she was still her friend. "Watch out!" called Humphrey.

Yrund dodged around one of the skeletal birches as an arrow pinged off the trunk. Another arrow cut through the ferns behind her. The woods were all a blur in the fog, glowing orange from the light of the airship's vaulted chambers.

Crap, crap, crap... She would never outrun an airship. Yrund veered back beneath the ship, arrows hissing into the snow all around, and crashed through the forest in the opposite direction, forcing the ship to turn, wondering what had become of the woodwin.

"Over here!" yelled Humphrey, but Yrund could not see him. "Here!" he yelled again, and she ran toward the sound of his voice, tearing through thorn bushes and tripping over branches.

The ship was banking around now, the orange light shining through the fog.

"Oh, little ratty!" called Veng, and a sharp pain drove through Yrund's shoulder. She stumbled, crying out—blood dripping from her hands to the snow. No—no!

A blurry arm reached out, pulling Yrund up onto the woodwin's back. "Hold on!" Humphrey bounded through the woods, leaping rocks and logs and half-frozen streams, the glow of the wield's airship growing closer. The pain was unbearable. Another arrow ricocheted off the back of her rucksack. The airship was gaining. Humphrey ran through the storm, dodging trees and heading deeper into the forest, branches flashing by in a black-and-white blur like a dream.

And then the airship was over them, its orange light like a cold sun. Humphrey never slowed, whistling as he headed straight toward an enormous tree. "Watch out," Yrund tried to say, but she was too weak, her words torn away by the wind. The tree shimmered in front of them, and she was dreaming again, for they had run right through its trunk and into the sky.

They dove through trees and stars and into a forest of pines, passing startled snowdeer and rising moons like eyes. It was all just a wild dream now, the woodwin's soft back her bed.

On and on the woodwin ran—the blizzard howling around them like wolves. Or were those real wolves, racing beside them?

Humphrey shook her awake. "Don't sleep!"

Yrund tried to cling on, forcing her eyes open. But they were so heavy, and she was so tired… Her grip began to loosen—

"Hold on! I can see lights!"

Lights, thought Yrund. Lights meant fire. Fire meant home… she was going home… She would see her mother and father, her pony and her goats.

Then Humphrey was swinging her down off his back and shaking her awake.

There was a funny little house, just visible through the blinding snow. Humphrey pounded his giant fist upon it, then pushed Yrund forward.

"Yaha?" someone called out as the thick door opened a crack. "Is that you, Hinri?"

Yrund willed her legs to move. Just one step. She teetered in the snow. The door began to close.

"Here!"

One more step… "I'm here!"

The door opened again, the shadow of a man blocking the light. Yrund teetered and fell into his arms.

CHAPTER FOURTEEN

Through the thick quilt of dreams, Yrund could hear her sisters giggling. She wished they would go away, but they wouldn't let her be, piling her feet with hot coals.

Yrund yelped as she woke. A rust-haired woman had one of Yrund's feet in a gentle grip. The other was in a pail of warm water. The woman dried and wrapped Yrund's feet in clean strips of cloth, being careful not to touch her serpentine anklets.

"You have frostbite," she said in Trade Tongue. "It's going to burn as your toes thaw." She was not much older than Yrund's mother, with weather-roughened skin that crinkled around her green eyes like dried apricots. At the neck of her thick coat she wore a silver locket, a heart engraved with delicate flowers. So Humphrey had delivered her to the Lumi as he'd said he would.

Yrund tried to untangle herself from the pile of felts and furs pinning her down but gasped at the sudden pain.

"Careful. You had an arrow in your side—stuck in a rib, thank Irsil and all her creatures, or you wouldn't be here now, but it will take time to heal." The woman's head swung back and forth in disapproval. "I don't know how you ever walked here in your state."

"Who…who are you?" asked Yrund. Her voice was hoarse, and her lips cracked as she spoke.

"I'm Tana Haya. These are my children." She turned her chin toward the staring faces behind her. "Anouk, my second-eldest daughter." The girl was taller than Yrund but looked slightly younger. She had light blue eyes, straight pale hair and a serious face that dimpled when she smiled. Around her neck she wore a locket like her mother's.

"And Jon-Luq, my middle son." The rosy-lipped boy was close to fourteen, Yrund guessed, with a flop of brown bangs under his cap and slightly gapped teeth.

"And the twins, Tir and Magrit." The youngest Hayas were perhaps three or four years old and spitting images of their elder siblings. The whole family wore heavily embroidered layers of snowdeer skins trimmed with dark fur collars.

"Say 'Good Way,'" Tana told her children.

"Good Way." They giggled behind their hands.

"And my eldest, Mila," Tana said, indicating a tall young woman at the stove who looked like a golden-beige lynx, her eyes and skin almost the same color as her hair. She whisked something thick and steaming into a bowl, then carried it to Yrund's bed, stepping gracefully over her siblings, too distracted with staring at Yrund to move out of the way.

"Good Way," Mila said, sitting down beside her. "What's your name?" She brought a spoonful of the liquid up to Yrund's lips.

"I'm Yrund."

"*Ah-roond?* That's nice."

Yrund opened her mouth to correct the Lumi girl's pronunciation, but just then Mila took the opportunity to pop the spoon in.

Yrund sputtered but swallowed. The drink was sweet and creamy and very spicy, a mix of flavors unlike anything Yrund had ever had—barks and fruit peels and even flowers. The color shifted from plum to feather green and back again, changing in the light of the stove like the feathers on a duck's neck. Floating on top were short hairs, which Mila didn't seem to notice, so Yrund ignored them. Mila spooned Yrund another sip of the iridescent cream.

Mmmm, Orelia purred happily, and Yrund nearly choked again. She had forgotten the gem.

"What?" asked Mila.

Ah-roond, I'm being good, Yrund! said the stone, and Yrund felt her mind tickle as if a wind had blown through.

Mila refilled the spoon, looking at her curiously. "What?" she asked again.

Hello? Yrund called silently.

Allo, said Orelia.

Yrund looked back at Mila for any sign she had heard, but the Lumi girl's face was a questioning blank. "Do you want to sit up, is that it?"

Yrund nodded.

"Yaha, of course you do," said Mila, setting down the bowl and helping her free of the bedding.

Yaha, said Orelia, trying out the new word. Just like with the Thinkers, no one else seemed to hear. At least the rucksack had made it with her. Yrund tried to remember the trip through the blizzard, a blur of pain and strange dreams—wolves and stars and trees that opened with a whistle. Another thought occurred to her. What if she was crazy? What if she was just imagining she could talk to the gem?

Humphrey can talk to me.

Yes, but what if Yrund had imagined him too? Some sort of way of coping or maybe a side effect of the explosion? But if the gem and the woodwin weren't real, how had she gotten out of the mountain or all the way to the Lumi's house?

Hesitantly, Yrund pulled her arms from the pile of furs. Two eyes stared back from her palms.

"What do those mean?" asked Mila. "We couldn't wash them off last night."

"They're a reminder."

"Of what?"

"A promise that I made." Yrund would have sighed but her rib was too sore. She saw that they had wrapped a wide strip of cloth around her chest and dressed her in clean woolen pants.

Tana draped a fur across Yrund's shoulders. "We'll get you a proper shirt when you can lift your arms. Your robe is soaking, but it will need patching. I'm afraid the other items you were wearing had too much blood on them to save."

"Good," said Yrund, who hoped Tana had burned them.

Yrund finished the rest of the spiced cream by herself, ignoring the spoon and gulping. It wasn't until she licked the insides clean that she saw the polished wood bowl was carved with small deer and leaves like those woven into the belts the family wore around their waists. She examined the rest of the small house, which was made of thick, insulating mud over branches. It reminded her a little of the round tents of her own people, the curved walls efficiently circulating the heat from the central stove, but in place of the browns and blues of the Sky Country, the Hayas' trunks were painted a vivid yellow, serving double duty as both storage and bed frames. She was impressed to see the family owned a cast stove and cook pots—metal of any kind was rare in the Sky Steppes.

"Would you like something to eat?" asked Tana, drawing Yrund's attention back to the family, who was watching her intently.

"Yes, thank you," said Yrund, inhaling as Tana pulled a dish of round buns from the oven's coals.

The children whispered to each other in their own language.

"Don't stare," said Mila. "She'll think you're *vandradolts*."

The buns were still hot from the fire, round and dotted with small, fragrant flecks. Yrund winced as she bit through the crust, burning her chapped lips on the steam.

"Don't you like cardamom?" asked Tana.

"It's my teeth—they're loose."

Tana came over to inspect Yrund's gums. "The same thing happened to Timo when they took him. You need milk. And minced meat. How the wields could starve a child…" She couldn't finish her sentence. She wiped her eyes with her apron and bustled back to the stove, where she banged pots around the one-person kitchen.

"Do you want some more alat?" asked Mila, looking uncomfortable at her mother's display of emotion.

"Alat?"

"The drink," she said, pointing to the empty carved bowl.

"I've never had alat before. What is it?"

"Nobody really knows," said Mila, springing back up to refill the bowl. It took her only three strides over the children to return. "Well, except the Alatis, who make it. And maybe Trader Ansyn. It's all the way from the Long Sea."

Yrund put the bowl down. Alat sounded rare, and here she was guzzling it.

Mila laughed. "Don't worry! Ansyn will bring us more. Or he'll have a revolt on his hands. He says we Lumi drink more alat than anyone else on the planet."

Yrund understood how they felt. The wields had put an embargo on all trade between Asteria and the Sky Steppes after their bridge had been destroyed. If it wasn't for the Windtraders crossing the Sea of Death in their sandships, the Sky People wouldn't have had any tea at all. Yrund picked her bowl back up, drinking more slowly this time.

The door blew open, letting in a jet of cold air and a man with a short brown and gray beard. He knocked his boots against the step and whistled. A thick-furred dog bounded inside behind him, shaking snow across the house.

"Sikka!" scolded Tana, closing the door against the wind. The dog came straight to Yrund and licked her face.

"How's the guest?" asked the man, taking off his mitten-topped gloves. His cheeks were chapped and bits of snow clung to his gray-speckled mustache and beard. His face was serious like Anouk's, but the same dimples appeared when he smiled. "Hungry, I see!"

Yrund had taken too big a bite of the bun. While everyone watched, she chewed and swallowed, face flushing.

"This is my husband, Timo," said Tana. "And Sikka, you've met."

Timo scratched the dog's head and pinched a bun for himself, switching to Lumi to catch up with his wife, both glancing at Yrund as they spoke. Lumi sounded much like the language of the camel herders that lived on the eastern borders of the Sky Country. The accent was different, but some of the words were the same. Like *wields* and *danger*.

"Don't mind them," whispered Mila in Trade Tongue. "We know you must have escaped from the silver mine at Sea Throat. Apa's just confused why the wields are bringing in rabu from the north."

Yrund shook her head.

"It's all right. You're safe with us," Mila reassured her.

"But, I wasn't at a silver mine," said Yrund.

"You weren't at Sea Throat?"

The whole family had now turned to listen.

"I was at Devil's Crown."

Timo looked at Tana, but she was just as perplexed.

"We don't know that mine. Which direction is it?"

"It's in the High Aeries," said Yrund.

"You cannot walk to the Aeries from here. Not without going north first. Perhaps you mean the Kalans? Even that's a long way to come with an arrow stuck in your rib and your feet half-frozen."

Of course the Lumi didn't know there was a way across the woodwins' land to the Aeries. Not with the gorges in the way. Nor could she tell them.

"Why did they shoot you?" asked Anouk.

"Because she tried to leave, obviously," said Mila, answering for Yrund.

"It would take a week to walk from the Kalans," said Tana, perplexed. "And your wound looks much more recent than that."

"How long have I been here?"

"Just since last night."

"That must have been when it happened. They have an airship." She still didn't understand how Humphrey had gotten them away. Fear came over her like a heavy blanket. "They're probably still looking for me."

"An airship?" Tana seemed astounded. "Near here?"

Yrund understood her disbelief. It was hard to imagine anything bad happening within the Hayas' safe walls, but she nodded nonetheless.

"I thought the wield's navigational instruments didn't work this far south," said Mila.

"They didn't," said Timo, squinting as if he might understand. "Unless they've come up with something new. Which is always possible with the wields..."

"Be that as it may," said Tana, "we still have our herd to get to Last Lake."

"Right your mother is," agreed Timo. "So finish up your breakfast. There are sleds and skis to finish." The children reluctantly got up, assembling buns stuffed with black sausage for their breakfast.

That was it? "But what about the airship? If the wields find me with you—"

"The wields can suck a troll's egg."

"Mila!" said her mother.

"It's true. The Asterians think they own the planet, but this is our country. We can take in whomever we like."

"What Mila means to say is that many families gave shelter to our Timo when he escaped Sea Throat, and now it is our turn."

"You don't understand," said Yrund. "They have bows, and strikers."

"We may not have strikers, but we have bows," said Mila, pointing over at the wall, where indeed half a dozen of the weapons hung, all twice the size of Yrund's compact bow back home. "I was the best shot at Winter Fair last year, and I'm not nearly as good as Apa and Katrin. They'll have to kill us all if they want to take you back."

"Yaha!" agreed Jon-Luq, though Anouk looked less pleased.

"Hold your dogs," said Timo over his daughter and son's protests. "No ship could have gotten through that blizzard, whatever new instruments they've got. Nor would they have reason—not with winter come early. The Mining Wield's boats will have already left Sea Throat."

"With the Lumi they've captured," said Mila darkly.

"Enough of such things. You'll go with us to Last Lake for the winter," said Tana, smoothing Yrund's hair. "We can discuss how to get you back home in the spring. Your family must be sick with worry…"

Home. Yrund had spent so long dreaming of the Sky Country it no longer seemed real. She tried not to think about Brandul and his men, hoping it was true his ship had turned around.

"The Asterians are all cowards," complained Jon-Luq. "Sending potchy pirates to do their dirty work for them. Let's see them come without their memluks to take our silver." He punched his fist into his palm with a loud smack.

"That will never happen," said Mila disparagingly. "Asterians can't stand to be cold."

"Except Ansyn," said Anouk defensively.

Timo downed a bowl of alat and pulled his mittens back on.

"Speaking of Trader Ansyn, it will take a smuggler to pack every-thing in time, so hurry up with your breakfast. There's much to do and not enough time to do it." He departed with the dog, letting in another cold blast of air.

Smuggler, said Orelia, tittering.

"You haven't seen my bag, have you? It was brown, about this big." Yrund tried to sound casual.

"Here," said Mila, pulling the rucksack from behind Yrund's head. "Can I get something out for you?" She undid the tie that held the pack shut.

"No!" said Yrund, taking the bag with a jerk that made her ribs hurt. "I mean…no, thank you."

Mila's golden eyes lingered on the rucksack. "What have you got in there?"

"Just some things."

"Like what?"

"A telescope," said Yrund, pulling the brass instrument out of the top. "And a book." There was a scar across the cover that she didn't remember. She laid all of Humphrey's treasures out across the bed for Mila to see. The pack looked empty now, with a hole near the same side the arrow had gone in—the book must have slowed its path. Thank the Sky, Humphrey couldn't help picking up human things. Yrund put the pack with only the stone left inside it beneath the blanket, praying Orelia would stay quiet. Somewhere in her mind, she had the odd sense it was she who was in the dark rucksack, smothered and bored.

"Wows!" said Mila, picking up the telescope and examining it. The young Hayas stampeded over from putting on their boots to see what she held. "Careful!" Mila cried, holding it above her head.

"They can look, too," said Yrund. "It's all right." The children handled the items one by one, passing them around to each other.

"Where'd you get all this? Did you steal it?" asked Jon-Luq, impressed.

"Jon-Luq!" scolded Tana.

"A friend gave it to me," said Yrund.

"What friend?" asked Anouk.

"Let the child be," said Tana, wading in. "She needs her rest."

Indeed, the pain in Yrund's feet was becoming impossible to ignore. Beside them, the arrow wound felt like a mere scratch.

"Hey, can I borrow this scope?" asked Mila.

"All right," said Yrund, who could hardly argue after they had clothed and fed her and tended to her wounds.

"Great," said Mila. "I'll bring it back."

As the younger children took their buns and left to help Timo, two new heads popped through the door. "Our brother Hinri," introduced Mila as she put on her coat. He was a solid-looking man with a shy smile and sandy beard like his father.

"And his wife, Katrin." The young woman was taller than her husband with startling blue eyes set off by her fair skin and black braid.

"Good Way," they said in Lumi.

"Good Way," Yrund said back, wondering how she would ever keep anyone straight.

"When you all are ready, we'll start fitting skis," said Hinri, accepting a bowl of alat from Tana. "We should leave soon. This snow could still melt again, especially if we're going through the lower lakes."

"But that's longer," said Mila.

Her older brother tilted his head at their guest. "But flatter."

"Oh, right, she might not be able to walk," Mila said bluntly, earning a glower from Tana.

"I'll be able to walk," said Yrund. "Won't I?"

Tana paused just a moment too long before speaking. "I added some bee balm to your alat. It will make your pain much worse, but it will keep the blood moving."

"I have a *numbli* if it would help," said Katrin.

"What?" said Tana. "You have an anodyne? I thought they were all taken in the last raid."

"I found one tied to a harness the other day, probably left over from the spring birthing. It's been so busy getting the herd gathered, I had forgotten all about it."

She held out a small green rock on a chain.

Yrund looked at it blankly.

"It's just a mallowkite *numbli*. For your feet," she gestured. "It will lessen your pain."

"I don't think I should..." Even after all the stones she'd handled in the mine, and all this time with Orelia, still she had never actually worn a gem.

"I insist," said Katrin, her black-ringed blue eyes boring into Yrund like a rabbit in the sights of an eagle. "Really," said Katrin, more gently. "You can give it back when you're better."

Mila agreed. "Take it, Yrund. Don't be an idiot."

With mixed feelings, Yrund let Katrin fasten the dark green gem around her neck. It was undeniably beautiful, rippled like wood grain.

Thbbt, said Orelia in Yrund's head, annoyed at the interloper. *Dumbly numbly.*

Don't be childish, Yrund thought back, still marveling she could hold a conversation with the gem without anyone else hearing. *Look how small it is compared to you.*

When the others had gone, Yrund lay back to rest, her feet so painful it was hard to know where to put them. She hoped Timo was right about the airships. If Brandul returned now, she would not be able to run away. He could kill her and likely the Hayas, too. The mine boss's face came back to her, sharp and furious. *The rat has the allstone!* Yrund could not make sense of it. Gem Beard had said Brandul's finder agyt was gemcrack. He'd said allstones weren't real.

What, what? asked the stone, sensing Yrund's worry.

That man that shot at us thinks you're an allstone.

Allystone! crowed the stone before asking: *What's an allystone?*

I don't know, but it must be valuable. Or Brandul would not have intended to give one to Niloofar Damantine.

What's valuable?

Something rare. Something Brandul would kill for.

SLOWLY, the burning in Yrund's feet and side began to lessen. She shifted restlessly in her bed, finally able to lift her arms without wincing.

"How are you doing over there?" asked Tana Haya, who was bustling back and forth around the house, kneading dough, and rearranging the contents of the family's yellow trunks.

"Better," said Yrund, for it was true. "Isn't there something I can do to help?" She felt useless lying there in bed while everyone else worked. And guilty. She'd never used a gem before. Not like this. It was cheating, and yet, there was no denying the mallowkite was effective.

Hmmph, said Orelia as if she were the only stone that was allowed to exist.

"Just because the mallowkite improves the pain does not mean you are healed—it is still an anodyne, not a halestone," cautioned Tana. "If you really want to help, you can eat—you will never survive a Lumi winter without building back some flesh." She pulled another batch of buns from the coals and brought one to Yrund drenched in cream and red syrup.

"Syrup!" Anouk dropped the logs she was carrying in a pile by the stove. "I wish I had frostbite." She released a sigh so big that the ribbons on her cap blew straight up in the air.

"What a silly thing to say," said Tana. "Then who would chop the wood? Now, sweep up your mess."

Anouk looked at Yrund as if the chores were her fault, then

stomped back out. It seemed not everyone was glad she was there.

IT WASN'T long before Yrund's bladder was bursting. She held it as long as she could, but there are some things willpower alone cannot fix, especially after three bowls of alat.

Tana called Mila to carry Yrund to the outhouse, forbidding Yrund from putting any weight on her feet. Mila, inexplicably, changed into a full fur suit complete with hood and boot covers before they went out.

"You'd better not be thinking you can sneak off to go hunting," warned Tana. "Not with all the packing to do."

Mila looked wounded. "I'm just trying it on—I haven't worn it since last winter." She hitched Yrund up onto her strong back.

"You're lucky she's letting you out at all," said Mila, snorting when Yrund tried to apologize. "When Jon-Luq got frostbite on the fall drive two years ago, she made him go in a bucket for a week. Now, he's got a carnelian, lucky dog."

"What's a carnelian do?" asked Yrund, trying not to inhale the white fur on Mila's suit.

"Warms you up," said Mila, giving Yrund a look back over her shoulder. "How come you don't know anything about gems?"

"My family is gem shy."

"Really? Wows. That must be hard—no sweepstones, no digestgems?" Mila was quiet a moment, considering the implications. "Is that why you didn't want the *numbli*? Trolls...do you want me to tell Ama and Katrin? I'm not sure they'd understand you turning down an anodyne, especially with your feet as bad as they are..."

"No, it's all right," said Yrund, not wanting to offend the Hayas so soon. "It's not like I've never touched one, working in a gem mine all these months."

"Well, you don't have to worry—we had almost all ours taken, all the good ones anyway, so you can't get in too much trouble around here."

Outside, the tall, bushy trees wore snow sleeves and snow hats—those that they could see, that was. The rest of the valley was hidden behind low puffy clouds, their edges like wispy breath. The Hayas' wasn't the only home. There was a scatter of round houses between the pines, each with the same thick walls, but only one other with a chimney smoking. Behind the houses was a three-sided shed from which emanated the sounds of sanding and sawing. There was also a cluster of small smoke huts and what looked like a well, everything topped with a matching snow cap. Mila paused at the corral on the way back from the outhouse so Yrund could see the family's herd of ivory snowdeer. The deer were enormous, bigger even than the horses of the Sky Country, with majestic antlers that clacked against one another in a pleasing percussion as the herd circled restlessly in a fog of their own breath.

Wows, said Orelia, imitating Mila.

"They're so beautiful," said Yrund, letting a snowdeer nuzzle her hand.

"They are, aren't they?" said Mila with pride.

The deer had large dark eyes and twitching ears, which followed every movement they made, flanks poised to run even as they bumped Mila for treats.

Yrund absorbed it all with wonder—she could hardly believe there were still humans living normal lives like this away from the wields and the mines.

Sikka nipped at Jon-Luq's heels as he skied past, trying out a new set of poles. He turned to smile at them, nearly running into a small tree. To her surprise, Yrund waved back at the boy, her cheeks stretching into a wide, stupid smile. She jerked her hand down.

Jon-Luq is nice, said Orelia.

Is that you making me act like an idiot? demanded Yrund. *I'm not your puppet! You can't just make me wave at a boy. If you do that again I'll...I'll drop you down the toilet.*

Thbbt! said the stone.

Thbbt! yourself, retorted Yrund, scowling at the gem just as they passed Anouk by the woodpile. Thinking the look was meant for her, the girl recoiled and stuck out her tongue.

"Careful or your face will freeze like that," said Mila, earning both herself and Yrund a snowball in the back.

Back inside, Yrund was sent back to bed, where she watched Tana knead batch after batch of buns and bread for their upcoming trip, all the while tending to a boiling pot of soup started from a cauldron full of snow and strips of dried meat. The Lumi woman added more ingredients as the day went on—onions and parsnips and handfuls of dried herbs—the rich scents mixing with the glorious smell of baking bread.

When they grew too cold to stay out with the others, Little Tir and Magrit returned, helping each other up the house's stone steps. After a hot bowl of cream, they came to sit by Yrund's bed, as if her mere presence was sufficient entertainment.

Tana retrieved a book from one of the yellow trunks. "Maybe you can read to them while I go try on my skis? The book is in Trade Tongue. You can read, can't you?"

Yrund nodded, caressing the book's leather cover embossed with silver letters: *The Moon Thief.*

The twins listened, eyes wide, as Yrund read them the tale of the Night stealing a moon and Irsil riding a wolf to bring it home. Orelia was as entranced by the stories as the children. *More,* she said. By the third tale, Yrund's throat was growing hoarse. Tana rushed in to stir the pot, then went right back out to chop more wood as Anouk was gone trying on her skis and Mila, it seemed, had disappeared.

"Tell us another story," said Little Tir, hanging on the edge of the bed. His sister, after much yawning, had fallen asleep on the floor, scrunched up like a bug.

"What kind of story?" asked Yrund, who was also growing bored. She had only been in bed half a day and already she felt trapped.

"The one about the yowi."

"What yowi?" Did the Lumi know of the woodwins?

"He lives in the woods and eats children," whispered Tir in delighted fear.

"Have you ever seen him?" she asked warily.

"Mila has, but Ama says they don't exist."

"And what did Mila say this yowi looked like?"

"He's hairy with red eyes and uses bones as toothpicks."

"Oh my," said Yrund, relaxing. "Where did you say he lives again?"

And so Tir wound up telling Yrund a story instead of the other way around.

When Tana finally returned, he had talked himself to sleep, and Yrund was silently reading the book of moonstales to an enthralled Orelia. Her mind wandered as she read, still trying to make sense of how far the Hayas had said it was from their home to the Aeries.

Slowly, the Hayas trickled back in for their evening meal, flushed with cold and smelling of wood shavings, all except Mila.

"Where's that girl gone?" asked Tana, serving up bowls of soup and buns filled with soft cheese.

"I sent her to test her new skis, and she never came back," said Timo, blowing on his fingers after trying to pluck a piece of savory meat from the pot.

"I saw her take her bow," tattled Anouk.

Mila didn't return until the suns had almost set, wearing her white fur suit and carrying the bodies of two limp hares by their feet.

Tana wagged her finger at Mila, voice tense. "Don't think a

couple rabbits excuse you sneaking off, especially if there are wield ships about."

"But, that's why I went," Mila defended herself. "I took Yrund's scope up the ridge to look around."

"And?" asked Timo, looking up from the harness he was repairing. Yrund held her breath.

"Nothing," said Mila, tossing Yrund's scope back to her.

After the young woman had eaten her late dinner, she pulled a basket of trimmed feathers and a quiver of arrow blanks from the rafters, coming to sit beside Yrund.

"Can I help you?" asked Yrund.

"You can make arrows?"

"My grandmother taught me."

Mila passed over the basket, nodding as Yrund selected three fletchings the same length. They worked together, wrapping the feathers around the notched blanks with thin strips of sinew.

"Oh, I almost forgot," said Mila, pulling a golden-black arrowhead from her coat pocket. "I filed it so you could wear it." As she spoke, she tied the point up with sinew and a thin scrap of hide so it formed a necklace.

"Is that—"

"Yaha, the one Ama pulled out of you. Obsydaline. Definitely Asterian."

"That's sick, Mila," said Anouk. "Why would she want to wear something that almost killed her?"

"Because it didn't!" said Mila as if this were obvious. She reached over to tie the arrowhead around Yrund's neck, where it dangled on top of the anodyne.

Yrund ran her fingertip across the arrowhead's smoothed edges. If it hadn't been for Humphrey and his book...

"Thank you," she finally told Mila. It would not hurt to have a reminder Brandul and Veng were still out there.

Orelia huffed jealously at the new ornament until Jon-Luq spoke.

"I think it's wolvy," said the boy.

Anouk rolled her eyes. "Have you ever smelled a wolverine?"

"Who cares what they smell like? Even white bears don't bother them."

Wolvy, said Orelia, and Yrund had the distinct impression the gem had tried on the obsydaline's golden-black color inside the bag.

"I can't remember. Are you supposed to mix obsydaline with mallowkite?" asked Timo.

Everyone looked to Tana for an answer.

"As far as I know, they're not contragems," she said. "Agnetha says obsydaline isn't very active, whatever those sellers in Windmarket might claim."

See? said Yrund. *It doesn't do anything anyway.*

The Hayas discussed the routes they would soon take and who would be assigned what duties, switching rapidly between Trade Tongue and Lumi. They considered what would happen if a sled broke or wolves attacked, adding new to-dos to their packing list. Yrund had grown up traveling. The familiarity of the preparations was both comforting and painful, reminding her of her journeys with her own family. Where were they now? she wondered. Were they even alive? Were they trying to get back?

Before bed, Tana unwrapped Yrund's feet. They were a blotchy red and white and covered in watery blisters.

"You must keep them moving," said Tana with concern. "Wiggle, wiggle, wiggle."

"I promise," said Yrund. If she couldn't walk, she couldn't go home.

<h1 style="text-align:center">CHAPTER FIFTEEN</h1>

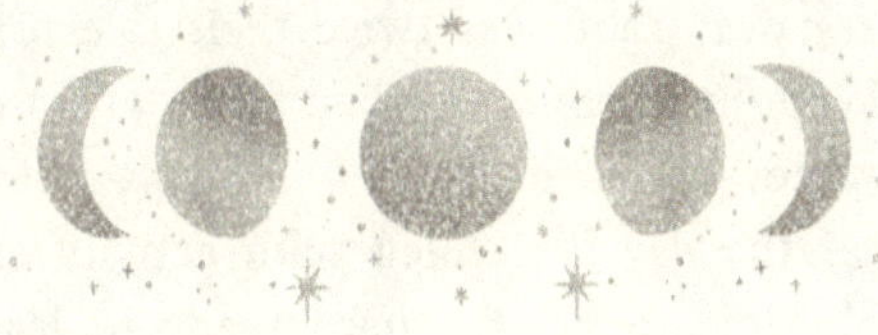

Tana checked Yrund's feet again before breakfast the next day, unwinding the old bandages to see what progress she was making. Underneath, Yrund's toes peeled back from the tip as if they'd been boiled.

"Gross," said Jon-Luq, coming over to look. "That's what my fingers looked like before the ends started coming off." He splayed his hand in her face so that Yrund saw that he was missing the tips of the last three fingers. How had she not noticed that before?

Yrund's eyes widened, and his mother pushed him away. "Enough, Jon-Luq! Go help your father."

But Jon-Luq was staring at the cold, metallic snakes wrapped around Yrund's ankles. Before they could stop him, he reached out and pulled on one, testing its strength. He and Yrund both jumped at the jolt that went through them.

"Jon-Luq!"

"I'm okay," he said, hair standing on end.

"Out!" hissed his mother. "I pray to Irsil that Trader Ansyn will know how to get these off."

"I don't think we should tell anybody about them," said Yrund.

165

"They mark me as a rabu." And this Ansyn, whoever he was, might have been the Hayas' friend, but he was still an Asterian.

"You're not a rabu. You're a girl," said Tana as if that were final, but Yrund had her doubts. Until those anklets were off, she belonged to the Mining Wield, and she wasn't keen to advertise that to a man who made his living smuggling. The reward for returning a runaway rabu was twice their sale price. Another deterrent to keep the prisoners in their place, and a sure temptation for any money-obsessed trader.

The rest of the day was filled with activity as the Hayas worked double-time to get the herd ready to leave for their winter home. Yrund watched the packing as she trimmed feathers for fletchings, one of the few tasks Tana would let her do. Back home, she would have helped her parents with rolling up their felt and frame house, loading the carts, and gathering in all the animals. But when Tana caught Yrund trying to get out of bed, she took away the mallowkite necklace. "The anodyne is for relief, not recklessness. I think a little time without it will be a good reminder."

It was only a few moments for the burning in Yrund's feet to return, and far worse than she'd remembered, a searing pain that took away her breath. Not to be outdone, her arrow wounds began to ache in a symphony of suffering. Almost immediately Yrund wished the stone back, impressed with its powers. Mallowkites, she hated to admit, were as useful as they were beautiful.

Ugly numbli—*I could do that*, said Orelia, whose language skills were fast improving here in the Hayas' house, where there was rarely a moment without conversation. The family mostly remembered to talk in Trade Tongue around Yrund, but she didn't mind when they slipped into Lumi. She couldn't understand all of what they said, but the similarities with the language of the herders that lived in the east of the Sky Country were enough for her to fill in most of the blanks. Yrund's family spoke at least a little of the language of every people they traded with. Her father insisted it improved negotiations. So Yrund was learning Lumi as fast as she could, a welcome diversion from the worry in her head and the constant chattering.

Quiet, Orelia!

Tana was saying something, but Yrund could hardly hear her over Orelia's sudden diatribe against the anodyne. *Stinky, turdy lump of goose poo…*, the stone was saying.

It doesn't stink. Don't be so jealous. Just because it can do something you can't—

Yrund's scalp went numb first, then her face and jaw, and next her spine down through the entire length of her body until she couldn't feel a thing. Not her lips or her tongue. Or her eyelids. She tried to sit up and fell over. Where her hand should have been to prop her up, there was nothing.

"Grawwr!" she drooled, unable to speak. What was happening?

I told you so! sang Orelia, who was learning a lot from the Haya children.

You're doing this? said Yrund inside her head. *Make it stop. Now!*

Sensation rolled back in, hot and prickling. Relieved, Yrund tried to lift her hand to wipe her mouth and smacked herself in the eye instead, still ungainly.

Orelia chuckled.

"Troll's balls, Yrund. What did you do that for?" asked Mila, who had come inside just in time to see Yrund hit herself in the face.

"Nuffing," she said, wiping away the drool with her sleeve. *Orelia!*

Tana came over to take a look at her. "I knew that mallowkite was too big for you. It was meant for a snowdeer, not a slip of a girl. You'll have to take it in smaller doses. Still, I've never seen it have that strong of a reaction. You haven't got a moonsstone hidden somewhere, have you?"

"No," said Yrund, finally able to move.

"Wouldn't do to mix those."

"You know, we should probably do something about her hair," said Mila, analyzing Yrund's head.

"That's not nice," said Tana. "It just needs a bit of a brush, is all."

"Naha, I mean, she doesn't look like a Lumi."

"It might not be such a bad idea to blend in a little more," Tana said, appraising Yrund, who felt suddenly self-conscious.

That night, Tana made a smelly concoction of snowdeer urine and wood ash, which she stirred into a paste and smeared onto Yrund's head. "Mila is right. Many Lumi have dark hair or eyes or even darker skin, but rarely all three, and your hair is the only one we can alter."

"Unless we had a vagary," said Anouk.

"A vagary?" Yrund repeated. Those seefires had been highly prized in the mine, though she hadn't ever learned what for.

"Turns your eyes the color of water lilacs," said Anouk, as if everyone knew that. "Like the queen's."

Ooh, said Orelia, intrigued.

Tana turned on her daughter, eyes full of fire. "There is no queen in our land. We answer to no one. If the wields want to put a spoiled few on golden thrones, that is their folly, but within our borders, every man, woman, and child is equal. Do you hear me?"

"Yaha, Ama," said Anouk, contritely. "I'm only repeating what the glossies call her."

"Not in our house, or I'll have Ansyn stop bringing them. You don't need fashion advice from a bunch of snotty city folk that have never swung an axe or lassoed a snowdeer."

She turned back to Yrund's hair. "That's coming along nicely."

Yrund wrinkled her nose at the fumes. Snowdeer urine stank. It was a relief when Tana finally brought a basin to wash the mixture out. She left a fresh bowl of hot water and some clean rags for Yrund to bathe herself with, along with a chunk of lard soap scented with pine. Then she pulled the curtain around her bed shut.

When Yrund was almost done washing, a hand poked through the curtain with a small stack of clean clothes. "Ama says to give you these," said Anouk. "They're things I've outgrown." Though she was a year younger than Yrund, Anouk was already taller. The clothes had been darned many times, but they were soft and well made. Yrund wriggled into a long-sleeved chemise and drawers, trying not to bump her feet. Over the undergarments went a pair of blue woolen pants and a thick woolen shirt embroidered along the arms and, finally, a padded suede coat stuffed with down.

Anouk put her head in to see how Yrund was coming along. "The clothes are okay, I guess, but your head looks like a pinepig." Tir and Magrit poked their heads in to see and retreated in giggles, pudgy hands covering their mouths.

Yrund tried to run her fingers through her damp hair before remembering she had Humphrey's comb.

"That's pretty," said Anouk admiringly when she dug it out of the rucksack and began working it through her bangs. "You want me to do the back?"

"Sure, thanks," said Yrund, surprised. Mila had been friendly from the first, but Anouk still seemed undecided about the new guest.

Anouk crawled onto the bed next to her, lowering her voice so her mother couldn't hear. "In Asteria, short hair is very fashionable right now. Even the qu—I mean, Niloofar Damantine's mother has cut hers in the new style. It's shorter than yours with little curls around the ears." Anouk talked on about hair and clothes, and Yrund pretended to listen, but all she could think about was sitting outside her family's tent back home, watching the clouds while her mother combed out her long hair. That was before Yrund had come home with a head full of briars from chasing down a goat. Her mother had both laughed and cried when she cut it. She could remember her mother collecting the locks in her pockets. She had been planning on weaving them into a new rug pattern to be called "Girl in the Briars".

A tear trickled down Yrund's face, and she rubbed it angrily away.

"What did I do?" asked Anouk.

Tana came and took the comb gently from her daughter. "Yrund has a lot of healing still to do. Let her rest now." She helped Yrund lie down, pulling the blankets up to her chin. "There is no shame in tears," she said, brushing Yrund's wet cheek with her calloused thumb. "The strength of a woman is in her heart as much as her arms. We may bend, but we will not break." She slipped the mallowkite back over Yrund's head. "Sleep until dinner, for tomorrow we have a long journey, and you will need your strength. I wish we didn't have to move you yet, but we must get ahead of the next storm."

"I don't mind. I like to keep moving." It was the way of her people.

"Then who knows where your Way will take you?" said Tana. "To the stars and back again, as the song goes." She sang to herself as she went back to work:

> We went dancing
> To the stars
> And back again,
> Da-da-da-da-da-da...

THE HAYAS LEFT their autumn camp to winter's invasion, their painted yellow trunks packed onto sleds led by teams of belled and harnessed snowdeer. Unlike the Sky People, they could not take their house with them, leaving the cozy mud dwelling and its stove behind along with a crate of provisions for any passing travelers. This seemed unusually generous to Yrund until Mila explained all the Lumi left their seasonal huts this way for each other—a necessity in a land of surprise storms.

Before their departure, Tana had outfitted Yrund with an oversized pair of socks, fur-lined loose boots with tipped-up toes, and a second and third pair of thick woolen pants. Over Anouk's old inner coat, she wrapped a hip-length felt jacket, and over that a long hide-and-fur coat that closed up to Yrund's mouth. They slipped a wide ring of dark fur over her head and around her neck, showing Yrund how to pull the cowl up to protect her face from the wind. Then they strapped a belt around her waist, attaching a carved mug and two knives—one straight and the other curved. Yrund pulled the blades from their worn sheaths, examining them like treasures. The cold metal was dinged but sharp, fashioned not for fighting, like Veng's blades, but for the daily tasks of cutting ropes, stripping branches and eating dinner. Lastly, Mila had lined Yrund up with the others, painting dots of black unguent beneath all their eyes to combat the glare off the snow.

"You look like one of us now," she said.

"A bit scrawny for a Haya, though," said Anouk.

Mila punched her. "You're a bit scrawny," she said.

The sisters were still taunting each other hours later as Yrund, bundled on a sled with the twins, watched the scenery slide by. The world was an endless white sheet, sky and land indistinguishable at the horizons. Katrin stood behind them on the sled's runners, steering, while the twins alternately napped and fought. Yrund scanned the distance with her scope, listening to the tinkle of the lead deers' bells and the yipping of the dog driving back wanderers from the herd.

The Lumi stopped frequently, too frequently for Yrund, who felt exposed traveling along in the open and at such a slow pace.

"Does it always take this long to get anywhere?" she asked as the Hayas stopped yet again to make alat and warm themselves over a small fire.

"Yaha, always, when we're with the herd," said Mila. "They need time to dig for moss. It's more efficient in the end for us too, though. It's hard to do anything once your blood is cold. By going slower, we actually get there faster." The breaks also allowed the family to trade places between sleds and skis, alternately resting and getting warm. Tana wrapped up rocks from each fire placing them beneath Yrund's boots, before once again checking over the harnessed snowdeer for any injuries to their cloven hooves or from their harnesses.

During the long nights, the Hayas slept in windproof hide tents, taking turns watching for wolves among the herd, setting off again at the silvery promise of first dawn.

To Yrund's eyes, the terrain was monotonous with few landmarks, but to her companions, the land was full of insight. Mila showed her how to read the long ripples in the snow, formed by the prevailing wind like waves in a lake. They pointed from north to south as the wind blew, giving the Lumi a constant bearing even when storms hid suns and stars.

Despite the open air, Yrund felt trapped in the slow sled, jealous of the others on their skis, especially Mila. The tall young woman went swooping after straying snowdeer as easily as a hawk flying, occasionally tossing out her lasso to rein one in. She wore a bow and quiver across her back, which, like Timo, she rarely took off. For wolves, Mila assured Yrund, mistaking her stare for worry. But it was envy Yrund felt. Her fingers itched to hold the polished weapon, though she doubted she would be able draw it back more than a few inches—the bows had been custom-made for someone tall with long arms. Back home, bows were much smaller and curved, so they could be used while riding horseback, perfect for hunting fat marmots or scaring off yotes. The others too had bows, which they rarely carried when they weren't on watch, keeping them stored on top of the sleds.

Yrund followed the snakelike tracks the skis and sleds left behind them, her scope an extension of her arm. Once, she thought she saw a blurry spot loping between the white trees. She waved her arms, imagining the blur waved back.

"Everything okay up there?" called Katrin from the runners. "Do you need a break?"

"Just stretching," said Yrund. She lifted the telescope again, but the blur was gone.

Is it Humphrey? asked Orelia.

I can't tell. The shifting snow played so many tricks on Yrund's eyes, she sometimes thought she saw an entire herd in the distance.

"Snow mirages," explained Timo when she mentioned it. "Don't ever follow them. Or you'll never come back. That's how the *spookli* lure their victims away."

"*Spookli?* What are they?" It sounded like one of Gem Beard's superstitions.

"The ghosts of lost travelers."

The days went by with the scenery blending together in freezing white sameness for Yrund, whose only distraction apart from talking to Orelia, who was equally bored, was practicing her Lumi with the twins and Katrin. Yrund liked Mila's sister-in-law, who did not mind the long silences when Yrund's thoughts turned inward, content with her own reflections.

Finally, on the ninth day, Tana said Yrund could try a few steps around camp. Her feet hardly hurt, but her muscles had grown weak without walking and the ground beneath the snow was full of hidden rocks and ice. Stubbornly, Yrund used a pair of ski poles to help herself along, but even such a simple errand as going for a pee behind a large pine ended in disaster.

"You can't get too close to the trees. Everyone knows that," said Anouk, grumbling as she and Mila pulled Yrund out of the well of snow hidden beneath the branches like a trap.

"I'm sure if Yrund took us to the Sky Country, we'd have just as much to learn from her," said Mila when she was done laughing.

After that, Tana gave Yrund a pair of snowshoes. "This doesn't mean you are allowed to wear yourself out. Those feet are still healing," she cautioned. But Yrund soon learned to position herself on the other side of the sleds away from the Hayas' nagging mother. For her feet felt fine, and the snowshoes were a marvel. Yrund could climb right up a snowbank without falling through. That was, until Tana took the snowshoes away. "You're as stubborn as a Haya," she complained.

As consolation, Mila let Yrund try her lasso, though aiming the stiff, looped rope was surprisingly difficult.

"Wows, you're terrible. Don't you use ropes with your herds back home?" asked Anouk, who could catch Little Tir with just one throw.

"Not like this," said Yrund. "Only if they go off a cliff or into the river. The Kyshkri have something sort of similar they use for catching wild horses, but it's attached to a long pole." She tried again, missing an unimpressed Sikka by several feet.

"Maybe you can help with making the alat," suggested Tana, sensing Yrund needed a job. "Jon-Luq can show you," she said, waving the boy over.

A-la-la-la-la-lat, sang Orelia in Yrund's head.

"Warm the cream and snow first," instructed Jon-Luq as he put two round kettles over the fire. Then she watched him portion out brilliant green powder from a painted tin. "This one's for mornings—one scoop per cup. Don't let the cream boil if you can help it, but the water has to, yaha?" He opened a second tin, this one a deep, smoky purple.

Ooh, said Orelia, and Yrund felt a flash of purple cross her eyes. She shook her head, trying to listen.

"This one's for evenings, so you just use a quarter amount now. As the day goes on, you do it the other way around—less green and more purple."

"Why is that?" asked Yrund.

"Too much green will keep you from sleeping. It's the purple that relaxes you."

"What's it made from?" The green tin didn't look or smell like tea, more like fruit rinds, while the purple mixture smelled of woods and hot spices.

"No one knows," said Mila, skidding to a halt by the fire. "Probably bad little brothers," she added, provoking a snowy kick from Little Tir.

"I think it's made out of gemstones," said Anouk.

"I swallowed a gem once," said Yrund. "Made me sick."

"See?" said Mila to her sister. "Even the Asterians aren't that stupid, stupid."

"What does Yrund know about gems?" asked Anouk. "She's gem shy."

"I knew I shouldn't have told you that—" Mila started to say, but Yrund spoke over her.

"I know enough! I know people like me wouldn't be sent to the mines if the rest of the planet didn't rely on gems to do everything for them."

"You don't seem to mind relying on our mallowkite."

The words hit Yrund like a slap, guilt and shame boiling up in a tempest.

"I do mind, actually, but…"

"But what?"

"Shut up, Anouk," said Mila, getting between them. "You know why she's wearing it. You saw her feet."

"Well, she could act a little more grateful instead of lecturing us while she's eating our food and wearing our stones…"

Yrund felt her ears go hot. She pulled the mallowkite off and, without a word, threw it at Anouk's feet.

"For Irsil's sake!" said Mila, retrieving the necklace. "Put the *numbli* back on, Yrund."

"No, Anouk's right," said Yrund, trying to ignore the burning in her feet. "This isn't how my family raised me—relying on gems for everything. It's not the Way."

"It's better than being a *vandradolt*."

Yrund ignored what she figured was an insult. "Don't you see? This is how the wields have so much power over us!"

"The wields have so much power because they're thieving cheats," said Mila, contradicting her. "They don't have to send rabu to the mines. They do it to scare us into submission. You could get rid of every gem on the planet, and we'd all still have the wields scheming to charge us for something. They'd tax the snow if they could."

"Yaha," said Jon-Luq. "Roads and Ways, probably."

"What's going on over there?" called Tana. "Are you girls fighting again? Why hasn't that alat been made yet? Yrund? Jon-Luq?"

"On our way," Mila called back, holding the marbled green stone out to Yrund. "Look at you—you can barely even stand. Is now really the moment to start a revolution? Can't you wait until we get to Last Lake, at least?"

Yrund wavered, the pain in her toes growing.

"Girls!" Tana's voice was thick with annoyance. "Am I going to have to collect the herd myself?"

"Come on, tell her, Anouk. Unless you want to explain to Ama how all this got started."

Anouk pushed her braid out of her face, huffing. "I didn't mean for her to take it off!"

"What did you think would happen—calling her out for being gem shy?" asked Jon-Luq.

"All right! Fine! Put it back on, Yrund. Mila's right. Like she always is—" With that she skied off, leaving Mila to help a reluctant Yrund put the necklace back on.

"Gems aren't the enemy, you know. The wields are," Mila reminded Yrund before she too skied away.

With a combination of simmering anger and shame, Yrund

turned back to the alat lesson. If only she didn't need the bogging anodyne. Her dependence on it stung as much as her feet.

I can do anything that dumb mallowkite does, said Orelia.

You can't, said Yrund, taking out her resentment on the gem. *Last time you tried, I couldn't move.*

But...

Shhh! said Yrund, seeing Jon-Luq was waiting for her.

"You okay?" he asked.

"Yaha. Anouk just hit a sore spot."

"That's her special talent."

"Hey, what's a *vandradolt*?" asked Yrund.

"*Vandradolt*? It's a person that doesn't know better than to get lost in the woods."

Yrund imagined it wouldn't be hard to get lost in Lumi Land, with its thick forests. Not like the Sky Country, where she could just climb up a little higher to see where she was.

"But don't worry. You're not a *vandradolt*."

"How can you be so sure?" asked Yrund. She was a thousand miles from home, after all.

"You found us, didn't you?" Jon-Luq smiled, dimples showing.

Yrund felt her own mouth pull up at the ends, forced into a smile. "I like your face holes," she heard herself say.

"My what?" said a startled Jon-Luq.

Argh! Orelia!! Yrund yelled silently. *Those are dimples, not "face holes". And how dare you speak for me?*

Why don't you have dimples? asked the stone, unperturbed.

You have to be born with them. Now get out of my head! Yrund tried to block the stone out, but it was like blocking sunlight from a sieve.

"You sure you're all right?" asked Jon-Luq.

"I'm fine, go on with the lesson," said Yrund, ignoring Orelia's giggles. Vengeful little pain in the—

"So like I was saying, you measure out the alat..." Jon-Luq showed Yrund. "Then you add half a bowl of cream for the little

ones, and whisk, whisk, whisk until it foams—that bit's important. You might even say there's an art to it," said Jon-Luq, tilting
the pan for Yrund to admire the rainbow of bubbles that formed
across the top before handing her the whisk. "You try it."

"An art to it?" said Hinri, skiing over to fill his mug. "I thought
you hated making alat."

Jon-Luq flushed at his older brother's words. "I never said I
hated it. I just prefer not to do something unless I have the time
to do it right."

"Oh, is that it?" said Hinri. "I'd always wondered."

Yrund watched Anouk moving around out in the distance
with the herd. She didn't mind when the family squabbled. Not
with each other. But she was ashamed she'd fought with Anouk.
And ashamed of what the girl thought of her—a burden. And a
fraud.

CHAPTER SIXTEEN

Yrund measured and frothed the alat by herself that night. She was nervous at first, afraid she would forget a step or spill something, but gradually a calm came over her. There was an orderly precision to the work that was ritual-like, the scent of the powders stimulating to her senses.

Timo tasted the first cup. "Mmmm," he said, wiggling his eyebrows. "That might be the finest mug of alat I've ever had!"

Yrund knew he was teasing her, but Tana pronounced Yrund the family's official new alat maker. "That will keep you away from the snowshoes at least, and I could use the extra hand while I see to the deer."

For her part, Yrund was glad to have a job, even if it was just making the alat as they traveled, and she had soon learned how each of the family took theirs. After a few days of drinking her own mug with cream and sugar like the other children, she decided to try it straight like Mila and her father. Without the snowdeer milk, the alat was spicy, almost bitter, with a heart-racing kick.

Oooofoo! said Orelia.

"Good, huh?" said Mila, looking on one morning. "Really makes you feel alive."

It did. Yrund felt like she could walk a hundred miles. She refilled Anouk's mug with a new spirit of forgiveness, accepting the lack of thanks without complaint.

"Anouk talking to you yet?" asked Mila.

"Barely," admitted Yrund.

"Lucky," said Mila, helping her pack up the kitchen for their next leg. "Wish she'd stop talking to me."

"You don't really," said Yrund, looking up at the same gray sky that had been hanging over them for days. "I'd give anything to argue with my sisters again."

"Trolls, I forgot. Sorry," said Mila, slapping her forehead with her glove. "She's just such a twit sometimes."

"She had a point, though. About the mallowkite. Who am I if I'm not gem shy?"

"Wows, you're pretty philosophical for this early."

"It's the alat, I think." Yrund felt like her mind was a drawer that had been opened to the fresh air.

"It does that sometimes," said Mila, saving the coals from the fire inside a pot for the next break. "But, honestly, it's just a mallowkite." *Crapkite,* said Orelia. "It's not like it's something frivolous, like a blushfire or a…a… I don't know—a giggle beryl. I mean, is it even the gems that are the problem or is it what people do with them?"

"I don't know." For Yrund didn't. Not anymore. She missed the certainty of her youth, when the Way had been clear. "And what about the mines? Humph—I mean a friend, said that the Asterians rerouted an entire river. Even if you could make an argument for gems, what good are they if there's no water for our herds? Or if they cost us our family and our neighbors?"

"Are those really the only choices?"

"They are with the locusts in charge."

"The who?"

"The Asterians."

Mila nodded. "So what are you going to do?"

"Me?" All Yrund wanted was to go home.

"You're the one always talking about a revolution."

"Actually, you're the only one that ever used the word *rev—*"

A loud whistle interrupted them. It was Timo. Three memluks had just broken from the woods to the south.

"Get your bows close," said Hinri, lifting a gloved hand to show his father they saw. Mila had an arrow nocked before she'd even stood up.

"I said get your bow close, not shoot them," said Hinri, pushing the weapon back down. "And someone grab Sikka."

Yrund yanked her scope from her coat. The memluks wore enormous fur coats and large packs with the usual assortment of clanking weapons and tools at their belts. They were ungainly on their skis, their poles out of sync with their legs.

What, what? asked Orelia.

Bad men. Like from the mine. But not from Devil's Crown. She didn't recognize any of them. With a sudden fear, Yrund looked down at her boots, conscious of the snake anklets hidden beneath them.

"Just act like one of us," said Mila. "And hide that scope if you want to keep it."

"Looks like a scouting crew," said Timo, gliding over to join them.

"Scouting for what?" asked Mila. "They should be long gone by now."

"They ski like buffalo," said Anouk.

"You've never seen a buffalo."

"We could outrun them easy," said Jon-Luq.

Tana and Timo traded a long look that, Yrund did not miss, included her.

"We stay," said Timo, hand on his bow's handle. "They look

like they're just passing through. If we run, it will look like we're hiding something."

Tana called the twins to her side. "All of you—behave. They've no business with us, so keep your heads on. Katrin, Mila—you know what to do. Stay on the other side of the herd. The rest of you go on with your jobs." Yrund drew her large fur hood closer around her face, pretending not to watch the nearing men who were arguing in Douarr, the harsh sound cutting through the air like flying metal.

The memluks skied straight over to the Hayas' fire, ignoring the family and bickering over a hide map. One of the men was small for a Sea Hammer, though still towering over Timo and Hinri, with a sunsburnt pink nose that had been broken at least once. His orange beard was cut short, but there were gems aplenty studding the amulets he wore around his neck. The other soldiers were taller with braided blond beards, each woven around one large green gem like a third eye. Orange Beard grunted at Timo, waving him over to look at their map.

"If you're trying to go north to Windmarket, you took the wrong turn at Graupel," a perplexed Timo explained, running his finger toward the coast. "Going to take you three days to get back to the fork." He pointed to the suns and held up three fingers. The men grumbled as if they didn't believe him.

"You going take us," commanded one of the Blond Beards in broken Trade Tongue.

"Me? What about my family? And my herds?" Timo said, pointing at his responsibilities.

"Leave my father. I'll be your guide." Hinri stepped forward, as Timo's jaw tightened.

"Good. Both go," said the memluk.

"No!" said Anouk, who was holding back Sikka.

Timo motioned for Tana to calm her. "We only need to get them back to the coast. We can catch up with you in Last Lake."

Magrit began to cry, and Jon-Luq picked her up.

Unlike his sister, Little Tir stared openly at the memluks, mesmerized with their every movement. With Tana's attention distracted, he took a tentative step closer. Without warning, Orange Beard lunged toward the boy, letting out a loud growl.

Tir's eyes went as white as the snow. Then, standing his ground, he opened his mouth and let out his own growl.

"Har, har!" Orange Beard bellowed with laughter and crooked a finger for the boy to come closer.

"No, Tir!" said Tana as she tried to pull him back, but the boy wriggled from her grasp, darting forward and punching Orange Beard in the leg. Shock stiffened the man's face, and he fell back in the snow as if he'd been mortally wounded.

This was too much for his blond-haired companions, who threw Tir up onto their shoulders, bouncing him like a hero and kicking snow on their fallen comrade. Sikka broke free of Anouk's grasp, leaping onto the man's chest and licking his face. Orelia laughed along with the memluks.

They might seem fun now, but just wait, said Yrund, who knew how fast these men could turn.

"Perhaps you'd like to warm up before we travel?" Timo gestured at the fire, his words polite but strained. "Have some alat while we gather our things?"

"Alat! Yes."

Tana moved towards the pots, arms still full with a sniffling Magrit.

"I can do it," said Yrund, stepping in. It was her job now. She kept her face down as she retrieved the coals Mila had stowed and stoked the fire with fresh wood, trying to ignore the memluks pilfering through Tana's stores behind her, helping themselves to frozen snowdeer cheese and dark sausages.

Soon the men's curiosity shifted to the family's sleds. Jon-Luq's nostrils flattened, but none of the Hayas tried to stop them. Clearly, they'd been through raids before. As the snow came to a boil, Yrund started to measure out the alat. It was just past the midpoint of the short day, so that meant an equal portion from each tin. She glanced at the memluks. The Blond Beards had the Hayas' trunks open, tossing out worthless nightclothes and stockings into the snow, too stupid to understand the Hayas' wealth was all around them. Not in their trunks, but in their herd. With a second thought, Yrund remeasured—a scant portion of the green with an overflowing scoop of purple—whisking quickly to combine them.

"That's not—" Tana started to correct Yrund, then gave her a pat instead, shifting Magrit onto her back. "I'll start some meat boiling. A hungry memluk's a mean memluk."

Yrund finished whisking in an extra dollop of cream and a generous handful of sugar just as Orange Beard lumbered over for a taste. "Good," he declared, filling the mug from his belt. The other two memluks, bored with the Hayas' lack of treasures, joined him in finishing the pot, draining their mugs without thanks. When they began to poke their noses in Tana's cooking, she shooed them off.

"It's not done yet!"

The memluks appeared in no hurry to leave with a hot meal on the horizon, taking advantage of the wait to do what any Sea Hammer would—have a quick gamble. They rearranged the Hayas' yellow trunks for what looked like a round of sticks-and-sevens, no doubt less risky than keeps with the thick snow all about. Only they were one player short. Orange Beard pointed at Timo, who was tying up his pack.

"If you insist," said Timo, reluctantly accepting a hand of the carved playing sticks and sitting down. "Though we shouldn't stay too long if we mean to be going, or we'll lose all our light."

Yrund felt Tana stiffen beside her. It was one thing to have your underthings strewn about camp, but another to know your husband and son would soon be taken.

The memluks, undeterred by Timo's sound advice, each put down their stakes inside a bowl in the middle—a jewel set pin, a heavy gold spoon, and a shiny, double-ended black crystal. When it was Timo's turn, he unclasped the silver necklace from around his neck. Though the metal was still bright, the old locket was dented, the simple design nearly worn off. Orange Beard flicked it open with a big thumb. The gem compartment was empty.

The memluks spread out their hands. Not good enough. He needed to put down something else. Timo looked around at his family. Hinri offered his locket next, but it was equally worn. And empty. The memluks cursed. Hinri pantomimed a big memluk coming along and stealing the gem inside. This made Orange Beard laugh.

With a frown, Tana gave him her locket. It held a tiny white stone with a green shimmer. One of the Blond Beards yawned and dropped it in the bowl, crooking his fingers to indicate they still needed to put in more. Stifling a sigh, Hinri dug through his hide and fur coat and came up with a silver flask. "There is a little flume left."

"Hoho," said the memluks, shaking it with delight. "Floom!" Thanks to his family, Timo finally had his stake. Now, the game could begin.

After stirring some herbs and dried onions in with the meat, Tana picked up the empty snow buckets and tipped her head for Yrund to follow her through the herd, leaving Magrit by the fire with Hinri. The memluks did not pay them any attention, already absorbed in their first round of play.

Behind the cover of the snowdeer, Tana waved Katrin and Mila in.

"I have a plan," said Tana quietly as they caught their breath. "I'm not letting them take Timo again. Or Hinri," she added before Katrin could speak.

"What sort of plan?"

"The simplest one. We'll wait until they're leaving. Then—as they ski away—we shoot the memluks in the backs."

Hu-huh. Orelia laughed.

Katrin and Mila looked at Tana as if she'd grown horns.

"You mean kill them?"

"Obviously. Yrund has already taken the initiative of adjusting their alat, thank Irsil for her, so their reflexes will be slow. Mila, Anouk and Katrin, you will take the tall pair. Jon-Luq and I will take out the short one. Go now—spread the word, but don't tell Hinri. Or your father."

"Why not?"

"Because it's safer that way," she said impatiently.

"What if the wields find out?"

"Who's to tell them? Their men are lost. They could have frozen to death or been eaten by wolves. Or fallen through the ice. We'll burn the bodies, and that will be that. Just wait for my signal. If anything goes wrong, split up and head south. Yaha?"

The women looked at each other for a moment, then nodded.

As she followed Tana back to the fire with their buckets of snow, Yrund's free hand moved to the belt knife the Lumi had given her, wishing she too had a bow. She remembered what Gem Beard had told her. If you have to kill a man, do it quickly, before he knows it's coming.

The game was in full swing now, though without the snappy clack Yrund had witnessed in the mine. Perhaps it was the thick winter gloves. Timo quietly kept pace, squinting slightly before each move. Sticks-and-sevens was a game of both chance and skill, but even the best hand could be foiled by a bad partner. Finally, Orange Beard threw down a trio of sticks with a flourish. The game was over. Ignoring the protests of his beaten country-men, the gloating memluk pushed the Hayas' lockets back to Timo, pocketing the rest for himself, all except the shiny flask, which he popped open.

"Flooom!" he cheered, taking a long swig. "Yom, yom, yom." Generously, or wisely, he passed the remainder on to the Blond Beards. The flask was empty in two more swallows.

"More!" they demanded without getting up.

Hinri mimed an apology. It was all the family had. But dinner was ready if the men were hungry.

Tana served the memluks first as she would any guest before allowing her family to line up for the rest. The wield men chewed slowly, yawning between bites as if their travels were catching up with them, paying little mind to the Hayas, who ate their own dinner in silence. That was, until Katrin slipped up to the pot to fill her mug. One of the Blond Beards elbowed the other. Yrund's stomach clenched as he called out to her in Douarr. She knew what memluks could be like with women.

Katrin ignored the man, who fumbled drunkenly to get up. He called again, this time in Trade Tongue. "Come here!"

Katrin finally turned toward the fire. All three memluks recoiled with a squeal. For the Lumi woman's normally striking face had transformed, one eye drooping as if diseased and her mouth slack with a droplet of spit in the corner. Jon-Luq coughed back a chuckle, while Yrund nearly dropped her spoon. Katrin smiled, even more hideous, and the spit turned to drool. Orange Beard touched the amulet around his neck, shaking his head in pity as Blond Beard sat heavily back down.

If the memluks meant to leave anytime soon, they gave no sign, signaling for Yrund to make more alat, which she did, exactly as before. Slowly, the suns dipped behind the gray clouds, and Hinri began to sing, his voice soft in the orange light. The memluks hummed along, staring sleepily into the fire, until they were yawning so wide Yrund could see their tonsils. Leaning against one another, the Blond Beards began to snore. Orange Beard too was soon out, head lolling against his hood.

Hinri hopped up. "Ready?"

"Ready," answered Timo, waving his family to their feet. "Get the sleds cleared."

"But what have you done to them?" asked Katrin, her face still twisted.

"Cloudstone," said Hinri, unscrewing a secret compartment in the discarded flask's bottom. A blue and white stone fell out into his glove. "Should buy us at least until morning. But we've got to move them deeper into the woods. No good them finding our tracks when they wake."

Katrin's slack mouth looked dumbfounded. "You could have told me," she said, alternately whacking Hinri and trying to kiss him.

He pulled away, shuddering. "Not until you spit out that screwberyl. One of these days your face will stick like that."

Katrin grinned, plucking something out from under her tongue. Almost instantly, her face returned to its usual symmetry.

Oh, said Orelia, impressed.

"Can I see?" asked Yrund. Katrin showed her an innocent-looking stone about the size of a bean with a twist at its center before dropping it in her pocket.

"It's lucky for them you had that cloudstone," said Mila, who had materialized to help the rest of them heave one of the Blond Beards onto a sled. The memluk grunted but did not wake.

"You mean lucky for *us*," corrected Timo, flopping a heavy arm back on top of the man.

"Maybe. You don't know what Ama had planned," Mila said doubtfully.

"What's this?" asked Hinri as they rolled the other two memluks onto the sled like dead fish.

"Your mother was going to shoot them," confessed Katrin.

"What? When?" Hinri's shocked gaze shot toward his mother.

"As you were leaving," said Mila matter-of-factly.

"Don't you think you might have told us?"

"You two didn't tell us you were going to gem them!" said Tana, giving Hinri a severe pinch.

"Owwwww! We didn't know if it would work."

"Nothing more dangerous than a moose protecting its calf," acknowledged Timo, clipping the memluks' mugs back on their belts.

"Did you just call me a moose?" demanded Tana.

"Only in the best way." Timo clicked his tongue at the team of snowdeer, who dug their hooves into the snow and set off.

Katrin drove the second sled, carrying the men's packs and skis, along with Yrund and the twins. The rest of the family skied, heading deep into the woods, where they started a large fire. After some discussion, they rolled the memluks off in front of the blaze, propping them up against their packs.

"What about their tents?" asked Jon-Luq.

"Naha, they'll be warmer out here."

"Oops," said Mila as Orange Beard began to slip sideways into the snow. He woke with a childlike start, his round eyes upon Mila's face as she hauled him back up.

"There, there, it was just a dream," she said, tucking his scarf in closer around his face. Wearing an expression of happy contentment, the memluk drifted back into sleep.

"That should do it," said Hinri after arranging several empty clay jugs around the men.

"One last thing," said Timo, marking the correct route on the memluks' map with a piece of charcoal.

The Hayas stood back to examine their work for a moment. Twilight was falling.

"You really would have killed them?" said Hinri, shaking his head at his mother, who'd already begun sweeping away their tracks.

"Swear to Irsil," said Tana.

Yrund knew she told the truth. And she would have helped her.

JUST A FEW DAYS out from the Hayas' winter home, autumn insisted on one last goodbye, melting the lowlands into a treacherous morass of mud and sharp ice. The sleds had to be emptied and dragged while the baggage was dispersed evenly among the snowdeer. It was an arduous task and took over half a day's light to accomplish, yet the Lumi's sprits were high. It was no small victory to outwit and evade the wield's men, even three lost memluks. Yrund did her part, keeping the skittish snowdeer distracted with handfuls of grayish lichen as they were loaded. She had fallen in love with the big, soft-nosed creatures and was beginning to tell the tamer ones apart.

"You'll have to ride too," said Tana, who had already boosted the twins up onto a snowdeer's blanketed back. "I don't trust your feet are healed enough for walking yet."

With that, Yrund was lifted onto her own cream-colored deer, who gave a small grunt of acknowledgment. Yrund took the reins with enthusiasm. In just a few strides, the gray horizon changed from bleak to full of promise. Past the branch-like antlers, a whole new world was waiting. She was no longer baggage, but a rider, and that made all the difference.

"Lucky dog," said Mila, who had been tasked with guiding the loaded snowdeer past the worst of the mud, then running behind to lift the empty sleds over logs and rocks they had caught on. The ground was too boggy for the animals to carry much additional weight without being mired, so even the older children had to slog through the slush to help the herd along.

"You look like you've ridden every day of your life," said Timo as he went past.

"Almost," said Yrund. "But horses and yaks, not snowdeer."

"Horses, I hear, are easier to train." He laughed and gently slapped the back of her mount.

"My father says a good horse shares its rider's mind."

"Yaha? We could do with a few of those."

Am I a good horse? asked Orelia.

We'll see about that, thought Yrund. *A good horse actually follows directions.* Which wasn't exactly true. Sky horses were notoriously wily when they wanted to be, but she didn't think Orelia needed any encouragement in that regard.

Yrund kept watch with the scope, but they met no more trouble on their journey. A few times, she thought she saw a blurry figure in the woods. She waved uncertainly. With each day that passed among humans, it seemed more and more impossible the woodwin had ever existed. And yet the watching eyes remained on her palms.

TWO DAYS before they reached the Hayas' village, winter came blustering back in like a new landlord, burying them in a storm so thick it was hard to tell night from day. When the suns finally rose the next morning, they had to burrow their way out of their tents, then dig out their empty sleds and reload them. It was an entire morning's work, but the Hayas were happy, boisterously talking of all the pleasures that awaited them in town while they reharnessed their teams. Katrin had to call twice for Yrund to get back on the sled.

"I could ski if you showed me how," Yrund told her, embarrassed to be riding with the twins again. "I'm doing fine walking."

Mila pushed her over in the snow. "Barely."

Katrin pointed, her blue eyes flashing, and Yrund got on the sled. In all truth, her feet had been feeling worse every day, something she'd been trying to hide. Back under the thick furs, she watched the iced forests and hills slide past along with countless lakes, each a flat expanse of white.

"How do you know we won't fall in?" Yrund asked, alarmed at the cracking sound below them.

"That's just the ice layers settling from the last melt," explained Mila, who had traded places with Katrin. "Don't worry. We'll stay close to the trees. That's why Apa goes first with his ice stick."

Yrund hoped Timo knew what he was doing. The twins, unconcerned, were fast asleep beneath the blankets.

"If you fall through, swim toward the side you came in from."

"Why?"

"It held you before, so it'll probably hold you again."

"And if it doesn't?"

"Might be until spring before they find your body." Mila lowered her voice. "I fell in myself last year, running from a bear over by Flori Creek. Balls, that was cold."

"Who pulled you out?"

"No one," said Mila matter-of-factly. "I was by myself. Luckily, the suns were out, and I could see where I'd broken through."

"I'm guessing you didn't tell your mother." Yrund was getting to know Mila pretty well.

"Are you kidding? Ama would have killed me. She lost a sister to ice break when she was little. I wouldn't tell her in a million years. Don't you tell her either."

"I won't, I promise, but why was a bear chasing you?"

"Wasn't ready to part with its pelt, I guess."

CHAPTER SEVENTEEN

Last Lake, it turned out, really was the last lake. The afternoon was turning a hazy gold when they finally slid into the Lumi village, smoke piping like fog out of chimneys and firelight already glowing in windows. The small town of round buildings covered in turf and snow had been built inside a curve of birch hills on the south end of the lake. A large peaked hall of weathered wood rose from the middle of the village while a scatter of ancient boats had been flipped upside down and turned into smokehouses and homes.

Swarms of heavy-coated dogs came running out of the village to greet them. Sikka bayed back, tumbling with old friends and fighting with new ones. Villagers too poured out of the houses to help the Hayas unload their sleds and corral the deer, greetings flying back and forth in the cold air as they thumped each other's thick coats with their mittens.

"Good Way?" came the questions.

"Good Way!" was the answer.

The Hayas said nothing of the memluks or the mud or the blizzard or even the wolverine that had disemboweled one of the snowdeer in the night. Their adventures could be recounted later over cups of alat around a warm stove. For now they were content to take in the familiar faces, beaming with excitement to be reunited with friends and relatives they hadn't seen in long months, some since the previous winter.

"But where's Petro? And Iric?" Hinri asked, looking around the crowd.

The Lumi shook their heads. The Hayas weren't the only ones who'd run across the Mining Wield's men. But they'd been the luckiest. Half a dozen of Last Lake's men had been conscripted the previous week when a large troop of memluks had come through with their Asterian commander. The Hayas frowned, the joy at their own good fortune clouded by the bad news.

"But why isn't the Mining Wield gone by now?" demanded Mila. "The Silver Narrows will be frozen over."

Her mother put up a hand, glancing toward the younger ones. "We didn't come all this way to stand around outside."

Yrund noticed a few curious looks her way before Tana bustled her indoors.

"Are you limping?"

"No," Yrund lied. "I'm fine." She knew how much there still was to do, and Tana wasted no time setting the family to bringing in trunks and splitting wood. The layout was much the same as the Hayas' autumn house, though nearly twice the size. There were carved nooks built into the walls for the bright trunks upon which the beds would be made, and a heavy metal stove in the house's center with a chimney that fed up the roof. Beside it sat a thick table for chopping food and rolling dough, with empty hooks dangling from the rafters above.

Before the first sun was down, the chimney of the Hayas' roundhouse was smoking merrily. By the second sun's fall, the floors were covered with soft hides, the fire glowing, and all manner of people were dropping in to say hello, bringing baskets of buns and pots of pickled fish to share as the Hayas unpacked. Orelia hooted at it all, delighting in every new sensation.

"Our *cousin*, Yrund, is spending the season with us," said the Hayas, making brief introductions with a special nod as they said the word *cousin*.

"Yaha," said their visitors. "Nice to meet you, *Cousin* Ahroond. Good Way."

"Good Way," replied Yrund in Lumi, as she had been practicing. Like the Hayas, the villagers switched between Trade Tongue and their own language constantly. She tried to catch names, but it was not going to be easy. To Yrund's unpracticed eyes, the Lumi, many of whom were related, looked confusingly alike. It had taken long enough just to keep the Hayas all straight.

Whatever curiosity the people of Last Lake had about Yrund's presence, they kept politely for later. Only one scowling man looked at her askance. He was older than Timo, with a grizzled, beardless face he had not bothered to shave. "Who's that, then?" he asked in Lumi from around a dirty, old pipe he had taken out but not lit.

"Pir Jaq, meet our cousin Yrund," Timo said.

"Whose cousin?" Pir Jaq was incredulous. "Not yours or Tana's."

"*Ours*," Timo said firmly.

The man tilted his head, unconvinced as he continued to stare at Yrund while Timo spoke to him in a low voice. Yrund caught the Lumi words for *wield* and *winter*.

"Maybe so, but it could also mean trouble," Pir Jaq responded with a last headshake, getting up to leave. "Seem to have enough of that already without inviting more in. Or maybe you haven't noticed all the memluks about."

"Why have they stayed?" asked Anouk, taking advantage of the one adult willing to talk.

"Not for anything good," said Pir Jaq, long eyebrows waggling as he went out.

Tana closed the door a little harder behind him than necessary. "We've still plenty of unpacking to do," she reminded her children, who'd begun to speculate about the Mining Wield's plans. "And someone needs to find the pots if you want dinner."

In their fall camp, the Hayas had been so busy catching and sorting their herds that many of their trunks were being opened for the first time since the summer, if you didn't count the rummaging of the memluks. Though their belongings were not new, the family greeted them like presents—a worn sytranj board, a beloved spoon. Anouk was especially excited to see her fiddle again, playing them all a cheerful song after she tuned the strings.

A loom appeared, too, making Yrund's heart wince.

What, what? asked Orelia.

My mother was a weaver. Is a weaver, she corrected herself.

"We use it to make belts, boot ties, shirt panels, anything—the larger strips can be bound together with a needle," said Timo as Yrund looked on. "I'll show you how it works one day, if you'd like."

"I would," said Yrund, surprised at herself. Back home, she had avoided learning to weave, despite her mother's fame at the art, preferring to be outdoors. Now, she suddenly saw the loom for what it was, not a device to keep her chained but a tool of limitless potential. She could make patches for her robe or, even better, a pouch to hold Orelia—maybe something with a strap to hang around her neck.

With yellow flowers! suggested the stone.

We'll see, said Yrund who was thinking more of snowdeer. "Did you weave those ribbons too?" she asked Anouk, who wore them in her hair every day, even when there was no one but the family to see.

"That's all she ever makes," said Mila, answering for her. "Ribbons, ribbons, ribbons…"

"And all you ever make are arrows!"

"That's not true," said Mila, indignant. "Sometimes I make bows."

Many neighbors came by to catch up that night. They brought braided breads and dried fish and other gifts to stock the family's larder. The Hayas seemed to have something for each of the visitors, too—small bags of dried mushrooms, berries, or acorns, the mushrooms in particular getting a warm reception—but quickly the conversation turned from greetings to questions about the memluks. Why had they stayed? What about the ice? Weren't they stuck for the winter now? The neighbors knew as little as the Hayas did.

"We only heard this morning," said a silver-haired woman named Didri, whose quick eyes sparkled even as she frowned. "Lut Celeste came to tell us. They've sent scouts to Sea Throat, but it will be several days before we know anything else."

"What you going to carve for the games this year, Didri?" asked Tana, turning the conversation to happier news. "Last year Didri's ice boat won first prize," she proudly explained to Yrund.

"And her silverwork, too—Didri is the best smith in Lumi Land," added Timo.

"Woo-hoo!" grinned Didri. "And wasn't Pir Jaq mad about that boat. You remember that ice troll he made?"

"That looked like it was eating your boat? I'll never forget it," said Timo, laughing. "He sure can hold a grudge. So, what about this year?"

"That troll of his actually gave me an idea. I think I'm going to carve a yowi crapping in his still." The silversmith took a small corked clay pot out of her pocket and handed it to Timo. "Almost forgot. Thought you'd want to try my latest batch of flume."

Timo took an appreciative sip. "Hmm, that is good," he said before Hinri took the pot. "Speaking of flume, we've a story you might enjoy."

And Didri did, clapping her hands with satisfaction that a countryman of hers had pulled one over on the wield's men. "Cloudstone, you say? In their flume? For that laugh, your first case is free this year."

"A case?" Tana shook her head. "We've no amethysts anymore, Didri."

Yrund looked to Mila for explanation.

"Didri has a flume still."

"Not here in town," the woman protested. "I wouldn't want to blow anything up."

"Not like some people we know," said Tana, crossing her arms.

"That was a very long time ago," said Timo, shame-faced.

"What is flume?" asked Yrund.

Flume! said Orelia, practicing the new word. *Floom, fl-ooooom...*

"It's a Lumi specialty," said Timo proudly. "Rutabaga and juniper—smooth as ice. You've got to try it to believe it."

"Don't believe a word of it, Yrund," said Mila, making a face. "It's rough as piney bark and burns like fire."

Tana clicked her tongue. "Flume is not for children, Timo."

"Or anyone with any taste buds left," said Mila.

After the visitors had all gone, Tana directed the children to bringing in kindling, washing up, and the various other chores of settling into their winter home. Even the twins were set to making beds. As before, each sleeping nook had its own curtains, and there were bunks for Anouk and Jon-Luq, stacked above their younger siblings'. Mila had taken the one above Yrund, insisting she didn't mind the climb.

"As for you, my dear," Tana said, taking Yrund by the shoulders, "you've already done too much today. Sit down so I can see your feet. Damn myself for not checking sooner!" Yrund's feet were swollen like small melons with red streaks, as if she'd been painted. "Take off that mallowkite! Quickly!" Yrund took the necklace off, groaning at the sudden pain.

"I should have kept a better eye on you," said Tana as she rummaged through her herbs, loose bits of hair falling from her auburn braid. "What you need is some of my valerian and willow bark tea. And a halestone. Pray to Irsil, someone in the village has one. Who can go asking?"

Suddenly, everyone had volunteered.

"I'll go!" said Mila, first to the door with her long legs.

"Me too," said Jon-Luq. In a matter of seconds, they had all put on their coats and ducked out the door, all except the twins, who Tana pulled back inside by their hoods.

Yrund soon found out why. Tana's tea smelled—and tasted—like dead frogs.

MILA RETURNED FIRST, and she wasn't alone. With her was a Lumi woman wearing a long cape over her coat, the green hood dusted with snowflakes. The healer carried a leather trunk and moved purposefully as she might be called away any moment.

"Agnetha!" Tana exclaimed, pulling the woman to her in a fierce hug.

While the two women kissed one another's cheeks and asked over each other's herds' health, Mila handed Yrund a lump of blue-green stone.

Bogging rock, said Orelia, disgruntled. Yrund hardly glanced at it. There was something familiar about the brusque and weathered woman standing in the Hayas' kitchen.

"Any news yet?" asked Timo, whisking up a bowl of alat for their guest.

"Naha, nothing. Jordi Silverfoot said he spent two days watching the prisoners on the south run, and there was no sign of them."

Tana held Agnetha's hand in hers. "Don't give up, Agnetha. Yrund here is proof there is hope."

Yrund raised her eyebrows at Mila, who whispered in her ear. "Agnetha's sister was taken by the Mining Wield from near Windmarket last spring. That's when her hair turned."

Yrund continued to look at Agnetha's face, recognition stirring inside her. "Do you want me to look at her feet while I'm here?" asked the healer.

"Do you mind?" asked Tana gratefully. "It would be a heartbreak for her to lose the toes now, and all this time, I thought they were improving."

The woman pulled down her hood, and a long white braid fell out across her shoulder.

Yrund felt as if she'd been dipped in ice. She had seen that braid before; it just hadn't been white. And she had seen those same gray-green eyes…though these were a shade more green-gray.

Agnetha flipped back the covers to examine Yrund's toes and frowned at her anklets. "Hmmm. I'm sure those aren't helping. Better put that skylite against your heart, child," she told Yrund. "Do you have a locket?"

When Yrund shook her head, the healer reached for her own.

"Wait—she can wear mine," said Mila, taking off her own necklace and opening it. "It's empty anyway." With a last look at her damaged feet, Yrund dropped the blue halestone inside.

Orelia grumphed. *I could do that.*

Don't you dare, said Yrund. The last thing she needed was Orelia experimenting with her. Not with her feet at stake.

"What is this?" asked Agnetha, noticing the arrowhead tied around Yrund's neck as she tucked the locket in.

"One of the wield men shot her with it when she escaped."

"Cravens!" The healer rewrapped Yrund's feet with a cold ointment from her trunk before inspecting the arrow wound on her side. "And what are these blue marks that have healed? Surely not cobaline? Only an Astrini would leave those."

"His name was Veng," said Yrund, his very name filthy in her mouth. "He was second-in-command at the mine."

Agnetha let out a string of obscenities that would have made a memluk blush. Orelia perked up, her vocabulary considerably extended. "Tana has done an impressive job with your injuries," said Agnetha when she'd calmed. "She would have made an excellent human healer, not just a deer healer, but those toes... It's a miracle you didn't lose them a week ago. It will be up to the halestone now." She closed her trunk and was about to stand back up when Yrund stopped her.

"What does your sister look like? Does she look like you?" Yrund asked, her mouth uncomfortably dry.

"She looks like me, I suppose, before my hair went white. And years younger. Why? You didn't see her did you?"

"There was a woman at the mine—" Brave Braid.

"What mine?" interrupted Agnetha.

"Devil's Crown. I...I didn't know she was Lumi. We barely spoke, but she had a braid like yours...and...and the same eyes."

"What happened to her?" The healer clutched Yrund's shoulder. "Is she still alive? Tell me now—you must tell me."

"I don't know," said Yrund, suddenly realizing the cruelty of her admission.

"But she was alive when you left?" The healer's fingers squeezed Yrund tight.

"She was then, but now..." With a thudding heart, Yrund explained about Brandul and his orders to leave the rabu behind.

"Were there other Lumi there? What about our brother, Amri, and his friend Lindin?"

Yrund could no longer meet the healer's gaze. "There were two men that tried to escape. I did not know them, but the memluks said they were Lumi."

"And?"

Yrund cringed at the memory of their burnt bodies. "They died trying to cross the deadlines."

Agnetha buckled, and Yrund regretted every word she had spoken.

THAT NIGHT, Yrund dreamt she was underground, locked inside the mountain with the ghosts of the prisoners she had left behind trying to bury her alive, each carrying a rock to place on top of her carved with an eye. She woke screaming to find Mila holding her down.

"It's just a dream," the girl said over and over, loosening her grip as Yrund got her bearings. "You're safe now. It was just a dream."

Except it hadn't been. Devil's Crown had been real.

CHAPTER EIGHTEEN

To Yrund's surprise, Agnetha was back the next morning after breakfast, this time with her medicine trunk and a heavily folded map. Yrund apologized for not getting up. The rest of the family was out doing chores, and Tana had forbidden Yrund from leaving her bed.

"No matter, I've already had my alat. Now, show me where this Devil's Crown mine is." Agnetha spread the creased map out on Yrund's lap. "You can work your way back from Last Lake, right here."

"I, ah…" Yrund hadn't been prepared for this. She examined the map in the beam that shone through one of the house's small windows into her bunk, wondering how much she could say without breaking her oath to the woodwins.

"Just do your best," said the healer, undeterred. "Here's the route the Hayas took to get to Last Lake from their fall camp, and here's Windmarket, near where Lili and my brother were taken."

Lee-leeee, repeated Orelia, playing with the new sound.

"Where are the Aeries?" asked Yrund, hushing the stone.

"The Aeries? Way up here, northwest of Windmarket."

Yrund soon found the peaks of Devil's Crown—the ring of

high mountains was unmistakable—then traced her finger down to the Lake Country. There was one gorge, but where was the other? It took her a few moments to realize the map's maker had never gotten past the first gorge to find out about the second. According to this map, the woodwins' forest didn't even exist. That would be a glad bit of news to pass on to Humphrey. If she ever saw him again.

"I was somewhere in these mountains, I think."

"You couldn't have been," said Agnetha, as disbelieving as the Hayas. "That's at least two months' walk from here."

Two months' walk? Yrund looked at the map again. She and Humphrey hadn't even walked for two weeks. The map had to be wrong, just as it was wrong about the Hidden Forest.

"You must have come from the Kalans," the healer went on. "There's a shortcut over this pass here…"

Humphrey has a shortcut, said Orelia. *Through the trees.*

No doubt he did, thought Yrund. Nobody knew the forests like the woodwins. But… Yrund did the math on her fingers. It still didn't add up.

"See?" Agnetha pointed. "There are mines up here in the north. Is this where you were?"

Yrund shook her head. "I know what you're thinking, that you could somehow get there to rescue her. But I promise you—the mine wasn't in the Kalans. It was in the High Aeries. You can't get in, or out," she emphasized, "without an airship."

"You got out."

Yrund could hear Agnetha's desperation, and yet she could not tell her the truth. Not all of it. To convince her, she needed a lie. "One of the memluks bought me from the wield. They put me on an airship, only I…escaped." Better to keep the details vague.

"Which is why they were chasing you…" The healer leaned back, bumping her head against Mila's bunk. "Maybe she got out too. If you really met my sister, you know how resourceful she is."

Yrund did know. Especially with a shovel.

"Maybe the wield didn't leave them after all," Agnetha persisted. "Maybe they changed their mind or went back…"

Maybe, thought Yrund, but even if that were true, the rabu would have been sent on to Smeralgdus. "I'm sorry," she said. "I just don't see a way."

"Well, we all know how mysterious the Way can be," said Agnetha, rolling the map back up and opening her tan medicine trunk.

Yrund said no more. It was clear the Lumi woman was not ready to give up her dead.

"Let's see those toes, then," said the healer, unwrapping Yrund's bandages. "How is the pain?"

"Fine, actually. I think that halestone must be working." Orelia snorted in Yrund's ears. *Shhh!* Yrund told the gem.

"Irsil's navel!" said Agnetha when the bandages were all off.

Yrund looked down at her feet. They looked perfect. No white spots, no black spots, no red streaks, no sloughing. It was like someone had traded her feet for a fresh set.

Agnetha poked and prodded and pinched, not quite believing it. "There's really no tingling?"

"No," said Yrund again. By the time Tana had returned, Agnetha had allowed Yrund to try to stand.

Yrund got out of bed, her bare flesh flinching at the cold.

"Well?"

Yrund flexed her toes back and forth, leaning from one foot to the other. "They feel great." She took a few small steps. Then a few more. Soon she was striding around the house. Agnetha and Tana both examined her feet again, making her stand in the light from each window, then the open door.

"Can I put some socks on?" asked Yrund, shivering.

Tana pulled out two pairs from her trunk.

"Let's see the arrow wound."

Yrund lifted up her layers.

"Remarkable. I've never seen anything like it," Agnetha said after spinning Yrund around to undo the rest of the dressing. "I've used that halestone on a hundred patients. If anything, it should be wearing out, not getting stronger."

"You have extraordinary luck, child," said the healer as Agnetha snapped her trunk shut.

"Not luck," said Tana. "It's her Way."

"A lucky Way, then."

A lucky stone, said Orelia, hmmphing.

Yrund practiced walking back and forth across the floor, excitement building. If she could walk, she could ski. If she could ski, she could go home. Just to think that one little blue halestone could do so much. No wonder the Asterians owned the planet.

"Do you think the halestone might have been strengthened by that arrowhead she's wearing?" Tana asked the healer as she started a pot of alat.

"I would guess the brightsilver before the obsydaline," said Agnetha, watching Yrund dance around. "Where did Mila get that locket?"

"It's the same one she's always had. Didri made it when she was born."

"Why would the silver make a difference?" asked Yrund, hopping lightly around the room, giddy with her new freedom.

"Lumi brightsilver is different from northern silver. It can double the strength of a weak or depleted stone."

Yrund stopped, one foot still in the air. "No wonder the Mining Wield wants it so bad. What with their wello shortage."

"There's a shortage of wellos?" the women said at the same time, putting down their mugs.

"Which kind—verdants or halestones?" demanded Agnetha.

"I don't know," said Yrund. She didn't even know there were different kinds of wellos. "All I heard was that the Asterians are looking for new mines." At least that was what Gem Beard had said.

All at once, her heart sank like a piece of iron.

New mines meant new roads. "You don't have a map that includes Asteria, do you?"

"Wait a minute, Ansyn brought Lotti that bigger map for the school last year. Let me go get it."

"There's a school?" said Yrund, getting dressed and putting her boots back on. They were too big now with the swelling gone down.

"Of course," said Tana, putting more water on to boil. "In the town hall. You'll attend with the others after the culling is over and Lotti's finished up at the smokehouse. Come, help me make more alat."

"But we haven't even finished ours."

Tana tsked. "You don't know Lumi yet, dear. We're about to have company."

Indeed, when Agnetha returned, she wasn't alone. Lotti, the teacher, was with her, along with her husband, Reviq, a boat builder, and Didri and Timo. Soon Hinri and Katrin had come too, the house growing crowded as Agnetha spread the new map out on the small kitchen work table.

"This is Lumi Land here," said the healer, orienting Yrund. "And here is Asteria."

"Where are your silver mines?"

"The biggest is Sea Throat down on the southern shores. The Mining Wield takes the bricks on ships from there through the Silver Narrows and on to the west."

"Why not overland?" It was still a long way but clearly shorter than by sea.

"You've obviously never been here in the summer," said Didri. "The mines and the mountains are separated by hundreds of little lakes when the snow melts. There aren't any roads to travel over, just mud."

"And mosquitoes."

Yrund ran her finger from the Lumi's silver mine to Asteria, her fear growing. The shortest distance to the capital from the Narrows was straight through her home.

"They are planning on taking the silver somewhere around here"—she tapped the coast below the Sky Country—"then going the rest of the way overland to Asteria." All the wields needed was to finish their road, and the Sky Country would be in the middle of a new silver highway.

The rest of the villagers crowded in to look at the map for themselves, their conversation flowing around Yrund, who imagined all the soldiers that would be flooding across her land soon. All because there weren't enough halestones. She didn't think so fondly of the blue gem now.

"That explains the new docks they're building," said someone behind her.

"But they can only go that way when the Narrows aren't iced in. Why leave the memluks here for the winter?" Lotti asked.

"The wello shortage means they intend to run the mine year-round," guessed Agnetha. "They're going to take it through Lumi Land in the winter and the Sky Country in the summer."

"Which explains all the snowdeer they've conscripted...," said Didri, leaning over the map. "They'd want to get the bricks to the Gem Road caravans before the snow melted." The silversmith's calloused fingers sparkled with silver flecks as she traced a second route from the silver mine north. "Windmarket would be their only choice."

"That means they'll be coming right through Last Lake," said Tana, looking at the frightened faces around her.

The Lumi's troubles with the wields had barely begun.

"What's going on?" asked Mila, who'd arrived with Timo. "We heard there was news."

"Nothing for you children to worry about," said Tana, pushing both her and Yrund out. The last thing Yrund saw was the Lumi adults close in around the map, her miraculous healing entirely forgotten.

"Children!" exclaimed Mila when the Hayas' door shut behind them. "I'm seventeen! You're—how old are you?"

"Thirteen. Fourteen soon."

"Exactly! And besides, you've already seen it all, haven't you? You've been to the mines. What do they think they're protecting us from? The truth? Our ignorance won't make things better." Mila raised her hands at the closed door.

Yrund agreed. Especially after she was the one that had put all the pieces together.

"They could at least tell us something!" said Mila, continuing to fume. "What did you hear before they booted you out?"

"A lot," said Yrund, helping herself to a pair of snowshoes in a jumble outside the house. "Let's go for a walk, and I'll tell you."

"Wait, what about your feet?"

"They're all healed," said Yrund, lifting them up high. "Thanks to Agnetha's halestone and your locket—" Orelia let out an annoyed whistle in her head. "That's what all this is about, actually—the memluks staying, me being captured—it's all about the brightsilver. And wellos…" As they tromped around the village, Yrund filled Mila in on everything she knew.

TANA, despite her distractions, found Yrund a pair of Anouk's old boots the next morning, worn but still beautiful, with little foxes embroidered up the sides. "Now that the swelling is gone, these should fit you better."

"Those are mine," said Anouk when she saw Yrund wearing them.

"They were yours," said Tana. "Now they're Yrund's, and when she's done, they will be Magrit's. Though I don't see what you're complaining about—you got a new pair last year you haven't even filled out yet."

"But they don't have foxes—"

"Enough," Tana interrupted. "Do you think the wield men will care what your boots look like when they come raiding for supplies? Now, go get those nails from the metalsmith as I asked. As for you, Yrund, if you feel good enough to be snowshoeing around town you feel good enough to help with chores. With Timo and me off to Floeberg in a few days, we'll need every pair of hands." Though they still wouldn't discuss their plans with the children, it was clear the Lumi were organizing themselves.

For the first time since her arrival, Yrund felt truly useful, strapping on a pair of snowshoes and heading over to the corrals. Her first job was searching for any antlers the bucks had begun to drop before the snow could bury them. Then she helped Mila check the fences, rebinding those that had come loose from the wind. After that, Timo sent her to trade places with Jon-Luq, cutting wood so the boy could help Mila round up the few snowdeer that had broken free in the night.

"You are wolvy," the Lumi boy said midway through putting on his skis to watch Yrund hurl the axe down into the end of another log. "You cut a lot of wood back home?"

"We don't use firewood much," said Yrund. But she had swung a rock pick every day at Devil's Crown—and wood was much easier than stone. It felt good to use all of her body again after so many weeks confined as a patient.

"If you don't use firewood, what do you put on the fire?" asked Jon-Luq, pushing his flop of brown bangs out of the way.

"Yak dung mostly," said Yrund. "Though in the summer, we use suns pots instead of the stove."

Dung, said Orelia. It was just the sort of word she liked. *Dung, du-dun-dung.*

"Eww," said Jon-Luq. "Doesn't it stink?"

"Not once it's dry. It doesn't rain much in the Sky Country."

"Suns all day!" said the boy dreamily. "Yaha, I could handle that. Don't you miss it?"

Yrund swung the axe down again, splitting the log so hard

that splinters flew through the air. "Yes." More than she could bear. Whatever suffering her people had already experienced was only going to get worse when the wield's road was finished.

What? asked Orelia, sensing her anger.

I need a plan, said Yrund.

What's a plan?

Something that will stop the wields from finishing their silver highway.

Like what?

That was what Yrund didn't know. Or what good any plan would do with her still a thousand miles away.

After lunch, Tana checked Yrund's feet one last time, then sent her to Katrin and Hinri's wood shop for a pair of skis. "I guess you've got to learn sometime. Anouk can start your lessons this afternoon."

Yrund was glad. She might not be able to keep the wield men from taking the Lumi's silver, but she could at least try to keep from getting caught. Right now she was the only person in Lumi Land above ankle-height who didn't know how to ski.

"I STILL DON'T SEE why Mila can't teach you," said Anouk, grudgingly showing Yrund how to put her boots in the curved wooden skis. "Aren't you two best friends and everything?"

"I guess she was busy with something."

"Like sneaking off to go hunting," said Anouk, handing Yrund her poles. "Follow me now." Yrund tried to imitate the girl's movements, pushing the poles through the snow to push off, first one leg, then the other. What looked so effortless and smooth when others did it turned out to be clumsy and hard for Yrund. Anouk outpaced her in moments. Stubbornly, Yrund kept on behind her, soon sweating beneath her furs. Eventually she arrived at the edge of town, where Anouk waited impatiently at the bottom of a low hill with few trees. "This is how we teach the babies," said Anouk, sidestepping up the slope with her skis.

Panting, Yrund copied her, fighting for breath when she finally reached the top to gaze out over Last Lake. The small hill seemed twice as high as it had from the bottom, the houses below them like little toys covered with sugar. "Now what?"

"Just slide down," said Anouk with a shrug.

Easier said than done. The next thing Yrund knew, she was headfirst at the bottom, Orelia's *Wheeeee!* turning to an *Oof*.

"That was terrible," said Anouk, skidding down around Yrund in a circle, spraying her with snow. "You really don't know anything."

Yrund pulled herself out of the thick white powder, shaking herself off. "That was the point of you teaching me, but if you don't want to help, you can bog off."

"Fine. I never asked for this job anyway!" said Anouk, leaving Yrund to retrieve her scattered poles and skis by herself.

Well, if memluks could learn, so could she. She sidestepped up the hill once again. It had started to snow again, the flakes as big as fingers. Yrund wiped her eyes. Anouk was not far off, hiding in the trees. Waiting for her to fall again, no doubt. Blast that, thought Yrund, who would prefer not to have a witness to her humiliation. She turned herself the other direction, away from Last Lake, to find another place to practice out of sight. At least if she fell again, no one would see. Laboriously, she stepped her way across the hill's crest, slipping on her skis' slick bottoms until she reached a smaller hill, whose backside was a long and gentle incline into a treeless clearing. Excellent—nothing to run into.

Ignoring Anouk, who had returned to yell more insults at her, Yrund slid over the edge, skis pointed straight down. For the first few moments everything was fine, the speed a soaring thrill. Until she began to lose contact with the snow. Crap on crap. She was going too fast. Yrund braked the only way she could think of

—with her poles—digging down so hard she vaulted herself right over them and into the air like a twisted bird. She was wrong side up now, cartwheeling toward the bottom in a blur of skis and white sky, gaining speed with every bounce. With a final jolt of pain, she crashed into something hard. She could hear Anouk yelling as she tried to sit up. Then the ground beneath her cracked, and the cold water rushed in like a heavy metal blanket.

Yrund, screamed Orelia. *Yrund!*

But the stone was still back inside the Hayas' round house, thought Yrund, confused, as she plunged through a cloud of blue bubbles.

Blast and crap! She must have gone through a lake. She kicked off her remaining ski, her limbs like dead weights, remembering what Mila had said. Go out the way you came in. Her head swung slowly, looking for the hole she must have made.

There—a shadow of an arm, and a head! Anouk. Yrund struggled up toward the surface, clutching for a handhold. "Here! I have you…"

Yrund watched the snow drifting like ashes from the sky as Anouk dragged her backwards to safety.

"Irsil's moons, that was close," said Anouk, whacking Yrund's back as she coughed. "Are you all right?"

"I will be if you s-s-stop beating me!" pleaded Yrund, who hadn't swallowed nearly as much water as the last time she'd almost drowned.

Anouk opened her mouth to retort, but whatever she'd meant to say came out in a sob.

"It's all right. I'm all right," said Yrund as Anouk wrapped her wet arms around her. Thank the Sky. Thank Anouk.

"You could've died!" Anouk wailed, rocking Yrund back and forth like a doll. "And it's all my fault. I shouldn't have ever left you alone… I never thought you'd get all the way over here. Ama will k-kill me."

"T—T—Tana doesn't have to know," said Yrund, shivering so hard she thought she'd break a rib. Bogging hell, she was cold.

"We've got to get you back," said Anouk, coming to her senses. "Wait here." She returned carrying her skis and poles. "Can you stand?"

With a little help, Yrund could. She could have sworn she'd felt at least one arm break in her fall if not two, but she wasn't even sore. Just cold. Miserably cold. "My skis, they're…"

They both looked out at the broken pond, shards of ice sticking up from the black water like fins. "Gone now," finished Anouk.

"I th-th-thought the lakes were all frozen over by now."

"They mostly are, except where there's a spring—you can never trust those."

"How are you s-supposed to tell?"

"You can't. Not until someone goes through." said Anouk. "It's not that far back to town, but the snow's deep. You'll freeze before we get there," she said, pinching at Yrund's wet layers. Her lips twisted as she thought. "Can you get back up the hill, at least?"

Yrund gazed up, determined. "Yaha," she said, chattering.

And she did, though by the top her clothes had frozen completely stiff.

"Trolls," cursed Anouk. "If you get frostbite again, Ama will—"

"Can you give me a ride?" asked Yrund, looking at the single pair of skis Anouk had dropped between them. Mila carried Little Tir around all the time.

"Yaha…why not? If you can hold on. I'll need my arms free." Anouk hoisted Yrund up. The Lumi girl wasn't much taller than Yrund, but she was strong. Factoring in her soaked clothes, Yrund must have been at least her same weight. Without complaint, Anouk slipped her boots into her skis, bent her knees and they were off—cutting back and forth down the slope in a clean ribbon. So that was how you did it, thought Yrund, feeling

Anouk's weight shift with each turn, her skis angling together at the tips when she wanted to slow their speed. As they approached the bottom Anouk straightened out, gaining enough momentum to shoot them through town like a beribboned rocket. Jon-Luq cheered as they flew past, coating him with fine snowdust.

Don't even think about it, Yrund told Orelia before she could make her wave or call back at the tousle-haired boy.

Anouk delivered Yrund to the sauna, putting fresh wood on the fire and bringing in a bucket of snow. They sat shivering on the warm benches until their ice-hardened clothes had melted enough to let them free. Then they stripped the leaden layers off onto the floor, soaking in the hot, fragrant steam. Yrund cheeks and hands burned as they thawed. She examined her toes, which were a bright shade of pink but still seemed to have feeling.

"I'd understand if you told Ama," said Anouk, her own skin blotched with orange and blue.

"I'm not going to tell." Not so much for Anouk's sake as her own. "It was pretty stupid of me to go off like that."

"It was, actually," said Anouk, her irritation coming back. "But, how are we going to explain about our clothes? I can say your skis got lost—that happens all the time, but Ama will notice our wet coats for sure."

Yrund, head still resting on the bench, reached out a toe towards the bucket of melted snow. "Oops," she said, tipping it over the wet heap. "Too bad we never listen about hanging up our things."

Anouk's head swung from the soggy mess to Yrund. "She'll still be mad!"

"Not *as* mad, though," Yrund pointed out, inhaling the wonderful scent of warm wood.

"You're really annoying. Did anyone ever tell you that?"

Yrund thought back to her own sisters and smiled as she closed her eyes. "All the time."

YRUND and the younger Haya siblings were playing a game of keeps after dinner with an assortment of buttons for stakes, shell being the most valued, when they heard the village dogs begin to bark. Sikka leapt at the door, scratching and howling to be let out.

"It's too soon for Apa and Ama to be back," said Anouk.

"Probably just Mila," said Jon-Luq.

"The dogs never bark at her."

Their parents had left early the previous morning for a meeting in Floeberg, leaving Mila in charge, but Mila, predictably, had sneaked off around midday and hadn't been seen since. Jon-Luq said she'd promised him a quiver of arrows if he would finish her chores, and her white fur hunting suit was not on its hook.

"Maybe there's a wolf back in the pens. Someone should go look."

"I'll do it," said Yrund, hoping it was Mila. She'd spent the day worrying the young woman had fallen through a river or pond, her body stuck under the ice until spring. True to her word, Yrund had not told anyone of her own plunge, and in gratitude (and likely guilt), Anouk had taken her back out that morning and given Yrund a real lesson, starting with showing her how to stop. With proper instruction Yrund had even made it down the children's hill without falling, but it would take far more than that to ever catch up with a skier like Mila.

Yrund cracked open the door to see a team of dogs pulling a man and a heavily loaded sled around the Hayas' house. A frantic Sikka burst out to chase them. "It's Ansyn! Trader Ansyn!" Now all the children were yelling and tripping over each other to pull on their boots.

The man threw an anchor overboard and the long sled slowed to a stop, dogs panting in the twilight and snapping at any village dog that got too close. In moments, the village had poured out to surround the man, laughing and shouting as if it were a holiday.

What, what? asked Orelia, burning with curiosity.

An Asterian, said Yrund, lips twisting. Whatever the Hayas seemed to think of Ansyn, he was from the land of the wields, and that alone was reason enough not to trust him. Still, she put another log on the fire and started a pot of alat, knowing it was the Lumi way.

"Ansyn's here! Ansyn's here!" the Haya children shouted, tumbling back inside with Sikka at their heels. They were followed by a tall, broad-shouldered man who had to stoop through the door. He wore a long shearling coat and matching hat, and his mustache was frozen solid above his thick collar. A pair of peculiar goggles hung loose around his neck—for wind or glare, Yrund guessed as she stared. This was the Asterian merchant? He was hardly older than Hinri. Except for the bold nose, his face was well-proportioned under its short dark beard, with long arched eyebrows and a wide smile that made his wind-burnt cheeks crease. He did not look like the Lumi—his deep-set eyes were brown flecked with green, his skin like baked clay.

"Good Way," the man said curiously when he saw Yrund. She returned the greeting, still disconcerted.

"This is Yrund, our *cousin,*" said Anouk, stressing the word with a wink.

"Oh? Nice to meet you, *Cousin* Ah-roond," he said, pronouncing her name as the Lumi did.

"It's Yrund, actually." Not that it mattered anymore. She was used to the way the Lumi said her name.

"Ih-roond?"

"Yaha." Close enough.

"Well, Yrund, I'm Ansyn if we're keeping it short."

"Naha, tell her the whole thing," said Anouk.

"Well, in that case I am Journey Trader Ansyn Eneldo

Angelica Bharat of the Merchant's Wield, though surely all that's not necessary among friends."

"What did you bring us?" demanded the twins, done with niceties.

"Who said I brought you anything?" asked the man, shaking them off with a laugh.

"Is it candy?" squealed Magrit.

"Or a chinchilla?" asked Anouk hopefully, going through Ansyn's pockets.

"Is that all I'm good for? You'll have to feed a poor trader before you get any presents." He winked over their heads at Yrund, who before she could stop herself winked back.

Bad gem! she told Orelia, who just clucked.

"I'm hoping that wonderful smell is Tana's mushroom soup. Might I beg a bowl of you after I've taken care of the dogs?" Without waiting for an answer, he stooped back out the door. The children went after him, jabbering for his attention.

Mushroom soup? There was only a bit of rabbit left, which she had saved to eat with Mila. It could be turned into soup, she supposed. At least that would stretch it to serve three.

Yrund got to work, rewarming buns and chopping and stirring and adding in pinches of spices from the tins Tana kept in the painted chest of drawers behind the stove. As for mushrooms, there was less than a handful left in the pantry cupboard. That wouldn't be nearly enough. Yrund knew there were more—the Hayas had given bagfuls to neighbors when they arrived. She looked through the rafters until she found the sack of the rest hanging beside an ancient-looking drum. She didn't have to trust the Asterian, but she did have to feed him or she'd have Tana to answer to.

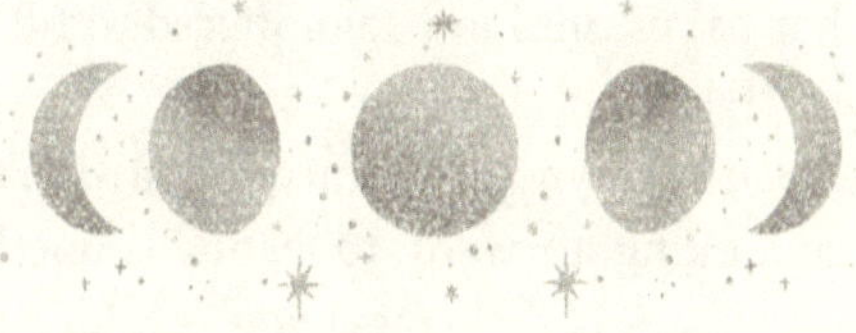

CHAPTER NINETEEN

"Where is everyone?" asked Mila, slipping silently in the door, black antiglare unguent smeared across her face. Her hair was matted with ice, and a putrid odor of decay wafted off her, making Yrund gag.

"What's that smell?"

Mila sniffed innocently at the air. "Must be the brains I was boiling. Didri and I started up our tanning camp again." She filled herself a mug full of the brown soup. "Why'd you make so much?" she asked, blowing on the top. "Are Ama and Apa back already?"

Yrund didn't have time to reply before Ansyn came through the door, loaded with heavy bags.

"Mila! How are you?" The trader's nose crinkled. "Woo! What's that smell?"

"Ansyn," Mila said, startled. "You don't usually get here until after New Suns." She gave Yrund an accusing look. "I, I—I'll be right back." She put her dinner down and ran out, grabbing her soap bag as she went.

Ansyn looked at Yrund for explanation.

"She was boiling brains today."

"Ah," said Ansyn, unsurprised as he dropped his luggage. Then, as if he'd done it many times, he folded his long legs underneath him and sat down in the visitor's spot to the right of the door, listening to the children explain that Tana and Timo had gone to Floeberg.

Yrund handed the guest a bowl of soup. His gaze lingered for a moment on her palms until Jon-Luq offered to fill the alat mug he carried Lumi-style on his belt.

"This is heaven," Ansyn proclaimed. "You don't know how long I've been looking forward to eating something besides biscuits and dog meat… Is that sorrel you've added to the mushrooms? Mmm, really gives it a nice zing."

Yrund took a bite. She hadn't put any sorrel in the soup, only some dried radish, which it turned out wasn't really to her taste. When no one was looking she dumped her mug back in the pot, opting for a bun instead. More for their guest.

"You ate one of your dogs?" Anouk asked the trader, horrified.

"No, thank the Way, just some of the meat I'd brought for their meals."

"What happened to your supplies? Did you run into bandits?" The kids crowded around to listen, the twins right up in the trader's lap.

"I did. Of a sort. There were two Roads and Ways stops outside Darban, not a day apart from each other. The first one was bad enough, the fossicking thieves with their Way taxes, but the second lot 'conscripted' my personal stores too. I'd bet a crate of my best pepper they weren't Roads and Ways at all—"

"Did they have an airship?" asked Yrund, interrupting.

Ansyn, who'd helped himself to another roll, looked surprised, his long eyebrows bunched together. "I take it you've run across this bunch?"

Yrund dodged the question. "Have you seen them again? Did they follow you?" A flush of nausea went through her.

"No. Wield ships don't like to go much south of the Gem Road."

"See? We told you so," said Jon-Luq to Yrund.

"Why not?" Yrund pressed.

"Up north the pilots can use a waystar if it's cloudy, but south of the Kalans, you have to fly by sight—the instruments just spin in circles down here."

"What did they get? Not the alat, right?" said Anouk with a note of panic.

"No. I'd had the foresight to bury all the tins inside bags of wheat." His mustache dripped into his soup as it defrosted. "They did get all the applesnap, more's the shame, and an entire bag of gemjellies." A wail went up from the children as the trader nodded sadly. "It's worse—nearly all the real stones I'd picked up in Orogaudi and Unsinn were in there, not that they could have known. Seemed in quite the hurry for tax men. Never once asked to see my account books."

"Did the bandits get our sugar mice?" clamored the twins.

"Yaha," said Anouk. "And what about our books?"

"*Your* books are all safe," said Ansyn, patting the lumpiest bag beside him. "As for your mice... I can't seem to recall if I picked them up or not... I might need a little more of that fine soup to help me remember," he teased.

The trader finished three more bowls and a fresh round of spice buns before Mila slipped back in, looking steamed and clean, the aroma of soap almost hiding the whiff of her day tanning.

"Ah! The great Mila returns!" said Ansyn.

Mila muttered something unintelligible and sat down in the corner against Yrund's bed, away from her usual spot by the stove.

Wiping his bowl clean with the last bun, Ansyn licked his fingers. "Oh, to be warm again—what a treat." He peeled his layers off, the firelight making the inlaid buttons of his travel coat shine an iridescent blue-black. Finally, he fished a wooden box from his pocket. The children squealed as he opened the seal and passed it around. Inside were tan-colored sweets shaped like perfect little mice. Even Mila took her share.

The creamy sugar dissolved slowly in Yrund's mouth. *Yomm-minomm*, said Orelia. *I like mice. Micey, micey, mice,* sang the stone, making up a new tune in Yrund's head.

"Can we see the books now?" asked Anouk when every last bit of sugar had been licked clean.

"So you've had enough of my company already?" Ansyn teased, pushing the lumpy sack toward them. "I was hoping your parents would be here, but seeing as how I am early—go ahead. After all, you did win first trade."

"What's that?" asked Yrund.

"Every year Ansyn gives the village a puzzle of some kind. Whichever family solves it first gets to have him for dinner the following year before anyone else, which means first pick of the goods he brings," said Jon-Luq.

Anouk untied the waxed canvas sack. Inside were bundles of books and papers tied together. Many were broken at the binding or missing covers, but the family was not disappointed.

"Look! *Tales of the Gem Folk,* and there are pictures!" said Jon-Luq before handing the book over to the twins, who spread the pages open on the floor between them.

"*The Daring Exploits of the Invisible Hand,*" read Anouk from a thin booklet at the top of the pile. "What's that?"

"Oh, the latest excitement the presses are on about," said Ansyn. "Someone's been stealing very rare gems, only to turn around and give them to fisherfolk and street sweepers. Popular person, the Hand," he said. "And good with his feet."

"A footfighter?" Jon-Luq swiped the garishly printed booklet away.

"Hey!" said Anouk.

The trader pushed a small stack of battered fashion glossies toward her. "Here," he said. "Consolation prize."

"Ooh, glossies! These are the good ones, too—you remembered! From Asteria, Paragon, Darban…" Anouk flipped through the pages, talking to herself. "Would you look at that!"

Orelia begged to see, but after a few pages looking over Anouk's shoulder, Yrund was soon bored. *It's just hats and clothes,* she told the gem.

Hats and clothes! repeated Orelia, enthralled.

Mila, unable to resist any longer, scooted forward and reached into the pile, turning books over and reading the covers. "*Great Families of the Green Mercantile. Secret of the Stolen Pearl—*what's that one about?"

"Adventure on the high seas escaping Sea Hammers and Silk Sparrows. Thought your father would like it."

"Sounds like him," Mila agreed, returning the book to the pile and picking up another. "*Petra's Guide to Herb and Jewel Tinctures.* Ama will want that one." Mila lifted up an especially battered volume next. "*Sailing the Silk Seas* by Sispel Finch."

"Brave lady, Ms. Finch," remarked Ansyn.

"You know her?"

"I once had the privilege to spend a night hiding in a nutmilk tree in Bindo with her during a local skirmish. Great company if you think you're about to die—she's been more places on the planet than the memluks. Sailing for Opaloosa last I heard."

Mila thumbed through the pages, examining the hand-drawn maps.

"I got this one just for you," Ansyn said, handing Mila the only new book in the pile.

"*A Memluk's Book of Weapons.*" Mila set the other title aside and opened the cover. There were sketches upon sketches of every sort of weapon imaginable, including several pages just of bows and arrows.

"Wows, look at that funny little curved one. It's like a toy it's so small."

"I believe that's for shooting from horseback. Popular in the Sky Country."

"Let me see," said Yrund, leaning in to verify this claim. Indeed, the bow was very much like those of her people, all except for the green stone set in its grip, a flight of Asterian imagination.

"Can't have much range," said Mila.

"A thumb ring adds a lot, actually."

"Do you know much about the Sky Country?" asked the trader with interest.

"A little," said Yrund warily.

"Some of the finest weavings on the planet. It's a shame I've never gone. I've always wanted to travel south of the Jaggedies." The Trader smiled at her.

Yrund looked away.

What, what? He's wolvy, said Orelia, who clearly didn't know how to use the word.

All traders are charming, said Yrund. *We don't know anything about him.* What if Brandul had hired him? Or the Mining Wield? An escaped rabu was worth a small fortune. He could be a bounty hunter. Or a spy. Then again, if he was who the Hayas thought, he could also be an asset. After all, who knew more about the wields than a wield man? She forced herself to smile. Either way, she'd do better not to make an enemy of him.

"Do you want another bun?"

"Me? No, I'm fine. Relax, Cousin, look through the books. It's first trade, after all," said Ansyn, waving with one hand and petting a contented Sikka with the other. The house grew quiet except for the turning of pages and the crackling of the fire.

Yrund picked up a dilapidated manual called *Cooking with Thrips*.

What are thrips? asked Orelia.

Bugs, I think. The Asterians eat them.
Next, Yrund thumbed through a small volume of what turned out to be love poems.

Pearl of my eye,
Halestone of my heart,
Beating drum in my veins,
Open your blushing...

She snapped the book closed, much to Orelia's disappointment.

At the bottom of the pile of books was one volume that looked older than the rest, a crackled leather tome bound with red thread and embossed in fading gold. She ran her finger across the battered spine. *Gempendium,* said the title.

"Don't judge that one by its condition—that's a true treasure you've got there," said Ansyn. "It's from the first run of gempendiums Barthalow Damantine ever printed. Not quite as valuable as it used to be with all the new gems that have been found, but still an impressive work of science and art."

Yrund opened the gempendium's cover. *Ohh,* said Orelia. The creamy yellow pages were filled with drawings of gemstones so fine they almost lifted off the page. Yrund flipped through the book slowly. Below each illustration was a short description. A shimmery blue-gray jewel caught her eye.

Hiraeth: Also known as storm opal. Iridescent gray with blue-black fire. Rules of the stone: Wear with caution—capable of inducing intense longing if worn for extended periods along with tendency to wander and hear voices, song, or music others cannot. Danger of catatonia when paired with forget-me-not seefire. Not to be worn with anything in the adularia family at risk of extreme melancholia and moon howling. Neutralized by ambergris and other resinous gems.

There were three small symbols beside the drawing: a flute, an eye with a teardrop, and a skull.

"Ooh—hiraeth! The most beautiful stone on the planet, in my opinion. And, alas, one of the most dangerous. You have to keep a bit of jet or red amber in your pocket if you're going to wear a hiraeth for long."

There was something odd about the gray stone, as if it could pull Yrund right through the page into its stormy depths.

"Did you say dangerous?" she asked, bringing herself back.

"Oh yes," said Ansyn. "There's an unfortunate tendency for wearers to walk into the sea. Interestingly, black opal, which looks very similar, merely makes you want to travel." He ran his fingers over the fiery buttons on his coat.

"I like the white ones the best," said Mila. "Apa gave Ama one when they were tied. She keeps it in her locket."

"White opal has just the opposite effect of black opal—makes you feel right at home wherever you are. A good gem for a marriage. Very different from hiraeth. They're an odd class, the adularia."

Yrund flipped backward through the book. *Violette... Agyt...Adventurum...*

Adularia: Those stones which have a milky or billowy glow, sometimes bluish, as moonslight on water. See moonsstone, agyt...oceanstar, opal, rose quartz, mermaid's fire, and sunsstone.

Yrund turned the pages of the gempendium with guilty fascination. *Pearls. Tiger's eye. Zargun.* Most of the stones Yrund had never even heard of. *Susurrus, dendronyx, mallowkite*—that one she knew from the anodyne Katrin had loaned her, what the Lumi called a *numbli*. Orelia took pleasure in farting at each jewel. *You're not any less special because there are other gems out there,* Yrund told her.

Wait a minute. She had passed an entry for agyts. Maybe

Brandul's finder stone was in there. She looked through the very long list: *Eye agyt...fire agyt...iris agyt...moss agyt...rainbow agyt*—there were at least two dozen varieties. She went back through them again. There were agyts for finding water, and metal, and snakes and love—though the author was more dubious about the last two—and suns on cloudy days...but nothing about gems that could find other gems.

Nor was there a single drawing of a stone that looked anything like Orelia—the closest were the vagaries with their changing colors or opals with their internal fire. Maybe she had missed one. *Let's start at the beginning.* She nestled back into a fur, reading the first page silently to the stone:

Yrund was nearly to the end of the *A*'s when she sat up. There was one description with no drawing attached:

Aubade: Known in modern times as allstone, aubade (or dawnstone) is the stone of all stones, the wonder of all wonders, the every stone. Purportedly of unsurpassed beauty and power...

What's unsurpassed? asked Orelia.

Well, with horses, it usually means they've won every race. The best of the best.

That's me! said Orelia, tooting. *Better than every stone.*

Let me finish reading, said Yrund, a worried flutter beginning inside her.

...able to take on the properties of any gem, for better or for worse. A popular subject of stories and songs, but almost certainly mythical. Today's gemists agree the wildly varying descriptions (and depictions) of such stones passed down through the ages (along with the peculiar tales, such as the gem coming alive to sing at dawn) indicate the much fabled allstones were in all likelihood merely vagaries with inclusions of mindturner (such as an eye or eartwister), which could naturally make the wearer see or hear any number of strange things. Note: The battle

for possession of such allstones is what led to the first wield wars. In fact, the very term wield was an extension of each house's belief that only they had the requisite skills to be the rightful wielders of the stones. The subsequent battles for the allstones and the untimely deaths of those that tried to wield them eventually led to the notion the allstones were cursed. It was not until their disappearance in the fourth century that the great star of our commonwield was formed—joining all six wields as equal points, the High Seat rotating peacefully every twelve years. In this light, perhaps it is best the aubades remain solely within the realms of myth. For more, see Ambryt Calenthrop's most comprehensive treatise: On Vagaries and Allstones.

Yrund sat lost in thought, ignoring the dishes, the other children, and their very full guest.

THE ROUND HOUSE was quiet but for the burning logs shifting in the stove and the occasional titter from the children as they read. The trader sipped his alat and rubbed Sikka's ears in satisfied peace, her tail thumping happily against his side.

"So, Mila, are you going to compete in the Long Shoot this year?" he asked, breaking the silence.

"Yaha," was all Mila said, still absorbed in the book of weapons.

"You know Koli Udnar is entering?" he said as if trying to goad her. "They say she's the best downhiller in the Windmarket Valley."

Mila put a string in her book and stretched her long arms out, then her legs, pushing Sikka out of the way. "She almost beat me last year. She's good. But I'm better," Mila said matter-of-factly, wet hair glinting in the stove light. "I'm faster than Apa now. And Hinri."

Yrund heard them as if their voices were carrying in from

another world, absorbed by the gempendium and Orelia's ongoing chatter. She was reading the page on aubades for the fourth time when something their guest said made Mila laugh, and Yrund finally looked up.

"It's good to be back," Ansyn was saying. He leaned onto his elbow, head in hand, taking in the warm scene as if it was something he had been looking forward to for a very long time—the round-bellied stove and brightly painted trunks, the children sprawled across the floor reading.

Yrund felt annoyed with his appreciation, as if an Asterian did not deserve such comforts, and yet, such a short time ago, she too would have given anything to be here. Even now, it was hard to believe she had a real bed and real clothes and no one waiting to whip her. In truth, some part of her hesitated to savor it too fully, as if the very acknowledgment of its preciousness would get it taken away. Sikka lay down beside her, and Yrund put down the gempendium and gave the dog a scratch, the thick, soft fur twining between her fingers.

"So what's the news around here?" Ansyn tilted his head toward Yrund.

Mila shook her head warningly. This amused the trader for some reason, and he shook his head back at her. Mila kicked his foot with her long leg, but Ansyn didn't seem to notice. He'd become extremely interested in his hands, moving them closer and then farther from his face as if waiting for something to appear.

Mila swung her foot toward Yrund instead, giving her a not-so-gentle tap. Reflexively, Yrund pinned Mila's leg between her own. Ground wrestling was one of her people's favorite sports.

"Where did a little rabbit like you learn that?" asked Mila, trying to get her foot back.

"I'm not a rabbit. I'm a badger." It was true. Her father was from the Badger Clan.

"Ha, ha…you're not a badg—"

Yrund squeezed harder.

"Ow! Okay, you're a badger."

Yrund released her grip, and Mila made a face at her, the dim light of the dying coals exaggerating her features. Yrund made a face back. Jon-Luq stretched to put more wood in the stove and noticed their game.

"Look what I can do," he said, flipping up his eyelids.

"Gross," said Anouk. Nonetheless she tried to fold her own eyelids on top of themselves.

Not to be outdone, Little Tir began to somersault around the room, leering at them like a monkey through his legs. Magrit, predictably, had fallen asleep. When Tir broke wind mid-roll, his siblings began to giggle. Which made Orelia giggle, tickling Yrund's mind as if with a thousand small feathers.

"What?" said Ansyn, putting down his hands. "Did I miss something?" Which only made the Hayas and Orelia laugh harder.

"What are you all laughing at?"

Now even Yrund's face had cracked.

"What? Is it me?" Ansyn asked bewilderedly, checking himself to see what was amiss.

The children clutched at their sides. Soon Ansyn too began to laugh, helpless against the tide. And as he broke down, Yrund felt something in herself give. She couldn't remember the last time she'd laughed. Not like this. It felt like rain soaking into dry ground.

"What is it?" asked the trader, trying to talk between howls. "What?" Then he melted into another laughing fit, even worse than the children's, which set them off all over again.

Yrund laughed so hard the muscles in her cheeks were like taut bowstrings. And the more she laughed, the more Orelia whooped inside her head.

"Stop, stop!" begged Ansyn. "I don't even know what's so funny!"

Little by little the house quieted as they all gasped for air. Then from just behind Mila—a small toot. So small it was as if she was practicing. But they all heard it.

"It's a good thing I've got my own cabin to sleep in tonight."

"That wasn't me!" Mila shrieked, horrified.

"Har-haw-haw-haw," howled the others as Orelia chortled proudly.

"I'm serious. It wasn't me!"

But only Yrund believed her. She knew exactly who had made the noise.

Tears streaming, Anouk began to choke on her own spit, so Ansyn had to pound her back. A frightened Magrit woke up in the midst of the chaos and began to cry.

Which was exactly when the door opened. Tana and Timo had returned.

"Apa! Ama!"

"Ansyn! You're early! Welcome!"

The trader got up to shake hands, swaying a little before sitting abruptly back down. Sikka licked his face. "Her head is so big," he said to no one in particular.

"Are you all right? Have they fed you?" asked Tana, going to the stove.

"Yrund made soup," said Mila.

Ansyn was waving his hands in front of his face again, first slow, then fast. "A most excellent mushroom soup, Tana. Nearly as good as yours."

"Weren't we out of mushrooms?"

"I found some more in the bag," said Yrund.

"What bag?" asked Tana, eyebrows twisting.

"The one in the rafters, behind the drum."

Tana had a queer look on her face. "Oh, no! Did the little ones eat it, too?" Tir was rolling around the floor giggling again while Magrit was sniffling and clinging to her mother's coat.

"No—naha, the others had rabbit earlier, but there wasn't

enough for the trader, so I made what was left into soup because that's what he said he liked." Dread prickled Yrund's neck as she wondered just what she had done.

"Those mushrooms are not for soup. They are for the snowdeer ceremonies in the spring!"

Ansyn no longer looked so relaxed. "You fed me rabbit?" he said, sitting up.

Tana's eyebrows had reached her hairline. She headed straight for her medicine chest. "You should be more worried about the flying mushrooms."

Yrund swallowed.

"Which of you ate the soup, then?" asked Timo calmly.

"I had a little, but not much," said Mila, looking worried. "I guess I got distracted with Ansyn arriving and all..."

The trader looked pleased at that.

"Yrund?" asked Tana.

"Just a bite. I didn't really like it," she admitted. "I thought I'd put too much radish in."

Timo peered into the pot. "You had the lion's share, then, Trader Ansyn?" he asked, eyes beginning to crinkle.

Ansyn nodded. "Serves me right for being so greedy. I'd been looking forward to a real meal for three days. Never occurred I'd been gemmed—well, I guess mushroomed is more accurate. Or is it rabbited?"

Everyone was looking at Yrund now, the children with a mixture of awe and pity, Timo with amusement, and Ansyn with an expression Yrund couldn't read.

"You know those men that robbed me outside Darban? They were looking for a girl about your size."

"Outside Darban? Yrund's never been to Darban, have you?" said Mila.

Yrund shook her head.

"And she couldn't have known about the mushrooms," said Tana, opening and closing drawers. "You're going to want some ginger and wort tea..." She talked to herself as she gathered ingredients. "Have you got a toadstone?"

The guest tried to shake his head, but it looked more like a wobble. "Just a violette."

"Woo-hoo, you're in for a long night," said Timo, clapping Ansyn on the shoulder.

"I'm sorry," said Yrund, though it seemed far too late for that.

"I should have warned you," Tana said. "It's just been so busy, and it's easy to forget you are still learning our ways."

Seeing Yrund's alarm, Tana tried to comfort her. "Ansyn has partaken in the rites before—this won't be his first time flying. Now, show me how much you put in."

Yrund showed her the box. "I used two handfuls. Is that a lot?"

"It's enough to get interesting," Tana said, dumping what little was left of the soup into the fire. Mila added the rest of her almost full mug after it. "Luckily he's a pretty big fellow." She looked over at the trader and sighed. He had taken off his socks and put them over his hands.

"Maybe it would be better if he stayed here tonight," said Timo.

"I agree. Bedtime, everyone. Timo, you'd better find Ansyn's amethyst, for as much good it will do. Then someone is going to have to scrub this pot."

"I'll do it," volunteered Yrund.

"Naha, I'll do it," said Mila. "It's my fault. I shouldn't have left her alone for so long."

"No—really, I feel just fine," said Yrund. "Let me do something."

"Mila, you can scrub the pot. And, Yrund, I suppose you can bring more buckets of snow if you're up to it."

"I am," Yrund said, already heading for the door. She needed time to think.

CHAPTER TWENTY

Outside, the night was quiet and cold with two bright moons already up, illuminating every snow-topped tree and roof, along with the puffs of smoke rising from Last Lake's chimneys. Small chinks of light marked the windows of neighbors still awake over a book or last mug of alat. Yrund strapped on a pair of snowshoes and walked straight up the nearest snowbank to fill her bucket, pausing at the top to look up at the stars. *You won't believe what a stupid thing I've just done,* she started to tell them.

"I see you are walking again," said a voice, interrupting her.

Yrund whirled. "Humphrey!" She hugged the fuzzy outline in front of her before thinking, but the woodwin did not seem to mind. "I was afraid I'd never see you again," said Yrund. "How have you been? Where have you been?" She had so many questions for the woodwin.

Hush, she told Orelia, who was whistling in her ear, despite being tucked in her backpack in the house.

"Oh, you know—here and there, but I've kept an eye on your progress," answered Humphrey, whacking Yrund's back and shoulders.

"If you hadn't gotten me away from that airship…" Yrund tried to find the woodwin's face.

"I regret I couldn't do it faster. You could have lost your feet."

"But I didn't."

"That's good. They were small enough to begin with. How do you like the Lumi?"

"They're very kind," said Yrund. "I'm going to miss them." She'd thought she could stay, find a way to help. But if Ansyn got it in his head to turn her in…

"Miss them? You just got here."

"They've got their own troubles. The Mining Wield will be coming south soon with caravans of brightsilver."

"So I gleaned," said the woodwin. "I've just come from Sea Throat. It seems the scarcity of wellos has made them desperate. You've probably already figured out that's why they're building a road through the Sky Country."

"Yes," said Yrund unhappily. And there was nothing she could do about it.

"Where is Orelia?" asked Humphrey.

"Inside—having a tantrum," said Yrund, who could hardly hear the woodwin. Without warning, Yrund's mouth opened and the noise in her head came out her mouth.

Humphrey listened, surprised, then whistled back.

Yrund forced her mouth closed. *Orelia! What did I tell you? That is not fair!*

"Does she do that often?" asked the woodwin.

"A few times," said Yrund furiously. "I don't know how, but I am going to drop her off a cliff if she does it again."

Sorry, said Orelia, though she didn't sound it.

"She is a strange stone, isn't she?" said Humphrey.

"Very. That's just the problem. I'm afraid she might be even more valuable than we thought. Those men in the airship, the ones that were shooting at us—they thought I had an allstone…"

"An allstone?" said Humphrey. "Have you heard the jokes she tells?"

"I know she's odd—"

"Decidedly—but there are many odd gems on Precios. There's a new adamantine out of Pullallawee that will make you dance around like a chicken. Why would they think she's an allstone?"

"Because of that finder's stone the mine boss has—it was pointing right at me. I think they can track her."

What is odd? asked Orelia, butting in again.

Special, explained Yrund impatiently.

"I've never heard of a finder stone that could find anything," said the woodwin dismissively.

"But what if it can? I was reading in this book that Trader Ansyn brought. It says the Asterians fought whole wars over allstones."

"And now they fight whole wars over spices. That is their nature."

"So, you really don't think she's an allstone?" Relief filled Yrund's chest.

"No, I don't. But that doesn't mean the Asterians wouldn't find a use for her. Remember the fire she started?"

Yrund would never forget. "Whatever she is, the Mining Wield wants her. And Brandul—that's the mine boss—he's crazy, Humphrey. He already tried to kill me once. Twice, actually. He won't stop."

"Then your Way is clear," said the woodwin. "If he wants the stone—"

"You just said not to give her to them!"

"I wasn't going to suggest you *give* Orelia to him. Merely use his desire against him."

"You mean set a trap?"

"Precisely."

"Then what?"

The woodwin knocked his knuckles against her head as though it were empty. "Kill him, of course."

Kill Brandul? Nothing would give Yrund more pleasure. "But how?"

"I imagine you can think of something. I always liked a large rock myself. You don't have to get your fur dirty. Anyway," he said as if that were that, "I have other news that will interest you. The rabu that were left at Devil's Crown escaped."

"What!" Yrund could not believe it. "How?"

"Mutiny from the sound of it."

"Where did they go?"

"We don't know yet, but they took one of the wield's airships. Speaking of which, maybe you could ask Trader Ansyn what he knows about rudders."

"Wait—how do you and Ansyn know each other?" The village sparkled as the fourth moon rose.

"We don't. At least, he doesn't know about me. But *I* know about *him*." Humphrey chuffed. "Let's just say he's more of an asset to the woodwin cause than most Asterians."

"He is?"

"Of course, he's a freewielder."

"Yrund!" called out Mila. "Are you okay? What's taking so long?"

"Coming!" Yrund called, then turned back to Humphrey. "When will I see you again? Or sort of see you. You're very clean," she said, trying to find his arm.

"'Cleanliness is stealthiness,'" the woodwin quoted. "I have some traveling to do, but I'll find you when I return. Give Orelia a message for me." Humphrey whistled something next that sounded like leaves dancing in the wind, then melted into the night.

"Oh, and one more thing," the woodwin said, making her jump. "It's the quality of the silver that gets to Asteria that determines the Lumi mine's worth." Then he really was gone.

"Yrund?" The Hayas' door opened wider now, the light shining out like a reverse shadow.

Mila came all the way out, taking away the empty buckets from Yrund, who had forgotten what she was doing. She filled the buckets with a light curse and pulled Yrund back inside.

"What were you doing out there?" asked Tana, looking worried.

"Talking to herself and looking at the moons," said Mila, pouring the buckets of snow into the pot on the stove.

"Oh dear, and I thought you were all right…"

"I am," insisted Yrund. It wasn't the soup that had her confused. Still, Tana forced a cup of tea on her.

For once, though, Tana's medicine didn't taste bad.

"Did you know that ginger and cardamom are related?" asked Ansyn, holding his own mug to his face. "And turmeric."

"I did not know that, no," said Tana. "Is turmeric the one that looks like saffron?" She'd arranged herself with a heap of darning, but one eye was on her patient.

"Not at all!" waxed Ansyn. "Saffron is golden-yellow, while turmeric yellow-gold. One is from a root; the other is from the stamen of the crocus plant, which is actually purple…though if you want purple saffron, you must find the red crocus, which is extremely rare outside of the islands of…"

"How interesting." Tana yawned, no doubt exhausted after the long ski back from Floeberg. The rest of the family had gone to bed.

As he talked on, Yrund observed the trader. He didn't sound like a man who would turn her in to the Mining Wield. He sounded like a man obsessed with spices. Then again, she'd thought she could trust Gem Beard.

The fire popped and a few embers shot out the small grate. Yrund ground them out with her heel, seeing Tana had nodded off, but Ansyn reached to catch a spark as though it were still flying. He bounced the imagined light between two hands, then tossed it to Yrund, who, unsure what else to do, pretended to throw it back.

"Those marks on your palms," said the trader, watching her as they juggled the light back and forth. "Do they have some significance?"

"They're a reminder," Yrund answered, just as she'd told Mila.

"That's funny you should say that. They remind me of something too, only... I can't remember what," he said sheepishly. "Do you remember your dreams?"

"Sometimes," said Yrund. Nightmares mostly.

"I feel like I'm having a dream right now. Did you know they've started a Dream Wield? Arts and Crafts, of course. We merchants are too sensible for such things," he said wistfully.

"What do they do, steal all our dreams?"

"Ha!" Ansyn seemed to think that was funny. "No, they sell dreams. Water dreams and flying dreams...you can pick anything."

"Is that even possible?"

"I suppose that depends on the dreamer. Honestly—I suspect they employ mindturners. Still...it's a lovely idea."

Was it? It was hard to imagine the wields did anything benign.

"I sometimes wish I was born to a different wield. Not that I don't like spices, I do, but I think I would have preferred to study the places they come from, like the Culture Collectors' Wield."

"Why can't you?"

"Exactly!" said the trader, losing the spark in his excitement. He leaned toward Yrund, dark eyes enormous. "Why can't we all be free? Just think of how many streetsweepers would be zeniths of gemistry given the chance? Or gemists that would prefer to sweep streets and plant flowers? How silly is a system where no one has a choice?"

"You have more choice than most of your rabu," Yrund pointed out.

A cloud crossed Ansyn's face. "Taking rabu is the biggest

mistake the commonwield has ever made, and it will be our downfall," he prophesied.

"Ah-huh," said Tana politely in her sleep. "You don't say."

Yrund stretched, wondering if she should go to bed. "Don't do that!" she said suddenly. "It's hot!" She jumped up, pulling the trader's bare hands back from the stove.

"I lost my light."

"Here it is," said Yrund, scooping up a pretend spark for him.

"Ah," said Ansyn, bouncing the light once again. "It's like a fire moth, isn't it? Did you know black peppercorn is excellent at dispelling moths…"

Yrund listened as Ansyn went on, his knowledge of various spices and herbs seemingly unending.

"Whoo, it's warm in here," said Ansyn, interrupting himself. He peeled off his opal-buttoned coat, sweat on his brow, then his under jacket and his shirt.

Yrund bumped Tana's leg. "What's wrong?" said Tana, waking up.

The trader was on his feet now, kicking off his pants. "I'm a moth," he said, fluttering his arms and twirling about.

"Yaha," said Tana, amused until he ran toward the door. Then she was on her feet after him. "Get his coat!"

Yrund followed them outside to see Ansyn bent over, vomiting into the snow. When he finally stood back up, he pointed a wavery finger to the south. "Look!"

There across the sky a giant light storm raged, ripping the night into shreds of blues and greens, shattering the stars into wild rainbows that crashed in violent beauty from one end of the horizon to the other. Ansyn raised his arms in rapture, and as he did, Yrund began to sing.

She tried to force her mouth closed, but still the music went on, both her and not her, calling to the stars and the storm, naming the moons, an impossible cascade of overlapping notes, higher than any human could produce. When she finished, the night shimmered with the silence.

"Irsil's navel," said Tana, staring at Yrund. "And I didn't even have any."

. *' ★ ✳ . ✦ * .

WHEN TANA finally sent Yrund to bed, Yrund's sleep was filled with exploding stars and strange markets where merchants sold dreams in glowing stoppered bottles. She woke once to hear the trader weeping and Tana's soothing voice telling him that was just the Way.

. *' ★ ✳ . ✦ * .

YRUND ROSE the next morning full of worry and fear, neck and jaw tight. Why did she have to go and poison the only man in Last Lake who knew Brandul was looking for her? And what was she going to do if the trader decided to report her to the Mining Wield?

I like Trader Ansyn, said Orelia.

So it seemed did everyone else, including Humphrey. But that didn't make Yrund safe. She should leave before he had the chance. But how? She could ski, but not well yet, and Brandul was still waiting. It was fine for Humphrey to talk of killing him, but what about the rest of his bandits? And what about the Lumi? Was she really going to abandon them now?

Yrund opened her bunk's curtains to see Ansyn was sitting in the middle of the floor, shrouded in his dark coat. One by one, the Hayas stepped around him to begin their day, hushing the twins when they grew too rowdy.

"Leave Ansyn alone," said Tana.

"What's wrong with him?" asked Magrit.

"Nothing is wrong. What goes up must come down is all."

241

"Maybe he just needs us to sing to him," reasoned Little Tir.

"Later," said Tana.

"No, it's all right," said the trader, looking up with tired eyes. "I wouldn't mind some music. Maybe Anouk could play her fiddle."

"Are you sure?"

Anouk washed the rest of her breakfast down, then got her fiddle from the wall. As she tuned it, the notes hung discordant in the air, the formerly cozy house close and foreboding, and Yrund wondered if she'd had more of the mushrooms than she'd thought. Even the falling snow outside felt suffocating, the filtered light coming through the window weak and dreary.

But as the Lumi girl began to play, Yrund's muscles softened. The music was weightless, meandering, in no hurry to go or stay, drifting on the wind like the lightest fluff of pollen. Ansyn swayed softly with the notes, a faraway look in his eyes. When the song was over, he clapped.

"That's a fine tune, indeed. I've not heard its like in all my travels."

"That's because she wrote it herself," Timo said, beaming at his daughter's talent. "Are you ready for bed yet, Trader Ansyn?"

"I think I am," said the weary trader, letting Timo put an arm under him and help him to the village's guesthouse.

"Did he really take his clothes off?" asked Anouk when he was gone.

Yrund covered her face with her hands.

Mila snorted. "Troll's balls, Yrund. It's going to be a long time before anyone lets you cook again."

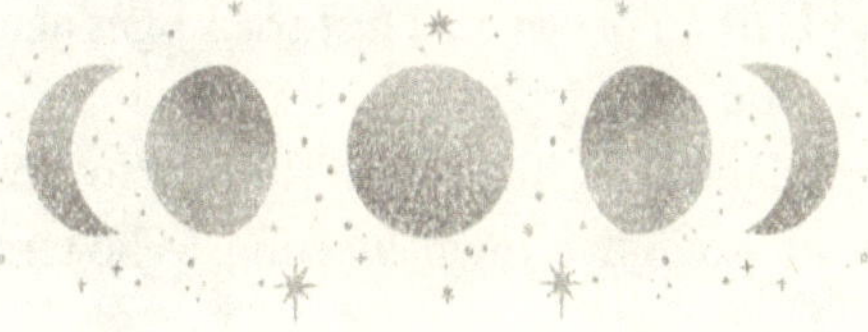

CHAPTER TWENTY-ONE

Despite his bloodshot eyes, Trader Ansyn appeared to be in good spirits the following morning, though he accepted a splash from Timo's flask in his alat when Tana wasn't looking.

Yrund kept her distance, unsure where she stood with the Asterian. The Hayas had no such reservations, serving up a breakfast feast of cloudberry cakes and fried fish, the latter supplied by Mila and Jon-Luq, who'd spent the previous day drilling a fishing hole in Last Lake's thick ice. Half the village was out there now with willow poles and stools, cheering as if it were a holiday. Not Yrund. She didn't think she'd ever go out on the ice again.

"This is better than Donkey's Day," said Ansyn, spearing another cake with his Lumi belt knife, the twin tips of which also served as a fork.

"What's Donkey's Day?" asked Anouk.

"In Asteria, the commonwielder, or high wielder as they are now insisting we call him—" Ansyn rolled his eyes. "That would be his wife's doing; Taliesin Damantine couldn't care less about titles. Anyway, he decreed that all beasts of burden must be rested at the end of every week, not just big market weeks."

"So, Donkey's Day is just Sunday?"

"Yes, except everyone actually stays close to home—like on New Moons—cooking and going to the fountains and putting business aside, a minor miracle for Asterians."

"What day is it in Asteria right now?"

"No clue," admitted Ansyn. "With Orogaudi insisting on five-day weeks and Darban on seven, I lost track ages ago."

"Is that why you're early?"

The trader glanced at Tana and Timo. "Not exactly, but all that can save for tonight's town meeting. Who's ready for first trade?"

"I am," said Anouk, bringing over her stack of glossies and a pile of handmade ribbons. "I want all of them."

"You can't have all of them," said Mila.

"Last year, Ansyn said he'd trade me one glossy for every ribbon I made," she said stubbornly. "There are twelve glossies and I have fourteen ribbons. That should be more than enough."

"And fair trade too," said Ansyn, admiring her weaving. "I'll give you store credit for the others."

"Well," said Tana, surprised.

"What about you, Tana? I've a few gems…" Ansyn pulled a small packet from his coat.

Tana unfolded the waxy paper to reveal a dozen cut stones. She held each one up to the light of the window.

Thhbt! said Orelia.

Shh. No one asked your opinion, said Yrund, patting the lump beneath her coat. She had woven the mischievous stone a new pouch the night before, in hope the closer she kept the gem, the better she might behave.

"No halestones?" Tana asked with a frown, closing the packet back up.

The trader shook his head. "I found a new seller in Orogaudi, but they were all taken outside Darban." He repeated the story about the conscripted gemjellies and other food stores. "Someone's going to be pretty surprised when they find a chunk of azulite in their tea."

"Imagine choking on a halestone—that would be ironic," mused Timo.

"Wouldn't that be a fine Way for those kicking thieves? It was bad luck to lose such a fine batch, especially with the price up so high."

"We heard about the wello shortage."

Ansyn nearly choked on his alat. "That's just a rumor, and a tightly kept one at that. How on Precios did news like that reach Lumi Land?"

"Yrund told us."

Ansyn pretended to take off a hat to her. "Poisonings and secrets. You, Yrund, would make an excellent Astrini."

"Is it true?" asked Timo.

"I believe it is," said the trader more somberly. "Which is why I came early. I overheard a bit of conversation in Darban about a caravan of brightsilver expected in the capital by the end of spring, and the only source I know for brightsilver..."

"Is Lumi Land," finished Timo. "They're preparing to leave Silver Throat as we speak. We found out the day before yesterday in Floeberg."

"So it's true. I hoped I might get here in enough time to give you some warning. I would have told you my first night..." But Yrund had poisoned him.

"We still appreciate it, Trader Ansyn. I'm sure you will have much good advice and insight as we plan for what is coming."

"Yaha, you can teach me how to footfight," said Jon-Luq.

Footfight! said Orelia.

"Me too!" Mila and Anouk cried.

Ansyn wobbled his head. "I'm not saying the Lumi shouldn't defend themselves, but if the wields believe you mean resistance, it will only be worse for you."

"Enough of this talk for now," said Tana. "We can save it for tonight. Show us what other stones you have brought. It's a shame about the wellos. We don't need any verdants, but a few more pieces of skylite would be nice."

Yrund cracked open the gempendium, which she'd spent most of the previous evening reading, and turned to the back of the book.

Verdants: One of the most common wellos—a type of Borosian jade with a clear apple-green hue. Easily confused with certain varieties of sea jade. Rules of the stone: A popular balm for the treatment of melancholia. Not to be mixed with topaz or citrine without risking mania. Other contragems include peardot, which in tandem can cause a mild blotch.

"I do have an excellent selection of rubilies," said the trader, reaching for another pocket, "but I didn't think those are much in need here. The Haya women could hardly get any better looking."

"Can I see them?" said Anouk, leaning in.

Tana stopped the trader with a firm shake of her head. "No."

"Aww," said her daughter.

Tana smoothed Anouk's braid. "Ansyn is right—you don't need any enhancers, you're already beautiful. Though perhaps a bee beryl...," she said, causing the others to titter.

Yrund turned back to the *B*'s.

Bee beryl: Golden, honey-colored topaz. Rules of the stone: Increases energy and focus, good for the shiftless and lazy.

She suppressed a smile and read on.

Caution: Not to be confused with beer beryl, which has the entirely opposite effect, or yellow beryl, also known as the beryl of laughs, which is more of a canary hue...

Ansyn put the rubilies away without opening them. "I'm afraid the price was outrageous anyway. Their color was pure pigeon's blood."

"Hey—didn't the Marquesa of Unsinn have her rubilies stolen?" asked Mila, who had been reading the posts Ansyn had brought.

Ansyn winked at her. "She did, and several fine seefires to boot. It was a fiasco, I'll tell you. Particularly with half of them showing up in the orphanage's porridge pot the next day."

"You were there when the jewels were stolen? Did you do it? Are you the Invisible Hand?" asked Jon-Luq, his cheeks burning with curiosity. "Did you take the mezmeralds? Can we see them?"

"Jon-Luq! Shame! Do you know what you're suggesting? Ansyn is not a thief. Apologize, right now."

"There's no need. I'm not offended at all," said the trader with a smile. "In fact, it's quite the compliment. The Invisible Hand, or hands as I think it must be, became quite a hero after Bittor Martzel had his mezmeralds taken at his own nameday party, including a rare red one."

"I read the Hand left gold in all the flower women's carts," said Mila.

"He did, or she did—I saw it myself."

"You were in Orogaudi, too?"

Ansyn nodded.

"But why was the Hand a hero if he's a thief?" asked Anouk.

"Because Governor Martzel, it turned out, had engineered Orogaudi's whole alat shortage. Blamed it on the Spice Wars while raking in a fortune. They ran him out of town last I heard. Not an easy place to be governor—Orogaudi."

"He kept alat from his own people? I would go to war with anyone that cut off our supply!" Mila threatened, outraged.

"You're not the only one," Ansyn said, continuing to go through his pockets for more packets of stones.

Tana ran her fingers over the new gems. "I'll leave that

anodyne for Agnetha as Katrin found hers, though that violette is tempting," she said, casting a glance at Timo, who looked affronted. "But what we need most are more halestones."

Yrund flipped back to the front of the gempendium.

Violette: aka amethyst. Purple, violet, or red-violet variety of translucent crystal. Sometimes found in conjunction with citrine, see citronette. Rules of the Stone: Prevents drunkenness when worn about the body; good for clear thinking. Caution: Not a reliable protection or antidote for many known poisons, particularly those of gem origin.

The trader packed the gems back up without complaint. "I understand. Perhaps there's something else I've brought that might be useful. It's all unpacked at the hall. You can come over for the rest of first trade whenever you like," he said, putting up his feet.

The family stampeded to get their boots on. Shopping was a rare treat when you lived off the land.

The merchant sighed and got back up, looking longingly at Timo's sytranj board. "Now is fine."

"Kids, put together all the books you want in one pile and help Ansyn carry the others."

Yrund closed the cover of the gempendium with regret. She hadn't finished the section on vagaries yet. Or the mindturners. According to Barthalow Damantine, there were at least six stones that could make the wearer hear or see things that weren't there, from susurrus to iaspis to hiraeth to moonsstone... If she could have just learned a little more about what Orelia was, whether she had any practical uses, for instance. Not for her own gain, of course. She was still gem shy. But if there was any reason to use a gem, surely it was against Brandul.

Then again, Yrund sighed, perhaps it was for the best. After what had happened with the little woodwin, Orelia might do more harm than good. She didn't know anything about using gems. She was better off with a plain old rock. At least she could throw it.

"Fine book, isn't it?" said Ansyn. "I can make you a good deal on it if you want to keep it—let's see, what did I pay? Forty something carobs times the latest exchange rate," he said, quoting numbers rapidly. "Converted to moons, at twelve moons to a sun…no commission as it's a cousin of the Hayas…" He paused to do the figures in his head as Yrund ran her fingers across her hands, multiplying.

"Sixty-one," said Yrund at the same time the trader did. The family gaped at her. "But I haven't got any money."

The trader pulled on his beard. "What's thirty-eight times seventy-two?"

Yrund added the sums across her knuckles.

"Two thousand seven hundred and thirty-six."

Ansyn whistled. "Not many folks know how to do finger counting anymore. Only merchants and tidecharters. And you can write, too?"

"Yes, my grandmother taught all of us to do our letters."

The trader grinned. "Then, if Tana can spare you later, I think that gempendium might be yours."

THAT NIGHT, all of Last Lake gathered in the lantern-lit town hall to welcome the Asterian trader back. The festivities started off with winter songs by the village's children, though many of the adults could not resist singing along too—nor could Orelia, who was humming so loudly in Yrund's ears she was sure the whole hall could hear.

"Thank you. That was beautiful. Good Way to you all," said Ansyn, taking time to greet the town elders individually.

"I've been coming to trade in Last Lake for seven years now," Ansyn said, standing before the gathering in Lumi coat and pants that were embroidered with sled dogs up the sides. "Not an easy journey to explain to my fellow Asterians, some of whom have never been outside their own wield's gates. 'Why go so far down south?' they ask. 'Nothing but meat eaters and snow,' they say. Now, you know how I feel about meat." The crowd laughed. "And I don't mind the snow, but the real reason I keep coming back is because of the friendships I've made. No people on Precios are more hospitable than the Lumi, and it's true, none buy more alat from me either." The crowd laughed even harder. "Speaking of which, there are still some crates left, but not for long. So stock up while you can."

The trader went on to report the news and gossip from the world outside. Interruptions were frequent with the Lumi throwing out questions or making a smart remark, which the Asterian took in good humor. The conversation switched from Lumi to Trade Tongue and back again, sometimes midsentence with Ansyn nearly as fluent in both.

"What's this year's puzzle?" someone yelled.

Orelia perked up. *What's a puz-zel?*

It's a game, said Yrund. *Like keeps.*

Puzzzzle. Puzzlllle, said Orelia, enjoying the sound of the word. Each time she said it, Yrund's head buzzed.

Stop! That tickles.

Ansyn smoothed his beard. "Ah, the puzzle, yes! This year is a riddle. Are you ready? What has a table but no chairs, has a rainbow but no rain, and is brilliant without a brain?"

He repeated it once more, then gave the crowd a chance to mull it over.

Yrund whispered her guess to Mila, but her friend was asleep, head resting on her furry hood.

"I have some more serious news too, I'm sorry to say. I have not arrived early just to trade. As you already are aware, Asteria has a wello shortage. And possibly a shortage of several other gems too if my sources are to be believed. They are scrambling to open other mines, but in the meantime, the price of brightsilver is soaring. No surprise when it makes a second-water stone work as well as a first-water. But it means the Mining Wield is moving to control the flow of brightsilver, and Lumi Land is both the nearest source and the richest."

"Hence the silver rush," said Didri.

"We don't need an Asterian to come tell us of the trouble we're in," said Pir Jaq loudly in Lumi. "So you can turn right back around. Unless, of course, that's not why you're here? How do we know you haven't come to spy for the Mining Wield? See what we're planning, then report it all back to your masters? All the while charging us double for your wares."

Old Nicolai called for Pir Jaq to be quiet. "You don't know what you're saying. Anysn's been coming here since he was a boy. Same as his uncle did. Our fight is not with the Green Wield."

"Maybe he's been spying on us this whole time," intoned Pir Jaq from around his old pipe.

The crowd wasn't laughing now. Yrund was still getting to know the townspeople, but Pir Jaq was by far her least favorite, though, according to Mila, he was no more popular with his neighbors. He'd been feuding with Didri since they were kids and had the habit of naming his sled dogs after neighbors he was mad at.

"I would have the same reservations in your shoes," said Ansyn, hands open wide. "You do not need to include me in any conversation you do not wish to—I will not be offended— nor will I stay if my presence is a source of strain. As for prof- iting off your suffering, that is the last thing I desire. If the Mining Wield continues its hostilities against the Lumi, it will hurt my business here, not increase it. Taliesin Damantine's father negotiated the trade accord with the Lumi in good faith, and it pains me more than anyone to see that goodwill destroyed. The commonwield is only made weaker when Asteria seeks to cheat friends. To that end, I have brought extra supplies this year as a gift to the town, including medicine and maps."

"We appreciate you coming early to warn us," said Didri, cutting off whatever Pir Jaq had planned to say next. "As you appreciate the injustice that we face. That trade accord has not been honored for the last four years. We rarely see a single trader besides yourself. Or any of the gemists or journey healers we were promised—much less any of the profit from the silver that the Mining Wield takes. We've had enough. It's time to fight back!"

This pronouncement was met with stern cheers, including from Mila, who was not asleep after all, it seemed.

"I don't disagree with you," said Ansyn. "But I've seen how it goes in other lands. And some of you are seeing the beginnings here—any dissent will just be met with more troops and more violence."

"This isn't how it was supposed to be," said Tana, speaking for the first time. "We were supposed to be partners, not be pillaged. Nothing in the treaty gives Asteria dominion over our land. Are we not a sovereign nation?"

The trader nodded as he listened. "They are asking the same thing in most of the Outlands. Yours is not the only treaty that has been broken. Taliesin Damantine is a good man, but he has taken little interest in the responsibilities of his position. Truth be told, his wife and brother do most of the decision making at the High Seat. Many of us suspect he has been gemmed, but that is not an easy thing to prove, and with the wields getting what they want, few would bother to try. This fight cannot be won head-on. Your numbers are too small—the Lumi would be destroyed in a prolonged conflict, especially while the Mining Wield can pay mercenaries like the Sea Hammers to fight for them."

"Yaha," said Agnetha, who stood at that back of the hall, arms folded. "But what choice do we have? We cannot let them continue to take our brothers and sisters, to steal our livelihoods."

"There are many types of resistance," said the trader. "Sometimes it is the long game that must be played. As we freewielders are doing in Asteria."

"What if there was a shorter game? What if the Mining Wield decided to leave on its own?" asked Timo, standing up. "A zugzwang."

"What do you mean?"

"Like in sytranj," explained Hinri, understanding.

"Ah. You mean force the enemy into failure," said Ansyn, steepling his long fingers together as he leaned in to hear more.

Zuga-zwang, said Orelia. Yrund had only lately started playing sytranj with Jon-Luq. Her father had tried to teach her many times, but Yrund preferred morrya, a finger-counting game popular with her cousins.

"That's exactly what I mean," said Timo. "What if it was the wield's own soldiers that refused to stay? Let's not forget it's a hardship posting already, and they've only been here in the summers before. They'll be up against blizzards, white bears, endless days without suns… Who's to say they couldn't be pushed to crack?"

"The memluks are a lot of superstitious fellows," said Timo. "When I was in the silver mine last year, they were afraid of every sort of *spookli* and ghost, even eye moons. They'd somehow heard the story about the lonely yowi."

"The lonely yowi?" repeated Ansyn. "I don't think I've heard that one yet."

"It's a good one for scaring the kiddies. Come over later, and I'll tell it to ya over a cup of flume," said Old Nicolai. "Might not sleep after you do, though."

"Well, if the Mining Wield's men are scared of yowis, why don't we give them one, then?" said Ansyn, looking straight at Mila in her shaggy fur suit.

"I'll do it!" said Mila.

"No, if anyone's going to do it, it will be me," said Timo. "You're not the only one with a yowi suit."

"It might work once or twice, but if you go out too often, they'll start to catch on," warned the trader. "And it will take more than a few yowi sightings to get the Mining Wield to leave."

"Yaha, it would take a flume shortage," said Hinri.

"That's not a bad idea," said Timo. "There are a thousand ways to sabotage the memluks without them knowing. Some we already know," he said, winking at Hinri.

"Like mushrooms in their soup," said Mila.

Yrund blushed and slid down in her chair while the Lumi guffawed. The story of the mushroom soup hadn't taken long to spread through the village.

"Laugh all you want," said Pir Jaq in Lumi, standing up. "This young *cousin*—how do you know she didn't poison the Hayas' soup on purpose? Where did she come from? You know nothing about her."

Shocked silence fell over the hall as the villagers' eyes turned to Yrund.

"You forget, it was not the Hayas that Yrund accidentally poisoned, but me—the Asterian," said Ansyn.

"Maybe you're in it together."

"Yrund is a victim of the wields, not a conspirator," said Tana, coming to Yrund's defense.

"Be that as it may," said Pir Jaq, "she's not one of us, however you dress her up. You're all fools sharing our plans with foreigners as if they were friends."

Orelia hissed in Yrund's ear.

"Bog you, Pir Jaq," said Mila, standing up to face him. "You're just a coward."

Pir Jaq shrugged. "I'm only saying what everyone else won't. Neither belongs here. If she's not a spy," he said, pointing his pipe at Yrund, "then she's a fugitive. What do you think they'll do to us when they find we've been keeping her?"

Jon-Luq stood up now too, facing Pir Jaq, fists clenched. "What do you think we'll do to *them* if they try to take her?"

"Yrund is part of our family now," said Timo. "As is Trader Ansyn, and we'll not hear any more nonsense about either of them. So if you don't have something useful to contribute, you can be on your way."

"Don't say I didn't warn you," Pir Jaq said and stomped out.

"Bah," said Old Nicolai. "My son's a *vandradolt*. And wrong— don't any of you listen to him."

Someone sitting behind Yrund patted her shoulder, which only made Yrund feel worse. Pir Jaq was right about one thing— if she was caught, she wouldn't be the only one the Mining Wield would punish. Misery filled her. She should never have stayed. As soon as she could walk, she should have left.

The hall swelled with voices, but Timo's cut through them. "There are real enemies we need to prepare for. I would ask the children to leave now so the adults can talk freely."

Predictably, the Haya children complained the loudest.

"Why shouldn't we hear what you're planning? This affects us too, you know," said Anouk.

"Because there are greater dangers than losing our silver. The less you know, the safer our real treasures are."

"You mean the herds?" asked Anouk, perplexed.

"He means us, you dummy," explained Mila.

"Why don't we just throw all the silver in the ocean?" said Anouk. "The Mining Wield would go away, then."

Yrund felt the back of her mind tickle. Something Humphrey had said…something about the silver… *It's the quality of the silver that gets to Asteria that determines the mine's worth.* "It's the quality of the silver that gets to Asteria that determines the mine's worth," she repeated out loud.

"What's that?" asked Mila.

"It's the quality of the silver that gets to Asteria that determines the mine's worth," said Yrund once more.

"Wait—that's genius," said Ansyn.

"You're talking about a swap, aren't you?" said Agnetha.

"It wouldn't be easy," said Timo. "Someone would have to distract the memluks while someone else traded the sleds out."

"For what, though?" asked Hinri.

"Plain silver, of course," said Ansyn. "So it looks like the brightsilver has finally played out. What does the silversmith say? Can it be done?"

"It could," said Didri, eyes glinting to match the locket around her neck. "The blacksmiths would have to make us molds that match those at Silver Throat so the bricks look just the same." She looked over at Lotti and her husband, the village's part-time smiths, who nodded as if they agreed. "Then we'd melt down a mixture of the plain silver with the bright. Iron would be too obvious..."

"We'd have to do it in stages," added Hinri. "Or it would look too suspicious. Make each shipment half the strength of the one before. They wouldn't be sure, at first, but as the shipments got weaker, their profits would drop."

"Don't forget, their margins are already tight. It's an expensive journey to get to Lumi Land over land *or* water—less than half of Asteria's ships get past the Silk Islands anymore. The Silk Sparrows have amassed a formidable pirate fleet in the west. And the wield's caravans will hardly fare better on the Gem Road. Not with the bandits growing more bold."

Yrund's heart gave a hopeful thump. If there was no silver to transport, there would be no need for a road through the Sky Country.

"A silver swap?" said Tana, considering. "It would take every village from Sea Throat to Windmarket to pull it off."

"Yaha," said Old Nicolai. "But it could be done!"

"Combined with the pressure against the memluks..." Timo

looked around at the other Lumi. "Why not? Better a secret war we might win than an outright one we will surely lose."

"A secret war will take twice the planning," cautioned Ansyn. "And in the end, it will come with the same dangers if we're caught."

"*We?*" said Hinri, clapping his friend's shoulder.

"You can't think I'm going to let you fight alone," said Ansyn. "Who would buy all my alat if you lose?"

"I want to fight too!" said Jon-Luq.

"And I," said Agnetha.

"And I," said Hinri.

"And I," said Mila.

"And I," said Old Lir, getting shakily to his feet. "You're not leaving me out of it."

"Or me either," said Old Nicolai. His friend helped him up.

Yrund felt herself rise. This was her fight too, whatever Pir Jaq said. It was time to stand up to the wields. For the Lumi. And for the Sky Country.

"I will fight," she said, adding her voice to her friends.

Fight! said Orelia. *Fight, fight!*

"And me!" declared Anouk, taking Yrund's arm.

"Quiet!" hushed Tana. "This is still a secret war."

"I will fight," mock-whispered Timo.

"I will fight, too," whispered another voice, and then another until the whole hall hissed with the sound. "I will fight," the voices whispered as one.

CHAPTER TWENTY-TWO

Since the night at the town hall, the children had been barred from village meetings. Tana would only say they had enough to do since school had started up again. Lotti, the village teacher, taught the morning lessons before she was off to her family's blacksmith shop in the afternoons to melt down silver with her husband and Didri—an undertaking the children weren't supposed to know about. But Last Lake was too small to keep many secrets for long. It was Ansyn who taught the evening classes, which were attended by adults and children alike, covering everything from memluk history and culture to the economics of the gem trade. How such a young man could know so much still boggled Yrund. Some lessons even included demonstrations on footfighting, everyone's favorite. The few short hours of wan suns in the middle of the day were saved for the Lumi to practice for the annual competitions in Windmarket. Winter Fair sounded much like the Sky Games to Yrund, only with skis instead of horses, and ice carving instead of wrestling. Today, though, the Hayas had skipped their usual activities to watch Timo test out his new yowi costume.

"I don't see why I can't be the yowi," pouted Mila. "I'm taller than you are."

"Watch yourself," said Timo, though it was true. Mila had at least six inches on her father. Timo Haya was an exceptionally fit man of great endurance and renowned marksmanship, but like most of the Lumi who'd lived through the Worst Winters, the elder Haya was being surpassed in height by his children. "It might sound fun to run around in the woods pretending to be a yowi, but this isn't a game, Mila. This is deadly serious. Those wield men are trained to kill people. It will require the utmost subtlety to pull this off right."

It might not have been a game, but the Lumi's enthusiasm for the project was obvious. The neighbors had contributed their extra scraps of fur and leather, and Ansyn had donated needles and thread. The Hayas had been working on the task after classes each night while Anouk read to them about the adventures of the Invisible Hand. Now, a week later, the get-up was finally finished.

Katrin and Hinri had constructed a light frame of thin bent wood to rest on Timo's shoulders, making him appear nearly eight feet tall and almost half as wide. On top of that was an enormous fur jacket with slits for Timo's arms and holes mid-chest for his eyes. The hood was stuffed with feathers and sewn shut, with little ears sticking out at what Yrund considered absurd angles on the sides. Underneath it all, Timo would wear his fur hunting suit for warmth. Yrund could not imagine what Humphrey would think of the poor caricature. The legs looked ridiculously short in proportion to the rest, which Mila did not fail to point out.

"If you want to be useful, you can help me get this blasted thing on," said Timo, his head stuck in one of the suit's arms.

It took two of them to help him on with the top of the costume, which barely fit between the rafters. Sikka barked, while Little Tir ran behind the curtain. "What do you think?" Timo asked, his voice muffled from within the layers.

"I don't think it's big enough," said Mila.

"I think it's too big," said Hinri at the same time.

"Well, which is it?"

The family shrugged at each other. "How should we know?" asked Katrin. "Yowis aren't actually real, are they?"

"Don't tell the memluks that."

Yrund stared up, trying to gauge where Humphrey would have reached. The shoulders were all wrong, but she supposed it didn't matter.

"Now for the true test..." Once they had released Timo from the top half of the suit, they followed him outside, where he tried out the snowshoes he had modified with leather pads. "How do the tracks look?"

"Those just look like a bear's," said Jon-Luq. "If he had two right feet."

"Huh," said Timo, disappointed.

"Maybe they should be wider," said Hinri. So Timo bound another layer to the soles.

"Now they look like an enormous goose," said Anouk, watching her father step around the yard for the second time. Sikka showed her opinion by peeing in one of the tracks.

"I give up for today. I've got snowdeer to see to," sighed Timo. "Anybody else want to give it a try? Yrund?" he said, catching her running a glove across a track. "You look like you have an idea."

"I, um—" She'd sworn a debt bond to the woodwins to keep their existence a secret. Then again, the Lumi didn't actually believe in woodwins—or yowis as they called them. It wasn't really breaking her promise to help impersonate a myth, was it? She took the snowshoe Timo was holding out to her.

After all, the woodwins didn't want the wields in this part of the world any more than the Lumi did. But she was going to have some explaining to do to Humphrey.

That evening after dinner and Ansyn's class, Yrund examined Timo's work. Humphrey's feet were not flat—that she knew. Also, the toes Timo had fashioned were not even close to long enough. She redrew the proportions with a wedge of charcoal, making the front of the feet wider and the heels narrower. Then she cut pieces of leather scraps, layering them so the pads curved in like a real foot.

"Yaha, that's pretty good," said Mila, impressed.

But attaching the new soles to the snowshoes wasn't nearly as easy. Mila offered her thread and needle, and they stayed up until late punching holes through the leather pieces so they could be bound together.

In the morning, Yrund examined the feet again. Something was still missing. She tried to remember Humphrey's feet and the prints he left in the snow. Then it came to her. Claws. The feet needed claws. She rolled pieces of hard leather and trimmed them at an angle, testing them with her thumb.

"Bog it!"

"What?" asked Mila from around a bun.

"The claws aren't hard enough," Yrund complained. "They'll never leave marks in the snow."

"I can make you some glue," said Mila.

"Really?"

"Sure—do you want pitch or bone?"

"I don't know. What do you think?"

"Bone should do it."

When Yrund got a whiff of the concoction Mila brought back from her tanning camp late that afternoon, she regretted her choice. "That's disgusting!" she said, holding her nose.

"Just hold your breath."

Pee-eww! said Orelia.

Yrund had to admit the stinking glue did work. By the next day, the leather had stiffened, adding strength to not just the claws, but the entire foot.

"Now *that's* an improvement," said Timo, taking the snow-shoes outside to try on. After a few yards, he reversed to examine the prints he was making. "You know, I feel like I've seen this track before," he said, his brows creased.

Yrund stiffened. Maybe she'd done too good a job.

"You know, my grandparents actually believed in the yowis. They used to leave offerings for them outside on full moons to keep them from stealing things."

"Like fat little boys," whispered Mila to Little Tir, who as usual was at her side. Despite her tales, or perhaps because of them, he could not resist her.

"Well, Yrund," said Timo, looking at the trail of prints, "I'm convinced. Let's just hope the wield men will buy it."

✴ ✶ ✴ ✴ ✴

"Did you enjoy the lesson?" Ansyn asked Yrund after classes that night, for Yrund had madly been scribbling notes onto her slate.

"Uh...yaha?" said Yrund, who hadn't meant to linger. She hadn't been alone with the trader once since the evening she'd poisoned him. He'd been friendly enough, especially after standing up for her at the town hall meeting, but a reserve of distrust remained. He was still a wield man. And unless the soup had magically wiped his memory, he still knew Brandul was looking for her.

"The applied mathematics of airship lift is marvelous, isn't it? I was afraid I was losing the rest of the students," said Ansyn. "But you seemed to get it."

Not really, thought Yrund, who hadn't been taking the notes for herself. It was only when Ansyn mentioned rudders that she'd remembered Humphrey's request and started paying attention.

"That reminds me—if you still want that gempendium, I could

still use some help with my account books. Maybe you can come over at lunchtime tomorrow?"

So Yrund was back the next day. The piles of goods the trader had brought were quickly dwindling from his end of the hall, but the Lumi hadn't cleaned him out entirely—there were a few bolts of fabric, one or two bottles of ink, a few gems, and a scatter of small wield-made baubles and toys. But it was the colorful spices she found most intriguing—powders and leaves and flakes and petals, all perfuming the drafty room with their exotic essences. She sniffed at a golden corkscrewed chili that had fallen off its pile.

"You're really not mad about the soup?" she asked, watching Ansyn's face for any sign of irritation.

"You mean about the rabbit? I admit it was tastier than I thought it would be. I mean, I eat meat when I have to—a trader's life is not always predictable. But rabbit?" He put his fingers up over his ears and twitched his nose.

Yrund looked at him as if he'd lost his mind. "I meant the flying mushrooms."

"Oh." Ansyn waved a hand. "No need to be sorry for that! I had a tremendous vision the other night—Asteria as it could be, free and open. No rabu, no wars, no birth binds... Do you know half of the wields' inventions never even get to market? They're so afraid it will be stolen, no one gets to enjoy them at all. Ah, well, listen to me going on. Do you want some alat?" The trader placed a hissing pot on top of one of the hall's iron stoves.

Next to the stove was a table laid with books and a sytranj set, and around the table were several chairs for customers. While the pot returned to a boil, Ansyn gestured for Yrund to hand him her belt mug, then began opening tins.

Yrund watched with interest as the trader worked. Ansyn had a carved wooden whisk that he spun between his palms, frothing the alat in the pot until it foamed. Then he poured it back and forth between the mugs to cool it, increasing the distance with each pour until it was hard to tell if the iridescent liquid was running up or down, as if he were pulling it rather than pouring.

"Where is alat from anyway?" Yrund asked the trader when he finished the pour with a flourish and set her mug before her.

"It comes from Alat, naturally. That's a peninsula in the Long Sea," he said. "The green portion comes from the Bindo region up in the hills, and the purple comes from the lowlands along the coast. You have to buy the two separately because the clans that produce them are always at war. Except when they're fleecing the rest of us."

"Is it true nobody knows what alat is made from?"

"I wouldn't say *nobody*," Ansyn said with a twinkle. "Now"—he tapped an open ledger on the table, full of scribbles and numbers, well worn around the edges—"let me show you why you're here. It should be simple enough for a girl that can finger-count."

ACCOUNTING FOR THE TRADER, however, turned out to be much harder than he'd made it sound. Yrund was sure of her numbers, but some of Ansyn's other bookkeeping tricks still weren't making any sense. Yrund's father had taught her finger counting as soon as she was old enough to ride a horse. Someday, he had promised, he would take her with him on his trading trips. She wondered where he was now—with the Windtraders? Or back in the Sky Country? Was he looking for his family? With effort, Yrund pulled her mind back to the task at hand.

"So you're saying I add up all the marks that represent the spices and other Green Wield stuff you sold?" she asked the trader.

"You have it. Plus anything I've sold for the Arts and Crafts Wield, like books or cotton. Then subtract that from my costs, right here in this column, to see my profits."

Zzzzzzz. Orelia was already bored with the job. Yrund

thumped the neck pouch in which the stone was hidden, forgetting Ansyn couldn't hear.

"So I don't do anything with these other columns," Yrund went on. "The ones with the little carrot things?"

"Nope."

"Why?" Though even as she asked, she was beginning to understand.

The trader tilted his head side to side in a noncommittal way. "There might be a few items I trade in that are not exactly considered within a spice merchant's purview."

"Like the gemstones you showed Tana?"

Ansyn took a sip of alat and leaned back in his chair, assessing her.

"For instance."

"Why aren't you allowed to sell gems?"

"I was born to the Green Wield. Lucky for me, I love my work, but in Asteria you do not get to choose your profession. Not unless you have an extraordinary talent or an even bigger wallet. That means you are not allowed to do business outside the wield you were born to, not without special writs and permissions. As a merchant I, of course, have many cross-wield charters. Just not with the Mining Wield."

"Why not?"

"The Mining Wield controls the price of every gemstone in Asteria. If they say a pomegarnet of this weight and that color costs such and such, then it is so everywhere regardless of need. In fact, the greater the need, the higher the price. If there's an outbreak of pox, the price of halestones is doubled."

"Then why would anyone buy from the Asterians if the prices aren't fair?"

"No competition. The Mining Wield owns every mine in the Aeries and the Jaggedies and is expanding farther every day. When you control the supply of a good, you get to set the price."

Yrund frowned. No wonder her family was gem shy.

"But you sell the Lumi gems anyway."

"I admit to evening things up here and there. Even the wield born feel constrained by the rules sometimes," Ansyn acknowledged. "They say there's more for sale in Asteria's backmarkets than in its shops."

"So what do you do with all the profit you've made that you can't declare?"

"You're asking a man for his trade secrets? You're obviously not from Asteria." Yrund started to apologize, but Ansyn stopped her. "I'm a freewielder. I'm all for sharing trade secrets. What would *you* do with the extra profit?" he asked, turning the question on her.

"Buy more gems, I guess? They'd be easy to hide."

"Spoken like a true smuggler," Ansyn said with a smile.

"Who's a true smuggler?" asked an apparition right beside them, covered in white fur and carrying a lunch pail.

Ansyn jumped. "Space apes, Mila! Don't do that. You're as bad as a Yavani, sneaking up on people like that."

Mila pulled down her hood. "Ama sent lunch over," she said, setting down the pail so she could rifle through the trader's wares. A spool of blue thread caught her eye. "You haven't got any white, have you?" she asked, testing its strength.

"Look in that trunk behind you," said Ansyn, swirling the last of his alat.

Mila dug through wound cards of ribbon and trim until she found the spool she was looking for. "Will you add it to my tab?" she asked.

"Of course," said Ansyn, without making any move to do so.

Mila pulled up her hood again and padded silently back out. The trader watched her go. Yrund noticed he was wearing traditional Lumi garb again and looked completely at home. They ate the lunch Mila had brought—sour black bread filled with pickled cabbage and sausage for her and cabbage and creamy snowdeer cheese for the trader. Ansyn sprinkled a heavy pinch of dried green leaves across the top. "Dill," he said, offering Yrund some.

She waited until he'd taken a bite before trying a pinch for herself. Good manners did not mean good intentions, but the herb tasted harmless, even good.

After their meal, Yrund returned to Ansyn's books. Unlike Orelia, she enjoyed the work. It was not as good as being out with her goats, by any means, but there was an orderliness to compiling numbers that soothed her feeling the rest of the world was in chaos, though the hall grew colder as the afternoon wore on. Yrund scooted her chair closer to the fire, stretching her legs out toward the warmth. No matter how the rest of her felt, the metal snakes around her ankles always stayed cold. She put her quill down when she thought the trader wasn't looking to rub at her boots.

"Tana told me about the ouroborus."

"The what?" said Yrund dumbly.

"Your anklets. May I see them?" Ansyn leaned toward her, elbows on knees.

Yrund hesitated. It didn't seem right showing the proof of her desertion to an Asterian.

"Sorry, that was rude of me," he said, leaning back again. "I wouldn't want others gawking at them either."

Yrund let out a puff of air. It wasn't as if he didn't know about the snakes. And hadn't he just been admitting his own crimes against the wields to her?

Checking around anxiously, Yrund unlaced her boot and rolled down her thick sock.

Ansyn sucked in his breath just as Tana had done. The metal snakes with their squinting gem eyes looked so unlike the suns-loving snakes of the Sky Country, who preferred to mind their own business, and who Yrund had always enjoyed seeing stretched across a warm rock.

"So it's true. Even children are being condemned. What has Asteria come to?"

"Do you know how to take them off?" asked Yrund.

"They are not usually meant to be removed. Not while you're alive."

Yrund pulled her sock back up. Just as she had feared. She would never be rid of them, then. Marked for life as a possession of those she hated most.

"That doesn't mean there isn't a way," said Ansyn. "The zeniths made keys to put them on, and the same keys can take them off. Someone, somewhere, will have one, probably in Wyn or Asteria…"

"Not that they'll just hand over to a rabu."

Ansyn wobbled his head, neither a yes or a no. "Don't forget. In Asteria, everyone has a price."

A price she didn't have the money to pay, thought Yrund as she watched the trader get up to refill their mugs.

"Or you might take a page from the Invisible Hand and just steal a key."

Yes! said Orelia. *I like the Invisible Hand. You should get a sword too.*

But Yrund's only experience stealing anything, apart from her mother's cheese stores, was taking Orelia from the mine, and that hadn't even been intentional. Not at first, at least. She settled back glumly.

"Here," said Ansyn, handing Yrund a large transparent stone the color of dark honey along with her mug of alat. "Take this for a while," he said. "You could use it."

"I don't think I—"

"It's just a topaz, if that—the price was a little too good to be true. But, you never know…"

The golden-brown stone was cool and smooth, faceted on one side, flat on the other. "Just hold it?" she asked nervously, wondering if this was some sort of payback for the soup. A customer arrived, distracting the trader's attention, and unsure what else to do, she dropped the gem in her pocket and went back to work.

After a scatter of villagers had come and gone, Ansyn came back to the table, opening up a red embossed tin of flecked biscuits and putting it on the table between them. "Cookie?" he asked, munching. The biscuit was rich and buttery and smelled strongly of licorice—her favorite.

What what? asked Orelia, waking up.

It's a cookie, said Yrund, reading the label.

Mmm, cookies. More, please.

Yrund returned to the account books, slightly more hopeful. Why couldn't she steal a key someday? She was small and fast, wasn't she?

"Please forgive my prying," said Ansyn, wiping some crumbs from his beard. "But how on Precios did you wind up as a mine rabu?"

"We got in the way," said Yrund. "My people, that is."

"Who are your people? Your Lumi isn't too bad, but I detect a hint of something else there—the Jaggedies, maybe?"

"I'm from the Sky Country," said Yrund with both pride and reticence. It felt odd sharing so much with an Asterian.

"The Sky Country?" Ansyn repeated, startled. "Your people's weavings are famous. Surely the wields would indenture a family like yours if you crossed them, not send them to the mines? With your talents, you'd be worth much more to them wield-bound."

"Wield-bound?"

"A prisoner to a wield, but working in your own trade. Asterians put a high price on craftsmanship. Many wields will even allow talented rabu to advance. The zenith of the Instrument Makers' Wield started bound. The memluks are another example —no one can match their fighting skills, and those that survive often retire quite wealthy."

Yrund was only following part of what Ansyn was saying.

"Would they keep the whole family or just those that could weave?"

"Just those that had a craft they wanted. But in your land, that's the women, is it not?"

Yrund been wearing her father's hat that awful night when the raiders came. She touched her short hair. "I think they thought I was a boy. Not that it would have made a difference. I barely know how to weave. I'm the eldest child—my place is with the herds."

"A shepherd would have been little use to the Mining Wield. Not with this wello shortage." He gave a small sigh.

But that was not what Yrund was concerned about any longer. "Are you saying there's a chance my mother might be in Asteria with my sisters? And my aunt, too?"

"If they are weavers, you can put your gems on it."

Could it be? After all this time not knowing where anyone was. A flush of hope went through Yrund. "You're going back to Asteria, aren't you?"

"I am," the trader said with a tilt of his head. "After Winter Fair. But via Siroc."

That was too close to Smeralgdus for Yrund's comfort. "What if I wanted to go straight from Windmarket?" Ansyn was a smuggler. Surely he knew a way.

"You'd do best to join one of the camel caravans. Traveling alone would be far too dangerous—with the sthaga and all."

"What are sthaga?"

"Bandits that strangle travelers in their sleep."

"What about these?" she asked, indicating the snakes around her ankles.

"It's a risk. But not everyone that travels the Gem Road reports to the wield. With the right introduction, someone like the Korundum would hire you on."

"And you're sure my family is there?"

"Not at all. It's likely if they're weavers, but nothing is certain with the Mining Wield anymore. Even if they are, you can't just walk into their wield hall and break them out. You would need a plan. Or better yet, something to trade."

The hall went quiet for a moment as they each sat with their own thoughts.

A plan to break them out… Yrund put her quill down again, suddenly remembering what Humphrey had told her outside the Hayas' the other night. "You haven't heard anything about a mine break at Devil's Crown, have you?"

Ansyn let the feet of his tipped-back chair return to the floor. "You mean up in the Aeries? Sure, it's all over the pigeon posts. They turned themselves in to the ambassador of the Mining Wield in Darban."

So it was true! "And then what?"

"The ambassador sent most of them on to Smeralgdus. Ungrateful fool. Though you know…there was one more ship. Crashed outside Unsinn and made quite a stir in the posts. Not many survivors."

"Where are they now?"

"Darban most likely. The wield sent a troop to round them up."

Yrund pushed her chair back from the table.

"Have you told Agnetha any of this?"

"No, we've been busy with other topics…," said the trader, digging in the cookie tin. "It's extremely unlikely there would have been any Lumi on those ships, not so far north."

"There might have been one," said Yrund, running out the door.

CHAPTER TWENTY-THREE

Yrund found Agnetha in her house, the door wide open to the frigid breeze.

The healer was wearing goggles, a mask, and long gloves and holding a glowing purple stone between a pair of tongs.

"Stay back," she told Yrund without looking up. "I'll be with you in a minute."

Yrund waited, watching the woman lower the purple gem to an ingot of what looked like a bar of brightsilver.

Jon-Luq came up behind Yrund. "Wows! What's going on?"

"Don't know, but we can't go in," she told him, blocking the door with her arm so the boy couldn't creep closer. By now she knew Jon-Luq's touch-first, ask-questions-later approach to life.

"Is that nepenthe?" he asked, breathing over her shoulder.

Yrund tried to recall nepenthe from the gempendium but couldn't remember what it did.

As Agnetha touched the stone to the silver, a wisp of purple mist swirled suddenly up, and Orelia began to whistle.

"Get back!" the healer yelled, the mist curling up and around her head. Then her face went slack. The tongs fell from her grip, the nepenthe bouncing off the reddish wood table and onto the floor, its purple fog spreading like fire.

Without thinking, Yrund ran inside, catching the glowing stone in her bare hand. She was looking around for where to put it when Jon-Luq called out: "In this!" The boy grabbed the wood box off the table as a puff of purple mist hit him in the face.

"Troll's balls…," he said right before his eyes turned purple.

"What in space are you guys doing?" asked Ansyn, bursting through the door.

"Throw me that box Jon-Luq just dropped! Quickly!"

"Is that nepenthe?" asked Ansyn, goggling just as Jon-Luq had done. "You can't touch that!" With that he raced straight for her, trying to knock the gem away. "Drop it! Drop it!" Now the hypnotic mist was enveloping him too, loosening the trader's grip as he forgot what he'd been doing. He stood there transfixed like the healer and Jon-Luq, the mist wrapping around them all like tentacles.

"Bogging hell!" Yrund wrenched the nepenthe away and retrieved the box herself, locking the misting stone inside and covering it with an upside-down pot.

Then, one by one, she dragged the others out into the fresh air.

"Agnetha!" she said, shaking the healer's arm. "Can you hear me?"

They all just ignored her, staring into nothing.

"Agnetha!" she yelled again. She reached up to pull the goggles off the healer's head and slap her face lightly. "Are you all right? Look at me!"

"Hello, Yrund," said Agnetha, green-gray eyes clearing. "What's happened? What's wrong with Jon-Luq?"

The boy's mouth hung open as if he were trying to recall something. Orelia chuckled. Troll's balls.

"Um—you were doing an experiment of some sort. With a purple stone? Jon-Luq said it was nepenthe. There was fog coming off it, and then you two got weird and then Ansyn came—"

"Nepenthe? What was I doing with nepenthe?"

"I don't know. Something with some silver, it looked like."

"I see…," said Agnetha, shaking her head as if she didn't. "But where is the nepenthe?"

"I put it in the box that was on the table. I didn't know what else to do…"

"You touched it? With your bare hands?"

Yrund nodded.

"And you remember doing it?"

"Yaha."

"That defies all reason. You could have forgotten your own mother's face!"

Agnetha examined the house, opening windows. Seeing the purple mist was clear, she came back out and took Jon-Luq's arm. "It should be fine now. Bring Ansyn too will you? We'll have some alat, and you can tell me just what stupid thing I've done."

Yrund gently slapped the trader's face as she had done with Agnetha. "Ansyn?"

"Hello," said the trader, his eyes blinking. "What are you doing here?" He smiled, and she could feel his soft beard. She pulled her hands away.

"Well, that must not have gone as I had planned," said Agnetha when they were all seated around her table with hot mugs. She stripped off her long gloves and set them beside her. "What a fool I am… What day is it, then? Let's see how much I've forgotten."

"It's Donkey's Day," said Jon-Luq, as if he'd just woken up.

"What?"

"I think he means Sunday."

"I would have said Moonsday. Which is it really?"

"Tidesday," Yrund told them.

"Tidesday?" said Ansyn. "Are you sure?"

"Oh dear."

"Trolls," said Jon-Luq, looking around. "I can't remember why Ama sent me over."

Agnetha tsked. "Tana will not be happy with me, I am sure. Nor should she be… What I can't understand is why I would ever let you two near any nepenthe. Ansyn, maybe…"

"I'm a little lost. Are you saying I got nepenthed?"

"Quite thoroughly."

"Well, that's a first." The trader looked bemused.

"What's the last thing you remember?"

"I remember working on my books. Yrund was helping me. We had cookies, I think. Then? Can't say after that."

They all looked to Yrund. "That was just after lunch. It's still midafternoon."

"So not too much gone. What about you, Jon-Luq?"

"Hmm?" asked the boy, who was staring deeply into his mug.

"What's the last thing you remember?"

"The town hall?" said the boy with an effort.

"That was over a week ago!"

"What have I done?" said Agnetha, clutching the table.

"It's not your fault," Yrund told the healer. "You told us not to come in, but then there was purple smoke everywhere—"

"And you three stepped in to help. Dumb as a dead fish! But… why didn't the nepenthe affect you, child?"

Yrund shrugged as Orelia tittered in her ears.

"You aren't still wearing that halestone, are you?"

"No, I gave it back to you, remember?"

"And no other gems?"

"I have a carnelian," said Jon-Luq helpfully.

"Which did you no good at all, obviously. It's what Yrund is carrying I need to know."

Yrund fumbled for what to say. "Oh, wait. Ansyn did give me something earlier." She fished around in her pocket for the brown gem and handed it to Agnetha.

"Topaz? Is this topaz?"

"I-I don't know. Maybe? You'll have to ask Trader Ansyn. It's his." Yrund still didn't know why he'd given it to her.

Ansyn took the clear brown stone, turning it over in his hand. "Might be? Looks like a topaz, doesn't it? Pretty big, though, for such clear color."

Agnetha scratched some notes in a book open on the table by the box. "Interesting. Very interesting... Can I keep this?"

"By all means."

"Can I see?" asked Jon-Luq.

Agnetha slapped his hand. "You've had enough gems for one day, Jon-Luq Haya. Go home now—tell your mother I'll be right behind you," she said, bustling him out.

Agnetha went back to the table and examined the ingot of silver on it, her braid falling forward. The silver was dull and gray as if it had tarnished. "You say I was trying to use the nepenthe on the silver? But this isn't brightsilver."

"Um, it might have been when you started—it looks a lot grayer now."

"Are you saying the nepenthe worked? Can it be?" Agnetha ran to her medicine trunk, wildly opening drawers and spilling out herbs and rough crystals. "Toadstone...bloodstone...no, no... none of that will do."

"What stones do you have on you, Trader Ansyn?"

But the trader couldn't remember. He fumbled through his pockets pulling out odds and ends. "There's usually a violette somewhere in case I run into Didri..."

"All too vague. We need something certain." Agnetha ran back to the open door, yelling for Jon-Luq to come back.

"I need your carnelian. And your locket, too."

Jon-Luq took off the necklace and gave it over, looking very confused. "But you said—"

Agnetha cut him off. "Go on home before you're late. I'll bring your necklace back later," she said before shutting the door firmly behind him.

"Take this in your hand," Agnetha said, shoving the silver necklace at Yrund, who tried to give it back. "No, just hold it for a moment."

Almost instantly, a pleasant warmth began to spread from the necklace to Yrund's hand.

"You feel that?"

Yrund nodded.

"Can I try?" asked Ansyn curiously.

"No, I need someone with their wits about them still." She turned back to Yrund. "So it's right? Pay very close attention to how warm." Then she took the necklace back, opening the locket and tipping Jon-Luq's carnelian onto the dull silver ingot she'd picked up from the table. "Now hold this. Keep the gem on top, that's right."

Yrund held the ingot and the stone together, waiting.

"Well?"

Yrund shrugged. "A little warm, I guess, but not like before."

Agnetha took them both from her, repeating the test. "No, definitely not, and this is ten times the amount of brightsilver as is in that locket." She looked up at Yrund. "Bless Irsil. It worked! It worked!"

"What worked?" asked Ansyn.

"I'll explain to you later," said Agnetha, pushing Yrund out. "I'll be in enough trouble with Tana as it is—" She tried to close the door on Yrund like she had on Jon-Luq.

"Wait!" said Yrund, only now remembering why she'd come. "I was over at the hall, and Ansyn said there had been a mine break in the Aeries…" Yrund told the woman everything she knew.

"Lili might be alive!" The door swung back open.

"She might," said Yrund, drawing in a deep breath. "Or she might not. I just thought—I thought you would want to know. Only maybe now's not the best time, with the nepenthe and all…"

For a long time, the silver-haired woman just stood there, lines of tears running down her cheeks.

"I'm sorry," said Yrund, wondering if she had made a mistake. "Maybe I shouldn't have said anything—"

Agnetha pulled Yrund close, looking straight into her eyes. Yrund could smell the light scent of alat on her breath. "Do not apologize for telling me this, child. Hope is a gift, not a burden. The silver is a sign!" She shook her gently. "Yaha?"

"Yaha," Yrund agreed softly.

✳ ✳ ✳ ✳ ✳

AFTER DINNER THAT NIGHT, Yrund looked topaz up in the gempendium, trying to ignore the gem farting in her ears.

Topaz: Commonly blue or golden-toned, though found in all colors except red; black rarest of all. Rules of the stone: Primarily affects temperament and disposition; see separate colors for details. Caution: Side effects vary from benign to imperiling. Not to be mixed with verdant without risking a bad case of blotch.

Brown Topaz: Hues range from pale tan to nearly chocolate producing moderate to extreme boosts in esteem and confidence. Easily confused with golden beryl, though the effects are quite different; see below. Rules of the stone: Best not worn with verdant to prevent irrational bravery and severe impairment of judgment. Unpredictable paired with diamants. Caution: Can spur dangerous feats of daring. Frequently produces loquaciousness in otherwise reserved persons.

Thbbt! I can do that, said Orelia.

Hush! said Yrund. *I'm trying to think.*

It was Ansyn that had wanted Yrund to hold the topaz. But why? So she would tell him all about herself? She barely knew the man, and there she had been, going on and on about her family and her goats and then running off to tell Agnetha that Lili might be alive—which now seemed so unlikely as to be impossible.

Anger rose inside her for trusting the trader—she had touched the nepenthe with her bare hands. What was it Agnetha said—she could have forgotten her own mother's face? Though to be fair, said a small voice, if he hadn't given her the topaz, she wouldn't have actually been protected from the nepenthe.

Or would she have? Yrund read the description again. There was not a single line about topaz blocking the effects of nepenthe. With a sudden wave of anxiety, Yrund turned to the *N*'s.

Nepenthe: A lilac-colored gem with strong luminescence. Used primarily to erase memories. Rules of the stone: Never touch the stone directly. Dilute in tincture. Caution—Extreme danger. Even small doses may lead to irreparable memory loss. Worse, with too great of exposure, the body can forget how to breathe. No known antigems.

Beside the description was a small skull symbol.

If the topaz hadn't protected her against the nepenthe, what had?

She didn't have any other gems on her besides Orelia.

Yrund jumped out of bed and threw on her coat over her pajamas.

"Where are you going?" asked Tana, who was blowing out lanterns. "I thought you already went to the bathroom."

"Agnetha might have nepenthed herself!" For the second time that day, Yrund ran for the healer's house.

Ansyn was still at the healer's, playing a round of sytranj with Agnetha. A stack of books lay beside them on the red wood table.

"Hello," they said when Yrund banged in without knocking, Tana and Mila fast on her heels.

"Where's the nepenthe?"

"In its box," said Agnetha. She was holding a playing piece shaped like a camel. "Are we having a pajama party?" she asked, looking at her visitors' nightclothes.

"So you didn't try to do any more experiments? With the topaz?" Yrund felt wobbly. The entire run through the snow, she'd had visions of the healer or the trader, or both, dead on the floor, having forgotten how to breathe.

"We did, actually. Just a small one, but it was a failure if you have to know. Luckily, we were prepared, and, thanks to Ansyn's quick reflexes, I don't think I lost more than an hour. To be honest, the day has turned into quite the patchwork. I suppose the children told you what happened earlier?" the healer asked, addressing Tana.

"They didn't tell me anything," said Tana, eyes wide, her hair tied up for bed. "One moment Yrund was reading that gempendium, and the next she took off like a fox on a hare. What's all this about nepenthe? Is that why Jon-Luq couldn't remember whether he'd had breakfast?" It took a while to catch her and Mila up.

"So you were reading up on nepenthe tonight?" said Ansyn, finally turning to Yrund. "What did Barthalow's old gempendium say?"

"That nepenthe doesn't have any antigems."

"Not topaz at any rate." The trader sighed.

"Though we haven't resolved how you managed to escape unscathed," said Agnetha, indicating the stack of books on the table. "You're certain you didn't have any other gems on?"

Orelia tittered, and a sudden suspicion rose inside Yrund.

"Yrund is gem shy," explained Mila before Yrund could come up with a reply. "Although—"

"You're gem shy!" said Ansyn, slapping his forehead. "That explains everything…I'm sorry, I should have known. You're from the Sky Country, and there I was giving you a topaz to cheer you up. In my defense, it was probably paffle…"

Paffle, repeated Orelia with disgust.

Wait—that was why the trader had given her the brown gem to hold? To cheer her up? According to the gempendium, topaz could cause irrational feats of daring. She could have been hurt—that topaz wasn't a fake. She'd raced right into the nepenthe's mist! Bogging gems! Though that still didn't explain how she hadn't lost her memory. If the topaz hadn't protected her from the nepenthe, that only left…

"You know, you actually do have a gem we haven't considered yet," said Ansyn.

Mila's mouth opened. "You mean—"

Ansyn went on. "Four, really—you have the ouroborus. The snakes' eyes are blue diamants. Those could be your antigem. Or, alternatively, it could be something in the metal. The Mining Wield's always creating new alloys."

"The ouroborus. I'd nearly forgotten!" said Agnetha, pushing aside the sytranj board and flipping through one of her books, labeled *Healer's Guide to Stones*. "Let's see—where is blue diamant? Here we go:"

Rules of the Stone: Popularly associated with bad luck and curses, though purely anecdotal. Good for endurance. Also, shows promise in experiments with energy capture and continuous currents. Do not pair with bee beryl at peril of exhaustion…

Agnetha looked up from the book. "Nothing about nepenthe."

"Well, the rules of the stones are always changing," said Ansyn. "Alternatively, Yrund might just be immune to nepenthe." As one, he and the healer appraised her.

"It's always possible," allowed Agnetha. "Many people are immune to certain gems—anodynes, for instance."

"I'm immune to topazes," offered Ansyn.

"I'll try again, if you want me to," said Yrund. She had said she would fight, and she meant it.

"No," said Tana. "It's too dangerous. You don't know what nepenthe can do. I've seen wispers in Windmarket who've forgotten their own names. For all we know, it was just a breeze that protected you. Or maybe it didn't. Nepenthe is famously unpredictable. Maybe tomorrow we'll find out you've lost an entire year."

"I agree," said Agnetha, caution overriding curiosity. "We'll find another way. In the meantime, this is to go no further than this room. Understand?" Agnetha pointed two fingers at Mila and Yrund. "If the Mining Wield even gets a hint of us trying to change the silver, the game will be up."

"How come you never told me you were gem shy?" asked Tana.

"Because I told her you wouldn't listen," said Mila. "Not with frostbite."

"Well, that's true—" admitted Tana.

"But why mess around with the nepenthe at all if you can just swap the brightsilver for the plain?"

"That's enough for tonight," said Tana, taking Mila by the shoulder. "You'll know *what* you need to *when* you need to."

Yrund followed them back to the house and to bed, wondering exactly what had happened with the nepenthe. Was it the ouroborus that had protected her? Or had it been someone else? *Tell me the truth, Orelia. Was it you?*

I am the best, the stone answered proudly.

The best? Or the most jealous? Yrund wondered to herself. Knowing her distaste for other gems, she could well believe Orelia had blocked the nepenthe's effect on her. Though the more important question was, would it work next time?

CHAPTER TWENTY-FOUR

"How do you all make it look so easy?" complained Yrund, spread-eagled in the snow at the bottom of yet another hill.

"You're much worse than I thought you'd be," said Mila, genuinely surprised.

Today's lesson was proving exhausting. Yrund wondered if she was getting sick. She'd been tired all week, but Tana had insisted Mila take her out. In fact, she'd sent all the kids outdoors. Another meeting with the adults, no doubt.

"It would help if the skis would stay on for two snaps. Can't we tie them to my boots or something?"

"Naha, they're made like that so you can kick them away if you go through the ice."

Of course, thought Yrund, remembering the day out with Anouk.

"Now, remember, when you get going too fast, turn into the slope and dig in your edge."

Easier said than done. Even at low speeds, turns became falls without any warning. The Lumi, who had learned to ski as soon as they could walk, were greatly entertained at Yrund's progress.

Even Ansyn, a spice trader from balmy Asteria, was an expert. As soon as Yrund had mastered one thing, there was another to learn, and Mila, it turned out, was even less patient than Anouk.

"And stop flapping your arms all over the place. You look like you're trying to fly, not ski. Do you want to look like a Lumi or not?"

"I do," said Yrund, looking around for her skis. "It's just—"

"Just what?"

"I just wish I could do more than not get caught. I want to fight the wields."

"I know," said Mila. "Me too. Ama and Apa act like we can't be trusted. It's always—keep your head down and don't attract attention." She lifted her bow and pretended to let an arrow go. "Never—kill the blasturds—like they deserve. It's too bad Agnetha won't let you try to change the silver."

Yrund jabbed the snow with one of her ski poles. The healer had decided it was too dangerous. Tana's influence, no doubt. "I bet Agnetha and Ansyn would have let me if your mother hadn't been there."

"Yaha, Ama's convinced you were just lucky—standing upwind or something."

"I walked right through it. Twice. No—three times."

"Hey, you don't think it was that funny sunsstone of yours that protected you, do you?"

Yrund's heart gave a lurch.

"What funny sunsstone?" she asked, her voice sounding like someone else's.

"The one you made the pouch for," said Mila as if Yrund were quite stupid. "I don't know why you're so secretive about it. We've all seen it."

"You have?" Yrund was nearly squeaking now.

"Sure. You sleep with it every night. Like the twins with their bunnies."

"I do? How come you never said before?"

"Ama said we're not supposed to tease you, what with your nightmares and all. I'd want a sunsstone too if I had the dreams you did." Mila looked sympathetic. "Though you haven't been sleeping much lately, have you? Not since Ansyn brought the new books."

Yrund had no idea what Mila was talking about. "Are you saying I've been staying up reading?"

"Don't you remember? Anouk is pretty miffed you got jam on her glossies."

Was that why she'd been waking up with sticky hair?

No wonder Yrund was so tired. She'd just assumed it was all the footfighting and skiing lessons. *Orelia!!! You are a bad, bad stone!*

Mila contemplated Yrund with her tan eyes. "Maybe the nepenthe did get you. Unless it's possible to sleep-read. You sleepwalk all the time. But so did Apa after he came back from the silver mine."

All this time, Yrund had thought Orelia had been a secret. "What else do I do at night?" she asked nervously.

"Read, mostly. And eat. Kind of weird stuff too. Last night it was pickles with jam."

Yrund's head shook in anger.

"Do you want to see Agnetha? She's got some sleep herbs that might help, and you can show her your sunsstone while we're over there. In case it's the antigem."

"No! You can't tell anyone about the stone."

"Why not?"

Yrund looked down at her icy boots. "I…I'm not supposed to have it."

"Why not?" Mila said again. "It's not a banned stone or anything. My grandama used to have a sunsstone before the wield took it in a raid. Oh…" Mila stopped. "You mean you're not supposed to have it because you're gem shy? Agnetha won't care about that."

"No, listen! I took it from the mine," said Yrund. "It belongs to the Mining Wield."

I do not! said Orelia, peeved.

Try explaining that to them!

"You stole it!" Mila punched Yrund in the shoulder. "Wows! You are wolvy. Good for you. You're just like the Invisible Hand—" Mila's gaze suddenly shifted to something in the woods. "Ooh, hey, can I borrow your scope?"

Yrund handed it over, glad for the interruption.

Mila turned in an arc, searching the edge of the tree line for her quarry.

"Fox!" she said excitedly. "I won't be long!" The words trailed after her.

Yrund waved goodbye with her mittened hand, unsure whether she was anxious or relieved the Hayas knew about the stone. Though it seemed Orelia hadn't revealed all of herself yet. She sighed and closed her eyes, feeling the snowflakes falling silently on her lashes.

Yrund? Don't be mad, Yrund.

I'm not talking to you, said Yrund, blocking out the stone's voice.

She had too much to think about.

A faint shadow fell across her face. Yrund opened her eyes to see a blur hanging over her.

"Humphrey! How long have you been there? Did you see me fall?"

"Which time?" asked Humphrey, sitting down beside her after he had said hello to the gem, who was whistling ecstatically from beneath Yrund's layers.

"Ha." Yrund watched her invisible friend rustle through her rucksack to see what she had packed for lunch.

"Ooh, buns!"

"Help yourself," said Yrund, just grateful to see the woodwin again. "I was beginning to think I'd made you up."

"You mean like an imaginary friend. Young woodwins have those, too."

Yrund tried to get her head around that—would they also be invisible?

"Why would you think I wasn't real?"

"Well, this gempendium I've been reading says some stones called mindturners can make you see and hear things that aren't there. I thought maybe that's what kind of stone Orelia could be."

Humphrey reached over and pinched Yrund.

"Oww!"

"Guess I'm real," he said. "Where did your Lumi friend go?"

"After a fox," sighed Yrund.

"Why does she hunt all the time? The Lumi have pens full of snowdeer to eat."

Yrund got up, brushing the snowflakes off her nose. "She wants the pelt—she's been working on a white suit to blend in with the snow so nothing can see her. Good thing she doesn't know about you guys. She'd kill for your fur."

Humphrey opened his mouth, revealing the large teeth inside.

"I mean, well…she'd probably try, at least," said Yrund, regretting her words. "She's a little stupid like that."

"Trying is not succeeding." Humphrey helped himself to another roll. "She's killing animals for their fur, so she can hide better to kill more animals?"

"Pretty much. She says they suffer less if they don't see it coming. And the meat tastes better."

"Humans!"

"You brought me here."

"I thought they were treating you well. The buns are certainly good." Crumbs floated in the air near the woodwin's hidden chin.

"They are," said Yrund, her voice falling.

"So what's wrong?"

"The Lumi are preparing a secret war, and I said I would help them fight. But they won't let me do anything."

"I'm sure you have many skills to contribute—you helped Timo with his yowi suit."

"You saw that? I was going to tell you."

"I saw," chuffed Humphrey, amused. "They got the shoulders wrong."

"I know…sorry. It doesn't bother you they're trying to use woodwins to scare the memluks off?"

"Not at all! Imitation is the sincerest form of flattery, as they say. Besides, we woodwins love a nice bit of sabotage. I hear the Lumi are planning to spoil the wield men's beer and wet their firewood."

"You have been eavesdropping. That's more than the adults would tell us."

"Gleaning, I think, is a better word. I also heard the Lumi are planning a silver swap—"

"Yaha, that was your idea."

"But they don't have enough plain silver. They're working out a plan to trade with Orogaudi, but that could take until spring."

"Oh, no…" Dread flowed through Yrund, making the dying afternoon even colder. "That must be why Agnetha was experimenting with the nepenthe."

"Nepenthe?"

"It makes you lose your memory."

"I know what it does," said Humphrey. "Just because your gems don't work on us doesn't mean we are entirely ignorant. But how would nepenthe help the Lumi? Unless they're planning on gemming the wield men…" He seemed to like that idea.

"Not exactly," explained Yrund. "The healer figured out the Lumi could weaken the silver with it. It's not as good as a swap, since the brightsilver gets ruined, but at least it wouldn't be worth as much when it finally got to Asteria."

"War always means sacrifices. Surely the Lumi would give up their brightsilver to be free?"

"The silver, yes. But everyone that's touched the nepenthe has lost their memory. Everyone except me," she added.

"Oh?" said the woodwin with interest. "Why are you different?"

"I think Orelia must be able to act like some sort of antigem when she wants to. Or…it could be something to do with the ouroborus."

"I'm great," said the gem out loud. "The best of the best. The every stone."

"Really?"

"She's still convinced she's an allstone."

Humphrey chuffed.

"I am. I can do anything those other rocks can do."

"Now's the time, then. The wield's first caravan will be coming through with the brightsilver in a few days."

"A few days! No wonder everyone's in such a bad mood."

"I'd help if I could, but there's someplace I need to be. Speaking of which, you haven't gotten anything from Trader Ansyn about rudders, have you?" asked Humphrey.

"Actually…," Yrund said, reaching into her coat for a small strip of paper she had torn off the edge of a glossy when no one was looking. "I copied this from my slate." She handed him a drawing and several equations from one of Ansyn's math lessons. "I can't say I understood any of it, especially the parts about pressure differentials and drag co-whatsits…"

The woodwin, however, seemed captivated with the drawing, reading it carefully before tucking it deep into his fur. Sometimes she wondered if woodwins were born with pockets built into their coats. "Was he curious why you wanted to know about airships?"

"I never had to ask," Yrund admitted. "Most of his lessons are about Asterian technology or trade. Compasses, airships. Next week is strikers."

"He does have the most knowledge of the enemy."

"Oh," said Yrund, suddenly realizing the importance of the lessons. "Why do you think he's really helping the Lumi?" She didn't want to sound like Pir Jaq, but it was still hard to understand what was in it for the Asterian.

"Because he's a freewielder," said the woodwin as if that explained everything.

"Which is what?"

"The freewielders, or Free Wayers, believe entry to a wield should be based on merit, not birth or wealth. They believe humans should have the freedom to choose their own Way. They would abolish the rabu system entirely if they were in the High Seat."

"The Mining Wield would never allow that," said Yrund.

"Which is why the capital is not a particularly safe place for him anymore."

So even the Asterian was fighting the wields.

Yrund watched moodily as an ermine dove through the snow as easily as if it were swimming. "Hey, I have a question, speaking of math. I was looking at the healer's map—the Hidden Woods aren't even on there. Nor is the second gorge."

"It's not on there *yet*," said the woodwin with a sigh so deep Yrund could feel the puff of warm air. "But with more airships coming, it's only a matter of time."

"You know what else was strange? The other distances are all wrong too. Agnetha said Devil's Crown is hundreds of miles from Last Lake."

"It is." They watched another ermine join the first, their spotted white fur breaking the surface of the snowbanks like fish through a stream.

"But, Humphrey, I did the math…there's no way that can be right. You and I were only together five days before you got me to the Hayas'—that's a hundred miles. Then, from their fall grounds, we couldn't have covered more than ten miles a day to Last Lake. Add it all up—that's two hundred miles at most! The map has to be wrong—no one could travel that far in such a short time."

"They could if they used the trees," said Orelia.

Humphrey whistled so loudly it was nearly a bark.

"Used the what?" asked Yrund, uncovering her ears.

"Woodwins know the forest paths much better than humans do with all their herds and sleighs," explained the woodwin. "It's only natural you would travel faster when you're with me."

"But that doesn't explain—"

"The important question right now," said Humphrey, not letting her finish, "is what are you going to do about the caravan on its way?"

That was the important question. Yrund looked down onto Last Lake with its little round houses and smoking chimney. A team of snowdeer was pulling a sled full of cut logs in from the forest. There was only one thing she could do. "I'm going to take the nepenthe and change the silver."

"You really think that Orelia can protect you?"

"I'll have to take my chances." After all the lost sleep this week, the stone did owe her something.

"Wish I didn't have someplace else to be, or I'd stick around for the fun." He sounded sincerely sorry to miss it.

"I'll help," said Orelia. "It will be wolvy!"

"That's the spirit!" said Humphrey, finishing the last of the buns. "Just don't forget anything important. Nepenthe is dangerous stuff. I would stay if I could..."

"That's all right," said Yrund, saying goodbye. She had another accomplice in mind.

"OF COURSE I'll help you nepenthe the silver caravans!" said Mila when she heard Yrund's plan. "I'll wear my yowi suit, and while I chase the watchmen off, you do your thing. I bet we'll scare the bezoars out of those silver-stealing thugs."

Yaha! said Orelia, as excited as Mila.

"There won't be any scaring," said Yrund, tamping her hand for Mila to calm down. "What if they started yelling and everyone came out to see?"

"Hmm," said Mila, taking target practice at a stump. The long arrow hit with a thwunk, the white feathers on the end bouncing. "Quiet distractions aren't as easy as loud ones."

Yrund wished she had a bow to shoot while she thought. It had seemed like such a simple plan when she'd discussed it with Humphrey.

"What would get a memluk's attention without raising any alarm?"

"I don't know. Finding something they didn't want to share?"

"Like what? Beer?"

"Beer could work," said Yrund, watching a pair of winter swans glide over the village. "But that could make them rowdy."

"What about Hinri's cloudstone?"

They raced over to the wood shop, but Hinri declined to let them borrow the stone, saying he needed it, though for what he wouldn't say.

"Probably needs it for the wield men inside," Mila surmised. "Don't worry, we'll think of something."

They discussed the plan every chance they had—which wasn't often. Yrund suspected Tana was trying to keep them too busy to get in trouble.

"Hey," said Mila while they chopped wood the next day. "What if we dug a hole and filled it with—"

"Don't forget we're trying not to kill anyone," Yrund reminded her, setting another log upright on the block.

"Right, right...," said Mila, disappointed.

"What are you two whispering about?" asked Anouk, coming to load a sled with the sharp-scented kindling.

"What we're making you for New Suns," said Mila, her face a picture of innocence.

"Yaha, right," said Anouk, stacking wood.

"Why are your lips so pink?" asked Mila, pointing her axe at her sister's face. Anouk's lips were unnaturally rosy, matching her cold cheeks.

"Ama let me try her new batch of berry stain. What's it to you?"

"Nothing," said Mila. "It looks good."

Anouk gave them both a squinty look before dragging her sled away.

Mila stuck her tongue out at her back.

"I know," said Yrund when Anouk was out of earshot. "What if we give the watchmen some beer but make it really hard to open?"

"That's good!" said Mila, impressed. "I can glue the stoppers shut. That would keep them busy for a while."

"Though I don't know if they'll just trust us walking up and handing them something to drink," said Yrund, realizing the flaw in their plan. "Memluks might be superstitious, but they're not idiots. At least, not all the time."

"Then we have to make the galoots think it's not for them," said Mila.

"How?"

"Stop worrying," ordered Mila, looking after her sister. "I know just what to do."

But Yrund did worry. After all, she was the one who would be out in the open trying to gem the caravans. If such a thing was even possible. It was one thing for Agnetha to nepenthe a spoon or a locket, but several tons of brightsilver? That could take all night. Or longer. If the nepenthe was even strong enough. What if it was used up after one brick? Or Orelia couldn't protect her after all? She could lose everything. The war might be secret, but it definitely wasn't safe.

CHAPTER TWENTY-FIVE

Five days later a messenger from Frazil arrived. The memluks were on the way. They arrived at dusk, drawing up outside the town hall—six teams of snowdeer, six sleds of brightsilver, six conscripted Lumi and five hammer-carrying memluks. As expected, Tana and Timo had ordered the children to stay put as soon as the village dogs began to bark.

"Mila—you're in charge. No one is to leave this house until we come back. Keep the curtains drawn and the noise down."

"What will you be doing?" asked Anouk with worry, for Tana and Timo had refused to tell them anything of their own plans to host the wield men.

"We'll be showing the wield men our best hospitality. Just as we've always done."

"But what about the secret war?" asked Jon-Luq.

"Part of it being a secret war is we keep our plans secret," said Timo. "We can handle tonight as long as you lot don't cause any problems."

"What about swapping the brightsilver?" asked Jon-Luq. "I heard there wasn't enough plain silver to switch even one sled."

"Then you've heard more than you should have," said Tana, putting on her coat and loading Timo up with baked goods.

"You don't win a war in one night," Timo told his son. "It's like a game of sytranj—all the pieces need to be in their place. Tonight our move is to keep the memluks happy and prevent any violence. If we do that, today's battle is won."

"Don't worry about us," said Mila, putting her arm around Yrund. "We'll all be right here."

Magrit started to cry as Tana and Timo left. "Who wants to play a game of keeps?" asked Mila brightly.

"Now? With memluks in town?" Anouk crossed her arms.

"Do you want to listen to the little ones cry all night?" asked Mila with a glare.

"Fine," said Anouk, getting out the buttons.

It might have been easy enough to distract Little Tir and Magrit, but the rest of them took turns peeking out the Hayas' small window toward the town hall.

The evening was torturously slow as they waited. Were the memluks eating a quiet dinner or taking prisoners? And what were the Lumi doing? Playing sticks-and-sevens with the enemy? Gemming them?

"What do you think is happening over there?" asked Anouk, echoing what they all were thinking.

"Do you hear that?" said Jon-Luq, cupping his ear to the window. "I think they're singing."

"Then everything is going to plan," said Mila.

"How do you know?"

"I heard Ansyn telling Hinri the memluks liked music. He says soldiers need entertaining or they'll find their own."

Memluks did like to sing, thought Yrund. And drink, and gamble, and fight—usually all at once. But there was no sound of yelling or furniture breaking as the night went on, just another hour of increasingly slurred singing in Douarr. Someone, it seemed, had gotten the memluks to perform.

"I think it's time," whispered Mila. Yrund put down her keeps buttons and put on Timo's furry yowi suit.

"Where are you going?" asked Anouk, looking up.

"Ama and Apa have a special errand for Yrund and me. We'll be back in a little bit."

"Liar," said Anouk. "You're sneaking off to do something you shouldn't."

"Then you don't want to be part of it, do you?" shot Mila right back.

"I do!" said Jon-Luq. "Can I come?"

"No," said Mila flatly. "But you can help."

"I'm going to tell," said Anouk, getting up for her coat.

"No, you're not. I need you."

"To do what?" asked Anouk, disbelieving.

"I want you to make my hair look nice," said Mila as if this were a common request.

"Why?" asked Anouk as Yrund wondered the same thing. Mila was an attractive young woman—healthy and strong—even beautiful with her wide eyes and matching golden skin. But she did not spend much time brushing her hair.

"Do you want to be part of the secret war or not?"

Anouk got out her brush, pointing for Mila to sit down. Deftly she pulled out the knots and straightened Mila's part, then lifted each side up into a comb.

"What can I do?" asked Jon-Luq, bouncing on his feet.

"You can sharpen the axe," said Mila, checking her reflection in the small mirror.

Jon-Luq excitedly fetched the sharpening stone from its drawer and the axe from its hook. "What are you going to do with it?"

"Nothing…yet," said Mila, giving him a meaningful glance.

"Right," said Jon-Luq, going to work.

Yrund tugged Timo's hunting suit up. It was better than Mila's but, while Timo might not have been taller than his eldest children, he was taller than Yrund—the suit hung in puddles around her ankles and drooped lazily at the crotch. She borrowed the snowshoes too. Just in case. Yrund looked around the small house, sure she'd forgotten something. Startled, she saw Anouk had not only done Mila's hair up but was applying plumberry stain to her cheeks and lips.

"What in the moons do you need all that for?"

"You'll see," said Mila, who was checking she had her knives in her belt. Then she slung her bow over one arm.

"No bow," Yrund reminded Mila, making her put the weapon back.

"Sorry, habit," said Mila, reaching instead for a heavy basket covered with cloth. It clinked as she lifted it up.

"I really don't think you two should—" Anouk started to say.

"Nobody asked you," said Mila, helping Yrund pull up her hood and mask. "Ready?"

Yoo hoo! said Orelia.

They slipped out the door, Yrund doing her best to ignore the betrayed faces of Anouk and her brother. "We won't be long. Promise," said Mila. "And we'll tell you everything as soon as we get back."

THE FIRST MOONS were still low, providing deep shadows to hide in. As they'd hoped, the nepenthe was still on Agnetha's shelf. They took their time approaching the wields' caravan, skiing between houses and keeping an eye out for any adults that might send them home. From the hall behind came the sound of music and what sounded like yaks dancing.

"Six sleds and two memluks on watch," whispered Mila in Yrund's ear as they crouched behind Didri's silver shop. The snowdeer had been moved to a corral with fresh fodder, so the six sleds of silver sat in their heavy row, harnesses empty. The two watchmen had a fire in the snow at one end of the caravan and as usual were playing a game of some sort.

Yrund slowed her breath. "You know what you're going to do?" she asked Mila.

Mila checked her basket again—four pots of beer, the lids of which had all been glued shut, and a half dozen cakes they'd stolen from Tana's cooling racks and covered in sticky boiled sweet cream. "Yaha, it's all there."

"Be careful. You know how memluks can be with girls."

"I'm counting on it," said Mila, pinching her cheeks.

Yrund finally understood the makeup. "No, Mila! All you have to do is drop the beer and keep going. Don't be stupid."

"You said you need time, I'll get you time," said Mila. "Don't you think I can be a convincing flirt?"

Yrund looked back at the girl who spent her days tanning hides and boiling brain glue. Who still hadn't caught on that Ansyn had a crush on her. "Not really. No offense."

"Well, I'll bet you five arrows you're wrong."

Bogging hell, thought Yrund. She had a bad feeling about this. "I'm not betting you. Just stick to the plan. And hurry up before someone sees us!"

"I'm going," said Mila.

"Wait! Why did you tell Jon-Luq to sharpen that axe?" The last thing she needed was another surprise.

"No reason, except Apa's been on me to do it all week." Mila grinned and pushed off into the shadows, reappearing several houses away, where she slipped off her skis and leaned them against a wall. She lifted a hand to show she was ready.

Yrund unslung Timo's snowshoes from her back, then cinched them on over her boots. She took a few steps, checking the set of yowi prints they left in the snow. Then she returned Mila's signal.

Mila never hesitated, setting straight off through the deepest snow towards the hall's steps. She pretended not to even see the memluks on watch as she trudged past with the heavy basket, straining once to adjust her grip. Yrund nearly snorted. Mila could carry a deer carcass by herself. The watchmen looked up, whistling appreciatively. For a moment, Yrund thought Mila was about to tell the men off. Then, acting completely unlike any Mila Yrund had ever seen, the young woman ducked her head shyly, switching hands once again as if the basket's weight was too much to bear. The memluks stopped their game entirely, mesmerized by the young woman.

Then Mila tripped, sending pots of beer and iced cakes all around, and the men wrestled each other to be the first to reach her.

"Oh no!" exclaimed Mila.

That was Yrund's cue. She took the nepenthe box from her pocket and crept towards the sleds. It was only when she'd reached the first one, she suddenly realized she had no idea what to do. The silver wasn't just lying there exposed in neat stacks. It was bound in hides and felt. Bogging hell. How could she have not thought of that? Yrund struggled to get an arm out of the sleeve of Timo's loose suit and to the knife belt she wore underneath.

Hurry, said Orelia.

I'm trying, said Yrund, glancing toward the watchmen and Mila. As soon as the men had handed her back one bottle or cake, Mila had somehow slipped and dropped it again. Yrund sawed through the felt of the sled, down near the bottom where she hoped it might look like a tear from a branch. The brightsilver gleamed in the light of a rising moon.

"I am Yrund of the Sky Country, daughter of Wian of the First Moon and Gantul of the Badger Clan," Yrund reminded herself before tipping back the lid of the nepenthe's box.

But the box was empty.

She hadn't thought to check if the nepenthe was inside. Yrund wanted to scream. Agnetha must have known she might try this.

Yrund tried to signal for Mila to leave, but the girl was giggling with the memluks. Giggling, for Troll's sake!

Let me do it, said Orelia.

Shhh! said Yrund, trying to think.

Timo's suit began to glow purple from within. Blooding hell!

It wasn't possible. Yrund wriggled the gem out from her pouch. The stone looked exactly like Agnetha's piece of nepenthe only ten times as large. Cautiously, Yrund reached Orelia out to touch the edge of silver brick. Purple mist began to rise from the brightsilver, just as it had in the healer's kitchen.

"I am Yrund of the Sky Country, daughter of Wian of the First Moon and Gantul of the Badger Clan," Yrund repeated under her breath as the lilac fog enveloped her. "I am Yrund…"

She jumped to the other side of the sled to cut a new hole, but the bricks had already caught Orelia's mist, the entire sled glowing through the heavy wrappings.

Yaha! Finally, something was going right. Yrund ran to the next sled, tearing her blade into the felt and exposing another brightsilver brick to Orelia's touch. The purple glow spread through the second sled as easily as the first.

Mila, Yrund saw when she popped up to check, was trying with feigned effort to open a pot of beer. One of the men took it from her, keen to show her how it was done, but the stopper would not budge. Now, the other memluk wanted to try, tugging at the well-glued bottle.

Yrund raced to the third sled. "I am Yrund of the Sky Country, daughter of Wian of the First Moon and Gantul of the Badger Clan," she repeated under her breath. "I am Yrund…"

"Hey!" said Mila, her voice raised, as Yrund finished the fourth sled. "Stop that!"

Through the thick mist, Yrund could see the watchmen had dropped the beer and were now pulling Mila back and forth between them like a toy. Blast. She should have known this would happen.

Mila's hand moved to her knife belt.

Orelia—do the woodwin whistle! The scary one like when you lit that fire in their woods. Yrund pulled up her hood.

"Arooo-wuff-wuff!" called the gem, making Yrund's ears ring. The memluks turned toward the sound, letting Mila go.

"Hoy-hoy!" they cried.

Yrund gave a yowi-like shake of the arms, glad she'd worn Timo's suit. The watchmen stumbled through the deep snow toward her. Time to go. But Yrund's body was no longer her own. Her face twisted into a mask as if she'd eaten twenty screw-beryls. She leapt onto one of the glowing sleds, then off, stomping and howling and circling the memluks. The men had their backs to each other now, hammers drawn, but their eyes were as round as moons.

Yrund beat her chest, lunging like an animal.

"Aroooh-ooooooooh!" she howled, the sound coming from her throat like nothing a human could make—the call of a yowi ready to feed. The men broke and ran screaming.

"I SHOULD HAVE KNOWN you girls couldn't be trusted!" fumed Tana, pacing the Hayas' house.

"What?" said Mila. "It worked, didn't it? Yrund nepenthed the sleds, most of them, at least. And the memluks got to see a yowi. You should have seen Yrund. Wows! Even I believed she was the real thing."

"We saw enough! You could have been killed! Or taken. Or worse," said Timo, shaking with rage. "What did I tell you? This is not a game!" Yrund had never seen Timo so angry.

"We know it's not a game!" yelled Mila, losing her own temper. "Don't you remember—I saw them drag you away when I was just fifteen. Do you think I would ever forget that? And Yrund—she's seen worse than any of us. This is our life too now

—losing the people we love. Not knowing what the future will bring. How can we stand by and do nothing?"

"What if Yrund had been caught?"

"But she wasn't. That's why I went—to create a distraction."

Tana clutched her head. "Timo, you explain."

"What your mother is saying is it wasn't worth the risk. You're the eldest, Mila, think! Do you want her blood on your hands? And what about your own safety? Those men…you might have been…" He could not say the rest.

"It was my idea," said Yrund. "I was the one that talked Mila into it all."

"I told Agnetha to hide that nepenthe better," said Tana, swearing in Lumi. "You're as foolish as Mila."

"I think it was pretty wolvy," said Jon-Luq, defending them.

"I agree," said Anouk, to everyone's astonishment. "If you don't want us going off and doing stupid things on our own, then maybe you should start including us in your plans."

Her parents exchanged a very long look. It was after midnight.

"We'll talk about this in the morning. After you two have scrubbed down the hall. One of the memluks was sick in there."

But Yrund didn't care what their punishment was. It had been a foolish plan. She should never have let Mila within reach of those memluks, and that wasn't even including Agnetha's nepenthe not being in its box. If it hadn't been for Orelia…

I'm great, said the stone.

You're deranged is what you are, said Yrund, climbing into bed. *Don't think you're off the hook either just because your crazy stunt worked.* The watchmen in their panic had run right through the purple mist. The last Yrund saw as she loped away was them wandering open-mouthed in the dissipating glow. *There are rules, Orelia! Rules for how you treat people.* How was she ever going to make the gem understand?

Like the Rules of the Stone?

Yes. Exactly like that. The Rules of Yrund. She rolled over, exhausted and annoyed but, if she had to admit, also a bit pleased. Despite all the terrible things that could have happened, they'd won a small battle.

"Pssst."

Yrund opened her eyes to see Mila's head hanging over her bunk. There was still a trace of the plumberry stain on her lips. "I have an idea for next time," whispered Mila.

"No," said Yrund, rolling back over before she could hear it.

"Wait—just listen. We get a big pile of rotten fish and a pinepig and…"

Yrund's lids dropped shut. Next time, she was going to plan the distraction herself.

The doors of Last Lake had been strung with bells for New Suns, and they chimed cheerily as the Lumi went to and fro on holiday-related errands, borrowing handfuls of dried plumberries or spools of ribbons. Rows of cinnamon- and cardamom-scented delicacies lined the rafters of every home, cooling beside bundles of mysterious wrapped presents. The youngest Hayas spent the morning of New Suns Eve carrying loads of firewood to the middle of the village for the evening's bonfire while Mila and Yrund collected armfuls of evergreen garlands to decorate the town hall.

Though the skies were dark and gloomy, the suns barely creeping over the horizon, the Lumi had grown more festive by the day. Relatives and friends had been arriving from nearby villages to help celebrate the new year, but with every sleigh full of someone else's family, Yrund's spirits fell lower. When it seemed Tana had finally run out of chores for her, she slipped away.

The corrals were a haven of tranquility after the constant noise of the house. She liked the Hayas, but they never stopped talking. Yrund leaned over the log fence to rub the velvet nose of a snowdeer, whose breath curled around her hand like a small cloud. It was impossible not to wonder what had become of her own family's horses and herds. And her family. Her sisters would have enjoyed playing in the snow with the village children.

Footsteps crunched up behind her.

"I thought you'd be out here." The rest of the deer came over to nuzzle Mila for treats. "Missing home?" she guessed, leaning on the fence beside Yrund. "Ansyn told us your mother and all could be in Asteria."

"Asteria's a long way away," said Yrund, scuffing her boot against the post. Over a thousand miles. And Brandul and Veng were still out there. But Mila didn't know about them, and Yrund had not told her. The Lumi had enough of their own worries.

"You got this far, didn't you?"

Not by herself, thought Yrund, wondering what Humphrey was up to.

"I'm not supposed to tell you, but Ama and Apa have already decided you're to go with us to Winter Fair in second month. Of course, they think you're coming back home with us..." She left the rest hanging.

"Well...since you brought it up," said Yrund, glad Mila understood. "I did talk to Ansyn, and he said I might be able to travel with one of the caravans going west, only..."

"Only?" repeated Mila, following the curve of a fernlike antler with a glove.

"What about the secret war? And Hinri? I can't just leave you now."

"Hinri will be all right," said Mila confidently.

Yrund hoped so. The memluks had decided they needed another Lumi guide on their journey north, taking Hinri, who it seemed had won them over the night of their stay in Last Lake. She would never forget the sound Katrin had made as the caravan had pulled away. His loss added to Yrund's heartache. "I still feel terrible about them taking him."

"It's not our fault the memluks are as scared as rabbits."

"What if it is? If I hadn't made them think yowis were real, they wouldn't have needed a Lumi guide to protect them on their journey."

"Pssshaw, they took him because he beat them at keeps, the dummy. They just wanted to get their gems back. Even Katrin says so now. Singing and gambling all night with them, pretending to be friends… I'm blaming Ansyn. It was his idea to entertain them. Anyway, you shouldn't worry about Hinri. He'll come home as soon as he's gotten the caravan to Windmarket. Or sooner. He knows the woods a thousand times better than those wield men."

"I hope so," said Yrund as a snowdeer nudged her. For whatever Mila said, as long as he traveled with the fickle-hearted memluks, Hinri was still in danger.

"Cheer up. We'll get Hinri back, and by the time spring comes, you'll be on the road to find your family. Not to mention we gemmed the silver—don't forget that! We should be celebrating, not moping. Think how annoyed the Mining Wield will be when they find out how useless most of it is."

Yrund's spirits climbed up a notch. They had accomplished something, despite their poor planning. If only her Way proved so lucky when it was time to get past Brandul and his men.

"Hey, can I borrow your scope?" asked Mila.

"Actually," said Yrund, bringing her mind back from its worries, "I was going to give it to you tomorrow for New Suns—as your present, but…you might as well have it now." She took the filigreed brass scope from her coat and held it out to Mila.

"Holy Troll, Yrund. Are you sure? That's a much better gift than what I made you."

"You made me something?" asked Yrund, wondering when Mila had had the time.

"Come on, I'll show you. I hope you like it." Back at the Hayas', Mila pulled a bundle wrapped in a pillowslip down from a rafter.

Inside, Yrund found a quiver of arrows and an unstrung bow with a coil of loose sinew. She stared at the familiar shape, not quite like those in the Sky Country but very close. It must have taken Mila weeks to make.

"Hinri helped me. We copied the one from that book of weapons Ansyn brought, but we couldn't figure out how to string it."

"You have to do it like this," said Yrund, sitting down to show her. The motion was as natural as putting on her boots. "That was why you were measuring my arms the other day! I was worried you were making me a shirt, and knowing how badly you sew…"

Mila kicked her.

"Ow! I meant thank you! I'm just sorry Hinri couldn't be here when I opened it."

"You can thank him soon," said Mila optimistically. "Well?"

"Well, what?"

"Let's go see how it works!"

Tana shook her head at them when they got back. She was securing Anouk's long braids in tight crowns around her ears while Little Tir and Magrit looked red from scrubbing. "Heavens to Irsil! Where have you girls been? I should've known you would go sneaking off somewhere today, Mila. But taking Yrund, too? You're a bad influence on her."

"I probably am," said Mila honestly.

Tana had a basket ready, filled with dried bundles of spruce and grass and fresh bars of soap. "Be quick about your bathing. The suns will be setting soon," she said, still tsking.

The sauna was empty, but the bed of rocks at the center was hot enough to release a geyser of sizzling steam when Mila poured a bucket of water on top. Into the steam, she placed the fragrant branches. When they had steamed and scrubbed and rinsed, they held their hair over the smoldering grass to absorb the sweet scent.

Mmmm, said Orelia, who liked new smells as much as almost anything.

Go away, said Yrund. *We talked about you snooping while I was in the bath.* The stone, as always, could not resist prying into everything Yrund did, infinitely curious and infinitely bored. Like the memluks, she needed constant entertaining. It did not matter if Yrund left her behind. Their mysterious bond seemed to reach from one end of town to the other.

Yrund and Mila returned to find the family had gone on without them, leaving an annoyed Sikka indoors. Yrund and Mila hurried to get ready. Tana had basted the fringe from a shawl to one of Katrin's old dresses, and the long strips of leather whipped and twirled fetchingly against the tops of her high boots. Yrund, to her pleasure, had been loaned soft hide pants and a coat embroidered with cloudberries and birds. On top she wore a shawl decorated with fur poms. Even Orelia was impressed, whistling loudly in her ears.

Yrund helped Mila twist her wet hair into loops, securing them in place with carved antler combs. Her own hair was hardly long enough to pull back, so Mila tied two entwined ribbons all the way around Yrund's head in a band, letting the ends dangle prettily down the sides of her face. Then, to Orelia's great pleasure, Mila tinted their cheeks and lips with plumberry ink Tana had left out.

"I don't know if we should—" Not after Mila's trouble with the watchmen.

But Mila was having none of it. "There aren't any memluks invited tonight. And, even if there were, those blasturds didn't lose their manners because of a little stain. They take what they want because the wield lets them. Next time one tries to get that close—I swear to Irsil—I'll cut his hammer right off. Speaking of which, you owe me five arrows. You said I couldn't flirt."

"I'm not giving you any arrows. It was a terrible plan, and I told you not to do it."

"Blah, blah," said Mila, ignoring her. "What do you think?" She held up Timo's shaving mirror for them to see.

Yrund was taken aback—she hardly recognized the young woman staring back at her, and not just because she had forgotten the blond hair. Where was Yrund, daughter of Wian of the First Moon and Gantul of the Badger Clan? She touched the scar Veng's knife had left under her eye, cursing him.

Pretty, said Orelia.

"Except for the scowl, you don't look too bad as a Lumi," said Mila.

"Thanks, you either," said Yrund, jumping to avoid a punch.

LAST LAKE'S town hall was so crowded Yrund could hardly make out who was who. The air was warm and close, the stoves stoked to a hot crimson. At the nearest end of the packed room were tables stacked with platters of fat sausages and long fried lake fish, crocks of bright pickled sorrel and pink neeps, and troughs of spice-flecked buns. Beyond those were planks holding golden jams and thick creams and great round plumberry pies dripping with red juices—all of it completely untouched. It was as if the Lumi were waiting for something.

Yrund was about to ask what was happening when unseen drums began to pound, and the center of the room cleared. Mila pulled Yrund with her through the crush around the sides until they found Jon-Luq and the twins. Jumping up and down, Little Tir waved to Anouk, who was up on a stage with the musicians, her fiddle at the ready. Magrit slipped her hand into Yrund's, squeezing tight as the drumming built, reverberating through the floor and into their bones.

From among the crowd, dancers dressed as deer emerged, stepping with the heart-like beat. The hall had gone dark except for a circle of lanterns hanging from the rafters, their flames casting long shadows across the deer, who were prancing in a counterclockwise circle. When they bowed low to each other, their antlers clattered. A high-pitched flute joined the drums, sending the herd scattering, eyes alert and wild, until the fiddle came in like a calming wind, weaving the animals back together. Then a forest of branches appeared, moving opposite the herd as they migrated through their lands. Drumbeats matched hoof drops, the eerie cadence making Yrund shiver.

The deer danced through the green forests of summer, then the burnt leaves of fall, finally staggering through the blizzards of winter before two large suns rose and spring came again. Males rutted, antlers clashed, wolves stalked, and new deer were born. All the while the drums continued to beat like a heart, thumping into Yrund's veins. Upon the ceiling and walls, the dancers' shadows leapt from human to deer and back again, herder and herd as one, mixing with the musicians and then the villagers, herding them out the doors of the hall and through the village toward the last, low red glow of the setting suns. Yrund was carried out with the procession, a lit candle placed in her hands as she circled the corrals in a daze. Together the Lumi sang, raising their voices in thanks to their herds and reminding the suns to come back tomorrow. Yrund held her candle up with the rest of the Lumi, ears ringing. One of the loudest voices was coming from inside her coat.

THE LAST DAY of the year was done. The Lumi returned to the hall, adding fuel to the stoves and relighting the lanterns before joyously toasting each other's health with little wooden cups of plumberry wine and throat-scorching flume. Then the feasting began.

Yrund filled her plate to heaping, balancing a few cardamom buns and a square of oozing plumberry sponge on the top as Mila did, a hot mug of alat crooked around a finger. Ansyn went by carrying a plate even higher than her own—the trader had cleverly made a dam of mashed turnips to hold his dinner in. Yrund found a seat on a bench next to Didri, who handed her a tiny cup of tart wine. "Good New Suns!" they told each other, touching elbows together in the traditional Lumi toast before drinking it down.

Eventually, the musicians filed back to the stage to tune their instruments. After a few final swallows of wine, they gave each other a nod, starting up a jig-like tune, feet tapping on the floor. At the sound of the music, the villagers wiped their mouths, put their spoons and mugs back on their belts, and began to take partners. What started as an organized line of leaders on one side and followers on the other quickly turned into a complex and changing pattern, the dancers swinging and circling up and down the hall like giant erratic snowflakes. Everyone was laughing and shouting and then mid-bite Yrund too was pulled into the chain.

Jon-Luq had her by the arm and was trying to tell her which way to step. "Left foot left, right foot right, swing on my arm, put your wrist in. Take a step back, and on you go!" Old Lir had her next, then Agnetha, then Mila. Yrund had no idea what she was doing, but nobody minded. They just turned her the right direction and sent her on down the line.

"What did you think of the deer dance?" yelled Timo, swinging Yrund by the elbow.

"It was incredible," said Yrund. "Did you miss it? I didn't see you and Tana anywhere."

"We were the deer!" Timo laughed before twirling her over to the next partner.

Yrund danced until her stomach cramped, and she had to sit down. Immediately a neighbor handed her a yawning baby to hold, and she jiggled it while she watched the dancers spin by. Then the baby was retrieved, and Yrund was pulled back into the fray.

"WEEEeeeee!" Orelia laughed out loud and would not be hushed, unnoticed by anyone but Yrund amid the drink and noise.

Yrund stamped her feet like the rest of the Lumi, ignoring the ache of the ouroborus rubbing against her legs, lights whirling by as she passed under the lanterns, swinging from partner to partner and clapping her hands until they burned. Her body had taken on a mind of its own, as Orelia screeched happily in her ears. Yrund felt her feet moving as much in time to the gemstone as to the band, or maybe the band was in time to the stone.

As the night went by, piles of sleeping children began to accumulate around the hall's sides while the adults danced and ate on. Anouk, foot tapping and face stern, played a tune of such joyful beauty Yrund thought she might weep. Jon-Luq joined in, his voice shimmering and bright. When it was over, Yrund could hardly drag herself out of the dance and over to the side.

Noooo, Yrund! Dance! commanded Orelia, but Yrund ignored the greedy stone, fanning her face with her hands.

Mila came prancing over. "Look what Ansyn gave me!" On her belt, next to the old one, was a splendid new knife with a polished shell handle. Mila beamed, cheeks shining.

"It's beautiful!" said Yrund. Indeed, the inlaid weapon suited Mila perfectly.

Ansyn handed Yrund his mug of wine before pulling Mila back to the dancing. The graceful young woman moved easily through the steps, laughing merrily when the trader kept changing places to be her partner. Yrund roamed the hall, listening in on the clusters of Lumi taking breaks to tell stories near the stoves and refilling her mug with alat, brewed to keep everyone awake. A game of keeps had started in a corner with Jon-Luq challenging Old Nicolai two agyt gembles for an ice bear tooth.

The only problem with drinking so much alat was how fast it

went through you. Yrund was making yet another trip to the outhouse when she ran into Katrin on the same errand.

"So what do you think of your first New Suns Eve?" Katrin asked.

"I'm falling asleep on my feet," admitted Yrund, who was impressed Katrin was able to celebrate anything with Hinri gone. She knew what it was like to be separated from those you loved most and her heart ached for the woman, as much for her grief as her determined hope. "But I don't want to miss anything. I don't know how you do it—staying up until the suns return."

"I took a long nap this afternoon, and it's a good thing, too. The band is really something this year. I could swear there were a hundred instruments in there tonight."

Yrund suspected at least one of those went by the name of Orelia—the stone was still humming in her head. Yrund opened the moons-carved door of the icicle-strung outhouse. A candle flickered in a sconce hung on the wall. Blast, it was cold. She'd heard stories from Mila of people freezing to death on the pot. Now she believed it.

"Oh, crap! I must've sat in some plumberry wine." No, not wine. Yrund was wide awake now. It was blood.

"Holy Troll! I think my sweep has started!"

"What? Now?" called Katrin through the wall.

"I think so," said Yrund.

"It's not your first one, is it?"

"Yaha, it is, actually." She didn't know if it was the alat or the cold, but her hands were trembling. "What do I do?"

"Irsil's ears! Stay there! I'll be right back."

Yrund could hear footsteps racing away through the snow.

She had known this would happen someday, but Yrund was still caught off guard—and off balance—as her world shifted.

"Here," said Katrin, handing a bundle of supplies through the door.

When Yrund came out, they stood staring at each other. It was the same night, the same moons circling overhead, and yet… "I feel strange," said Yrund. "Maybe I shouldn't have had the rest of Ansyn's plumberry wine."

"You could probably use another mug," said Katrin, squeezing her arm. "You are a life maker now—a woman!"

"It doesn't seem like it's going to be very comfortable," Yrund said, shifting awkwardly in her padded pants.

"Naha, it's not really. I'd loan you a sweepstone if I had one, but the wield men took them all last year."

"What does a sweepstone do?"

"Don't you know? It will stop your cycle. Though I won't be needing one for a while."

"Why?" asked Yrund naively.

Katrin patted her abdomen, eyes sparkling.

"Ohhh! Congratulations!"

"You're the first to know. Besides Hinri."

"I'm sorry," said Yrund. "It's not fair he's not here."

"No," said Katrin bravely. "But he'll be back. He's got an extra reason now."

"What's going on?" said Mila, trudging by on her way to the bathroom.

Katrin and Yrund both looked at each other.

"Yrund's started her sweep!"

"Katrin is going to have a baby!"

"Really? Wows! What a way to start the new year." Mila hooked them both by the elbows and swung them into a circle with her, howling at the fading moons. Arm in arm, the three women danced, crying and laughing, welcoming life and the silvery light of the rising dawns.

CHAPTER TWENTY-SEVEN

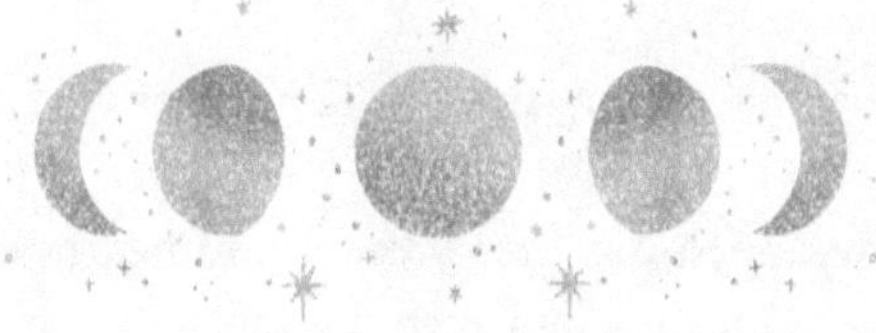

The new year's first day was not what Yrund had hoped—the novelty of becoming a woman had worn off as soon as the cramps had started.

"My sweep's no big deal," said Mila, surprised at Yrund's discomfort. "I can't believe you're hurting so bad. Maybe you just need to get up and move around."

Yrund threw a pillow at her.

"Instead of gloating," said Tana, "why don't you go find Katrin's mallowkite? Last I heard, Old Nicolai was wearing it on his knee, but I'm sure he'll give it up for a few days."

"He hasn't got the *numbli* anymore," said Mila. "Agnetha left it in Locchen. One of Vitra's cousins is expecting twins."

"Damn the Asterians," said Tana, waving a long spoon around.

"I'll be all right," Yrund said before another bout of cramps took her breath away.

"Mine were awful at your age, too, so don't feel bad. Everyone is different," Tana said, bringing Yrund hot stones for her abdomen and a mug of rose and ginger tea.

"I hope you still have an appetite, at least. It would be ill luck to miss the first meal of the year." Tana called the children to set out warmed soft cheese and braided loaves of golden bread.

"I'll do my best," said Yrund, inhaling the enticing scents. Having slept all day, none of them had yet eaten.

Timo and Katrin came in with a burst of icy air, carrying mysterious bundles inside socks and pillowslips and even old flour sacks.

Once everyone had a small pile in front of them, Timo said, "Go!"

Yrund unwrapped her first present and nearly laughed. Jon-Luq had made her a sling and even thoughtfully included a heavy sack of lake stones, each of the same size and heft.

"Don't you like it?"

"Naha, I do! Now, open your present from me," she told him. It was Jon-Luq's turn to laugh, for Yrund had made a sling for him as well. For Anouk she had bought a small box of hairpins, something she knew the girl had wanted. "Wows, thanks, Yrund!"

For her part, Anouk had given Yrund half her stack of glossies. "Since you're always borrowing them anyway…"

Ooooh! Yrund was as touched as Orelia. Despite her own lack of interest in the gaudy fashion pages, she knew how much Anouk treasured them. At least Orelia had gotten a present. Two, actually, as Yrund had also sewn her a new neck pocket, this one with a button.

From the twins, Yrund received a new feather pillow they had helped their mother stuff. In fact, all the Hayas got pillows, which according to Mila was a New Suns ritual. Already, the children were using them to beat each other, making Orelia laugh so hard Yrund thought her head might split.

Tana and Timo could not seem to believe Yrund had gotten them presents, too, as pleased with their respective tea and chisel as if she had brought them rare treasures. "I don't know how you could afford them," said Tana.

"Ansyn gave me a store credit for working on his accounts."

"But that was so you could buy that old gempendium."

"It was, but then he gave me the gempendium as a present for New Suns," said Yrund, still surprised at the trader's generosity. Especially since she hadn't thought to get him anything.

"Open this one now," said Mila, handing Yrund a small gift tied with string. Inside the simple wrapping was a pine box carved with snowdrops and squirrels.

"Wows, it's so beautiful," said Yrund, admiring the delicate work.

"Hinri and Katrin made it."

Yrund turned to thank Katrin, who gave her a wink.

"That's not all. Look inside!" said Timo, as excited as his children. Yrund flipped the box over, perplexed. There was no way to open it. And yet, she could hear there was something inside. As the others watched, Yrund ran her fingers across the carved animals, searching for a secret catch. Finally, she noticed the fine seam on the ends. With a smooth movement, she pushed the hidden lid out with her thumbs. The Hayas clapped. Inside was a gleaming heart-shaped locket just like the other Hayas wore.

Mila fastened the brightsilver necklace behind Yrund's neck while Sikka licked her face. "It's from the whole village. For gemming the silver caravan with the nepenthe."

"We still don't approve of you sneaking off to do it, though," said Tana, shaking her finger. "That was very dangerous. Agnetha still doesn't know how you managed it."

Yrund was nearly speechless. "Thank you," she said, the words sounding inadequate.

"Didri made the locket. There isn't a gem inside. We didn't know if you'd want one, being gem shy, and with so few to be had…"

"It's perfect just how it is," said Yrund.

Ahh, said Orelia, who apparently didn't have a problem with brightsilver.

There was also a pile of presents saved for Hinri. "He'll just have to open them when he gets back," said Tana, trying not to cry.

"Now, for the twins' surprise," said Timo after the rest of the gifts had been exchanged and everyone had eaten. "For that, we'll have to go outside."

Timo, Hinri, and Katrin had made Little Tir and Magrit a new sled. Whooping, the children raced out into the fresh snow. Fortified by Tana's tea, Yrund ran out with them.

⁕ ⁕ ⁕ ⁕ ⁕

THAT NIGHT AFTER DINNER, Anouk brought Yrund one of her glossies and the box of pins.

"I want to do this, but I can't figure it out," said Anouk, pointing to a well-worn page of a woman wearing a complex braid across the back of her head in the shape of a bow.

"There's no way I can do that," said Yrund.

"Yaha, you can! It's just a four-strand braid, like for reins. You can do that—I've seen you."

"It looks more complicated than reins," said Yrund doubtfully, looking at Anouk's picture again.

Undeterred, Anouk handed Yrund an antler comb. "I'll read to you," she bargained, holding up the battered copy of *The Daring Exploits of the Invisible Hand.* "Your fa—vo—rite!" she sang.

Yrund stifled a sigh and motioned for Anouk to sit down in front of her. Despite all the sleep-reading Orelia had made her famous for, Yrund couldn't actually stand the stories about the Invisible Hand. They all seemed to end with the hero barely saving yet another teary-lashed and swooning woman from certain death before disappearing into endlessly setting suns. It was drivel, but the Hayas, otherwise intelligent and unsentimental, not only didn't mind the stories but looked forward to Anouk reading to them. Tonight the whole family stretched out on the floor around the fire to listen, soaking in the last of their holiday.

Anouk had just gotten to the part about how the handsome thief had fought off ten bandits while blindfolded when someone knocked at the door. "Yaha!" called Timo.

Sikka jumped on Ansyn as he let himself in. "Good New Suns!" he greeted the family.

"You've just missed a dinner of leftovers," said Tana, "but we can rustle something up."

"That's kind of you, but I already ate with Agnetha and Didri."

"Working on the holiday?" guessed Timo.

"We were going over the maps again," said Ansyn. "Thought maybe a game of sytranj would clear the mind. If you're up for it."

"Sit down, sit down." Timo waved the trader to the guest's spot by the door and got out the sytranj board with its antler and wood pieces. "I'm always up for a game with a friend. Anouk was just reading to us about the Invisible Hand. Things were becoming very exciting."

"Ah—that rogue the Invisible Hand! By all means, continue," said Ansyn, sitting down. "We can play while you read."

Anouk picked the book back up.

He grasped the jeweled sword between his bound hands, swinging left and right, slashing through one bandit and then another, spinning to meet their blades as if he had a thousand eyes. One by one they fell before him, three, then four, his sword darting between their ribs and through their hearts until the rest of the cowardly bandits fled screaming, the treasure abandoned. The Hand flicked the blade one last time and his blindfold fell. With his teeth he untied his binds, then kissed the poisoned Moon Maiden, laying the sword's jeweled hilt upon her still chest. As the gem touched the Moon Maiden's heart, her golden skin bloomed and her lungs filled with air."You came back," she breathed, violet eyes fluttering open, but the Hand was already gone, the long curtain blowing behind him in the wind.

The cabin was silent but for Sikka snoring by the door. Tears gleamed on Anouk's cheeks. Yrund pretended not to notice as she continued to braid and pin the girl's hair.

"That was beautiful," said Tana, also sniffing. The whole family looked moved.

Yrund tried not to roll her eyes. *You can't fight ten men blindfolded,* she complained privately to Orelia. *You couldn't even fight one probably.*

The Invisible Hand can, said the stone, defending him. She had obviously enjoyed the story as much as the Hayas had.

"I bet it was a blood-amethyst in the hilt," said Jon-Luq, slashing a piece of kindling around as if it were a sword. "What do you think, Ansyn?"

"Hmm?" said the trader, looking up from his game.

"What sort of gem do you think it was that brought the Moon Maiden back to life?"

"Violettes are only good for flume and ale," interrupted Mila, who was fletching a pile of arrows.

"Can't they work against any poison?" asked Jon-Luq.

"No, not any poison," said Ansyn, moving a goat on the board. "Mila's right—there are a few gems violette protects against, but it's most effective against spirits."

"Weren't you listening?" said Anouk, annoyed. "The Elder Mystic said only an allstone could undo a white rubily's poison."

An allstone? Yrund was listening now.

"I didn't know there were white rubilies," said Mila.

"There aren't that I'm aware of. There are white seefires, which can have odd effects, though hardly poisonous, and white adamantine, which in and of itself has no power at all...but no white rubilies," said Ansyn. "But then, there probably aren't any allstones nowadays either."

"How do you know for sure?" Yrund asked the trader. "If they existed once, couldn't someone find one again?"

"If they had, we'd all know about it. No doubt Niloofar

Damantine would be wearing it smack in the middle of her forehead."

"How something so valuable could just disappear is what I never understood," said Timo, taking one of Ansyn's pieces off the board. "So many people must have been looking for them."

"Well, thank Irsil they are gone," said Tana. "Who can imagine what the Asterians would do with such a thing if they had one now? They get up to enough evil with the gems they do have."

"I read that the Astrini have poison jewels," said Jon-Luq with great interest.

Ansyn nodded over the sytranj board. "It is true, I regret to say. And the Yavani. There are many gems that can be used as weapons—red adamantine, cianite, orpiment. But then, any gem can be dangerous if you aren't careful."

"So allstones aren't real?" Yrund pressed the trader. "You're sure?"

"No more real than yowis."

I told you so! said Orelia smugly.

"Owww!" said Anouk as Yrund accidentally tugged her scalp.

Mila looked up. "What in the world did you do to her hair?" The rest of the family turned to see. "She looks like she has horns!"

"What?" cried Anouk, feeling her head.

Jon-Luq began to laugh.

"It's not funny!" said Anouk, running to the mirror.

"It's supposed to be a bow, I think," said Yrund, holding up the glossy Anouk had given her. "I told you I wasn't good at doing hair."

Timo guffawed while Ansyn tried to hide a smile. Even Tana suppressed a giggle. "It doesn't look so bad," she told her daughter. "The tops of the bow got a little pointed is all. From the back it looks just like the picture. Really."

Mila took the glossy from Yrund. "Huh, it does, actually,

Anouk. It's only from the front that you look like a troll. You'll just have to walk everywhere backward."

Jon-Luq wiggled his fingers over his head like horns. "Troll head," he said, and soon Tir and Magrit were copying him.

When Orelia snorted in her ears, Yrund had to suck back her own laugh. "Let me see!" she told Anouk, who turned around to face her, two large horns of hair sticking out from her head. Despite herself, Yrund's face cracked.

"You did it on purpose!" Anouk declared. "You and Mila are always making fun of me!"

"No, I didn't. I promise," said Yrund. "Let me try again. Maybe if—"

Someone banged on the door, interrupting the squabble.

It was Timo's brother, Sirj, who had just arrived from Floeberg. The second caravan was on the way.

"WELL, Yrund, you think you can manage the business while I'm away?" asked Ansyn, loading belongings into a pack. "Don't let Pir Jaq try to get the price down on anything."

"I won't," promised Yrund. It was the least she could do with half the village leaving. The caravan would miss Last Lake, but now Floeberg would play host to the memluks as they traveled north. From what Yrund could gather, the wield men would arrive to find a feast in process, just as they had in Last Lake. Only this time the Lumi had melted down enough plain silver to trade out nearly all the sleds. The rest of the details were a mystery though Didri had let slip that the seaside town had been practicing for the swap in the late night when the marine fog was thickest. Even Agnetha went along. With so many hands to help, the swap should hardly take a few minutes, Ansyn guessed. How they planned to distract the memluk watchmen, the adults wouldn't say, though Yrund noticed the trader had packed the cloudstone from his collection.

There was plenty to do for those that stayed behind—wood to chop and kindling to stack and herds to gather—all of which took on a hurried intensity that afternoon. A storm was pushing down from the north, driving a biting wind ahead of it. Yrund watched the snow flurrying outside the hall windows. She had just decided she would close the trader's shop early and go help Jon-Luq and Anouk bring in the rest of the snowdeer when Pir Jaq arrived.

Sure as Ansyn had warned, Pir Jaq wanted a discount on everything from a hammer he said looked scratched to the last tins of alat, but Yrund held firm on the trader's prices. She'd seen his books and knew he was already taking a loss on all the goods he'd brought with him.

"You're as pinching as the Asterian. Sure you aren't one of them?" the man said in Lumi, squinting at Yrund. He had a bit of lunch still stuck between his teeth.

"My family is from the Sky Steppes," responded Yrund in her best Lumi. "We were invaded by the wields just like you were."

"So you say, so you say…" He held a green gem up to the weak light filtering in the window. Outside, the snow was blowing like curtains of gray-dotted lace in the wind. "What's this one do again?"

"Ah…" Yrund tried hard to remember what the little stone was. She opened the gempendium sitting on the table by the stove and flipped through it, searching for something that might jog her memory.

Peardot, yawned Orelia, waking up.

"Peardot," repeated Yrund, relieved for the reminder. "It's good for…"

Old men with stinky breath.

"Old men with stinky—um." Yrund caught herself as she realized what the gem had said. "Pains in the limbs," she improvised.

"Old man, huh?" He glowered at her for a moment before noticing the gempendium spread open on the table. "How much for the book there?"

"It's not for sale," said Yrund, shutting it quickly.

"Everything's for sale with the Asterian," scoffed the man. "You just have to name the right price."

"Not this," said Yrund, wishing for a new customer as yells erupted outside. Yrund swung open the hall's door. To the north, an airship was bucking and bouncing to a landing on the ice of Last Lake.

An airship meant only one thing. Wield men. Yrund tried to think through her shock. The wield men weren't supposed to be here. They were supposed to be in Floeberg. And why did they have an airship? Unless—

"My flume!" Pir Jaq pushed Yrund out of the way.

"Bogging hell!" Yrund went back inside, scooping up Ansyn's small collection of gems and dropping them into a basket of buttons, which she shook to cover the stones. Next, she hid the trader's private account book under some dusty fabric, then added the gempendium for good measure. She was wondering what to do with Orelia, in her new pouch under Yrund's coat, when Mila flashed past the open door. The young woman was headed straight for the airship, and she was wearing her bow and quiver.

"No! Mila, no!"

"I'm just going to slow them down. Help Ama with the twins! Get Katrin and Didri!" yelled Mila, looking back but not stopping.

Yrund jumped down the hall's steps and into her skis, skidding around the corner to the Hayas' hut at the same time as Katrin. They found Tana already at the door, the scope to her eye.

"What are they doing here?" Katrin had to yell over the wind. "I thought the caravan was to go to Floeberg."

None of the other villagers understood either, only that the ship had come from the north, barely ahead of the blizzard on its tail.

"Tana!" said Yrund, tugging at her coat. "Tana, please, I need to see!"

Wordlessly, Tana handed Yrund the scope. There were ten passengers unloading from the ship. Yrund scanned through them with her heart in her mouth. Eight memluks, a tall man in a fancy coat, a woman whose hood hid her face, and Mila—who was leading the arrivals the long way around the lake. At least she hadn't shot anyone, thought Yrund.

There was no sign of Brandul or Veng. But Yrund did not relax.

What what? asked Orelia.

Trouble, Yrund answered, watching the wield men's clumsy progress.

She handed the scope back.

"Not the men who gave you those scars, then?"

"No," said Yrund. Still, she pulled her hood a little lower around her face.

"We've never had an airship here before!" said Little Tir as he and Magrit stood on their toes to catch a glimpse of the exotic sight through the snow. Even Orelia was curious, oohing at the large ship with its slowly deflating silk chambers. Only Anouk looked as frightened as Yrund felt.

"Should I get the dogs harnessed?" yelled Katrin.

"Naha, we'll never outrun what's blowing in," said Tana. "Gather everyone in the town hall. Tell them to bring food and alat—they'll be half-frozen."

"Maybe now's the time to kill them. While they're too cold to fight," observed Didri.

"Whoever it its, they're important, or they wouldn't have a ship. It's not like a few lost memluks disappearing in the woods. There would be an investigation. Retribution."

The villagers dispersed, grumbling but resigned.

"And bring instruments, but no flume! Anouk, get your fiddle." Tana looked to Katrin.

"Yaha, I'll stay with the twins," said Katrin, answering before even being asked. She pushed the little ones back inside.

"What can I do?" asked Yrund. Only she and Didri were left.

"Find Jon-Luq and gather every axe and bow you can find and hide them in the snow behind the hall's back door—hurry, you mustn't be seen. Have Lotti's children help you. And, Yrund," she said, holding her gaze, "keep your hood up tonight, understand?"

Yrund nodded.

"Didri?"

"Ready," said the silversmith, cinching her coat to conceal the ice axe hanging from her belt. Tana threw her skis down and they were off.

Yrund turned to see Jon-Luq already had the family's axes in his arms, plus his own bow and arrows. They stopped at the wood shop to gather more tools, recruiting helpers as they went. There wasn't much time. Despite Mila's detour, the line of visitors were halfway up from the lake.

CHAPTER TWENTY-EIGHT

Snow still clung to Yrund and Jon-Luq's gloves when they let themselves in the town hall's back door. They had collected and buried enough weapons to arm almost every adult in Last Lake, though Yrund didn't know how much good that would do when half of them were in Floeberg. Even if the wield men didn't have strikers, one trained memluk was a match for at least three untested Lumi, maybe more.

"I don't see why we can't just shoot them all," said Jon-Luq, jumping up to see out the crowded hall windows. "Like Ama planned to do with those dolts in the woods. Who cares if they're important?" The boy had clearly missed his mother's speech about not inviting retribution.

Yrund shared his frustration. She too wanted to set the wield's airship on fire, but she put a hand out. "If you piss off the Mining Wield, they won't just take your bright silver, they'll take your family—your mother, your sisters, even the twins. I know…"

Jon-Luq flicked his bangs out of his eyes. "So what are all those weapons for, then?"

But Yrund didn't have to say. The boy knew as well as she did. They were the last resort.

The scent of brewing alat filled the hall, its comforting aroma incongruous amid the tension. Ansyn's tables had been cleared to make room for hastily gathered plates of food near one stove. Near the other, Anouk was plucking at her fiddle. It looked like the beginning of a party, only the guests were all terrified.

"That's the ambassador of Darban!" The villagers surged closer to the windows, trying to get a look.

"And Lili! They've got Lili with them!"

The memluks climbed the steps up into the town hall, scattering snow across the wooden floor as they looked around at the assembled Lumi. Seeing no threat, a tall man wearing a long golden fur and hat entered next, followed by a woman. A hush fell over the hall.

Yrund's chest pounded. The woman had pushed back her hood. It was Brave Braid.

"Lili!" Several of the Lumi rushed to her, crying out, but the memluks forced them back, holding up the same big fighting hammers the guards had worn at Devil's Crown. The woman's gray-green eyes took in her people's faces as if they were water after a drought.

Tana led the tall man to the stove. "As I said, Ambassador Boole, we have food and alat for you and your men. When you have warmed yourselves, you can tell us more about what has brought you to our far corner of the south."

The ambassador, who was blue with cold, couldn't put one foot in front of the other without trembling. He and his men approached the stoves as if the fires were altars, hands outstretched in supplication. While the visitors thawed and ate, the Lumi whispered among themselves, staring at Lili, whose eyes darted from one side of the room to the other.

Looking for her sister, no doubt.

Someone mouthed something to Lili, and her face fell. Agnetha was still in Floeberg.

Finally, the ambassador turned from the warmth to address

the villagers. "I am Am-Am-Ambassador Binjin Boole of the Mining Wield of Asteria," he said, unable to control a lingering shiver. "We are seeking a missing airship. It was s-s-stolen from Darban last week, and reports claim it was sighted crossing the Lumi border. Anyone caught stealing Asterian property or assis-ss-ss-ting in such a theft will be subject to the highest penalties under Asterian law. You would do best to tell me what you know now before we discover it for ourselves."

The Lumi looked at each other with blank, confused faces.

Old Nicolai spoke first. "We've heard nothing of a missing airship," he said. "In fact, that airship out there is the first that Last Lake has ever seen." To prove his words, the windows were still crowded with children trying to get a look for themselves through the swirling snow.

"May I ask why we would go all the way to Darban to steal an airship?" asked Didri. "Aren't there much closer ships in Wind-market?" A few of the Lumi tittered.

The ambassador looked to his memluks, but they did not seem to be following the conversation, either because it was in Trade Tongue or because they were too caught up in the platter of blood sausages.

"The stolen ship was seen heading over your border," the ambassador said, his navy eyes flashing in the stove light.

"Don't know why anyone would think they'd come here to hide," said Pir Jaq in Lumi. "There's wield eyes all over our land nowadays."

For once, the man wasn't wrong.

"This is an absurd accusation," said Didri. "What would we do with an airship? Take our snowdeer flying? It is the wields who steal from us, taking our silver and people." A ripple of angry agreement went through the hall.

The ambassador's long nose flared, anger flushing the cold from his deep golden face. He seemed about to say something, then thought better of it and sat back in his chair. "Your village, what is it called again?"

"Last Lake," said Old Nicolai.

"Last Lake—hmm, this is farther south than we meant to search, but our instruments stopped working below Windmarket, and the winds took us off our course."

"You were lucky to have landed at all in this storm," said Tana. "You could have been blown right out to sea."

"So we found out. Your Lili here was the one that convinced our pilots to land. That will do well for shortening her sentence, let me assure you." He held out his empty mug, and Tana refilled it, her movements polite but stiff.

"Don't you think it could have been the Invisible Hand that stole the airship?" asked Anouk, still holding her fiddle.

Ooh, said Orelia. *The Hand is very handsome!*

How would you know? asked Yrund distractedly.

The story said so, said Orelia. *And he can fight ten men blindfolded.*

You can't believe everything you read in a story, said Yrund. No wonder Orelia thought allstones were real.

The ambassador smiled as he spoke to Anouk. "The Invisible Hand? You sound like my sister. Can you play that violin?"

Anouk tested a few notes when Tana nodded at her, then played a short song. The memluks listened with interest, and the ambassador clapped. Anouk was a fine musician, even when she was nervous.

"Very pretty," said the ambassador—whether he meant Anouk or the music was not clear.

"Perhaps after you have eaten, my daughter and the others could play a few more songs," said Tana.

"We would be honored," the ambassador said, his tone warming even further as a villager offered him a heaping plate of fish and turnips. "Mmm, buttered neeps!"

"Is Lili to stay here?" asked Tana, keeping her tone level. "We have missed her greatly since she was taken."

Ambassador Boole swallowed. "Your friend Lili, as I understand it, was caught trying to evade the tax stop outside Windmarket."

"Why should we pay Asterian taxes?" said Didri. "Since when did Lumi Land become part of Asteria?"

"We had a trade agreement with the Lumi," said the ambassador testily. "It was your people's failure to hold up their end of the bargain that led to our having to manage your commerce ourselves."

"Perhaps you are not aware, being all the way from Darban as you are, that the trade agreement to which you refer was supposed to provide the Lumi with goods and services that Asteria failed to send," said Didri, her jaw tight.

"Enough, Didri," said Tana. "The ambassador lives in Darban. Our complaint is with the capitol. Perhaps he is unaware of the unfair treatment we have received and would be glad to relay our concerns to the Commonwielder."

The ambassador flushed again, a bun partway to his mouth. "As you've said, this is not my area of jurisdiction—the ambassador in Windmarket oversees Lumi trade. Any complaints should be directed to her. In any event, Lili will return to Darban to finish her sentence. She was lucky not to be sent to Smeralgdus like the other rabu—it turns out the cook has found her to be invaluable."

"Lili is a herder, not a servant. Her place is here with her people," insisted Didri.

"No, her place is in my kitchen. Unless you can make puffovers as well as she does." Ambassador Boole signaled his memluks to his side, finished with the conversation. "We'll let you know when we need you again. Last Lake's hospitality will not go unnoticed by the wield."

Pir Jaq shuffled forward. "We want our Lili back," he

demanded in Lumi. The memluks towered over the man, who stood his ground, unfazed. Then Pir Jaq turned to point toward Yrund, hiding at the back of the crowd. "You can have that foreign girl for trade. She's not one of us. She's—"

A jarring chord cut through the air as Anouk stepped in front of Pir Jaq and launched into a rollicking flume song.

Lotti and Old Nicolai each grabbed one of Pir Jaq's arms, leading him forcefully away from the ambassador while over the noise Tana tried to explain it was all just a Lumi joke. Yrund stood paralyzed as Orelia buzzed in her ears. Lili was looking straight at her.

For a long moment, Yrund stared back. Then Jon-Luq was turning her and pushing her out the door. The other villagers pressed in to close the space behind them, joining Anouk in the loud drinking song. The last thing Yrund heard was the deep sound of a Douarr voice chiming in to hum the chorus. It seemed someone, at least, had found the plumberry wine.

YRUND STAYED with Katrin that night, listening to her curse Pir Jaq while they made dinner in her and Hinri's cozy house, decorated with carved wooden platters and a bark vase filled with dried willows. "That selfish, shortsighted old goat!" Katrin fumed as she dropped two small snowdeer steaks into a hot pan. "And Lili! Can you believe the gall of the ambassador, after she saved them from getting blown out to sea? Why can't he let her stay? What if we took his sister? I bet he wouldn't be so pompous then." She stabbed the steaks with her belt knife, lifting them off the heat and onto wooden plates.

They talked little as they ate, wiping up the pan drippings with some leftover bread. After dinner, they tried to play a round of sytranj, but neither of them could concentrate, repeatedly forgetting whose turn it was. Didri stopped in, but the news was the same: The ambassador and his guards had stuffed themselves on the Lumi's food and wine and gone to sleep early in the town hall. Lili was not allowed to leave or to speak to any of the villagers.

"Agnetha will be beside herself when she finds out!"

Tana had sent Mila to Floeberg to get her, but there was almost no chance the healer could return before the wield men headed back to Darban with her sister.

"At least Lili is still alive," said Didri.

It was a turn of events Yrund could not believe. Or stomach. For Agnetha to keep hope against all odds, only to have her sister ripped from her twice. It was too much.

"The ambassador looks easy enough to take down. It's the memluks that are the problem," said Didri. "I promise you I would burn that hall down if our Lili wasn't in there with them." She paced by the stove, the lines in her face accentuated by the flames.

"We could set fire to their ship," suggested Katrin.

"They would set fire to the village," said Yrund. Just as they had done to her own home.

"What, then? We can't let them take her away again!"

"I say give them Pir Jaq. Trying to turn in Yrund—he should be ashamed of himself," said Didri.

"If only the others were here," said Katrin, her hand moving instinctively to protect the child inside her. "Of all the days for everyone to be gone…"

"Better they are," said Didri with a sigh. "And Agnetha, too—she would die a thousand times to set her sister free." The silversmith looked at the sytranj board they had abandoned and moved a lion to take down a deer.

ALL OF LAST Lake was gathered outside the town hall the next morning. The storm had passed, leaving a fresh blanket of snow across the streets. Yrund didn't have to be told to stay home, but Tana told her anyway. "I'm sorry, Yrund, I thought you would be safer hidden among us, but after Pir Jaq…"

"I know," said Yrund, just glad they hadn't locked her in like the man. Katrin and Didri had nailed up Pir Jaq's doors and windows overnight, and they did not intend to let him out until well after the ambassador was gone.

After the others left, Yrund stood on a chair to see what was happening through the Hayas' little window, the twins balanced precariously in front of her. At second dawn, they watched Lili come down the hall's steps between two memluks, her arms tied with rope, followed by Ambassador Boole, who paused at the top to say a few words to the villagers amassed below him, his striker belt on the outside of his coat. Whatever the man was saying, it was short, for just a few moments later the ambassador gave a little bow. Then, almost as an afterthought, he stopped in front of Tana and made a small fiddle-playing gesture with his arms. Tana shook her head, pushing Anouk behind her. The ambassador gave the slightest shrug.

With no warning, the memluk beside him knocked Tana down while another heaved a screeching Anouk up over his shoulder, as if she were no more than a sack of grain. Anouk began to shriek, striking out, until the first memluk hit her with the back of his boulder-sized fist and pulled a bag over her head. The Lumi went mad, attacking the man like fleas on a dog.

Fear like Yrund had never known slammed through her as the villagers went down.

Topaz me! she told Orelia. *Topaz me now!* She couldn't just stand here and do nothing. Yrund untangled herself from the twins. *Give me courage!*

"Stay here!" she yelled at Tir and Magrit, grabbing up her bow and quiver and slamming the door on their wails. Blood roaring through her ears, Yrund ran toward the melee, nocking an arrow as she went.

Tana was struggling to get up, Didri beside her with her ice axe ready. The silver-haired woman got in one good swing before the memluk's hammers took her down. Jon-Luq and Old Nicolai rushed in with nothing but their belt knives—they hadn't had time to get to the buried weapons. The ambassador turned with his striker, releasing a blazing ball of fire straight through the old man and sending Jon-Luq staggering back from the flash, blinded, unable to see the memluk's fist swinging down into his blistered face. Too late, Yrund's arrow bounced off the man's belt. Yrund released a second arrow, which sank into the man's arm as his hammer crashed into a screaming Tana. No, no, no, no, no!

Yrund shot again, the shaft splitting as it was stopped by an amulet. The memluk broke it off like a twig, not even looking where it had come from. Yrund let loose again as the man collided with another memluk covered in Lumi. Lotti screamed as Yrund's arrow hit her thigh. Blast it to hell!

Yrund only had one arrow left.

The village was in chaos, women and children crying as the memluks tore through them with their hammers. Fury cut through her like a flame. In her ears she could hear Orelia howling to kill them, destroy them—burn them. And suddenly Yrund was charging.

"Hey, you *rppty fynryg mzrylycks!*" she screamed, using every Douarr curse she knew. The memluks turned to see who was yelling, pausing their assault.

"Yaha! You blooding *fynryg mzrylycks!* Is this how the mighty Sea Hammers make the Sea Mother proud—attacking deer herders and children? *Rppty* cowards," she yelled. "Is this what you gave up your boats for? To sell your souls to the Mining Wield?" She threw down her bow and last arrow and reached for the pouch around her neck, her anger a fire ready to break free.

"*Fynryg mzrylycks?*" one of the memluks asked the other, hammer paused midswing.

"Yaha, you *fynryg mzrylycks!*" That seemed to be the only part the men understood. "Come and get me," she yelled. She would burn them like kindling.

The memluk lowered his hammer and laughed—a big, booming guffaw that spread through all the men.

"*Fynryg mzrylycks!!!*" they howled, slapping each other on the back.

The ambassador looked around at the few Lumi still standing. Blood and bone littered the snow.

"Come get me!" screamed Yrund again, but the men were done with her.

"Enough," said Binjin Boole, signaling for the memluks to regroup. "We need to go before the next storm comes." One of the memluks, still chuckling, repeated the order in Douarr.

The memluks hauled up the bound Lili, who had been knocked down in the fighting, and gave the still-yelling Anouk another thump before they closed ranks around the ambassador.

"You can't take them!" Yrund ran after them through the snow.

"No? Is a child going to stop me?" asked the ambassador, almost amused.

Finally, Yrund saw what they saw—a girl in an oversized coat who had dropped her bow and last arrow. While they were eight memluks and a man with a striker.

Burn them! said Orelia. *Burrrrrrn them!*

But doubt had crept in. How? She struggled to get the stone free from its pouch, suddenly unsure what to do with it. With the little woodwin in the Hidden Forest, it had all happened too fast to follow. Did she just run over and touch Orelia to the ambassador? What about the striker? Was she supposed to throw the stone? She hadn't even thought to bring her sling. And what then?

Maybe Orelia could light one man on fire, maybe even all of them, but what about Lili and Anouk?

The image of the little woodwin rose up before her, crying in pain. She did not know how to wield the stone without hurting her friends. In fact, she didn't know how to wield it at all. Not as a weapon. As a nepenthe, perhaps. On a pile of silver bricks. But on a person?

"Take the little brat, too," she heard the ambassador say, as if through a fog. "We can always use more bodies in Smeralgdus."

CHAPTER TWENTY-NINE

The trip to Darban was freezing and miserable, the suns a wan silver above the high clouds. At the ambassador's orders, the pilots cranked two sets of gears, rotating one and then another glowing gem into position. The airship flew north and east, cutting across a black sea rough with white waves, the engine burning hot and bright. Yrund had been thrown beside Lili and Anouk at the far end of the ship, away from the pilots and the single fur-lined chair upon which the ambassador sat bundled, a long brass scope to his eye. He faced north, calling out landmarks to the pilot at the rudder, a term Yrund only knew because of Ansyn and Humphrey—neither of whom she would ever see again.

Through one of the hull's triangular drains, the hundreds of lakes that formed the Lumi's country went by, their snow-covered depths occasionally mottled with blue ice or a trail of footprints strung out behind a family of plodding moose. Anouk groaned, trying to wipe the frozen snot and blood from her face. They had removed the bag from her head, but she still looked dazed. Lili hushed her when she tried to speak.

Bored, one of the memluks shook a small keeps sack at the

others, looking for a game. Anouk followed him with angry swollen eyes.

"Stop glaring at them!" whispered Yrund. "Act like you're afraid!" Yrund knew memluks. To fear them was to respect them, and respect was not optional.

"I am afraid," Anouk hissed back. Blood had dried into a mat in her blond hair and the white of one eye was red with burst vessels. Was she afraid enough, though? Anouk was Mila Haya's sister, after all.

"Where are they taking us?"

"Darban," whispered Lili from Anouk's other side, gesturing for her to hush.

"Why? What are they going to do with us?" asked Anouk stubbornly.

"Highsmith Boole needs a wawa, so do as Little Thorn says," said Lili under her breath. "If you make trouble, they'll only send you to the mines."

Anouk's face crumpled, and she began to cry. Yrund wrapped her arms around the girl, looking up at Lili, whose hands were still tied. A world of silent understanding passed between them. Though they had never spoken in Devil's Crown, Yrund had more in common with the Lumi woman than almost anyone on Precios.

The memluks did not bother to offer them anything to eat or drink as the hours floated past, although they did throw some frosty blankets toward the women when the ambassador told them to.

"*Fynryg mzrylyck*," parroted the men to each other, the joke seeming to tickle them more every time they said it.

Dirty trolls, said Orelia.

Not trolls, thought Yrund. Just humans. Humphrey was right. They were an abomination.

A great sorrow came upon her, dark as the sea they were approaching.

Yrund...? asked the gem. *What's wrong, Yrund?*

Everything, she answered.

The Lumi would lose their silver and their herds and their loved ones until there was nothing left to take. The Mining Wield would finish its road through the Sky Country, dividing her people from their land. They would keep her mother and her sisters and her aunt and her cousins—

And, they would take Orelia. They would cut her and set her and give her to Niloofar Damantine.

No! said the stone as if reading Yrund's mind. *I won't go!*

But it was too late. Yrund had put Orelia right in the hands of the enemy. She could have learned how to use the stone. To fight with her. To wield her. But she had been too afraid. Afraid of who she might become. Afraid of what she might lose. Afraid, no matter what she did, she would fail. Who was she to wield a stone that could burn forests or erase memories? She was just a shepherd. And a gem shy one at that.

I'm sorry, said Yrund. *I can't let them have you.* She pulled the gem's pouch over her head, clutching the stone one last time. Then she dropped her into the rippling sea below.

EXCEPT THE GEM did not drop. Yrund shook her hand, thinking the fabric had frozen to her glove, but the gem would not budge.

I'm sorry, Orelia! But they will find you...and use you...to do terrible things, and I will not be able to stop them.

She shook her hand again, but the gem was stuck fast.

I can stop them, said the stone as if that were that.

No, you can't—none of us can.

I can burn down this ship.

We're on this ship! said Yrund. *What good would that do?*

It wouldn't save the Lumi. Or the Sky Country. No, it was over. She had missed her chance, and now it was too late. She didn't know what to do with a gem like Orelia. She didn't even know how to make her be quiet half the time. But the wields would. The wields would find a way. And it would be the innocent that suffered.

It's too dangerous, said Yrund. *You cannot stay with me.*

Still Orelia would not listen. And she would not let go. Yrund began to beat the stone against the ship's bottom, trying to dislodge it.

"Wh-what are…are you doing?" whispered Anouk, breaking out of her shivering stupor.

Yrund looked up at Anouk and Lili's cold, confused faces.

How could she possibly explain?

Then before she could even try, Yrund's body went limp. She slumped into Anouk and Lili, unable to even lift her hand.

Orelia! Don't you dare gem me! she thought desperately. But a gentle warmth was spreading through her, slowly quieting her mind. The warmth spread out of Yrund and into her friends, stopping Anouk's chattering teeth and returning the color to Lili's cheeks.

Orelia! pleaded Yrund one last time before a forgetful calm came over them all, like a fog of fragrant purple flowers.

Hush, said the stone, and Yrund did.

CHAPTER THIRTY

They flew through the day and all of the night, arriving in Darban the next morning.

Yrund woke to a memluk hauling her up by her collar and throwing her in the back of a black sleigh painted with gold eagles and snakes.

What was happening? Yrund wiggled her fingers and her hands, feeling returning, and realized she no longer held the stone.

Orelia!

I'm here, said the gem from the pouch beneath Yrund's coat. Yrund didn't know when she'd put her back.

The driver clicked his tongue, and the sleigh slid forward. He wore a belted felt jacket and thick padded mittens, which held the reins lightly.

What are they? asked Orelia about the long-legged, long-eyelashed creatures, whose big, wide feet acted like snowshoes as they pulled them along through the snow.

Camels, said Yrund, who had seen them many times at the Sky Games back home, though never in snow and never with such soft and thick coats. The animals carried them from the airfields through a light snowfall toward the city. Darban was a hundred times the size of Last Lake, with pointed black-tiled roofs and thousands of slender chimneys, each piping up a line of gray smoke.

They slid through the city's narrow streets behind the camels, Yrund and Anouk goggling at the tall houses with their colored glass windows and carved wooden gables and the other sleds, pulled mostly by yaks. They eventually turned between two towering homes and into a hidden yard lined with bare trees and iron gates. As they did, a gold-painted door at the top of a flight of stairs banged wide open, rattling the enormous mural windows that stretched up two stories from a delicate gilded balcony.

"Binjin!" said a dark-haired woman in a sweeping blue dress coat from the top of the stairs. She was tall and broad-shouldered with the same dark navy eyes and strong nose as the ambassador and the same deep golden skin, but without the long chin. "Where in the five continents have you been? We expected you home two days ago! You were only supposed to go to Wind-market and back! I sent ten pigeons!"

"Hello, Banny," said the ambassador, getting out of his sleigh. "Sorry to scare you—there was an unexpected storm that blew us down into the Silverlands…blinking instruments useless in the south…then we were against the wind all the way back. But don't be mad—I've brought my favorite sister a present!" He spread his arm toward Anouk with a flourish.

"What would I want with that?" said the ambassador's sister, looking down with disdain at the half-frozen girl the memluks were hauling out of the sleigh.

Anouk Haya had never looked worse, hair matted and face filthy and eyes swollen red with crying, a small crust of bloody snot beneath her nose.

"She plays the fiddle like a dream—just wait till you hear!"

"Are you suggesting this is my new wawa?" Her lip curled.

"Just get the keeper to clean her up, and then you'll see. She's a pretty little thing underneath all that…that…" He finally seemed to see Anouk as his sister did. "Well, you'll see…," he said lamely again.

"At least you've brought back Lili." His sister sighed dramatically. "The cook can hardly be expected to cater Lady Darbana's party all on his own!"

"Lady Darbana!" said the ambassador, putting a hand to his face as he went up the steps. "I'd entirely forgotten!"

"Obviously," she said, opening the door for him to enter. She looked back down at Yrund, whom the memluks had forced out of the sleigh beside Lili. "Does that one also play the fiddle?"

"That's Highsmith Boole," whispered Lili.

The ambassador turned as if he'd forgotten Yrund existed. "Oh yes, the little brat was shooting at my men. Put her in the stables or something until I can put her on a ship to Smeralgdus."

"The stables? With all this work there is to do? It was your idea to throw Lady Darbana a nameday party before the trade route talks."

"Yes, yes, I know. But my airship was spotted and—"

"And it couldn't wait until after the deal was signed? You are a man of feeble brains, Binjy. We'll put her in the kitchens." She turned back to face Lili, who had a large bruise across her face and a trickle of dried blood above her ear. "What happened to you?" Then back to her brother. "What have you done to my cook?"

"Don't blame me—it was those squalid Lumi people that started it…" The rest of what he said disappeared inside with him.

Ms. Boole leaned over the stairs' railing, pointing a gold-ringed finger at the memluks and speaking harshly in Douarr. The men looked sheepish, untying Lili, then beating a quick retreat.

"Well, then," said Ms. Boole to Lili, who stood in the snow

with Yrund and Anouk. "Get yourselves a scrub and some real clothes—there's a party to prepare for, though I don't see how we'll possibly be ready by tomorrow night—I still haven't finished Lady Darbana's new scent!" She pulled up the neck of her coat against the wind. "And for the sake of the Way, go get Bezel to find you some halestones for those bruises. I won't have my house girls looking like common potch and paffle."

As the door at the top of the stairs slammed shut behind High-smith Boole, a second door swung open on the ground floor.

"Took you blooding long enough," said an enormous red-haired man with a towel over one shoulder and flour down his apron. He was leaning lightly on a cane. "Thought maybe you'd gone and tried to throw the ambassador over the—" He paused, mouth open above his gem-woven beard, as he saw Lili's bruises. His gaze swung from her to Anouk and then Yrund, where it stopped.

Gem Beard. Yrund didn't think her heart knew how to beat any faster. She stumbled backward in the snow, and Lili reached out to catch her.

"It wasn't me this time. It was the ambassador and your beastly memluks attacking my sister's village," said Lili defiantly, pushing a resisting Yrund straight toward Gem Beard.

What, what? said Orelia. *Who is that?*

A traitor, said Yrund.

Wowwa, said the stone, clearly impressed.

Lili forced Yrund through the door. "Inside now, quickly. Melmeth's the least of your problems."

Yrund felt herself being propelled past the big man, felt his eyes on her back as she entered a large, low-ceilinged kitchen, followed by Anouk, looking both frightened and confused.

Gem Beard closed the kitchen door behind them, then cursed

at the half dozen servants that stood gaping. "Back to work, or I'll break all your bones and boil them for broth!"

He motioned Lili and the two girls into a side pantry, still unable to take his eyes from Yrund.

"Chicken?" he said, reaching out to touch her bleached hair. "Is that really you? Or are you a ghost?" His own face had lost much of its color.

Yrund knocked his hand away, scowling.

"Yup! That's the chicken," the memluk said, beaming at her and shaking his great beard. "Thought you were dead."

"I hoped you *were* dead!" she spat back. "Leaving me with Brandul—"

"You're alive, aren't you? So there you go—just wasn't your Way. Though I don't know how in the Mother of the Sea you got out of that cave-in…it gives me the jeeblies."

Yrund sputtered, unable to find the words the traitorous memluk deserved.

"You know him?" said Anouk, alarmed.

"I thought I did," said Yrund, still glaring at the big man.

Gem Beard was as threatening in an apron as he had ever been—muscles bursting from what appeared to be a custom-made tunic embroidered in the Mining Wield's colors below his vest. Instead of his usual hammers, though, he wore several thick-handled spoons like clubs and a row of gleaming cleavers, which hung at his belt like instruments of war. And he had a new tattoo on his forearm—the razor peaks of Devil's Crown. Seeing Anouk staring, he flexed it and growled. When she jumped, he laughed.

"Leave her be," said Lili. "She's been terrorized enough for one day. Your Sea Hammers cut down her family right in front of her."

To Yrund's surprise, the memluk stopped laughing.

"Melmeth!" called a sour voice. "Where have you gone?"

"Be right there, Bezel," Gem Beard called back in an exasperated tone. "Skinny little ninny-hag, I'd like to put her through the ricer. These girls down here with us, I hope? I could use a few more hands."

"For now," said Lili, her face troubled.

Ninny-hag, said Orelia, giggling, before Yrund told her to shut up.

"Allyright, then! It's about time you were back," Melmeth told Lili. "My puffovers still aren't rising up right." As Yrund followed Lili out of the pantry, Gem Beard gave her head a happy thump.

"Aren't you one lucky little chicken!" he said, still amazed.

That was not at all how Yrund would have put it.

LILI GUIDED Yrund and Anouk through the bustling kitchen and the still-staring servants, up several flights of narrow stairs, and into a long corridor on the fourth floor. She led them through the first door on the left, which turned out to be a sort of indoor outhouse with wood-partitioned toilet rooms and sinks that drained through a maze of pipes. Yrund had heard of such things but never before seen them, nor apparently had Anouk, who also gawked at the gleaming taps and polished mirrors and glowing sunsstone sconces. A row of metal tubs stood at the end of the tiled floor, larger than any wash buckets Yrund had ever seen.

"This is where you live?" asked Anouk, slowly spinning to take it all in with her good eye, fear temporarily overcome with awe. "I thought they sent you to the mines."

"They did send me to the mines," said Lili. "And if it wasn't for Melmeth, they would have sent me to Smeralgdus."

"Who's Melmeth?" asked Anouk.

"She means Gem Beard," answered Yrund.

"Gem Beard? Yaha, that does fit him, doesn't it?" said Lili, almost smiling.

"How did you escape from Devil's Crown?" demanded Yrund,

who had even more questions than Anouk for the Lumi woman. "We heard there was a muti—"

Lili put her finger to her lips. "I might ask you the same question, Little Thorn, if we only had the time. But Bezel, I mean Keeper Antonina, will be up to check on us soon. I must get you washed and dressed—"

"Why do you call her Little Thorn?" asked Anouk. "Her name is Yrund."

"Yrund…," said Lili, savoring the name. "I'm afraid we didn't know each other's names at the mine," she explained to Anouk. "So you come up with your names in your head—and Yrund here, well—Little Thorn just fit," explained Lili. "I don't suppose you ever had a name for me…"

"I did," said Yrund. "It was Brave Braid."

"Brave Braid? Me?"

"You did save me from Veng, remember?"

Lili's auburn eyebrows rose up as her mouth made an O. Then she turned away, wiping her eyes and moving with purpose around the strange room and gathering stacks of undergarments and dresses from a wall of cupboards at the end. "We haven't got long to bathe. You can leave your clothes and boots there—I'll take care of them."

Anouk began to do as she was told, but Yrund just stood there, a new dread rising. "I'm still wearing the ouroborus," she confessed to Lili. "Around my ankles."

Lili swore. With her coat off, Yrund could see the Lumi woman's wrists were ringed, not with the ouroborus, but dull gold bangles—each stamped with an *MW*. "Even more reason to hurry," Lili said, going over to one of the large metal tubs and turning the taps. Steaming water poured from the pipes like magic. "Try not to let anyone see the ouroborus—not until after the party. The highsmith will be in a good mood then… Between Melmeth and me, well…we'll think of something to convince her you would be wasted in the mezmerald mines. Now, into the baths," said Lili, passing them scented soap and towels.

"Don't they have a steam room?" asked Anouk, getting into one of the steaming metal tubs.

"No, this is how Asterians bathe," said Lili, slipping into her own tub. "Hush with your questions—there is much I need to tell you about working for the ambassador and his sister."

Yrund stripped off her layers and boots, the eyes of the gray, snake anklets sparkling hatefully up at her.

"Damn the Mining Wield," said Lili under her breath. Then she gasped as her gaze rose from the ouroborus to Yrund's arrow wound and the blue stains Veng's stars had left. They were not Yrund's only scars, but they were the ugliest.

"Did the Astrini, Veng, do all that to you?"

Yrund nodded, seeing Lili had plenty of new scars of her own.

"I should have killed him when I had the—"

The door opened, and they all fell silent as a maid ran in to use the toilet. Yrund sank low in the tub, trying to hide her ankles and washing herself quickly.

When the maid was gone, Yrund jumped out to get dressed again, pulling the socks on first, then her boots before the undergarments and itchy woolen dress.

It was Anouk that broke the silence, her voice trembling. "Will they beat me here, too?"

"Not if you do as you are told!" said Lili, drying off. "You will be working for the highsmith, and she does not believe in beatings, despite her brother's attitudes to the contrary. She is still a cruel woman in her way, but with her it is words, not fists, though, well…she does like to throw things—"

"When do you think they will come for us? Apa and Mila and Agnetha?"

"Agnetha," said Lili, letting out a little breath. "I wish I could have seen her…just for a moment."

"She never gave up believing you might still be alive," said Yrund, feeling guilty she had doubted her.

"No—Agnetha does not believe in giving up," said Lili with a bittersweet combination of pride and regret. "But, for now, we are on our own. So get dressed, both of you. The sooner you prove your worth, the better—"

"But they will come, won't they?" said Anouk, her voice rising as she pulled her own yellow dress on. "I want to go home! I want to see Ama and—" Her eyes closed as the day's events replayed in her head. "What if…what if Ama and Jon-Luq are dead?"

Lili took Anouk's chin firmly in her hands. "All you can worry about is what is in front of you. They might be dead. They might be alive, but if you don't survive today, right now, you will never find out."

"I just want to go home!" said Anouk, trying not to cry. "I want everything to go back to how it was."

"Nothing will ever go back to how it was—but you are still Anouk Haya. They cannot take that away from you. Not by making you scrub toilets or wash a bitter woman's hair or walk up and down the same flight of stairs a thousand times. And someday, the tide will turn, and we will be free again. But for now, you have me and you have Yrund, and we have you, and that is a great deal indeed. Yaha?" she said.

"Yaha," said Anouk, putting her arms around them.

Yaha, added Orelia.

"Besides," said Lili, squeezing them back, "sometimes even the dead come back to life. Yrund here is proof."

When they had all finished dressing, Lili bundled up their Lumi coats and clothes and then, looking up and down the hall to see that no one was watching, hid them away under a bench at the back of a dusty closet.

"Why are you putting them in there?" said Anouk.

"Because Keeper Antonina will throw them away if she finds them, and—"

"We'll need them when Agnetha and Apa come for us?"

"For instance," said Lili, inspecting them in their new clothes. Then she lowered her voice. "From now on, you must keep your head down, but your eyes and ears open—"

"For what?" asked Anouk.

"Anything," said Lili, "that might help us give the tide a little push."

"You mean like a secret war—like in Last Lake?" whispered Anouk.

Lili looked to Yrund for explanation.

"The Lumi are sabotaging the wields any way they can, but secretly so..." The rest didn't have to be said. Lili knew exactly what would happen to those that were caught.

"A secret war," said Lili, nodding. "That's just what it is. You are spies now—" She cut herself off. Someone was coming.

"Aren't you done yet?" asked Keeper Antonina, stomping up the stairs to check on them. She was a narrow-faced woman with dark pulled-back hair, wearing a garish rouge the wrong hue for her purple-tinged skin. She was taller than Yrund and unattractively thin, her bony wrists poking from her gold sleeves. Small gray stones the color of ashes bobbled from her ears as she looked them each up and down.

"Good Way, Keeper Antonina," said Lili. "We're almost done." She finished braiding Anouk's hair and pinned it up into coils. Yrund's wilder locks were more difficult to tame, barely flattening even with a comb.

"Just get her a bonnet," complained Keeper Antonina, foot tapping with impatience. "Is that cobaline?" she asked suspiciously, trying to wipe the blue scar off from under Yrund's eye. Orelia snarled in Yrund's ears.

"It's from an old case of blotch," Lili interjected, retrieving two flouncy white hats from the cupboards. "A bad azulite when she was small."

"She doesn't look Lumi," said the keeper. "She looks like a westerner."

"Her father was a sailor." Lili shrugged. "You know how it is."

"From where—the Silk Sea? What's your name?"

"Yrund."

"What kind of name is Yuh-roond?"

"Not Yuh-roond. Yrund."

"Eh-roond?" The keeper shook her head. "I suppose it doesn't matter. You'll be in the kitchen, anyway. For now... But you're a fright, aren't you?" The keeper turned to Anouk, who still bore a face full of bruises and a swollen dark eye. She took a string of small blue-green beads from a purse at her waist and fastened them around Anouk's wrist. "That's as good as I can do. Why the ambassador saw fit to bring me back an illiterate outlander to serve the highsmith—well, you'll all be gone soon enough. The Booles don't like outlanders. Come on, then, pick up your feet, girl. There's work to do..."

Anouk took one last nervous look back at them before the keeper led her down the stairs.

CHAPTER THIRTY-ONE

Yrund followed Lili back down to the kitchens, counting the number of doors and floors as they went, an old habit left over from the mines, for the grand four-floored house was just as convoluted a maze with its multiple sets of stairs and warrens of rooms. The entire bottom level was for the cooking and laundry and other business related to running a large house, and the only place kitchen maids were ever allowed to go, besides the fourth floor that housed the servants' dorms and bathrooms. The second, she was told, was for the ambassador's entertaining and diplomatic business, and the third for the private quarters for the ambassador and his guests, including his sister, who had three entire rooms all to herself. Lili said one was just for making perfume.

Downstairs, behind the kitchen, there were maids arranging flowers made of gems under Keeper Antonina's watchful eyes, and boys shining shoes and replacing sunsstones in dead lanterns. There were servants with pigeon posts and trays coming and going every which way and the cacophony of dozens of people at work, including a troupe of musicians who seemed to be lost. Lili soon kicked them out, but not before they pilfered an egg and currant pie.

The kitchen was at its highest roar yet—the ovens blazing and pots boiling and maids scurrying beneath Gem Beard's arms to set down a tray of plucked quails.

"Lili! Get those birds buttered and stuffed," he commanded with a point of a large knife before turning to Yrund.

The memluk guffawed at Yrund's puffy, starched bonnet. "You look like a marsh-meringue!" Then his scarred face grew serious. "We've got sixty people coming tonight and ten courses to get ready, so put your fighting jewels on, little chicken." He tossed her a small knife from his belt. "Milly—show this new runt how to roll the moon pies." Then he returned to the great stove with its dozen flaming burners, flipping sizzling pans with two hands at once.

"I'm Tilly," said a slim girl, rolling her black eyes. "*That's* Milly," she said, pointing to a round maid with pale skin who gave Yrund a red-cheeked smile as she bustled past with a stack of clean plates.

"You'd think he'd have it straight by now," complained Tilly, leading Yrund to the far end of the kitchen's long central table, where rows of tiny pies gleamed with spirals of caramelized pears beneath a crescent-shaped crust.

"He just knows it annoys you," said Yrund, who knew full well that the memluk could tell the difference between five shades of blue seefire, much less a dark willowy maid and a short pink one with a turned-up nose and freckles. They were as different as night and day. Tilly had straight, shiny black hairs peeking out of her bonnet and a curved rosebud mouth, while Milly had red curls like the memluk's and a little pointed chin.

"Oh," said Tilly, as if this had never occurred to her, rolling out a fresh crust of cool dough. "I don't know why it bothers me —Tilly isn't even my real name. I'm called Zhenyi back home, but the keeper couldn't pronounce that. Your name isn't really Chicken, is it?"

"No, it's Yrund."

"What's your birthstone, Eeh-roond?" asked Milly as she went by again, this time bearing a leaning pile of mixing bowls.

"I…I don't know."

"Mine's rubily, but I've never had one," Milly shared, narrowly avoiding the end of Gem Beard's towel.

"I'm not paying you to jibber-jabber!" he yelled.

"He's not paying us at all," said Tilly in a low voice. "Well, except for news from upstairs or next door."

That sounded like Gem Beard. Always looking out for himself.

Yrund watched the dark-eyed maid cut moons out of the dough with fast flicks of her sharp knife.

"Got it?" Tilly asked, fanning the pears into the small pan.

Moon pies! said Orelia, and Yrund felt her hand reaching towards one of the desserts.

Stop that, she told the stone. *They aren't even cooked yet.* Nonetheless her mouth watered. She hadn't eaten anything since the morning before.

"I've got it," Yrund told Tilly, taking the knife.

"Good," said the maid, for Gem Beard was roaring for someone to come get the blinking cheese twists from the broiler.

It was hard and busy work, but Yrund had to admit it was still a thousand times better than working at Devil's Crown. So Yrund rolled and trimmed out pastry moons as best she could, trying to make them look just like Tilly's. Then she was on to kneading bread dough and peeling carrots and painting egg whites onto loaves and pulling boiled turnips from a pot and washing dishes and pots and sweeping up a broken bowl. After that, Milly showed her how to hedgehog parsnips and drizzle them with duck fat. The work went on and on with no breaks, except to dunk a mug under the tap for a quick drink before starting yet another sink full of pans that needed scrubbing.

"I need a taster," yelled Gem Beard, searching around the kitchen, which had suddenly gotten even busier if that were possible. "Lili?"

But Lili had popped upstairs on an errand. "Milly, then!" The girl appeared reluctantly by his side.

"Well?"

Milly took a tiny mouthful. "It's good, boss!" said the little maid, looking eager to get away.

"Useless little sea slug—you, chicken," he commanded Yrund. "Come here and taste this. I burnt my tongue on the jam."

Yrund came over, still holding a crate full of beets. The memluk shoved a spoon of sauce in her face.

"Well?" he asked again.

The kitchen paused to hear Yrund's answer.

Yrund swallowed, then winced.

"That bad, huh?"

The pale sauce was rich with cream and wine but bland. Very bland. "Bleh, it needs salt." She'd never had anything like the food in the ambassador's kitchen, but that was obvious even to her.

The maids exchanged a worried glance.

"Uh-huh." Gem Beard nodded, tucking his beard back into his apron so it wouldn't dangle in the pan. "That's what I thought. At least someone besides Lili has some spine around here."

"Did I hear you saying nice things about me again?" asked Lili, returning.

"Not a chance, you uppity snoweater." The memluk threw another pinch of salt into the sauce, along with a sprinkle of crimson spice. Yrund tasted again, expecting little difference, but the sauce was transformed. She licked her lips, suddenly ravenous. "Better, eh?" said Gem Beard, elbowing her out of the way.

Lili traded Yrund the beets for an even heavier crate of plump cabbages. Yrund nearly dropped it.

"Have you eaten yet?"

"No," said Yrund.

"What?" said Gem Beard, who seemed to be able to hear even the smallest gossip or mistake over the rest of the kitchen's noise. He handed the pan over to Lili to watch. "There's no one that's allowed to starve in my kitchen," he said, wiping his hands. "Been wanting to have a little chat with you anyway." The aproned memluk steered Yrund toward yet another of the house's larders as he limped behind her with his cane.

"Have as much of anything in this pantry as you can eat yourself. Touch anything in the others, or try and sell anything to the chef next door, and I'll cut your arms off."

Yrund looked around at the great wheels of cheese and baskets of bread and crates of apples and pears. "There's boar sausages in that ice box," said Gem Beard, pointing a big finger. "I'll take one, too, while you're at it."

Yrund ate ravenously, stuffing the sausages into her mouth along with a hunk of sour bread Gem Beard tore off from a round loaf.

"So, tell me," said the memluk, looking around to see that no one was watching before he sat down on a cask and began to massage his leg. "Which ship was it you stowed away on? 'Cause I know that's how you must have done it—found an old adit after the cave-in to squeeze out…then snuck yourself on board as we were leaving. I bet it was the second ship when it was raining— am I right? Just squeezed in with the others?"

"Uh-huh," said Yrund, ripping off some more of the sour bread. That was as good an explanation as any since she wasn't about to tell a man who worked for the wield about Orelia or the woodwins.

"You stowed away—I knew it," said Gem Beard, clearly proud of himself for figuring it out.

"Yrund?" asked Milly, poking her head into the pantry. "Where'd you put the rest of those drippings?"

"In that brown bowl with the towel at the end of the poultry larder…or—" It was hard to remember with so much happening. "Maybe the—what do you call that cupboard thingie where you keep the milk?" She was trying to keep up with the kitchen's many Asterian inventions and devices.

"The ice cabinet," said Milly, dashing back out.

"Eeh-roond, huh?" said Melmeth, who was using the break to sharpen his knife. "That really your name?"

Yrund straightened her shoulders. "Yes, *Yrund* of the Sky Country, of the First Moon and the Badger."

"You don't say," Gem Beard said, testing the edge of the shining blade on his arm hairs. Flecks of red hair floated onto the stone floor. "I've got a good thing here at this house. You're not going to do something stupid and ruin it for me, are you now, Little Eeh-roond, Thorn in the Arse?" he asked, the knifepoint right on her heart.

"Because from what I heard—you haven't changed a bit since the mine," the memluk went on. "Still pissing off the wrong blooding person at the wrong blooding time, and this party tomorrow night is my ticket to staying out of any more stinking mines. If Lady Darbana signs that deal, the highsmith is going to take me to Asteria to run her kitchen, and then I won't be just a useless, limpy memluk anymore, will I? I'll be a kitchen boss in the biggest capital on the planet."

"I won't piss off anyone tomorrow night," promised Yrund, looking down at the knife.

"Allyright, then, just so we're all rowing to the same song," said Gem Beard, spinning the large blade back into its scabbard. "And one more thing—for the next time you want to rile up a bunch of Sea Hammers? It's *fynrryg,* not *fynryg,* and *mzryllyck* has two *L*'s."

"You heard about that?" Yrund said, biting her lip.

"A Douarr-speaking little chicken? I heard…" A smile cracked across his scarred face.

"Why is it so funny?" demanded Yrund. "What did I call them?"

"You…you called them a sack…a sack…" He roared with laughter as he slapped his giant thigh. "A sack of hairy onions!"

Which wasn't nearly as funny to Yrund as it was to the memluk. She eyed the crate of apples behind his shoulder, and in good cheer Gem Beard tossed her one.

Yrund caught the apple with both hands as Gem Beard went white. "Where'd those come from?" he asked, pointing to her palms. "You didn't have those in the mine."

The eyes looked up at them, inscrutable yet knowing. "The mountain spirits gave them to me," she said, telling the closet version of the truth yet.

Gem Beard's big bulk shivered up and down. "The *eye-eyes* gave you those?" he asked, grabbing her wrist.

"Yes. So they can watch me." Also the truth. Mostly.

With a hork, the memluk spat in her palm, trying to wipe the marks off. "Can't be…" But even using his sleeve, the eyes remained. Gem Beard made the sign of the mermaid, touching his amulets. "Storm's a-coming."

YRUND PEELED SO MANY POTATOES, turnips, and carrots that the peelings filled an entire trash can, but the work was not over then. After they finished sending up dinner for the first guests that had arrived, there was breakfast and lunch for the next day to prepare, all the while still cooking and baking and simmering and chopping everything needed for Lady Darbana's party. Not to mention feeding themselves and all the other rabu and servants filling the house.

Then Keeper Antonina descended, saying the alat samovars

were empty, and where in the feathers was the black walnut cheese the highsmith had requested? Then, after dessert was delivered, she was back, accusing Gem Beard of stealing the Orogaudian port.

He chased her out of the kitchen with his rolling pin, informing her it was the ambassador himself who had taken it.

"Not bad for a runt badger," said Gem Beard, dumping yet another load of dirty bowls and spoons in the sink at the end of the night, drenching Yrund's already thoroughly soaked apron.

Yrund did not know what was happening in the rest of the house, but there was a constant line of boys lugging baggage past the doors to the kitchen. Sometimes a weary servant or rabu would come in looking for a quick slug of alat or to gobble one of the sausage or cheese rolls Milly and Tilly had made. When Yrund wasn't doing one of another dozen things, half of them all at once, she was sent to refill the platters with more rolls or a fresh brick of dark cake she could have sworn Tilly said was made with honey and crickets. Occasionally Yrund caught sight of Anouk, at the door, sent down to retrieve a tray of sweet rolls or a thermos of extra dark alat. The keeper's blue beads seemed to have done their work, for except for a few scabs and some bruising around the eyes, Anouk's face was quickly healing. Though she hadn't lost the scowl.

"You don't have to smile," said Lili, taking her aside. "But if you walk around with that expression, they'll think you mean to poison them."

This brought a look of interest to Anouk's face.

"Don't even think about it," said Lili.

"I wouldn't mind poisoning that keeper. Who does she think she is? Do you know what she said? She says the Lumi don't wash! Just because we don't do it in those dumb metal tubs doesn't mean we don't bathe!"

"She's just an ignorant fool, but she's a fool with power, so keep your mouth shut and your face blank. Ignoring insults inside a warm house with good food is a thousand times better than dying of damp lung starving in the mines! Now, what did the highsmith send you down for?"

"A bottle of coriander."

"Coriander?" Lili shook her head. "It's never a dull moment…"

But Anouk was back a few minutes later.

"She threw the bottle out the window! She said it was caraway, not coriander, and if I don't bring back the right one this time, she's going to sell me to the scrap man."

Lili fetched her a new bottle, chewing a seed just to be sure. "Here, take her this one. Tell her it was my fault."

"Who puts coriander in perfume?" asked Milly. "Wouldn't you just smell like an armpit? Or caraway for that matter. Unless you were a pickle."

"She might be eccentric, but Highsmith Bannia is the most sought-after perfumer on the planet. If anyone could make someone want to smell like a pickle it would be her," said Lili before sending Anouk off with a pocketful of buns and another prayer to Irsil.

"The highsmith hasn't gotten rid of her yet," noted Gem Beard. "That's better than the last one." Lili nodded as if the memluk's words comforted her. How those two had made an alliance was beyond Yrund's understanding. She hoped the Lumi woman knew she couldn't trust him.

They did not drag themselves up from the kitchen until well after midnight, meeting a hollow-eyed Anouk on the stairs. There was a fresh slap mark across her cheek and she smelled not unlike a box full of mice. "What is it?" asked Lili, taking her by the apron.

Anouk just shook her head in mute fear as Keeper Antonina came up behind them.

"I hope you're not coddling her," said the keeper. "I'm arranging for her to be sent to the stables in the morning. She's more useful than a white diamond. She didn't press a single piece of the highsmith's laundry or clean out the grate! And she mixed the highsmith's stockings with her slips! I don't know what she's been doing all day, little snow savage."

For a moment, Yrund thought Lili was going to push the keeper down the stairs. "Are you saying the highsmith fired her?"

Keeper Antonina flushed an even deeper shade of purple than normal. "She will when she realizes what's going on!"

Lili's jaw twitched. "Well, that is for the highsmith to decide, isn't it? It's not the girl's fault she has not had the time to be properly trained. I'll see to it myself as soon as the party is over."

"It won't make a difference," said Keeper Antonina. "There's some that aren't fit to work inside is all. And certainly not to wear seefires!" She opened a door with one of the many keys hanging from her belt, revealing a tiny but private bedroom. Without a good night, she slammed the door behind her.

"Just ignore that beet-faced weasel," said Lili as they got ready for bed in a small dormitory packed with sleeping women and girls. "If the highsmith hasn't fired you herself, it doesn't matter what anyone else says. Especially not Keeper Antonina." She helped them get a stack of worn blankets from a cupboard and make a spot on the floor. "Move over!" she commanded, pushing a snoring hall maid over with her foot.

"I wouldn't mind being sent to the stables—" said Anouk.

"Shut up!" yelled one of the servants, trying to sleep.

Anouk lowered her voice. "But she said she was going to have the ambassador send me to the mezmerald mines. And she called me a snoweater."

"Well, she's a bugeater," said Lili. "Though if I were you, I'd catch up on the highsmith's laundry tomorrow. It is a wawa's job."

"I didn't have time!" said Anouk. "She's had me grinding up something that looked like mouse poo all night!" Her nose wrinkled at the memory.

"Hirax feces. It's for perfume, believe it or not. Just a touch or it ruins it. This is good, actually. She wouldn't let the last wawa near her work."

"She's making a special perfume just for Lady Darbana," Anouk whispered as they made their beds on the hard floor. "And did you know she's made scents for the Fan-Fan Girls? And even Niloofar Damantine?"

What's purrflume? asked Orelia.

Perfume, corrected Yrund, who'd only ever read about it. *It makes you smell like flowers or fruit or something.*

"What was that about a seefire?" asked Lili, rolling her dress up into a pillow.

Yrund copied her, so tired her eyes burned. Someone shut the dormitory door, blocking out the light from the sunsstone sconces in the hall. Yrund lay back, listening to Lili and Anouk whispering beside her in the dark, and missing her bunk at the Hayas'.

"Oh, the highsmith said she'd give me a blue seefire if I lasted the week, and a whole new wardrobe of clothes, too."

"No wonder the keeper hates you already," said Lili, yawning. "The highsmith's probably never given her anything but a bee beryl."

"But I don't want any of it…" Anouk sniffled. "I just want to go home."

"Will you *shut up?*" A shoe flew across the room in the dark.

Yrund reached out to hold Anouk's hand. As she fell asleep, she imagined delivering the ambassador and his sister to Devil's Crown.

✴ ⭐ ✴ ✴ ✴

"Who is Lady Darbana?" Yrund asked Lili the next morning. They rose before first dawn, fighting their way to the bathrooms, where a line had already formed.

Lili answered in a low voice, though the other maids were so loud—gossiping and sharing news—Yrund didn't think they could have heard them if they'd yelled their conversation. "Lady Goldrina Darbana is the head of the largest family of timber lords in Qalami, while her sister's husband has ties to Unsinn."

"So?"

"Orogaudi has recently discovered a new source for wellos, which the Mining Wield is keen on securing, but the Asterians need permission to go through the Qalamish territory to get to Orogaudi. And Unsinn."

"Everything comes back to the shortage," said Yrund, putting it together. "Lady Darbana is just a sytranj piece."

"You wouldn't think there's a shortage of anything in Asteria," said Anouk as Yrund helped her twist her hair up for the day. "Highsmith Boole has drawers and drawers of jewels—ear dangles and stacks of rings, and every sort of necklace and bangle, even perfume bottles made of gems—"

"Don't forget your bonnets," cut in Lili.

"Ugh, do we have to? They look absolutely ridiculous."

"The highsmith doesn't like hair on her carpets... Oh dear, all the small ones are gone," said Lili, handing Yrund a bonnet that would have fit Gem Beard. A few of the other maids laughed, but Yrund just ignored them. She had something else on her mind. After they had finished in the bathrooms, she pulled Lili and Anouk to the far end of the hall, where bells had started to chime.

"What is it? If we don't hurry, Melmeth will salt cure us."

"How big a deal is it that Lady Darbana likes the perfume the highsmith makes her?"

"Don't even think about it," warned Lili, reading Yrund's mind. "The last time the ambassador was unhappy with some rabu, he had their heads put in the town square, and you're already on spring ice with the man."

They plunked down the stairs, saying goodbye to Anouk on the landing of the highsmith's floor.

"You'll be fine," Lili told Anouk, straightening her fresh apron.

"Just keep your head down and do as the highsmith asks. Bezel Antonina is not the worst problem you could have. All right?"

Anouk's head wobbled. The shock of her capture was wearing off, and the reality was setting in. "Aren't you ever afraid?" she asked Lili.

"Of course I'm afraid," said Lili. "Who said I wasn't?"

"Then…then, how do you do it—how do you keep going?"

"Honestly? I just imagine what Agnetha would do, and then I do that. She was always the brave one, so I just pretend I'm her. The Yavani say fear is just a mist. You can walk right through it."

"If I imagined what Mila would do, the highsmith and her brother would be full of arrows," said Anouk.

"I wish they were," said Yrund.

"And what is your secret, Little Thorn?" asked Lili, lifting up the edge of Yrund's flopping bonnet. "You're the most fearless of us all."

"I am afraid, though," said Yrund. "All the time."

"You wouldn't know it to look at you."

"Yaha—you tried to save us," chimed in Anouk. "In Last Lake. Just you against all those memluks, and the ambassador. He could have shot you."

"Maybe you two just don't know what my normal face looks like," said Yrund. The truth was she had been terrified. If it hadn't been for Orelia…

Anouk's lips twisted. "That's not supposed to be funny, is it?" she said. Nonetheless, she looked heartened, straightening her back and marching toward the highsmith's door.

"Your normal face…," said Lili, snorting behind Yrund all the way down to the kitchen.

Yrund was glad to see the others smile even if for a moment. But the truth remained. They had everything to fear. Perfumes and parties aside, it would only take the flick of one perturbed finger to get them all sent to Smeralgdus. Rabu were not safe. Not ever.

CHAPTER THIRTY-TWO

There was barely time for Yrund to eat a boiled egg and bun before Gem Beard had her chopping celery roots and whisking gravy, which sloshed all down her front when a young man playing a flute bumped her as he pranced through the kitchen.

"Hoy!" yelled Gem Beard. The musicians, hired all the way from Unsinn to play for that night's party, had all come down to serenade him as thanks for their breakfast.

"And thank *you*," the memluk said with a bow before giving them his boot. "Now get the hell out!" He continued to hum, though, as he pulled a pan of perfectly golden little birds from the ovens.

I like Gem Beard, said Orelia.

No offense, but you like anyone who sings, said Yrund.

The memluk's good mood did not last long, for a smirking Keeper Antonina soon came in to say the lunch order had changed. It had slipped her mind the night before, but the ambassador wanted ham instead of quail. Yrund ducked along with the other maids as a roasted bird flew past her. Tilly just picked it up and washed it as if used to the cook's moods.

"Blooding, stinking little turd keeper couldn't have told me last night when we discussed today's menu?" Gem Beard fumed.

"One more thing," said Keeper Antonina, coming back down the stairs. "I need the maids to come up and try on their new uniforms for tonight." She crooked a bony finger at Milly and Tilly. "You too," she snapped at Yrund, who was trying to clean the gravy off her apron. "Though it's a silly waste of fabric, if you ask me, when no one's going to see them." The keeper pinched Yrund's arm as she pushed her through the door and up the stairs with the other maids. "All to impress Lady Darbana with her face full of moles…" Her face showed what she thought about spending money on new uniforms for kitchen maids and moley women.

They joined the line of house maids already waiting in the girls' dorm. Two seamstresses stood in the middle of the room with a measuring tape and pins. There was a stack of satin gold dresses on a bed, and as each girl came forward, they fitted the uniform to her frame. A third woman sat in front of a metal contraption built into a table, pumping a foot crank and running a dress beneath a furiously jumping needle. Thread whirled off the bobbin and magically through the fabric.

"Enough staring!" snapped Keeper Antonina. "Take off your clothes."

Milly and Tilly did as they were told, lifting their old dresses right over their heads.

"What are you waiting for?" said the keeper. "We haven't got time for shy little outlanders today."

But it wasn't shyness that stopped Yrund from undressing.

"Come on!" Keeper Antonina clapped her hands. "Get it off her!"

Yrund stood frozen as the two seamstresses came over to pull the dress off. Orelia growled in Yrund's ears. Bogging idiot! Yrund cursed herself. Why hadn't she hidden the gem? She could have put Orelia with their coats, or in the larder! With a last tug the dress was over Yrund's head.

"What are these?" demanded the keeper, ripping the silver locket and arrowhead necklace from Yrund's neck. "You can't have these." Then she saw Orelia's pouch, brown with the gravy that had soaked through Yrund's apron. "And what is that?" She pointed, nose wrinkling in disgust. "Some kind of disgusting outlander gimgem? What's inside there?"

Yrund's mouth had gone so dry her lips tore when she tried to speak. "It's a…a sweepstone," she lied.

"You don't look old enough for your sweep," said Keeper Antonina.

"I just got it this month."

The keeper shook her head, annoyed. "Fine, let her keep the stone for now," she said. "We can hardly reuse the new uniform if it's covered in blood." She was about to drop Yrund's necklaces into her belt purse when she paused. "Pitch and potch! I almost forgot," the keeper said, lifting out a pair of glittering metal snakes. Their tails were tucked into their mouths, beady eyes glowing. "The ambassador gave me these for you."

Ouroborus.

Ouroborus meant Smeralgdus.

Only the ambassador and the keeper didn't know Yrund already wore the snakes beneath her boots.

"Hold out your wrists!" the keeper told Yrund, who heard her as if through a long tunnel. "Don't be one of the difficult ones."

Yrund wasn't going back to the mines. She wasn't! She wasn't going back—

The keeper reached for Yrund's arm.

"Are you growling at me, rabu?"

Hush, Yrund admonished Orelia. *You're a sweepstone now—you have to act like one!* She tried to recall the picture from the gempendium as she held her arms out for the woman. What did it matter if she wore four snakes or two—either way, the ambassador was going to send her back to the mines.

"Isn't it just my Way!" cursed the keeper, finally noticing the snake anklets were still locked closed. She dug back through her waist purse, then checked her pockets. "Where is that feathering key? I told the ambassador we needed a ring for it—"

A bell rang insistently on the landing. "That'll be the highsmith wanting to see if her bottles have arrived." The keeper dropped the ouroborus back in her purse and spun out of the room, still talking to herself as she went. "Of all the times for the secretary to have caught himself a blotch—I'll blotch him if he ever recovers."

When Yrund was finished being measured, she hurriedly got dressed and ran back down the stairs to the kitchen, where Milly and Tilly were already back at work.

"Which way is the ambassador's office?" she whispered.

"Third floor at the east end," answered Tilly. "Why? Does he want some more alat already? I just sent a tray up with the floor maid."

"Yes," said Yrund, thinking quickly.

It was just as Lili said—sometimes it was up to them to turn the tide.

"Keeper Antonina told me on the way down."

"Better be quick, then," said Tilly, pointing toward where the alat pots were stored. "And change that apron—you've got gravy all over it."

✳ ✷ ✳ ✦ ✳

YRUND KNOCKED on the door at the east end of the third floor, balancing the tray of alat on her hip.

"Come in if you must," called the ambassador after a moment.

Yrund let herself in, keeping her face down.

"Yes? Has another pigeon arrived?" Binjin Boole asked,

glancing down from the post in his hand. "Freewielders Protest Alongside Streetsweepers' Wield," said the title across the front. The ambassador wore a pair of oblong lenses on his long nose and a golden velvet jacket and matching house slippers, which seemed deliberately chosen to set off his blue eyes. Behind him was a small table teetering with books and random piles of ore samples. On the wide, carved desk in the center of the room were yet more samples along with messy stacks of letters and half-read pigeon posts, the edges still curled.

"It's not a post. The cook thought maybe the cream had gone off and wanted to send up a fresh pot just in case," said Yrund, trying to sound as much like Tilly as she could.

"It tasted fine to me." The ambassador shrugged, looking annoyed to be interrupted. "But do as you will."

Yrund set down the tray beside the first one, surveying the crowded room the best she could from underneath her large bonnet. There was a fireplace and some chairs and thick rugs stacked with more books and chunks of raw stones and a table by the window filled with hundreds of wax packets like those Ansyn carried gems in. They were all arranged, unlike everything else, in neat little rows with coded labels across them. At the table's edge was a small vessel crammed with a dozen miniature scopes and a round viewing glass that made the vase of flowers behind it look double its size.

Orelia, curious to see everything, tried to swivel Yrund's head. *Stop that!* snapped Yrund. *He can't see my face.*

"Was there something else, Tilly? Or are you Milly?" asked the ambassador, sitting back down in a chair by the fire with his post.

"Tilly," said Yrund, waiting by the door. "The keeper, Ms. Antonina, said she would be needing your key." Yrund tried to keep her voice steady, head still down, as if she didn't care at all whether or not he gave it to her.

"Which key?" asked the ambassador, growing more impatient.

"The one for the ouroborus, she said..."

"Hmm?" The man had already returned to his reading. "Oh yes, of course."

The ambassador got back up with a sigh and put the letter aside. Mumbling to himself about too many interruptions, he opened a drawer in the desk, rifling through quills and nibs and blotters. "The key...the key," he said, hunting around. "That blinking key—I never can find it. Maybe Antonina's right about a ring..." He lifted a post and looked underneath, then lifted the lids of several inlaid boxes on a shelf. "Oh yes, here it is. Now, go away," he said, holding out a long, pronged instrument shaped like a forked tongue. In its end was a blue gem the same color blue as the eyes of the ouroborus.

Yrund's hand was just closing around the malevolent-looking key when the ambassador pulled it back. "Actually, tell Keeper Antonina I'll only let her have the key if she finds me that fiddle I asked for." With that, Binjin Boole closed the door in Yrund's face.

YRUND CURSED to herself as she walked back down the stairs. She had been so close! So close! Now what was she going to do?

"Where have you been?" said Lili, forcing a colander into Yrund's hands. "The radishes haven't been peeled yet!"

The afternoon was a miserable flurry of sauces and puddings and tray after searing tray of moon tarts to rotate in the vast ovens so their fragile edges wouldn't burn.

"Keep the pace," commanded Gem Beard, but Yrund couldn't keep up, thoughts of the mezmerald mine weighing her down.

Finally, the memluk pulled her aside to a corner. "Thought you were going to pull your oar right—what you dragging around like a blubberbuss for? You were scooting along just fine until Bezel took you up—" Then he understood. "What did that witchbone keeper go and tell you? She's always making my girls cry." He tore her off a hunk of braided white cheese as if food could fix everything.

"She said I'll be sent to Smeralgdus tomorrow."

"No, she blooding well did not!" The memluk hit the counter next to them so hard the alat cups rattled on their shelf. "Listen to me, Little Thorn. That Bezel is going to Lady Darbana's tomorrow. She doesn't know it—but I finagled for the highsmith to send her over as a present—sweeten things up before the trade deal. So she's not going to be around to send you anywhere."

"It doesn't matter," said Yrund, slumping onto a crate of potatoes. "It was the ambassador's decision."

"The ambassador's decision—" He snorted as if this were a joke. "It's the highsmith that runs this house, and I run the kitchen. If I want you to blooding stay, you *will* blooding stay. Got it?"

"Not when they find out I escaped from Devil's Crown."

"Well, I'm as sure as shat not going to tell them!"

"I'm still wearing the ouroborus," said Yrund, defeated. A hot tear leaked out from one eye.

"Oh...yeah, I didn't think about that," said Gem Beard. He beat a drumroll on the shelf, thinking for a moment. "Allyright, so you've got the snakies on still—that's not good, I'll admit it."

"Fire!" called Milly from the stove, where flames had engulfed a pan of oil.

"Gemcracked piece of... We'll talk later," said the memluk, racing back to the ovens, his limp hardly slowing him.

Seething, Yrund returned to her work. Talking wouldn't do a thing to get the ouroborus from around her ankles. Gem Beard had betrayed her at Devil's Crown—what would he do for her now with a fancy job in Asteria at stake?

"Ow!" Distracted, Yrund had splashed the hot oil she had been straining all over her arm. Crap on crap. She ran to rinse the burn under the cold tap.

Then Tilly was beside her, jumping to pull down a tin from a shelf above their heads. It was decorated with a painting of a blue stone coming out of the ocean. The maid popped the lid open to reveal a matching aqua-colored salve. "Here, put this on it," she said. "It's infused with aquamarines. It's Mellymeth's, but he lets us use it for the bad burns."

Yrund lifted her arm out of the stream of cold water and rubbed the salve into her skin, holding her arm up to the small window above the sink. No redness, no blisters—no pain.

"That was fast," said Tilly, grabbing Yrund's arm and twisting it in the light.

"Ow!" said Yrund again, taking her arm back.

"You wearing a halestone?"

"No—just a sweepstone."

"Really? Lucky you," said Milly, coming over to drop a burnt pan of pies in the sink. Her freckled face was red from the heat of the ovens. "Keeper Antonina doesn't usually let kitchen maids wear gems. I don't know why—I heard Highsmith Boole lets all her rabu wear gems in Asteria. I hope I get sold to someone in the capital someday!"

"You what?" said Yrund, in disbelief.

Milly shrugged. "It's better than being a field rabu." Tilly vigorously nodded her agreement, more shiny black hairs falling from her bonnet. "House rabu get Donkey Day off in the capital. Here in Darban, the keeper never gives us a day off."

"Don't you want to be free?" said Yrund. "To go home to your families?"

"I don't remember my family," said Milly.

"I do," said Tilly, her face shadowing. "And I'd rather be here."

"Well, I remember my family," said Yrund stubbornly. "And my horse. And my goats. And my sisters. And being able to go wherever I wanted, whenever I wanted without anyone beating me or threatening to send me to the mines..." Just three days ago, she had been free. Just three days ago, she'd had a plan. A plan to fight the wields. A plan to save the Sky Country. "We'd all be free if it wasn't for the bogging Mining Wield."

The kitchen maids looked at each other, eyes as wide as moon pies. "But, Yrund," said Tilly patiently, "if it wasn't for the Mining Wield, we wouldn't have any gems."

"I would like to ride a horse, though, someday," Yrund heard Milly say as they left her with the dishes.

Yrund shook her head in disgust and looked at her arm one more time. It really was impressive. She'd seen the skin blister. That salve was as good as Agnetha's halestone.

I'm better than a halestone, said a voice in her head. *I'm an every stone.*

What do you mean? Are you saying you did this? You can really fix burns?

Yup, said Orelia, who seemed to be picking up some of Gem Beard's vocabulary. *I can do anything.*

Then take me home.

I...I can't do that, admitted the stone, losing her bluster.

That's all right, said Yrund, already feeling guilty. No gem could do that. *Thanks for fixing my burn.* She should have been mad at Orelia for gemming her again, but what did it matter now? They would be sending her to Smeralgdus soon. And she'd never see the stone again.

What am I going to do with you? asked Yrund, scrubbing the burnt pans.

What what?

They'll never let me take a sweepstone to the mines. Just the thought of going back into a dark mine made Yrund want to weep. *Would you let me give you to Lili? She might know what to do with you. She knows about gems...and her sister is a healer. At the least they can use you to nepenthe the silver.* Yrund stood up from the sink for a moment to stretch her back.

Use me now.

How? You're a gem, not a sword. What am I supposed to do with you? Offer to heal Gem Beard's blisters? Nepenthe the ambassador so he doesn't remember what he had for breakfast?

Why not?

Yes, why not, thought Yrund. If he couldn't remember what he'd had for breakfast, he couldn't remember to send her to Smeralgdus. She'd only been thinking of how to use Orelia as a weapon, a weapon the wields would just take away. But what about the secret war? She could still fight. She would still fight!

Lili dumped another armload of dirty dishes in the sink. "When you're done with these, I need more carrots peeled," she said. "Then chop them and add them to the soup."

"Lili! We have to talk," said Yrund, grabbing her sleeve with a wet hand. She had an idea.

The Lumi woman shook her off, for Gem Beard was yelling for her. "Later—I've got to get the meringues in the oven!"

Yrund was about to call her back, then thought better of it. No reason to drag anyone else in yet. Lili had a good position here in the kitchen. Compared to going to Smeralgdus, that was... And that, Yrund realized, was how the Mining Wield kept its power— it was the threat of being sent to the mines that kept the other rabu in place. But Yrund was already being sent to Smeralgdus. She no longer had anything to lose. Why shouldn't she use Orelia?

Orelia!

Yrund!

Will you help me nepenthe the ambassador? And the keeper?

Of course, said the stone.

Yrund finished the dishes and moved on to peeling carrots, thinking hard. How was she supposed to nepenthe the ambassador without anyone seeing? She cut the peeled carrots into pieces and carried them to the cauldron boiling on the stove. Soup. She could nepenthe some soup. Just like with the mushrooms.

Can you nepenthe the soup? No, not the soup, she decided,

remembering the nepenthe's purple mist. It would be too obvious in soup. Yrund looked around the kitchen, then the pantries. It was in the ice larder she found what she was looking for—a large bowl of plumberry punch. That was perfect! Why not gem the whole party? Then an even better idea came to her. Why not poison the party? That would be the end of the ambassador and his sister and Lady Darbana and who knew how many other allies of the wields. The thought of it filled Yrund with power. She would finally get revenge. For her family. For Pit and the other ratters at Devil's Crown. For Tana and Jon-Luq and everyone else.

Can you poison the punch? Yrund asked the stone.

Poison?

Like the black rubily in the story of the Invisible Hand. Or cianite? Yrund tried to remember the other poison gems.

No, said Orelia. *I can't do that.*

Yrund cursed. For a moment, she had begun to believe Orelia was an allstone after all. That together they would wipe out the Mining Wield, free the rabu, burn Asteria to the ground!

She sighed with disappointment, unwilling to let go of her vision of the ambassador dying a miserable, slow death. *You know, I'm actually sorry you're not an allstone*, said Yrund.

I am so! I'm better than every stone. Just like the Gempendium said.

But you can only do three things. And even those not very well, thought Yrund, remembering the gem trying to mimic Katrin's anodyne. *I mean, you can still sing and be pretty and light up. And you're good company...* Most of the time.

I can be a mallowkite and a halestone, listed the gem. *And a cloudstone, and a screwberyl and a nepenthe...*

A cloudstone and a screwberyl? She'd never seen Orelia do that. Without warning, Yrund's face contorted into the same hideous yowi face from the night she'd chased the watchmen back in Last Lake. Bogging gem! thought Yrund, forcing her face back to normal. *That doesn't make you an allstone, just because you can mimic all the gems you're jealous of.* Not even all of those—just the few Yrund had gone as far as to touch…

Yrund dropped a plate, shattering it across the floor. How had she been so stupid?

"Chicken!" bellowed Gem Beard. "That's coming out your wages."

"You don't give me any wages," she shot back.

"Huh," said the memluk. "That is the downside of not paying you twerps. Nothing to do but beat you. Well, remind me tomorrow to give you a kick. There's no blooding time today."

Yrund cleaned up the plate, mind running wild. What if Orelia really was an allstone? *You can't be a stone you've never met, right? That I haven't held? Is that it?* Yrund asked.

Eh…, said the gem.

Don't be embarrassed. That's just learning. We all have to learn. Even herself, she realized. Nobody was born knowing how to wield an allstone. Especially not a gem shy like herself. Though many wouldn't mind trying. A man like Brandul, for instance. He'd see it as his right, waving Orelia around, telling her to do this or do that—lighting forests on fire, paralyzing rabu… poisoning punches. Yrund wanted to slap herself. What if she'd poisoned someone innocent? No wonder the gempendium said allstones were cursed.

Let's just stick to nepenthe, she told the stone. *And just a little.* As much as she'd like to see the ambassador forget how to breathe, she'd never forgive herself if she hurt Milly or Tilly.

In fact, as she considered it, the nepenthe was far better than poison. The ambassador and the keeper would not only forget Yrund was supposed to be sent to Smeralgdus, the whole party would be so forgetful, no one would remember her breaking into the ambassador's office. She could take the key for the ouroborus! Yrund nearly skipped out of the larder on her way to find Lili.

"Oh good, take this icing bag," said Lili. "I need another hand."

"Psst, Lili," said Yrund as she helped the woman squeeze meringue stars out onto baking trays. "How many memluks do you think will be on duty tonight?"

"All of them. The ambassador likes to show them off, especially after all those reports of the Invisible Hand…" Her eyes crinkled. "What are you up to, Little Thorn?"

"Nothing," lied Yrund. There was no point incriminating anyone else.

"Tonight is not the night to go and get yourself in trouble."

But Yrund wasn't planning on getting herself into trouble. She was planning on getting herself out of it.

Yrund spent the rest of the afternoon watching and waiting. Finally, when Gem Beard was busy with a delivery, she sneaked back into the ice larder. She didn't know how long it took to nepenthe a bowl of punch, but the longer the better was her guess.

All right, are you ready? Yrund asked the stone, slipping her out of her pocket and stepping between the bottles of wines and gem brews crowding the floor.

Ready, said the gem, despite still having a sheen of gravy on it from the morning's spill.

Here goes, then.

Yrund was just reaching to drop Orelia into the punch bowl when she heard the distinctive sound of a large person with a slight limp approaching the larder's door. Bogging hell! Gem Beard. Yrund put the stone back and ducked down, pretending to be looking for something on the bottom shelf, where a row of cakes were precariously perched.

"What do you think you're doing in here?" Gem Beard asked, giving Yrund a squint not unlike Lili's. He was carrying a case of wine in his arms, his cane in his armpit. "I'll pull your fingers off if you're in my cream cakes."

"I was looking for the…sultanas." Yrund tried to stand up, accidentally knocking over a bottle of applejack. As it fell, it knocked over another bottle, then another. The sweet scent of liquor rose up as glass cracked and the precarious cakes toppled.

"You, dumb clucky," roared Gem Beard, trying to set down the crate and hit her with the cane at the same time. "I'll put you on the ship to Smeralgdus myself!"

Yrund felt the cane crack against her back.

"Get out! Get out of my kitchen!"

CHAPTER THIRTY-THREE

Yrund ran up four flights of stairs to the bathroom on the top floor and hid herself in the toilet stall at the end. Tears poured out in a flood. What had she thought would happen? That one girl could actually beat the wields? Even with an allstone, she would never win.

She pulled Orelia from her pouch, rubbing the gravy stain off her surface.

The gem shone on as bright as the suns in a deep summer sky. Yrund sat watching the colors change through her tears until Milly came and knocked on the door.

"Lili sent me to check on you!" said the maid, sounding worried. "She said not to worry about Mellymeth. We've all broken things. Even him. He'll forgive you in a few days."

Yrund blew her nose. She doubted it. Not if she'd cost him his only chance at making a life for himself in the capital that didn't involve fighting or mining.

"It's all right," the maid whispered through the door. "We all cried when we got here—but Mellymeth is good to us. You'll see. He just has a big bark."

But Yrund knew better. The only person that Gem Beard

cared about was himself. He'd left her to die in Devil's Crown, and now he was sending her to Smeralgdus.

"Anyways, I wouldn't take too long," warned Milly. "He says you're to come back and wash the pots. They're stacking up something bad."

"I'll be right there." Yrund listened to the footsteps retreat. What choice did she have? Rabu followed orders. This was her life now. And tomorrow, it would be worse. Tomorrow, she would be sent to the mezmerald mines.

Orelia?

Yes, Yrund.

Will you topaz me, please? I could use some courage now.

I can't, the stone said.

Yes, you can—you did it before! That's how I stood up to the ambassador's men! For all the good it had done.

Nope. Ansyn's topaz is gemcrack...

No, it's not. It worked! I ran right into Agnetha's house, right into the mist. I wasn't afraid at all.

That was you, the stone said begrudgingly.

Me? But you're the allstone.

I told you so.

No, I mean... Yrund reeled as this revelation sank in. The trader had said the price he'd paid for the brown gem had been unusually low. And he was immune to topazes.

So—she was braver than she'd thought. Or crazier.

Yrund wiped her eyes on her sleeve and put away the stone. She didn't feel brave. But if Lili could fake it, so could she. She'd escaped from one mine, hadn't she? She could escape from Smeralgdus too.

Dread still weighing her down, Yrund opened the door and caught her reflection in the mirror. She forced herself to stand up straighter, lifting her chin. Hands on hips, she regarded herself. It wasn't over yet. Perhaps she'd still get a chance to nepenthe the punch. Bogging Gem Beard couldn't be looking all the time.

Yrund washed her face and hands and returned downstairs to the kitchen. As she passed the hall for the third floor, something blurry caught her eye. Something blurry and big.

Orelia whistled.

The blur whistled back.

"Humphrey!" Yrund stepped out of the stairwell and onto the thick carpet. "Is that really you?"

"Ah, Yrund—there you are," said the woodwin, clapping her on the shoulder. "I didn't recognize you in that bonnet."

"What are you doing here?" Yrund grabbed his invisible arm, hugging him tight.

"I heard you were taken. It's all over Lumi Land. They're on their way to retrieve you."

"Who is?"

"The healer and a few others." He tutted. "Very dangerous."

Yrund's heart lifted, then dropped. "They'll never get past the ambassador's memluks! They'll be slaughtered if they try."

"True, but *they* don't have to get past, do they? You just have to get out," said the woodwin. "That's why I've come. They'll be arriving late tonight."

"Tonight?" That wasn't possible. "But Darban must be nearly three hundred miles away from Last Lake."

"They're taking turns, swapping out fresh sled dogs at every village. Even I couldn't keep up with them."

"But then how did you get here first?" Yrund was so confused.

"Woodwins have our shortcuts, but that doesn't matter now. What matters is getting you three out."

"That won't be easy—there are memluks stationed front and back."

"Yes, I saw. You'll have to wait for my signal. It's too bad the ambassador ordered the men aren't allowed to drink tonight. It's not really fair considering..."

"No, it's not, is it?" said Yrund, catching on. Even the indoor servants were resentful at the extra-long hours, and that was without having to stand out in the cold all night. "Maybe the ambassador might reconsider once the party has started. Send a few bottles out as thanks."

"That would be a nice gesture for such hardworking soldiers."

"But how will I know when it's time?" There was so much to do. She still had to find Lili and Anouk—

"You'll know," said Humphrey, chuffing. "I promise."

"You there!"

Yrund swiveled her head.

A tall woman in a deep yellow dress had appeared down the hall. "Come here!"

"Me?" Yrund looked around. Humphrey was gone.

"Yes, you, you stupid rabu." The woman snapped her fingers, rings flashing.

Yrund approached reluctantly. Kitchen maids weren't supposed to be on this floor, and she had places to be.

"Smell my wrist," the woman commanded, holding out a long arm.

"Have her start with the left one, Lady Darbana!" came Highsmith Boole's voice from the open door, though she did not bother to come out.

"No cheating! Don't influence her!" Up close Lady Darbana was even more impressive, with rows of golden pearls lighting up her deep, mole-sprinkled skin. She wore a stitched brocade pant dress that accentuated her long legs while her short yellow-dyed hair was highlighted with matching topaz-colored jewels. She was a similar age as the highsmith and radiating the same self-importance.

Yrund leaned in to smell the woman's outstretched wrist, encircled by a bracelet of enormous citrines, which were cold and hard as they bumped Yrund's nose.

"Well? Be honest. What do you think it smells like?"

"It...it smells like...burnt squash?" guessed Yrund. She was hardly trained as a kitchen maid, much less a perfume tester.

The woman laughed, an abrasive, off-note sound. "What about this one?" she said, holding out the other arm.

Yrund inhaled again. "That one smells like...like a flower. Rose, maybe." But not the soft wild roses of the Sky Country. This rose was hard-edged, almost stinging.

"That's all?" said the woman gloatingly.

"Don't rush her," called the highsmith. "Let the bottom notes kick in. A rose and what else?"

Yrund sniffed once more. The floral scent was layered over something biting and unpleasant. Like reins that chafed.

"Well? Be specific. It's something a rabu should know well."

"It smells like a whip," said Yrund, repulsed.

"Bravo!" said Lady Darbana, turning around and going back in the door without another glance. "You were right again. It's just what—oooh, I just love what your new wawa's done with your hair, Bannia! Maybe you should give her to me instead of—"

Yrund crept closer.

"Keep away from her," Yrund heard the highsmith reply. "I'm taking her to Asteria. She'll be a present for Niloofar."

"Oh, you are clever. As always."

There was high laughter and the clinking of glasses.

So, the highsmith was planning on taking Anouk to Asteria. Not anymore, thought Yrund as she ran back down the hall.

YRUND RACED BACK DOWNSTAIRS, getting a hard thump from Gem Beard as she went through the kitchen door. "Next time you disappear, it's because I drown you in that dish sink!"

Blooding memluk. He was the one that had told her to leave! And, she saw, he had added a lock to the ice larder door. Yrund went back to the sink, forgetting for a moment there was a new plan now. Humphrey was here! And the Lumi were coming!

As dinner grew nearer, the kitchen became a complete blizzard of dishes and pans. They took their meals standing, and the giant alat pot was hardly emptied before Yrund was sent to refill it. Once or twice she felt Gem Beard watching her, and she tried to look busy. Bog you, she told him in her head. We're leaving! Only she still had to somehow find a way to get some hard drink out to the memluks in the back, and, just as important—warn Lili and Anouk. And what about their coats and skis? Yet every time Yrund tried to get Lili alone, something came up—a delivery or a spilled crate of beans or Keeper Antonina shrieking through the door.

The keeper called the maids back up to change before dinner, complaining again at the waste of good cloth. "Nobody will see the little rabu anyway!" she exclaimed to herself before rushing off to answer a bell ringing on the guest floor.

By the time dinner was served, there were so many pots and pans piling in the sinks even the shoe boys had been requisitioned, though they weren't much help, preferring to blow bubbles rather than dry dishes. Through the sink window, Yrund could see half a dozen memluks standing in the back around a fire. Gem Beard might have locked the ice larder, but there were bottles of brandy and cherry port and every other sort of liquor on Precios stacked in the halls. A glob of bubbles caught Yrund in the face, making Orelia laugh. Yrund was about to kick the nearest shoe boy in the pants when she had another idea. "Are you two hungry?"

The boys nodded eagerly.

"I'll give you a moon pie for every bottle of applejack you can get out to those memluks. You tell them it's a gift from Gem Beard, but don't let the keeper catch you, or you won't get paid, understand?"

No strangers to intrigue, the shoe boys swore they wouldn't get caught and disappeared. A short time later she saw them taking out the trash, the bin so heavy it took two of them to carry it.

That was one thing done. Yrund looked around for Lili, but she was still helping Gem Beard. The two of them moved like whirlvishes, checking every single plate before it went out—scattering herbs and mica-flaked salt. Yrund jittered with impatience, wondering if she should go try and find Anouk first, but every time she slid toward the door, someone called her back. "Help me with this sauce!" begged Milly, trying to watch four pans at once. "I have to get the fish out!"

Finally, a brigade of shiny-shoed footmen came to carry all the dishes up the stairs—platters of golden trout followed by tureens of red onion and carrot soup, each floating with puff swans. There were salads and cheese and tiny black peppers stuffed with even tinier pink beets and gold-rimmed bowls of minced reindeer and neeps brined in vinegar, along with silver dishes of pickles and jellies—an endless parade of food disgorging from the kitchen's full larders. Lastly, Gem Beard unlocked the larder and sent the footmen up with the punch.

Music trickled in through the ceiling and down the stairwells—a mix of horns and strings and a few instruments Yrund had never heard—Asterian, Darbanian? Lady Darbana's party had begun. Yrund whirled between the stove and the sinks as Gem Beard barked orders, wondering how she would know when Humphrey made his move. Bog this, she had to find Anouk.

She was headed toward the door again when Gem Beard forced an icing bag into her hands. "Pipe those blinking sponges—quick."

Yrund squirted the yellow cream haphazardly across the cakes. "What is that?" said Milly with horror. "It looks like a bird shat on it!" She grabbed a long wooden scraper and spread out the sides. "Quick, give it here before Mellymeth sees it and boils your ears—"

Hu-huh, boil your ears, said Orelia, who had been no use at all, wanting to stick Yrund's finger in every pie and tart that went by.

No, commanded Yrund, pulling her hand back. *Remember: the Rules of Yrund.*

"Where have all the footmen gone?" demanded Gem Beard, sending Lili upstairs to check.

Lili returned bearing a pile of empty platters, eyes wide. "Half the footmen have disappeared, and the others could use a good strong amethyst—they must have gotten into something…hopefully not the punch!" she said with a knowing glance at the memluk. "Speaking of which, Melmeth, you should see the guests. They're already on the last course. We'll have to send dessert up early."

"Son of a sea snake!" The memluk pumped his fists. "It worked!"

"Maybe too well. Lady Darbana told the ambassador she won't sign the trade deal unless she can have you as part of the terms."

Gem Beard's scarred mouth puckered in shock. "What did the highsmith say to that?"

"That Lady Darbana could suck a—you can guess the rest."

"Excellent!" said Gem Beard, his big head bobbing. "That will give me leverage negotiating my terms." He did another dance around the kitchen, rolling pin lifted as he sang: *"Asteria-Ho! We will go! Asteria-Ho! We will go!"*

"You can celebrate later!" said Lili, exasperated. "Are the tarts ready for me to take? They're like wolves up there."

"Asteria-Ho, we will go…" Gem Beard trailed off, head cocked toward the door. "What's all that ruckus?"

Yrund's heart beat faster. Was it Humphrey? Or the Lumi to the rescue? Crap on crap. It was too early. She still hadn't had a chance to tell Lili or Anouk!

Tilly leaned her head out of the kitchen to investigate. "The footmen are having a kicking fight over who the ambassador likes best," she reported.

"I knew those blasturds would get into the port!" said Gem

Beard, stomping off to separate the footmen. He called back over his shoulder. "Hoy, you maids, help Lili up with those moon pies and tarts. And don't forget the cream cakes."

Lili layered Yrund's arms up with heavy platters as the shoe boys went by with another bin of trash and a wink.

"Lili!" hissed Yrund when they were halfway up the stairs. "Stop!"

"I can't stop now," said the woman. "It's chaos up there."

Yrund waited for Milly and Tilly to get ahead. "They're coming for us, Lili!"

"Who's coming for us?" asked Lili from behind a tall cake.

"Agnetha and… I don't know who else—but they're coming!"

"How could you know that?" asked Lili, turning sideways on the landing so she could see Yrund.

"Because…the ambassador got a post," said Yrund, flailing for something the Lumi woman would believe. "The pigeon boy told me. They were spotted on their way here. We need to get ready. We need to get Anouk!"

"They'll never get past the guards," said Lili, shaking her braid. "What are they thinking?"

"They can't, but *we* can. Please," Yrund begged. "This might be our only chance."

Lili looked hard into Yrund's face. "You didn't drink any punch, did you?"

"No, I promise. You have to believe me."

"Irsil's navel," said Lili. "If there's anyone I would believe it's you. Let's go get Anouk—she's up in the dining hall."

"Why is she in there?"

"I don't know, but she didn't look happy."

"WHAT ARE ALL the kitchen maids doing up here? You can't send them in with the guests," exclaimed Keeper Antonina, who was stationed outside the dining hall like a gatekeeper. Or a zookeeper based on the sounds coming from within.

"I wouldn't have to bring up my girls if your serving men hadn't dipped into the punch," countered Lili.

"But she's still in her apron!" said the keeper, looking aghast at Yrund.

"The guests were wearing their napkins as hats the last time I was in there—I don't think they'll notice!"

"I told the ambassador not to put a hoopoe in…" The keeper raised her hands to show it wasn't her fault.

"You put a dupestone in the punch?" said Lili, pausing on the threshold. "When? We locked the larder!" It seemed Yrund hadn't been the first with plans for that punch.

"Right before they served it. I tried to tell him not to, but he never listens to me, does he? And now they've let the Alatis bring that thieving monkey in! It's already stolen two candlesticks!"

Lili and Yrund pushed through the heavy doors. "Irsil and her wolves," said the Lumi woman, surveying the chaos.

The Booles' dinner hall was like nothing Yrund had ever seen —as big as Last Lake's town hall and covered with tapestries. On the far end was a set of cut-glass doors rising up into a sweeping wall of colorful stained glass reflecting back the room's sunsstone chandeliers, while the nearer end of the great room housed a gilded fireplace big enough to roast a memluk. Opposite the tall entrance doors was a raised dais upon which a lone harpist was trying unsuccessfully to be heard over the half dozen more musicians scattered around the hall, none of whom were playing the same song. The tables and chairs had been pushed back for the guests to dance, though it was not at all clear which tune they were following. As Lili had noted, they wore their napkins on their heads.

Orelia chortled while Yrund gaped, for the bejeweled guests were even more spectacular than the lavish hall—aqua drops on ears and hyacinths on wrists, black opals for buttons…

A bald man knocked Yrund from behind, spilling tarts off her platter. "Moon pies!" he cried, tussling with two identical women in rubilies and pearls. The women looked torn from the glossies, skin glowing like candles and cheeks as red as cherries.

"Ooh! Tarts! Tarts!" A tiny woman wearing a bat brooch jumped for the rest of Yrund's platter. "Tarts!!"

Yrund pushed her off, grappling with another guest, whose eyes glittered silvery-pink to match his strangely translucent skin.

"Let them have them," advised Lili, who'd lost her own trays.

"Where's Anouk?" asked Yrund as a lithe brown animal swung past, veering from one chandelier to another.

A monkey! sang Orelia, overcome with joy.

Yrund could only guess how the gem knew that. Probably one of the books she'd stayed up reading in Lumi Land.

"This way," said Lili, dragging Yrund along behind her through the crowd.

The guests were babbling in a dozen languages, shrieking and laughing as if they were having the time of their lives. Above it all were the musicians, who'd come together now, playing their horns and flutes and fiddles in a merry dance that only a few of the inebriated guests still seemed able to follow.

"Who are all these people?"

"Diplomats, mayors, merchants...road builders, jewelers, furriers, winemakers...friends, enemies, glossy artists, post writers—you name it, really. They're going to be passed out in every stairway tonight. I told that Douarrian galloot not to leave the appetyt in overnight..."

"You two gemmed the punch too?!"

Lili tamped down her hand for Yrund to lower her voice.

"It was just supposed to be a little appeteaser is all—nothing dangerous, but look at them. It must be a reaction with the ambassador's hoopoe... I've always heard dupestones were unstable—wait, I think I see Anouk!"

"Where?" asked Yrund, who was nearly the shortest person in the room.

"There, with Ambassador Boole—"

The ambassador had climbed onto the low stage with the band. Anouk stood unhappily beside him and Highsmith Boole, who was resplendent in a velvet cape.

Yrund hardly recognized the Lumi girl. She was no longer wearing a bonnet and uniform like the other maids, but a new blue dress and matching ribbons in her hair, and were those seefires in her ears? She looked like…like an Asterian.

At the ambassador's wobbly gesture, the band wrapped up their song.

"That wasss splendid. Ferry, ferry splendid," said the ambassador, leaning on his sister. "And now, I haff another treat. Antoninaaaa," he cried, looking around for his keeper. "Antoniiii-iina! Where is that fiddle you promised??"

"Here it is," said the keeper, carrying an ebony instrument above her head, which she presented to Anouk.

Anouk took the fiddle uncertainly as if it were a foreign object. Half the crowd had turned to watch her.

"Go on," said the ambassador. "Play Lady Dar-ban-ana a nameday tune."

Anouk looked desperately around the room as if looking for an escape before catching sight of Lili and Yrund. Taking their waving for encouragement, she placed the fiddle beneath her chin and closed her eyes.

"Yaha, go on, Anouk, you can do it!" whispered Lili, squeezing Yrund's arm with the tension. Yrund wondered what time it was and how they would possibly get Anouk away.

Anouk plucked the first note. It hung discordantly in the air. "I…it's…it's not tuned," she apologized.

"What silliness is this, Binjy?" demanded his sister.

"You fellow," said the ambassador, pointing an unsteady finger at the band. "Let her have yours."

One of the musicians came forward, giving up his fiddle and bow with an elaborate curtsy. Anouk blushed at the gallantry. But as soon as she plucked the next note, full and on key, her expression changed to one of concentration. She ran her fingers up and down the instrument, testing the tuning. Finally satisfied, she drew the bow across the strings.

The hall's great ceiling lifted up the sound, carrying it over the room like a summer breeze. Slowly, the remaining guests quieted. The song wound its way through the party like a bewitching dream, stirring memories of warmth and light and wildflowers fluttering in the suns. Even the monkey dangled down by his tail to listen.

When the last note faded to silence, the swaying crowd erupted in applause—clapping and whistling and saluting the Lumi wawa.

"See??" bragged the ambassador to his sister. "Didn' I tell you?"

"Very pretty," acknowledged Highsmith Boole in her dry voice, not nearly as drunk as her brother. "She will come in very useful. A reminder even seefires are found in the dirt. Now, let us raise our glasses to Lady Darbana!"

"Tooooo Ladeeee Barnana!" cried the room.

"May I also take this moment to unveil the new scent I have created in her name as a token of the friendship between our two countries." The highsmith produced a slim yellow bottle, holding it out grandly.

"How luffly," said Lady Darbana, splashing her bare wrist with the new perfume.

Anouk took the opportunity to hand back the fiddle and escape to where Lili and Yrund stood by the door.

"Well done," said Lili.

"Yaha, well done," said Yrund impatiently. "But we have to go." She hoped they hadn't missed Humphrey's signal. They still needed their coats. With a twinge she remembered the key up in the ambassador's office. With the punch gemmed, no one would ever notice her upstairs. But there wasn't time for wishes. The night was growing late. Yrund tried to steer Anouk out the door.

Anouk resisted, looking back at the dais. "Wait for it," she said, watching intently.

First, Lady Darbana's nose wrinkled. Then she gagged. "What did you do to my perfume? This doesn't smell like leather and roses! It smells like cat tur—" Her expression changed suddenly from repulsion to horror. "My new bracelet!" Lady Darbana cried, no longer concerned with the perfume as she noticed her bare wrist for the first time. "It's gone!"

"And my rings!" shrieked a voluptuous woman from the crowd. "Where are my mezmerald rings?"

"My pomegarnet's missing!" cried the bald man.

Now the entire room was wailing. "My peardot!"

"My pearl!"

"My flute!" cried a musician.

"Call the memluks inside!" commanded the highsmith. "A thief is among us!"

"It's the Invisible Hand! The Hand has struck."

Humphrey's signal! thought Yrund. "It's time!"

"Time for what?" asked Anouk again as Yrund propelled her out of the hall.

"Time to go home."

"Wait—we'll need our coats," said Lili at the landing. "Get some food and some matches and whatever else you can from the kitchen, but quickly! I'll meet you by the back gate."

Yrund and Anouk skidded down the stairs three at a time, leaping off the landings and racing down the hall to the kitchen. They hurtled past a startled chambermaid, who dropped a pile of laundry onto a shoe boy, who dropped an armful of shoes, which tripped a chimney girl with a bucket, engulfing the hall outside in a cloud of gray ashes just as a troop of memluks rushed in, adding to the confusion.

"The Invisible Hand is in the dinner hall!" Yrund yelled as they ran into the kitchen. "A prize to whoever catches him!"

"The Invisible Hand is in the dinner hall!" Milly and Tilly relayed back through the servants. "A prize to whoever catches him!!" Soon everyone was out of the kitchen and up the stairs.

"A thief in the house?!" Gem Beard snatched his rolling pin and dove into the cloud of ashes.

Yrund found a turnip sack and dumped the contents in a corner behind a barrel. Better for them to get as far as they could before anyone knew they were missing. She filled the bag with a little of everything: a sausage here, an end of cheese there, half of a bread loaf and an armful of apples—but not so much of anything to notice at first glance. Then she pinched a few tins of alat and a box of matches from the stove.

"What else?" asked Anouk. She had gathered a fistful of sharp knives—still Mila's sister—putting two in her empty belt sheaths and the rest in the sack.

Yrund thought regretfully of the key upstairs, but it was too late for that now. "We just need Lili with our coats." And a ride back to Lumi Land.

CHAPTER THIRTY-FOUR

Yrund and Anouk edged out the kitchen door and into the yard, which was bumper to bumper with painted sleighs and their yaks. The animals' breath curled up into the night, little twin chimneys of steam. Overhead the clouds hung low, like a scatter of bones on a black shore. From the stables they could hear the disgruntled sound of camels squeezed in too tight for their liking and the shouts from inside as the search for the Invisible Hand began in earnest. The girls slipped between sleds and shadows, crouching when another line of memluks charged past headed for the house. Like a gift, the watch at the gate had been abandoned. Yrund sent a silent thanks to Humphrey, wondering how he'd known the Hand was going to strike. Unless…could it be? Was Humphrey the Hand?

No, said an adamant Orelia. *The Hand has silver eyes. And a sword.*

"Where's Lili?" asked Anouk, interrupting the argument in Yrund's head. "It's freezing out here." They looked longingly at the guards' abandoned braziers as the cold cut through their dresses like shears. "And where are the skis? How are we supposed to go home? You don't expect us to take a yak, do you?"

"Shh," cautioned Yrund. "Lili said she'd meet us here. We're waiting for Agnetha—she has a sled."

"Agnetha's coming? What about Ama and Apa?"

"I don't know any more than that," said Yrund, ducking her head out the gate for a peek, but the alley was empty.

"But how did you know—"

"There she is!" said Yrund as the door to the second floor opened. The ambassador's house was lit from the bottom to the top, every window shining with sunsstones and firelight. From their vantage point, Yrund could see the golden eagle of the Mining Wield in the immense stained glass side of the dining hall. Wings spread, the bird was diving down into a valley of gems guarded by rearing snakes. Below, Lili ran down the steps, carrying their wadded bundle of coats and something clutched in her hand.

They waved their arms for her to see them.

"Are they here?" she asked breathlessly when she reached them.

"Not yet," said Yrund, feeling the first twinge of panic. If they were caught outside, the memluks might mistake them for the jewel thieves. "And you're sure you heard the ambassador correctly? They'd have to have traveled nonstop to get here so soon..." Doubt began to creep across Lili's face as she handed them their coats.

Yrund replayed the conversation with Humphrey on the third floor. Could she trust him? Could she trust herself? Had she imagined the woodwin all along? She took a frosty breath. "Maybe we should try to meet them on the road." There was no point in waiting. If Humphrey was wrong, they still had a chance —but it wouldn't last long. "We'll have to find some skis."

"There's a ski smith on the south end. We can trade him these," Lili said, showing them a strand of large pearls knotted with multicolored gems.

"Where did you get that?"

"From the stairs—one of the guests must have dropped them," said Lili, stuffing them in her pocket. "Or the Hand. It doesn't matter now."

"We're really going home!" said Anouk, eyes sparkling in the reflection of the stained window.

"Yaha, the tide has finally turned."

They gave each other one last disbelieving look, then sprinted for the ambassador's gate.

Only it was blocked by a band of men wearing blue and brown Roads and Ways uniforms.

Yrund's stomach lurched as her head tried to catch up. Where had they come from?

"Let us pass," said Lili in her haughtiest voice. "We're on an errand for Ambassador Boole—we cannot be detained."

"What sort of errand?" asked a soldier with a stubbled beard. His face was thin, his dirty coat bearing the faded *R* and *W* of Roads and Ways. Yrund felt her legs give a little beneath her.

"To the healers. One of the guests from Alat has been sick."

"And he sent all three of you?"

"It's no business of yours how many messengers the ambassador sends—if you do not move this instant I will call for the memluks to arrest you," warned Lili.

"The memluks taking orders from rabu now?" the soldier asked as the men spread out to surround them.

"Not these rabu." Another soldier came into the house's light. He had the markings of a captain but his coat was too big, sliding off stooped shoulders to reveal the gem-jaundiced skin of his neck and a familiar scatter of amulets and talismans. In one hand he held a green-and-white agyt. In the other, a striker, its glowing gem casting a noxious light on the snow.

The tide had turned all right, thought Yrund. Just not for them.

"Think I wouldn't find you, rat?" demanded Brandul, jabbing his striker toward her in the air. "You should've stayed with those silver eaters down south. But you aren't that smart, are you? Or you wouldn't have taken my allstone." He emphasized the word *my* with another jab.

"An allstone?" said Anouk, aghast. "What is he talking about?"

Brandul's eyes protruded unnaturally from his wasted face, twitching from Yrund to the agyt. "Give it to me," he said, taking another step closer. "Give it to me now, or I'll kill you!"

"No." The word dropped from Yrund's lips like an axe. She had survived every beating, every horror, every insult. She had survived Veng's blade and his stars. She had survived the explosion and the cave-in and all the mountain's attempts to poison and drown her. She had survived the woodwins and their gorge and Brandul's arrows and the blizzard. She had even survived the ambassador and his memluks, but she would die now before she would give him Orelia.

"I will shoot you!" said Brandul, voice rising.

"Then do it."

"No!" said Lili, trying to shield Yrund with her body. Yrund pushed her away.

"Stay out of it!"

"Look, Bran—it's the Lumi wolf from the mine." The bandits parted. "Hello, *Lili*," said Veng, wiggling a bandaged hand. "Did you miss me?"

"Never," hissed Lili.

"You can have her later," said Brandul, annoyed. "Get the stone first."

"You heard the boss," said Veng, a blade appearing in his hand.

"Leave her alone!" said Anouk, holding up one of Gem Beard's knives.

"Ooh, hoo, hoo! Who's this little tidbit?" asked Veng, dancing around her. The Astrini was as light on his feet as he'd been at the mine. He darted in to lick Anouk's cheek. She lunged with the kitchen knife, which Veng easily sidestepped, delivering a quick stab of his own. Anouk gasped, her hand sliced open, and the blade fell from her grip.

"Enough! Get the allstone from the rat."

"Yes, the rat! You owe me a few fingers, rat." Veng was dancing around Yrund now, his sweat acrid in her nose, and she saw his eyes were unnaturally bright, the side effect of some gem, or some drink.

"We don't have any allstones—what kind of insanity is this?" demanded Lili.

Brandul swept the striker around. "Hurry up!" he told Veng.

"What fun is that?"

"Just shoot me," said Yrund.

Brandul hesitated, the wrinkle between his brows deepening. If he shot her, he might lose the stone. His eyes flicked to her friends, and the striker followed.

Yrund thrust herself in front of Anouk. "Get behind me!" she told Lili, but Veng was faster, dragging the struggling woman apart from them.

"Hold her!" said Brandul, advancing with the striker until it was inches from Lili's face. He flicked the spur lever at the back and light shot out, reflecting off her pupils. "What about now, rat? Will you give it to me now?"

Burn him! said Orelia, her fire filling Yrund's head.

Yrund pushed back her hood and took the stone's pouch from her coat. There was only one choice to make. "All right. You can have it."

"But…allstones don't exist," said Anouk with disbelief.

"They do," said Brandul, a queer expression almost like happiness transforming his gaunt face. He held out his hand. "You just have to know where to look."

Everyone was watching now.

Yrund threw the pouch up into the air, where it tumbled end over end, the woven strap catching in the breeze.

Brandul let the striker go, leaping to catch the allstone with both hands. He was gleeful, giggling. "I knew you would come to me! I knew it!" He kissed the gravy-stained pouch, panting with joy, not seeing Veng kick the fallen striker up into his good hand.

"Give me the allstone, Bran."

Brandul pulled his eyes from the pouch, so stunned his smile still remained. "What are you doing?"

"I'm doing my job. Did you really think Leolin would entrust a man like you with an allstone? You? Brandul Petrador? Whose own memluks turned against him? Who lost your fleet at Remora? Who let the rabu mutiny? You're an embarrassment to the wield."

"An embarrassment?" Brandul's joy drained away. "Who found the allstone? Not the Mining Wield! Not any of them." He was spitting now, his friend's betrayal cutting deep. "Who found the maps? Who read Dyrian's letters? Who," he demanded, "brought the finder's agyt back from Remora? You wouldn't even know about Devil's Crown if it wasn't for me! You would still be drunk in a hole in Borosia, gambling away your knives!"

"Say what you like. It's done, Bran—" Veng waved the striker's shining nose, and the bandits surrounded the mine boss.

Brandul cursed and flailed, but he was no match for five men.

"Well…let's see what we've been starving all kicking winter for." Veng shifted the striker to his bad hand and yanked the dirty pouch away. With his teeth he tore it open, dumping the stone out onto his palm and thrusting it toward the light from the windows. The bandits all crowded around, dragging Brandul with them.

"What the—"

Veng shook the stone, then tapped it, but the stone did not sparkle or glow or do anything at all. Confused, he spat on it, rubbing it and turning it over and over.

Realization slowly dawned. "Blooding gemcracked idiot!" Veng hurled the stone back at the restrained Brandul, bouncing off him and into the trampled and dirty snow. "Look at it!" Veng yelled. "Look at your allstone!"

Brandul's mouth sagged open, breath hanging in a sad cloud.

"You blinking fool! You blinking, blooding agyt-addled fool!" shouted Veng.

"But the agyt trembled! The agyt trembled!" said Brandul like a child.

A bandit with a ragged scarf grabbed the stone up from the snow and rubbed it hard on his sleeve. "It's not even a gem," he said. "It's just a rock."

They passed the plain gray stone around, some biting it, until the last bandit threw it back down in disgust. "How you going to pay us with a gemcrack rock?" The men had all turned on Veng. "You said you'd get us a thousand suns each when we got to Asteria!"

"Shut up!" said Veng, pacing back and forth as he thought. Then he spun to a stop. "We can still turn him in for the bounty." He raised the striker back at Brandul. "The twit ambassador will pay us."

"But the agyt trembled..." Brandul whimpered, clutching the green-and-white finder stone, which continued to point stupidly toward the rock on the ground.

Veng roared. "Can't you see? Your agyt's cracked! Leading us on a monkey's chase. For what? A bit of nothing stone."

"Then why did she take it? Why carry it around all this time?" asked the old mine boss desperately.

"Why do superstitious outlanders do anything?" With a savage jerk, Veng ripped the agyt and chain from Brandul's neck and flung them out into the night. "She's played you for the fool."

Brandul looked up at Yrund as though she'd betrayed him, as though *she* had destroyed all his dreams. Perhaps she had. Just as he had destroyed hers. "Worthless rabu!" he screamed. "You're worth nothing! Less than nothing!" Pulling away from the men holding him, he kicked Yrund's stone as hard as he could back at her, spraying her with snow. "You're not even a rat. A rat has a brain. A rat is clever. You're just an illiterate little sheep eater who's going to die in—"

"Oh, shut up, Bran!" said Veng, cracking him across the head as Yrund bent down.

"Though he is right," the Astrini said, turning the striker toward Yrund, its yellow-green beam marking her chest. "You are going to die. We've wasted months following your useless rock. Months!" he screamed, his temper finally cracking. "Did you think I would forget what you did to me?" He dangled his bandaged hand out in front of him. "I—did—not—for—get!" Yrund raised her hands as a blinding ball of lightning exploded from the striker.

But the flame did not reach her, ricocheting instead off the outheld Orelia, who swatted the ball of fire back the way it had come. In an instant Veng was gone.

The small crowd stood gaping at the puddle of melted snow and greasy ashes. All but Yrund and a figure in the shadows, whose attention was on the proudly shining rock in her hand.

Orelia! she said sternly, and the stone's light faded.

"Hoy!" boomed a voice from across the yard. "What in the sea snakes are you blooding doing here?" Gem Beard brandished a rolling pin, bellowing in Douarr as he charged. The bandits scattered, Brandul abandoned.

Goggle-eyed and speechless, Brandul swung his head from Veng's remains to Yrund, oblivious to the memluk towering over him. There were others crowding in now—Milly and Tilly and musicians carrying stolen breakfast pies from the kitchen and shoe boys stuffing themselves with tarts. Through them all crashed a dozen memluks running to Gem Beard's call.

"He's the thief!" said a quick-thinking Anouk, pointing the guards toward Brandul. "The Invisible Hand—it's him, and those are his men!"

"Mellymeth's caught the Invisible Hand!" shouted Milly,

holding hands with Tilly and jumping around in a circle. "Melly-meth's caught the Hand!!!"

There were more voices now, including the ambassador and the highsmith's. Someone had opened the doors from the dining hall to the balcony overlooking the yard. "What is happening down there? Have you really caught the thief?"

The entire party crowded out to watch as the memluks chased down Brandul's bandits in an entertaining game of hide and seek among the sleds. The musicians, always ready to enter-tain, finished their pies and started up a lively tune, marching around Gem Beard to the cheering of the crowd. "Mellymeth! Mellymeth! Mellymeth!"

"Well done, Melmeth!" shouted the ambassador. "I shall make you the head of our eastern command!"

"You shall not!" said his sister. "He's going to be my kitchen boss in Asteria!"

While they argued, the musicians started up a new song and the guests pushed down the balcony stairs to dance, kicking up their satin party shoes in the yak dung and the snow.

"What happened there?" Gem Beard asked them, pointing his rolling pin at the smoldering mess on the ground.

"Striker misfired, I think," said Lili, eliciting a giggle from Orelia.

"Anyone we know?"

"Veng," answered Lili with more than a little satisfaction.

"Veng? The Astrini? Good Way for that buggedy blasturd—"

Yrund didn't hear the rest, for above the din of the party-makers and Orelia crowing in her head came a new sound—the unmistakable whoosh of an airship, floating right over the ambassador's house.

"That's my ship they're taking!" The ambassador pointed up from the balcony, his face orange in the ship's light. "Get it back! Get it back!"

Everyone was yelling now except the musicians, who were

blowing their horns and their flutes and following the airship as it turned north. The rest of the party followed the band, chanting: "Mellymeth! Mellymeth!"

"For pissake," groaned Gem Beard. As the memluks gawked at the ship gliding over them, Brandul and his bandits had broken free.

"There they go!" yelled Lili. "They're getting away!"

"Catch the thieves!" commanded Highsmith Boole.

"No! Catch the ship!" commanded the ambassador.

The memluks were divided, half chasing the ship and half chasing Brandul and his men.

"Where are the pilots?" asked Anouk, for the ship appeared to be flying of its own accord.

A whistle floated down from overhead. Orelia whistled back.

Bogging hell. This was the sign the woodwin had meant!

"Out the gate! Now!" Yrund hissed to Lili and Anouk, just as a heavy hand clamped down on her shoulder.

"Hoy, where do you three think you're going?" growled Gem Beard, his scar gleaming in the airship's glow.

"Melmeth—please!" begged Lili, trying to peel back the hand that held Yrund. "It's our only chance!"

Gem Beard scowled down at the Lumi woman. "Hold your anchors. There's going to be a storm of ugly down on my head if you disappear. This's going to cost you."

"I'll pay! I found some pearls on the stairs—you can have them."

"Don't want your pearls," said the memluk grimly.

"What do you want?"

The memluk flipped the rolling pin in his free hand like a weapon. "You have to give up what's in those puffovers of yours. I know you're keeping secrets—trying to protect your place in the kitchen—but you'll blooding well tell me now."

Lili blinked. "My puffovers? They're the same as yours—the same recipe exactly."

"Can't be."

"They are. Your problem is your technique. You have to leave a few lumps—you're always overworking the batter…"

"Leave a few lumps," the memluk said dubiously. "That's all?"

"No, that's not all. Stop poking at it like you do, let it have a proper rest. While you're doing that, get the oven as hot as you can—with the pans in there, that's very important—and put on some alat. As soon as the alat starts to boil, not a moment sooner, then you put your batter in the hot pans."

Yrund looked around the yard helplessly. This was the time to go! Right now, with everyone distracted, yet here they were talking about bogging puffovers.

"You've always told me to put the batter in a cold pan!" Gem Beard protested.

"I know I did," admitted Lili. "But I'm telling you straight this time." She reached her hand out to the memluk. "I promise on my sister."

Gem Beard released his hold on Yrund to shake Lili's hand. "I'll come find you if you're holding back and turn you into chum."

"I know you will. Now, please, we have to go!"

"Well, Little Thorn in the Arse," Gem Beard said to Yrund, thumping her head one last time, "those eyes still watching?"

Yrund held up her bare palms. "Then you can tell 'em it wasn't me that stood in your Way." He took a loaf from his vest and shoved it in her pocket. Then he limped off to join his men and the chase. "That blooding thieving Brandul… I'm going to put a hammer through his—"

"Go!" said Lili, pushing Anouk and Yrund through the gemmed guests and angry yaks and out the open gate. The sound of shouts followed the departing airship, but except for a few wobbling musicians, the alley was empty. No guards, no Lumi. No rescue.

"We have to go south," said Yrund, orienting herself. If the airship was the distraction, and the airship was headed north...

"Right, out the front, then!" said Lili. "Follow me!"

They dashed back through the yard and into the kitchen, down the ash-and-slipper-littered hall, up the stairs still covered in laundry, and across the carpeted second floor, dodging drunk footmen and a few napkin-hatted guests who were trying without success to get the monkey down from the chandeliers.

They had nearly reached the great home's front door when the keeper cried out from the dining hall. "Where have you been?" she demanded. "I've been ringing the bell. Lady Blinking Darbana's been sick in the—why are you bleeding?" She finally seemed to notice the gash on Anouk's hand and the bulging turnip sack of supplies in Lili's arms.

Just as the keeper's mouth began to open again, Yrund reached out and touched her with Orelia. *Nepenthe*, she said silently.

The keeper tipped her head to one side, eyes misted over with purple. "What...what was I saying?"

"That the ambassador wants you immediately! He's waiting in the kitchen!" said Anouk, pointing back down the hall.

"The ambassador? Down in the kitchen?"

"Yes," Lili chimed in. "Something about a new seefire necklace —for your help catching the Hand!"

"A seefire?" said the keeper, her narrow face twisted. "For me? I caught the Hand? Was it that filthy memluk? I always said he would be—"

"Not Melmeth. It was..." Lili faltered.

"Lady Darbana!" said Yrund, knowing the keeper's disdain for her. "And you were the only one who suspected—the ambassador is very impressed!"

Anouk pulled the hall bell behind the keeper's back.

"That must be him now," said Lili, leading the keeper toward the stairs. "Quickly! You mustn't keep him waiting. He has a big toast planned and everything."

The keeper, eyes still misty, descended out of sight. "I knew that moley woman couldn't be trusted! Didn't I say? Didn't I? Probably in league with the cook…"

Lili cracked open the front door and peeked out. Chin nodding, she waved for Yrund and Anouk to pass through. They paused on the stair's landing, looking down. The white street was lit softly with lanterns, peaceful except for the faint snatch of song from the house. Too peaceful.

"I thought you said they'd be here!" said Anouk, worried.

Yrund fought back her disappointment. After all, would Humphrey have stolen an airship for nothing?

"Come on," she said, linking her arms through her friends. "We still have a plan. We'll get some skis and intercept them on their way."

"Actually, I think you'll find what you're looking for just around the corner."

They hadn't heard the tall man slip out the door behind them. He was wearing a traveling coat with black opal buttons and a familiar brown beard.

"Ansyn!"

"Follow me!"

They slipped and skidded down the stairs after the trader and through the snowy lane, Lili and Anouk uncontained in their glee.

As they ran, a small doubt pierced Yrund's relief. Something wasn't right. Why had the Asterian been inside? The question rolled through her like a log down a hill. What if this was a trick? Was he working with Brandul? Or the ambassador? What if he was a spy? What if he'd been scheming against the Lumi all along?

"Wait," she called, fear rising in her throat. "What if it's a—"

A trap, she was about to say as they rounded the corner.

There in the middle of the lane, two sleds sat waiting—Agnetha at one and Timo and Mila at the other. Ansyn beamed back at them, eyes moist. "Your ride awaits!"

"Apa!" cried Anouk, running into her father's arms.

"There's no time," said Timo, throwing her to Mila.

Lili had no words for her sister, merely accepting the hand up onto the sled, gray-green eyes meeting green-gray. Yrund and Ansyn had barely leapt on before the dogs shot off, heads down and paws pounding, hurtling them through Darban's narrow streets. Then they were out of the city, flying across the snow-covered fields and toward the forest to the south.

Mila caught Yrund's wrist as they hit a bump, hauling her back in with one hand. She said something to Anouk that Yrund couldn't hear over the wind, a grin stretched from one edge of her furry hood to the other. Beside them raced Agnetha and Lili, leaning side by side into the wind, one rein in each of their hands, while Ansyn lay in the back, holding on for his life.

"Wawoooo!" shouted Orelia.

"Wawoooooooooo!" shouted the others.

Yrund looked back at the dwindling chimneys of Darban. High above, a small glowing airship was still heading north into a sea of glittering stars.

We're going home! said Orelia in her ears.

Yes, said Yrund. Someday, they were.

THE END
OF
BOOK ONE

FREE BONUS CHAPTERS WITH
NEWSLETTER SIGN UP

Subscribe to the author newsletter and get the free ebook: *Gem Beard—Bonus Chapters from The Every Stone*! Plus you'll be the first to hear about new book releases in the *Gempendium* series, behind-the-scenes peeks and more!

Sign up now at theeverystone.com

GLOSSARY

The Aeries Mountains - the central mine-rich mountain range
that divides the largest continent on Precios from north to south;
it becomes the Jaggedies to the west and the Kalans to the east;
the High Aeries refers to the highest peaks in which Devil's
Crown is located

alat - a popular drink from Alat composed of two powders,
purple and green, whose respective soothing and stimulating
qualities are adjusted proportionately for the time of day or night

allstones - aka everystones, aubades, aka dawnstones; mythical
living stones believed to be able to take on the properties of
any gem

anodynes - gems with a numbing effect

appeteaser - gems or gem infusions or aperitifs served in gem
glasses, used to stimulate appetite

Asteria - a mineral-rich land that stretches from the Aeries and
Jaggedy Mountains in the south to the Chatoyant Sea in the
north; also the name of the Asterian capital, home to the

governing High Seat and the six wield halls which form the commonwield

Astrini - secretive Asterian spy wield

aubade - see **allstones**

backmarket - places to buy goods, often gems, for less than the prices set by the wields

banned gems - those most injurious, poisonous and dangerous of stones; includes but not limited to red adamantine, cianite, cinnabar, cobaltite, fangstone, orpiment, realgar

birthbound - those born to wields with the accompanying obligations and restrictions (birthbinds)

blotch - bad reactions between wearer and gem, usually involving contragems or counterfeits

Borosians - the inhabitants of Borosia who dominate the spice trade; known for their fierce merchant fleet

brightsilver - rare and precious silver that does not tarnish and enhances the properties of any gems it is near

Bringers - mythical beings who brought humans to Precios seven centuries ago

bugeaters - pejorative for Asterians, describing their custom of eating insects as part of their diet

calmstones - wello gems that reduce anxiety and agitation in some wearers (though not all), including jade, white opal, topaz

carobs - currency of Alat shaped like the edible seed pod of the same name

cobaline - a rare metal that dyes victims pierced by it blue; coveted for blades as it keeps its edge

colorchangers - aka vagaries; gems that change colors depending on the light and often produce a temporary change of eye color in user

commonwield - see **Asteria**

contragems - stones that are not compatible, the combination of which can produce unpredictable, unpleasant, dangerous, or even deadly, results

Culture Collectors' Wield - a wield of historians and anthropologists that collect stories about outlanders

Darban - city-state strategically located along the eastern portion of the Gem Road

dawnstones - see allstones

deadlines - glowing green ropes crafted to enforce Asterian mine boundaries

Devil's Crown - an ancient gem mine in the circular peaks of the High Aeries; inaccessible except by air; rich in seefires, rubilies, moonstones, and agyts, among other gems

diamant - aka diamonds; commonly used in energy transfer and other industrial capacities; colored varieties known to affect the wearer's mental state; despite popular belief, colorless diamants, aka greasestones, have no known effects

digestgems - gems that aid in digestion or with digestion-related ailments

dogstones - extremely low-quality gems

Douarr - the inhospitable and volcano-ridden land of the Sea Hammers in the farthest north; also the name of the inhabitants and their language

Double Deaths - two deep and deadly gorges (the Fast Death Gorge and the Slow Death Gorge) that form the northwestern and southeastern borders of the woodwins' Hidden Forest

dreamstones - gems and stones used for vivid and/or lucid dreams or dreamlike states

dupestones - gems used to trick their victims by making them gullible, talkative, inebriated, infatuated, and so on

Dyrian's letters - Dyrian was a treasure hunter who believed in woodwilds, Bringers, allstones and other mythical phenomena; he left hundreds of letters and maps behind after his death, charting his research, rantings and expeditions

eartwisters - gems that amplify, distort or otherwise affect the perception of sound; often cause the wearer to hear sounds that no one else can

enhancers - gems, stones and metals that strengthen the effects of other gems

everystone - see **allstones**

eye-eyes - mythical large-eyed beings who watch humans, playing tricks and seeking vengeance when offended

eyestones - any gem affecting the eyes; confusingly, also any gem that looks like an eye, regardless of its effects

eyetwisters - gems that enhance, diminish or distort the wearer's vision, sometimes to the extent of hallucinations

Fast Death Gorge - see **Double Deaths**

finder stones - gems and rocks that react to the presence of other minerals or substances, water being particularly useful; despite claims otherwise, not for the finding of most lost items— for that, try a memory stone such as a forget-me-not

first water - gems of excellent clarity and quality

flume - an alcoholic drink of the Lumi, distilled from rutabaga and juniper

footfighting - aka footboxing; combat done with legs and feet; created by sailors, so often incorporates surroundings for leverage

forget-me-not - a cornflower-blue seefire that improves memory and focus

freewielder - aka freewayers; those who believe that the wields should be free and open to all regardless of family lineage

Gelb - the desert that contains the mezmerald mines (Smeral-gdus) and night-harvested obsydaline of the Lightning Sands

Gem Road - the caravan highway and trade route that trans-verses the north end of the Aeries and Jaggedy Mountains

gembane - gems used to harm or trick a victim, the most vile of which are banned

gembles - a game played on the ground with low-quality round gems of varying sizes; the objective is to toss your gem piece into the winning position by knocking out the competition

gemcrack - a counterfeit or fraudulent stone that appears of fine quality but is in fact worthless

gemists - experts in gemistry and gem rules; prescribers of gems

gemistry - the study of gems, their properties and effects and their interactions with other gems and sources of energy

gempendium - any encyclopedia of gems; usually includes an illustration, description, and rules of each stone, including contragems and warnings

gempox - see **potch**

gemshine - liquor or spirits infused with gems; usually of extreme potency

gim-gem - stones used for good luck or as talismans or amulets; often carried around the neck or waist with other artifacts

glossies - printed illustrated guides of current fashions and trends

Great Ship - a boat-shaped constellation

guidestones - waystars, lodestones, sunstrackers, other navigational gems

Hidden Woods - aka the Hidden Forest; the secret and inaccessible land of the woodwins; situated between the Double Deaths and the south side of Devil's Crown

High Aeries - see the Aeries Mountains

High Seat - aka the common seat, aka the star seat; the residence and governing seat of Asteria's rotating ruler

high wielder - aka the commonwielder; the leader of Asteria, a position which rotates between the six main wields every twelve years

hoopoes - a type of dupestone used to make the gemmed victim agreeable and/or gullible

Horsefly - a tiny constellation beneath the Wild Mare

hypnogogs - aka hoopoes, aka dupestones; stones used to hypnotize and thus affect the mind of the wearer, for good or for ill

Irsil - the mother of Precios according to Lumi lore; her steed was a large flying wolf

Jaggedies - spiky gem-rich mountain range that borders Asteria's south end and the Sky Country's north end

Jaggedy River - a small mountain river over which the Asterians built a bridge which was blown up

jump-jewel - a game played by capturing an opponent's pairs of gem pieces

Kalans - a mountain range north of Lumi Land near Windmarket

keeps - a high-stakes betting game that involves luck and bluffing; usually played for gems

Kite - aka the Diamant; a kite-shaped constellation with a long tail; one of the largest in the southern sky

Last Lake - a small village in Lumi Land surrounded by lakes and forest; winter home of the Hayas

Lumi - the people of Lumi Land, mainly semi-nomadic snowdeer herders, silver workers, boat builders, and fisherpeople

Lumi Land - a snowy region in the far south, rich with lakes, snowdeer and silver

memluks - aka Sea Hammers; captured pirates from Douarr valued for their fighting and tactical skills; though prisoners in diplomatic terms, they are paid salaries, sometimes quite large ones, and sometimes advance to running their own businesses and even purchasing their freedom

mindturner - aka mindtwister; a gem that causes the wearer to see, hear or otherwise sense things that aren't there

mindtwister - see **mindturner**

moons - unit of silver currency in Asteria; valued above stars and below suns

moontales - myths and stories told to children of wild and fantastic creatures and events

morrya - a finger-counting game

mudstones - extremely low quality gems with an especially murky appearance

nazir - an apprentice to a wield; a novice

Opaloosa - a wild and sparsely settled land in the far east, rich with volcanoes, lakes and opals

Orogaudi - a land of harsh mountains, large tigers and rich silver and gold deposits

ouroborus - the snake-shaped manacles worn by mine prisoners; blue diamant eyes

paffle - gems of such low quality they have not been separated out from the ore

Paragon - a port on east coast of Asteria, famous for alat and pearl trade

peskies - mythical mountain spirits blamed for stealing gems and tools and playing tricks on miners; there are also house peskies in towns, who similarly steal gems, keys, socks and sweets

potch - aka gempox, blotch; an affliction of spots or stripes and other ailments caused by a bad reaction to a gem or gems that are contraindicated; occasionally fatal, such as with Barthalow Damantine; also refers to low-quality conglomerate stones, which are common sources of blotch/pox

Precios - a mid-sized planet rich with life and minerals; home to five continents and countless islands surrounded by salt seas; orbits two suns and is orbited by five moons

Qalami or Qalamish Territory - forested land with access to two oceans and a tradition of fine boat crafting

rabu - prisoners of the wields of Asteria; sentenced for life, usually to heavy labor

ratters - captured children sent deep into Asteria's gem mines to map deposits and plant explosives; valued for their small size and ability to reach difficult places

rumgem - rum infused with gemstones; unpredictable at best—drink at one's own risk

Saltlands - uninhabitable salt flats to the west of Devil's Crown

screwberyl - a peculiar variety of beryl that has the effect of the sourest of lemons on one's countenance; beloved by children and pranksters

Sea Hammers - see **memluks**

Sea of Death - the desolate desert wasteland west of the Sky Country, traversed only by the Windtraders

Sea Throat - a silver port at the southern tip of Lumi Land

second water - lesser-clarity gems, below first water and above third

Silk Isles - the islands in the far west, known for their highly secret silk production (including spider silk)

Silk Seas - oceans around Borosia and the Silk Isles

Silk Sparrows - lady pirates of Silk Seas

Silver Narrows - the island- and rock-strewn channel in the far polar south; impassable in winter when iced in

Silver Throat - a large silver mine near the south coast of Lumi Land

Silverlands - the Asterian name for Lumi Land

Singing Sands - a phenomenon within the Sea of Death where the shifting dunes make musical notes and hum

Skerry River - the river that flows from the Aeries Mountains through the bottom of the Fast Death Gorge and into the Skerry Sea to the south

Skerry Sea - the sea of the polar south that includes the Silver Narrows

Sky, the - sacred origin of the Sky People; giver of life and light

Sky Country - an arid land of nomadic herders south of the Aeries Mountains and north of the Silver Narrows

Sky Steppes - see **Sky Country**

sleepstones - gems used as sleep or dream aids, such as cloudstone and moonstone, or calmstones like white opal

Slow Death Gorge - see **Double Deaths**

Smeralgdus - mezmerald mines in the Gelb run by the Mining Wield

Southern Glories - roll clouds south of the Hidden Forest

Star Throne - the seat of power in Asteria during the Age of the Allstones that was occupied by a series of leaders claiming royal dominion, each toppled in turn during the centuries-long wars between the wields; according to a popular children's song, the Star Throne was literally toppled in a chain of events set off by a mouse

stars - unit of copper currency in Asteria; valued below moons and suns

Steering Star - the star that marks north

sthaga - bandits on Gem Road who strangle travelers in their sleep, then steal the entire caravan of animals and goods

sticks-and-sevens - a betting game with partners that uses numbered sticks instead of cards

striker - gem-powered personal weapons that shoot lightning-like bursts

suns - unit of gold currency in Asteria; valued above stars and moons

sweepstones - gems used for pausing a woman's monthly sweep

sytranj - a strategy game involving carved pieces in the shapes of humans, animals and boats

taw - a large round gem used for shooting in gembles

third water - aka last water; stones of poor color and/or clarity though not as valueless as potch or paffle

toadstones - lumpy green stones secreted by toads; used to reverse poisonings

touchstones - gems used for marking the quality of precious metals or as a standard for measuring other gems

Trade Tongue - the language spoken by traders and merchants and all of Asteria

Troll, the - mythical Lumi monster who starts rockslides, avalanches and other natural disasters through his clumsiness

True Way, the - how inhabitants of Precios distinguish their own

Way as the correct one, leading to infinite claims of the "True" Way

Unsinn - the city-state on the Unsinn River surrounded by the Qalamish Territory on the north, west and south and bordered on the east by Orogaudi

vagary - aka colorchangers; gems that cause changes in appearance, usually eye color, such as color-change seefires

verdant - green varieties of wello known for their healing and wellness properties, including jade, riverine and, falsely, mallowkite which is actually an anodyne

wakestones - gems that cause wakefullness, such as citrine, citronette, and certain jades

Way, the - the path of destiny or right living

waystars - see **waystones**

waystones - aka waystars; varied navigation stones used by caravaners, pilots and sailors; not reliable in certain geographic regions, such as Lumi Land

wellos - a class of gems that improve health and wellbeing, chiefly halestones and wellos, though sometimes stretched to included digestgems, eyestones, calmstones, sleepstones, and others; arguably the most most profit-generating gems on the planet

wield-bound - prisoners that are forced to practice a particular craft or trade for a wield's profit; the state of being bound to a wield

wielder - the elected leader of each wield in Asteria; almost always a zenith

wields - the powerful collectives that form the basis of the Asterian social and economic hierarchy; there are hundreds of sub-wields, but the six main wields that run the country are: the Arts and Crafts Wield, the Green Wield, the Merchants Wield, the Mining Wield, and the Roads and Ways Wield

Wild Mare - a constellation of a bucking horse

Windmarket - a market town on the portion of the Gem Road that traverses the Kalans; home to the annual Winter Fair
Windtraders - traders from the west who ride the seasonal wind- and sandstorms across the Sea of Death in their sandships
Winter Fair - aka Winter Games; the annual winter market and sports competition in Windmarket, marking the start of trading and caravan season
wispers - people who abuse nepenthe, thereby losing their memory until they no longer remember who they are
woodwilds - aka yowis; mythical enormous manlike creatures with big feet and fur coats; in the tales they are infamous for eating small naughty children; not to be confused with **woodwins**
woodwins - a hidden race of sentient forest-dwelling beings
Wyn - the location of Asteria's largest captured prisoner market
Yavani - an elite all-female fighting force that protects the high wielder and anyone else who can afford them
zenith - the highest rank attainable within a wield; ultimate master of a trade or craft

ABOUT THE AUTHOR

E.A. Sandrose lives in the mountains with her husband and many animals. She's an expert at cloud watching and picking up rocks. Tools of the trade include a library card, a squat brown teapot and wooden pencils. *The Every Stone* is her first novel.

www.theeverystone.com

www.ingramcontent.com/pod-product-compliance
Lightning Source LLC
Chambersburg PA
CBHW021328110726
47900CB00005B/1397